Brightfeather

Hannah Hounshell

Hannah Hounshell

Brightfeather

ISBN (paperback) 979-8-9924333-1-9

ISBN (ebook) 979-8-9924333-0-2

Cover Design and illustration by Hannah Hounshell

Editing by Addison Horner of Avocado Tress Press

Proofreading by Feathersword Proofing

To my husband, the hero of our story who has saved me more times than I can count and sweeps me away with swoon-worthy kisses everyday. You are my heart. I love you.

And to my aunt, who was always asking about my writing, even when my answer stayed the same for years. Your encouragement meant the world to me. Thank you.

Author's Note

Brightfeather is an upper YA romantic fantasy with NA crossover appeal that follows Bri and Adam through the streets of modern-day New York and into the enchanting—but often dangerous—world of the fae. As such, it includes instances of:

- Minor language (dammit)

- Violence (attempted assault of a female, hand-to-hand combat, blood, and multiple elements of fantasy peril)

- Brief mentions of past off-page SA

- Toxic relationships (NOT between the MMC and the FMC)

Also, this is a kissing book. Lots of kissing. So much kissing. It doesn't contain explicit or spicy content, but there's sensuality and sizzle leading up to a fade-to-black. Please make the best decision for yourself before joining the adventure within these pages.

Chapter One

I always forgot how quickly the winter sun faded in the evenings, dipping below that famous New York City skyline.

The wooden crate I hugged to my chest creaked in protest when I tightened my grip. I shivered as the late January chill nipped at my fingers through my knit gloves. My scarf wasn't quite thick enough to ward off the icy wind trailing down the nape of my neck, but the cold helped me focus on something besides my churning stomach. Even after two years of living in the city, being out after dark left me queasy with nerves.

I took the next corner at a brisk walk. The soft thud of my boots mingled with the music of footsteps and rushing traffic around me as I wove my way through the other pedestrians. Clay mugs clinked in my crate, drawing a faint smile from the midst of my anxiety. My boss, Sherrie, talked about my amateur pottery to anyone who came into her shop. The display in the front window of Sweet Haven Bakery had been her idea. Those sporadic sales often meant the difference between a full fridge and eating ramen for a month. Which was why I was out on the streets—far from the safety of my tiny apartment.

I threaded my way through a group of young women whose party clothes peeked past their winter coats. Their chatter followed me, a cheerful accent to the weight of the night. I glanced at the darkened sky, my gut clenching. One more block to go.

A bright trill from my pocket yanked my attention back to earth. I slowed, balancing the crate on one hip while I dug for my phone. My moment of inattention cost me. A shoulder collided with mine as a young woman in a long wool coat and glittery leggings shoved past me to join her friends. I lurched sideways, unbalanced by the heavy crate, and my foot caught on a snag in the sidewalk. I gasped, one arm flailing as I tried to stop the inevitable. The dirty cement rushed toward me—then, with a soft grunt, someone caught me and my precious cargo.

I froze. A woodsy, masculine musk surrounded me as the stranger shifted his grip and set me on my feet, his touch gentle and polite. A flush of embarrassment burned across my face. Readjusting my grip on the crate, I straightened and looked up.

My rescuer was huge—all broad shoulders and frightening height—his face mostly hidden by the deep hood of his sweatshirt. Next to him I was a tiny doll, easily broken and discarded.

I wrestled down a surge of panic, resisting the urge to bolt. No matter how terrifying his size, he didn't deserve rudeness in exchange for the kindness he'd shown me. I could do that much, at least.

"I-I'm so sorry, I—"

I wobbled, and he steadied me. A corner of the crate caught on the worn hoodie he wore, snagging a careful line of stitches in the faded black fabric. Another bitter gust of wind seeped past my scarf, and I shivered. He wore no coat or gloves, only the neatly patched hoodie. When I glanced at the bare hand cupping my elbow, my chest went cold. For a moment, his fingernails appeared long and dark, almost claw-like—and then they were normal and pink, and bitten short.

My gaze shot to his face. The deep hood of his sweatshirt swam with shadows that flickered as if alive. His face was a shimmery blur of pale skin and tangled dark hair. The shape of his nose was all wrong now, as if the hands sculpting it had forgotten their goal halfway through. As the headlights of a passing car washed over us, his eyes glowed, reflecting the light like a wild animal.

I took a deep breath, forcing a smile. My vision warped one more time, and his face retreated into a vague blur of normality.

It was happening again.

"Thank you," I said, somehow keeping my voice even and my smile steady despite the panic, hot and sour on my tongue. I clutched the crate of mugs close to hide my trembling hands.

The hood tilted and the stranger nodded, his hand falling from its place on my arm. "I'm sorry. I didn't mean to frighten you." His soft apology was voiced in a rich, velvety baritone.

I gave a jerky nod of my own and tucked a stray lock of hair behind my ear. Several inky strands snagged on my glove. "I-it's okay. I should've watched where I was going."

He started to speak but paused when something over my shoulder caught his attention. He stepped away as though I might burn him and shoved his hands into his hoodie's front pocket. A loud car honk jerked my attention to the street, and when I looked back, he was gone. I turned, combing the street around me, but it was as if he'd vanished into thin air.

As the noisy bustle of foot traffic flowed around me, a pool of stillness caught my eye. Several feet ahead, a man wearing a dark green beanie and heavy winter coat watched me, his gray eyes meeting mine with cold assessment.

Thoroughly spooked, I spun on my heel and broke into a brisk walk. The crate bit into my hands and chest, the mugs inside chiming as fear pushed my legs faster.

Sherrie would notice if I was late. If I didn't show up, she would know something was wrong. As long as I didn't stop, I would be okay.

I glanced back as I started down another street. The gray-eyed man hadn't moved from his spot. He pulled out a phone, his gaze following me as I stepped out of sight.

By the time I arrived at the bakery, I'd managed to find a scrap of calm. It was enough to let me greet Sherrie and unload the mugs without alerting her to the knot of anxiety lodged in my throat. I went straight home afterwards, navigating the streets in record time without encountering any more unsettling strangers.

Back in my apartment, I heated up some leftover soup for dinner. I ate it standing beside the stove as my thoughts returned to the memory of a blurring face beneath a deep hood.

"Breathe, Brianna," I whispered. "Just breathe."

Staying in the city was supposed to help, but how could I escape my nightmares if they followed me around and popped up on street corners?

A watery laugh slipped out, strangled and harsh, as I blinked back the burn of frustrated tears and stared into my cooling soup. I took a deep, shuddering breath and blew it out, focusing on releasing my tension with it. I might be going crazy again, but tonight I was still me.

My phone warbled from its place by my elbow, shattering the quiet of my apartment. It jolted me from my dark thoughts and banished them as the cascading chimes sounded again.

"Chris." I smiled and slid my phone over, accepting the video call as his ringtone sang out a third time. With a low chirp, his face filled the screen. For a second, I simply drank in the sight of him.

When we were kids, his innate charm and sly humor reminded me of a playful fox. As time passed, the resemblance had only grown. The once-cherub face now sharpened into sleek angles with sun-kissed skin. Blue eyes and dark blond hair, paired with his refined taste in well-tailored clothes, drew the eye and invited it to linger.

Everyone insisted we made a striking couple, but it was all Chris. People listened to him when he spoke. His accent and formal way of talking perfectly complemented his aura of capable and confident. I could've had the face of a boot, and no one would have noticed.

A thin scar saved his features from boring perfection. The faded mark rose from beneath his collar to root itself in the corner of his eye. I glanced at the side of his neck where the rest hid behind starched cloth and the silk of his loosened necktie. The silvery circle of scarred skin resembled knotted vines with something at their center. Although beautiful in its own way, Chris always viewed the scar as a flaw. In his mind, boring perfection was better.

I waved, prompting a smile that lifted some of the tiredness in his eyes.

"Hello, love. I hope this isn't a bad time."

I laughed, the sound still a little harsh and frantic despite the giddiness his smooth, cultured voice always inspired. "No, never. I thought you'd be asleep, though. It's almost eleven o'clock in London, isn't it?"

Sighing, Chris glanced over his shoulder. A heated debate in the background grew louder, peppered with jeers and laughter. "Well, my flatmates are discussing the merits of ordering in versus taking a night on the town. No doubt they expect to borrow my notes for studying instead of doing it themselves. Foolish of them but they never do listen to reason."

I set my phone on the counter, fishing a bit of chicken and noodles from my soup. "Will you let them?"

Chris snorted. "Of course not. They'll learn or suffer the consequences." He shook his head and smiled, his dry tone mellowing into a fondness I'd only ever heard him use with me. It always made me feel special. "Never mind them, though. How are you, love? Is everything alright? You don't sound yourself."

I sighed and set my spoon down. "I'm okay."

"Brianna..."

I cringed. Telling him about my little scare earlier would only make him worry more, and he needed to focus on his studies. I would manage. Somehow.

"I'm tired from working overtime at the bakery, that's all. And rent is coming up. I should have it covered, but I dropped off more mugs with Sherrie earlier to make sure."

He frowned and I winced, bracing myself for what I knew was coming next. "I could speak to your parents again, love. Perhaps your aunt has a larger place we might share."

"No, I couldn't—I mean, I—"

Chris chuckled. "Too much? Sometimes I forget how old-fashioned you are, Brianna. It's charming."

My face burned, but the right words eluded me. He was always teasing me about how I was born in the wrong era, especially when it came to relationships. He had started asking me to move in with him a few months ago, but I always made excuses. He wanted more, and I wasn't ready. I didn't know if I'd ever be ready.

Chris didn't know the truth about my past. The truth behind all the doctors and pills, and the years my parents kept me locked up in a house that held no warmth in it. The city was lonely and gray but better than what I'd left behind.

No doubt he could talk them into allowing us to live together, but still I balked. If we took that next step, everything would change. Our relationship. The way he saw me. Everything.

The silence between us stretched, and with a soft sigh, Chris changed the subject.

For an hour, he made me laugh with stories of the ridiculous pranks his flat-mates had pulled since the last time he'd called. We talked about the upcoming weekend, and before we said goodbye for the night, Chris assured me he would be there. He knew the perfect place for a romantic dinner, and he wouldn't take no for an answer. As usual.

I set my phone on the kitchen bar and finished my now-cold soup, then put the bowl in the sink. For a long moment, I stared at the meager pile of dirty dishes. The rim of the basin dug into my palms as my grip tightened, and I glanced up at the smallest of the three cupboards spanning the wall between my sink and my stove.

The door had sagged open, and the myriad of short orange pill bottles with their white caps winked at me. My gaze shot to the large tan container behind them, barely visible and dusty after two months of neglect. I went to close the cupboard and hesitated. My stomach churned as I debated with myself before reaching for the tan bottle to shake out one of the herbal pills.

The capsules were filled with a dark green powdery substance. Musty and bitter, the iron taste lingered in my mouth for hours, but they chased away my hallucinations completely. If I took one, I would be normal for an entire day. Tomorrow, I needed to be normal.

With a grimace, I grabbed a glass of water and swallowed the pill before I could change my mind. I fought the urge to gag and drank another glass before heading to my studio space to set up my makeshift potter's wheel.

I needed to go to bed. The morning shift at Sweet Haven Bakery started early, but strange dreams and old nightmares waited for me, stirred up by the strangers on the streets. Working the clay always helped calm the mess in my head. Besides, Sherrie might need more mugs for the display.

The hope that sparked in my chest brought a smile to my lips as I pulled out a fresh hunk of clay. I slammed the hapless lump down and relished the satisfying *thunk*. Again and again, I wedged it against the sturdy wood. The weight of the day melted away, and I found my rhythm quickly. By the time I went to bed, ten new mugs sat drying on my studio shelves.

The next day, I woke up early enough to carve four of the new mugs before I was forced to get ready or be late to work. By the time I arrived at the bakery, two of yesterday's mugs had been sold. Sherrie was well on her way to selling a third to a tall, thin woman wearing a sleek winter coat and earmuffs.

Sherrie smiled her usual wide, sunny smile and waved when she spotted me. The white apron she wore was one of the new ones she'd ordered with her bakery logo embroidered across the chest in glossy black. Paired with her cheerful yellow shirt and pale jeans, she looked more like my coworker than my boss. The lack of gray hairs in her double-handful of beaded braids only added to the impression.

I waved back, and as I stepped behind the counter, she pointed to a sweet roll set aside on a little plate by the coffee machine. The cream cheese frosting spread on top oozed over the sides to puddle on the plate. Rich and sweet, the aroma of cinnamon sugar combined with cream cheese frosting teased my nose. My stomach gave an audible growl. I flushed, and Sherrie winked, pointing at the treat again before returning to her customer.

There was no denying Sherrie's generosity. If I ignored her gift, she'd only box it up and slip it into my bag before I left. Besides, Sherrie's sweet rolls were delicious. I scooped up the little plate and grabbed a fork from the bin, only to pause as the feeling of being watched sent an icy finger tracing up my spine. I straightened and glanced back.

Cold gray eyes met mine as a man wearing a dark green beanie and heavy winter coat entered the bakery. The icy finger became a fist, squeezing the breath out of me while I stared, stunned. It was the same man who'd watched me walk away last night. Was he following me?

The fork I clutched dug into my palm as I forced myself to turn and head down the short hall to the breakroom. The comforting smells of fresh bread, honey, and butter swirled around me as I ate Sherrie's gift and donned an apron. By the time I'd clocked in and returned to the front, the man was gone.

Chapter Two

Almost home.

I cupped one hand over my purse, pressing it close as I walked. The bitter cold of winter had mellowed into the wet chill of early spring over the past two weeks, but I hardly noticed the nippy weather tonight. The old canvas handbag shifted against my hip as I turned a corner, muffling the soft click of worn wood.

A potter's studio near Sherrie's bakery was closing its doors. I'd stopped by during my lunch break to raid the wealth of secondhand tools heaped in a bin beside the cardboard sign announcing their closure. Now, most of the pile's contents filled the empty spaces in my purse. I'd even managed to find two small bricks of porcelain clay. Though I'd never worked with the stuff before, I couldn't resist the bargain. Besides, it was the only kind left, somehow overlooked by everyone else.

My brief stop meant I was running late, but if I hurried, I'd be home in time to video call Chris. A giddy smile curled my lips at the thought of surprising him for once.

A few hasty moments of conversation were all we'd managed these past two weeks. To make matters worse, Chris had been forced to cancel his upcoming weekend visit due to school, and I expected he wouldn't be making it to the States next month, either.

College kept him busy, and his degree was more important than a visit to New York. Besides, Chris had said he wanted to do something special for our next date. That usually meant more extravagant plans than a movie and homemade spaghetti.

The memory of our last date at his favorite café washed over me. I hummed happily, too wrapped up in the remembered taste of real hot chocolate and buttery croissants to pay attention to where I was going.

I splashed through a murky puddle, speckling my boots with city grime as I rounded a corner and stuttered to a halt. Unfamiliar buildings loomed in the graying twilight. Biting my lip, I glanced at the darkening sky before turning to retrace my steps. Someone whistled at me, and I flinched as I sped up again, forcing myself to focus on my surroundings this time.

New York City wasn't a bad place to live, but my apartment building skirted one of the rougher areas on the Lower East Side of Manhattan. For the most part, my neighbors kept to themselves. Still, it wasn't the best place to wander while lost in thought, especially once the sun set.

Raucous laughter spilled out of a crowded bar as I passed, the sour stench of alcohol and sweat washing over me. Wincing, I ducked around a group of rowdy drunks lingering by the door. One of them called after me, asking for my number and a smile in the same breath. I all but ran from their laughter, the sound chasing after me like a rabid dog nipping at my heels.

"Breathe," I whispered, forcing myself to slow as I left them behind. I shivered, then straightened my shoulders. Acting like a victim around here would only invite trouble. One hand slipped into my purse to palm the tiny can of pepper spray I kept as my constant companion these days. I hadn't had to use it, yet, thank goodness.

A flutter of movement jerked my head around. I slowed to a stop, unease creeping up my spine. Two streets down, a tall figure in a beanie and leather jacket eyed me for a second before starting up the sidewalk toward me.

I scanned the buildings around me, and relief swamped me. Another ten minutes—five if I ran—and I would be home. I could circle the block or cut through the alley up ahead. The alleyway was an old shortcut I usually avoided at night, but I knew the stretch of cracked asphalt well enough to make a run for it.

The stranger drew closer. Something familiar about him nagged at me, and I hesitated. He smiled, the bland gesture leaving his gray eyes cold.

I turned away, knuckles white on the strap of my purse as I broke into a jog. It was the man who had been watching me on the street two weeks ago. Last week, he'd come by the bakery to buy some of Sherrie's famous cinnamon bread. Then again yesterday for a dozen sourdough bagels.

I was almost to the alley. Twilight was fading fast, and the safety of my apartment beckoned. With a little luck, I could lose him in the shadows between buildings, if he was even following me in the first place.

Ignoring the jangle of nerves souring my stomach, I hitched my purse higher on my shoulder and plunged into the alley. I was only a few steps in when the scuff of a heel on concrete alerted me to the fact I wasn't alone. I clutched my purse to my chest and bolted.

The sound of approaching footsteps echoed off the alley walls. I was so focused on the man behind me, I didn't see the second one step out until it was too late. The unmistakable reek of cigarettes threaded with something sickly-sweet flooded my nose as I crashed into him and staggered back.

"*Hullo*, beautiful," he drawled, leering as his friend closed in behind me. His dark eyes were cold and calculating as he looked me over like I was a piece of meat on a butcher's counter.

I spun around to flee. Rough hands grabbed me, knocking my purse from my grip and covering my mouth before I could scream. I brandished my pepper spray. The man caught my wrist and twisted my arm up behind me. With a faint clatter, my last chance at salvation skittered across the asphalt.

He snorted as his partner kicked the can of pepper spray aside. "Wily little bint, isn't she? This is the one, then?"

"Unless there's another girl with black hair and freckles working at that ruddy bakery. Don't let her rabbit on you."

They pulled me into the deep shadows by a cluster of dumpsters. I stumbled, slipping on trash while they yanked me along. Broken sounds escaped in whimpers and gasps as I fought to breathe under the smothering hand clamped over my face. I bit and kicked blindly. My free hand clawed at any bit of skin I could find in a desperate bid for freedom.

The dark-eyed man holding me swore. His hand covering my mouth vanished long enough for a heavy fist to crash into the side of my face. I slumped back, stunned and tasting blood from where I'd bitten my cheek. Another curse and I was hauled upright again, sour breath washing over my face as they pinned me between them.

My hands were secured behind me with a thick zip tie. The gray-eyed man shoved me at his partner, scanning the buildings around us. "You better be right about this mark."

The man holding me let go of my mouth and turned me around. He grinned—his pale angular face too close. I shrank away with a swallowed whimper, my heart beating against my ribs like a butterfly in a jar. His grin widened. "Maybe we should have a bit of fun and sample the goods before we get down to business."

His partner hissed and sucker-punched him in the ribs, wringing a pained grunt out of him. "Don't get stupid. This is a job. You want to piss away your life being sloppy, be my guest. I'll make sure you get roses at your funeral."

"Shut up. What do you think'll bring it faster? The beastie was watchin' her last week, but it left when the old lady got mugged two blocks over. No way it saw us snatch her, but its den has to be close. A few screams—"

His partner shot him a look of disgust and hushed him harshly, reaching inside his coat as he peered about. My captor sneered at him and jerked me closer.

Mindless panic seized me. *No, no, no...Not again...please, not again*, I begged as he yanked my jacket open and palmed my hip. His bruising grip sent a sharp ache down my leg. Memories long buried began to surface under his rough touch to mingle with the now. The zip tie bit deep as I yanked helplessly against it, a plea caught in my throat.

He leaned in close, his breath hot on my neck. "Sing for me, little bird."

The harsh whisper scraped through me. He stank of sweat, cigarettes, and an animal musk—a nightmare come to life. A muffled sob slipped past the fear choking me. This time there would be no waking up.

He grabbed my belt and yanked it free, ignoring his partner's distracted cursing as the man tracked something on the roofs framing the night sky above us. A hand squeezed my thigh—and then there was a snarl as my would-be molester was ripped away.

"Dammit, you useless f—"

A roar shook the air, and I was knocked to the ground. Something snagged the zip tie around my wrists, and the plastic gave way with a wrenching snap. Sobbing and gasping for breath, I scooted away until I hit a wall and pushed myself up, staring.

A choked-off cry mingled with the sharp crack of a gunshot and a high-pitched scream. The thud of a body landing hard echoed around me in a muffled whisper as I stood frozen, my ears ringing. Another thud, and the unconscious body of the gray-eyed man landed at my feet in a careless sprawl of limbs. His gun slid across the cracked asphalt into a pile of trash.

I shrank back, cold brick biting into my shoulders through my jacket as I searched the shadows in the alley with wide eyes. A huge shadow separated from the other shapes in the alley and turned toward me.

Its eyes...its eyes were *glowing*.

I ran, not stopping until I reached my apartment.

***

Safe.

I clung to the thought as I slammed the door shut behind me. My hands jerked and shook, and I fumbled at the lock, shoving the deadbolt home before I sank to the floor with a sob. I huddled against the door, clutching my head and rocking in time with each gasping breath. "Breathe, breathe, breathe," I chanted in a harsh whisper, reliving the assault again and again in crystalline clarity. The greedy clutch of hands on me, the wrench of my belt being pulled free...

I moaned, scrambling for something, anything to anchor myself as mindless fear threatened to drown me. My nails dug into my palms until I knew I would have marks. The pain gave me a hold in the here and now as the panic attack tried to peel me apart. Each breath was a struggle for calm. I fought to see past the haze of a bruising grip and mocking leer. I was home. No one would touch me here.

"I'm okay," I whispered, clinging to the lie and forcing my racing heart to believe it was the truth, even as reality threatened to pull me under again. "Breathe."

Bit by bit, the panic attack faded. At last, I sucked in a deep, shuddery breath and let it go, pushing out the last bit of tension with it. Limp as a dishrag, I slumped against the door.

If only Chris were here. If only he hadn't been forced to cancel his plans to come to town this week. He would've insisted on taking me home himself, and those strangers wouldn't have grabbed me. It must have been a mistake—a horrible one. I was nobody special.

I missed him so much. If I closed my eyes, memory would bring the comforting warmth of his hands around mine. The miles between us would melt away, and I could revel in his easy smile and the way he loved to cradle me against his side. The gesture always surrounded me with his unique fragrance reminiscent of exotic flowers and deep forests. It hung in my throat, teasing my tongue as much as my nose.

As if my thoughts had summoned him, my pocket buzzed. It took me a bit to free my phone with my hands shaking, but I managed. The sour lump in my stomach melted away when I opened my alerts to read the new text from him. Chris's timing was perfect as always.

"'I miss you, love,'" I read aloud. "'I hope you can forgive me for having to cancel on you again. Study session tonight, but I'll call you tomorrow night if I can get free.'"

I shuddered, shoving away the flicker of recent memory his words called up. "Breathe, just breathe." It was past and done, and whining about it when he needed to focus on school wouldn't change what happened. Those men must've mistaken me for someone else. I was safe now.

I kept my reply brief, telling him I missed him, too, and promising to watch for his call. A fragile calm crept over me as we exchanged a few more messages before saying goodbye. I clung to it as I forced myself to my feet and double-checked the locks. And then checked them again before convincing myself to step away.

As I hung my jacket on the coat rack beside the door, the lingering stench of cigarettes caught in the back of my throat. My bruised cheek throbbed. I flinched, my stomach a queasy knot as I headed to the kitchen for some chamomile tea. Turning from the hated pill bottles in the cupboard, I let the familiar routine of filling my ancient copper kettle and brewing tea soothe my shattered nerves.

"So much for a relaxing night." I added a generous dollop of honey to my mug and collapsed onto my tiny couch with a sigh. My phone dug into my hip, and I freed it from my pocket, tossing it onto the coffee table.

The need to talk to Chris created a hollow, painful ache in my chest. I stared into my cooling tea and tried to think of something besides the lingering fear and panic of reliving my oldest nightmare. My purse was probably still in the alley. Thank goodness I'd put my keys in my coat pocket for once. No amount of new supplies or missing credit cards would be enough to get me to leave my apartment tonight.

A clattering crash sounded in my bedroom. I jumped, sloshing tea all over my lap. The sudden movement set my cheek throbbing again and I winced. "Dammit." Setting my cup on the coffee table beside my phone, I grabbed my old baseball bat from the closet and crept toward the open door.

A cautious peek revealed an empty room, but one side of my bedroom window hung open, its hinges squeaking. The bat was a comforting weight in my hands as I drew closer.

"Hello?" I whispered, but only the usual night sounds of the city answered.

A fresh gust of cold air seeped through my sweater, scattering icy trickles over my skin. I shivered and set my makeshift weapon aside. Wiping my clammy hands on my jeans, I reached out to close the window, then froze.

A familiar canvas bag dangled in front of my nose.

It still bulged with my new clay and tools, hanging from the brick ledge above my window. My hands trembled as I tugged it loose and peered inside. The pepper spray was missing, but my wallet was there. A lone credit card rattled against the tidy coil of my belt. Something bumped my foot when I started to edge away, and I jumped with a gasp. Spinning around, I watched my old beeswax candle roll to a stop on the colorful rag rug by my bed. It must've fallen off the sill when my window was opened.

"How in the world...?" I clutched my bag to my chest and turned to peer out into the night. The fire escape was on the other side of the building. While thin brick ledges circled each level, they weren't close enough to allow a person to scale the building. Yet someone had.

The memory of glowing eyes in the alley shadows flashed through me. I'd seen those eyes before, framed by a deep hood swimming with shadows.

A chill skittered along my spine. I closed the window with clumsy haste, double-checking the latch to make sure I locked it this time.

Chapter Three

"Late, late, late," I chanted, my breath coming in quick puffs. I pounded my way across the nearly empty walkway on the Brooklyn Bridge. *Maybe taking the long way home was a mistake.*

The city was never truly dark, but it was an hour past sunset, and my sculpting workshop hadn't ended until fifteen minutes ago.

I slowed to detour around a group of tourists snapping pictures of the twinkling skyline. My ponytail flopped over my shoulder as I ducked under a selfie stick, squeezing past a second group at a jog.

"Hey, watch it!" a woman yelped when I stumbled, banging up against her and ruining her shot.

"Sorry!" I called over my shoulder and ran on.

Two weeks had passed since the attack in the alley. I hadn't gone anywhere but work and the store since then, and never at night. I wouldn't have ventured out tonight, but I'd paid for the workshop six months ago. Only the thought of how hard I'd worked to afford the class pushed me out the door.

The men who'd tried to grab me were gone, hopefully for good, but it wasn't easy to leave the safety of my apartment behind. I'd spent too much time jumping at shadows to ignore the monsters hiding in them.

Although I wanted to get home, I couldn't help stopping when I reached the last stretch of bridge between me and my apartment. It was almost bereft of people. Cars flashed by on the bridge's roadway beneath me, their frenetic energy echoing the rush of the river below. Even so, if I closed my eyes, I could believe I was the only one here suspended between earth and sky. It was so peaceful.

Drawn by the sound of the Hudson flowing under the bridge, I went to the rail. The distant crash of water hitting the pylons below beckoned with a soothing wildness, but it wasn't enough to listen. After a moment of internal debate, I checked to make sure no one was watching and hoisted myself up. Butterflies filled my stomach as I shuffled along one of the wide beams over the roadway below. It was illegal to climb around on the bridge, but I'd never been caught before.

"Just for a minute to clear my head, and then I'll go home," I promised myself when I reached the far side and dropped to straddle the heavy steel beam. The cold metal burned my fingers, hard edges digging into my palms while I stared down at the Hudson unimpeded.

A tightness in my shoulders eased. I watched the eddies of froth and debris caught up in the murky water. The river was beautiful and frightening. The raw strength of the churning current washed away today's twitchy nerves better than any pill. A sigh slipped out, and my eyes drifted closed as I leaned into the cool breeze coming off the water.

A faint buzz in my pocket pulled me back to reality. I straightened and freed my phone, mindful of the river below. Quiet laughter bubbled up as I read Chris's response to the silly meme I'd sent him this morning. I was halfway through a reply when a flicker of movement below me made me pause. Returning my phone to my pocket, I scooted closer to the edge, peering into the shadows below the bridge. Maybe I had imagined it.

The distant wail of a police siren cut through the murmur of feet and voices on the bridge behind me. I jumped and looked around with a guilty wince. I really ought to be getting home before someone spotted me up here. I stood to navigate my safe return to the walkway, then paused. There it was again. A flicker of movement, like someone ducking out of sight.

My stomach lurched, and a chill swept through me. I scrambled back with a gasp—and one foot met open air. Crying out, I flung myself forward. I bounced and slid, then caught the edge of the beam. In one breathless moment, I hung there before the cold metal slipped free, and I was falling.

For a minute of eternity, the wind rushed past me. I flailed, my hands clawing the air for purchase while part of me braced for the harsh impact of cold water. A dark blur against the approaching waves was my only warning before something snatched me out of the air.

I choked and gasped, struggling for air as the impact knocked the breath out of me. A ragged grunt blew past my ear, warming my icy cheek. The world spun, and I scrunched my eyes closed, swallowing hard as bile rose in my throat.

We jerked to a stop. My eyes popped open, and I stared at the rocky pylons and rushing water below my dangling feet. Cold brick bit into my shoulder, and metal creaked overhead. I was under the bridge. An arm covered in worn, dark cloth was wrapped firmly around my waist.

Slowly my brain caught up with the rest of me. "W-what..." The arm around me tightened when I tried to twist around, and I started to thrash. I was trapped.

"Please don't—I won't hurt you. I promise."

I froze at the sound of the familiar velvety baritone rumbling in my ear. A woodsy musk teased my nose, like pine but sharper.

"I...um, okay," I whispered as he shifted his grip. There was a harsh scraping, like a clay shard being dragged over rough stone, and we started to move again in jerks and sudden halts. Cold brick pressed against my elbow for a second, and then we were flying again.

He must be really, really strong.

I closed my eyes with a whimper. We landed hard, and I waited for the rough-and-tumble ride to end as the world spun and lurched with his movements. I'd panic and feel stupid later. Right now, I just wanted to be back on solid ground.

A minute later, I got my wish. My mysterious rescuer set me down on the river bank. I staggered when he let me go, arms flailing like a scarecrow in an effort to stay on my feet. My eyes flew open, and I spun around—but he was gone.

A chill slid through me, and I scanned my surroundings. Glowing eyes met mine from the shadows below the bridge, but they disappeared before I could get a good look.

I swallowed hard, my heart in my throat as I turned to scramble up the embankment. As I headed home, one hand rose to my stomach. I could still feel his arm around my waist. I walked faster.

***

I made it.

Dropping my jacket, I hung up my keys and made my way to the kitchen as my phone beeped. *Thank goodness for small mercies. After everything else tonight, it's a miracle it's not at the bottom of the river.* Bemused at my good fortune, I wiggled it free from my pocket and leaned against the bar while I checked my text messages.

"Work, bill, bill, and...oh."

Queasy, I stared at the tiny picture of my parents on my screen. My thumb hovered over the familiar number. Before I could decide if I was going to open it, a video call alert flashed across my screen.

It was Chris. A wobbly smile slipped out, despite the numb fog in my head. I almost dropped my phone, fumbling to answer before it went to voicemail. A swell of pure relief sparked in my chest when I hit the right button and his face appeared on my screen.

"Hello, love. I had hoped to catch you before you turned in for the night." Chris's easy grin faded into a frown. "Brianna?"

"Hi," I croaked, wincing as I scrubbed my pale cheeks and tried to smooth my wind-blown hair. I was a mess. In contrast, the desk lamp beside Chris made his sandy brown hair gleam gold and limned the collar of his shirt with a crisp play of light and shadows.

"You look awful. Did something happen? Are you alright?" He leaned toward the camera, brow furrowed in concern. He glanced around his limited view of my apartment, his gaze lingering on the closed cupboard behind me. I flushed and started to reply when someone called his name.

Chris sat back with a frustrated sigh. "Don't mind that, love. I have a car waiting for us, and my friends are getting impatient. I wanted to check on you before I left, though. Are you sure you're alright?"

"I—of course," I said as he turned to answer them. "What's going on? Is something wrong?"

"No, not quite, but I wanted you to know I won't be able to make it to New York for some time," he said after a few seconds of hushed conversation. Probably telling them to keep the driver from leaving while he dealt with his phone call.

The sheepish smile he offered me next was tinged with more than a little regret. "To make a long story short, I've been offered a fantastic opportunity thanks to my studies. I know it's a bit sudden, but starting tomorrow, I'll be traveling around the country for several months, at least. Perhaps out of England entirely at some point, as well, but I'm not sure." Chris hesitated and his smile faded. He gave me a searching look. "We'll have to postpone everything until I return. I'm sorry, love."

"Oh." I swallowed thickly and forced a smile back in place. "This is what you were hoping for, right? Congratulations! I'm happy for you."

Two years ago, it would've been unheard of for Chris and I to go more than a week without seeing each other. This past month, he'd been canceling a lot. I'd barely seen him since his visit during his Christmas break, and now he would be gone all summer. It was only school, though. It would pass. I just needed to be patient. Chris was making enough sacrifices without me fussing over his choices.

Taking a deep breath, I pushed my turmoil aside the best I could. "It sounds great. I'll miss you, though."

Chris grinned and nodded, a faint air of smug satisfaction replacing the regret. He straightened the dark gray coat he wore, smoothing the lapels over his chest. "Yes, it is. I'll miss you, love. We should plan a night on the town when I return to New York. Perhaps for your birthday. It'll be my treat."

"It's a date," I said, finding my smile one last time as Chris stood to go. Someone called his name as we said our goodbyes, and the screen went dark.

"Right," I muttered, tossing my phone onto the couch. The giddy flush from seeing Chris for the first time in weeks faded, leaving me queasy and numb. I shivered and stared blindly at my empty apartment. I needed some air.

Making a quick cup of hot cocoa, I grabbed my jacket and headed for the roof. For once it was completely empty. Which was rare for a Friday with the warmer spring nights creeping in. Cradling my steaming mug, I straddled the wide ledge edging the roof and stared up at the stars, my dangling foot swinging absently.

Slowly, my stomach settled. The numb haze melted into simple exhaustion while I sipped my cocoa and tried to find constellations. As I finished the last mouthful and considered going inside, a faint movement pulled my wandering attention to the other end of the roof. I peered into the thick shadows around the stairwell and waited, my knuckles white as I clutched my mug to my chest.

"I know you're there," I called out as I stood and edged towards the hidden fire escape behind me.

The silence of the rooftop pressed close, mocking me. Doubt crept in, and I hesitated. The two older gentlemen down the hall from me kept letting their cat out on the roof. Maybe I'd imagined it. Feeling foolish, I started for the stairwell door and froze.

Glowing eyes reflected the street lights back at me. Slow and steady, they rose until I had no illusions about it being a wandering cat. Not this time. Eyes wide, I stared as they drew nearer, step by halting step, and the shadows peeled away.

He was *huge*.

The faded black sweatshirt hid his face with its deep hood, but did nothing to hide his height or the broad shoulders that hinted at the power to snatch a girl out of the air. *Or chuck someone across an alley.*

"I-it's you," I whispered, glancing at his neatly patched hoodie and the line of snagged stitches across his chest. I bit my lip, my stomach a sick knot. Panic at being trapped on the roof with a stranger—a *male* stranger—warred with an intense curiosity. In the end, curiosity won.

"You're the one who caught me on the bridge today." The deep hood tilted, and I took another halting step closer. "Why—"

A loud click from the door behind him announced someone else coming onto the roof. The big form flinched and turned to go.

"No, wait!"

For a split second, I stared into glowing eyes—and then he was gone.

"Don't...don't go," I finished as a giggling, tipsy couple spilled out of the stairwell. Hugging my empty mug to my chest, I slipped past them and headed for the safety of my tiny apartment. I had a lot to think about.

Chapter Four

Waiting on the roof quickly became an obsession.

Every night for a week, I sat on the ledge, wondering if he'd come back and if I really wanted him to. Maybe it was my self-imposed isolation talking, or the growing distance between Chris and me. Maybe I was going crazy all over again. It wouldn't be the first time.

Curious as a cat and twice as stupid. I need to get a grip. I hugged my knees against my chest. It was pathetic—haunting the roof and hoping to run into a mysterious stranger who'd saved me twice in impossible ways. Last night, I'd even dreamed of his glowing eyes, reflecting light like a wild animal's before he left me on the roof. The image haunted me all day.

"This is ridiculous." Uncurling from my perch, I stood and brushed away the crumbs of my snack. I had a batch of mugs to finish for the display at the bakery.

With a last look at the twinkling city lights, I gathered up my plate and cup—and almost dropped them when I turned to find a familiar hooded figure watching me from the farthest corner of the roof.

"Oh," I squeaked, fumbling the dishes and saving them from a spectacular death on the rooftop. Though I couldn't see his face, enough light came from the street below to show his jeans were as patched and worn as the hoodie. The neat stitches and tattered edges made him a little less frightening. *He's not wearing shoes.*

I crept closer, setting my dishes by the stairwell as I passed. "Hello."

"Hello." The low, velvety rumble sounded just as I remembered.

"You came back."

A hesitation, a slight nod, and he stood slowly. He loomed over me even after he stepped down from the ledge. I stared, eyes like saucers. The deep hood tilted, and he started to back away.

"No! Please don't go!" I wrestled with my nerves, stuffing them in a box to feel later. It wouldn't last long, but for the moment, it was enough to steady my hands, if not my voice.

He paused.

I shivered as the night breeze slipped past the collar of my jacket, ruffling my ponytail. "You're just, um...not what I expected, actually." The hood shifted again, and I caught an impression of shadowy shapes within. I offered him a shaky smile. "Could you take it off? The hood, I mean."

For a moment, I worried he would vanish again. The thought twisted in my stomach. I couldn't let him leave. I harbored too many questions and not nearly enough answers, even if I wasn't quite brave enough to ask those questions yet.

The deep hood turned away. "You may not like what you see," rumbled the deep voice. "I don't want to frighten you."

"Please?"

The silence between us stretched for a long minute. At last, he nodded. He reached up, and my eyes widened at the sight of his hands. They resembled paws more than anything human. Curving claws glittered in the dim light, savage and unsettling.

I flinched back, fighting to stay where I was as the urge to flee echoed through me. *Dangerous*, my thoughts whispered, sending icy trickles down my spine. I shuddered, my gaze shifting to the shadows hiding his face. *I don't care. I have to know.*

He paused, his hands on the edges of his hood.

"It's okay," I assured him. If he left now, I may never get this chance again. My nails bit into my palms, and I forced a trembling smile to my lips.

His hood shifted as he cocked his head. The silence between us stretched, setting my heart thudding against my ribs. Each stuttering beat tightened the thorny tangle of hope and despair forming in my chest. At last, he lowered his hood.

The light from the street below spilled across his face. My breath caught in my throat, one hand flying up to cover my gaping mouth.

Dark eyes met mine, set deep in a face both broad and flat, with a heavy brow and full lips. His nose was more catlike than anything human. Fur a few shades lighter than my own black hair covered his neck and edged his face, thickening along his jaw. It darkened the bridge of his nose, framing his eyes and cheeks before giving way to dusky skin in soft shades of umber. He tilted his head, and my eyes were drawn to the short, pale horns almost hidden in his tangled mane.

"Do you have a name?" I forced my hands down, clutching the sleeves of my jacket in a white-knuckled grip. My gaze traveled the length of his face before meeting his eyes again. Swallowing, I offered him another shaky, brittle smile. He hesitated, and I caught a glimpse of pointed teeth as he inhaled, nostrils flaring like a stag scenting a doe.

"I...I should go." He backed up and reached for his hood.

"No! No, I'm okay, really. It's just a lot to take in. Please don't leave. Please." If he left now, I'd never get any answers. If he even held any at all.

He paused on the edge of the roof. I crept closer. My hands shook as my grip on my nerves cracked, but I forced myself to reach out anyway. "My name is Bri. Brianna McKinley, actually. Thank you for helping me."

A hint of woodsy musk teased my nose—sharp and wild. His gaze dropped to my trembling hand, then returned to my face. Another beat, and he took my hand, cradling it as if he were afraid of breaking something. My pulse jumped, and I let out a shaky breath. His palm was warm and calloused, and real. I shivered as his claws skimmed over my knuckles. This wasn't a hallucination. At least, not entirely.

He released me. "You're welcome."

"Do you want to come inside?" I asked before I could reconsider. It was a horrible idea, but the thought of watching him vanish without getting a single answer was worse.

He cocked his head, an unspoken question in his eyes. I gestured to the stairwell door. "I'll have to take you through the building. You may want to, um, put your hood up. Just for a little bit."

He nodded, and I gathered up my abandoned dishes. Another fissure fractured my mental box as all the possible scenarios raced through my head. He waited for me, the hood casting his inhuman face in a smudge of shadowy shapes once again. My mug and plate pressed against my fingers as I led the way, praying we didn't encounter any of the nosier tenants in my building.

Luck was with us, and I ushered him into my little apartment with nary a soul the wiser. "I-I'll only be a minute," I assured him, shedding my jacket and setting my dishes on the kitchen counter while he looked around. He nodded, taking a special interest in the window by my studio space as I beat a hasty retreat.

Escaping to the bathroom, I cranked the faucet on full blast and shoved my hands into the scalding tap water as the box shattered and my panic attack broke through.

Gasps wracked me, and I forced myself to ignore the bright promise of the razor by my sink. Instead, I focused on the painful heat, keeping my hands in the water until my skin was lobster red and tender. "Breathe, breathe, breathe," I chanted as I cradled my hands against my chest and waited for the icy shards digging into my gut to fade.

At last, I rose and turned off the water. My hands were dry now, but I rubbed them down with the towel anyway. It was another routine, and I shivered as the lingering traces of the panic attack faded further.

"Okay, let's do this," I muttered, patting my cheeks and giving myself a good mental shake. "Breathe."

He was standing by my workbench when I finally convinced myself to leave the dubious safety of my bathroom. The unfinished sculptures on the set of shelves beside the workbench held his attention, and I took the opportunity to really look at him.

A bewildering mix of questions, both familiar and frightening, echoed through me as he lifted one of the plastic shrouds hiding my work. He was impossible, yet no matter how I wanted to deny what I saw, I couldn't. Even with the efforts he'd made to hide what he was, the massive clawed hands and feet would never appear entirely human. Though, with his body tucked into a pair of fraying jeans and a faded hooded sweatshirt, it was enough to fool a passing glance. Only if he hid his face.

"It's not done yet," I said as I joined him, gesturing to the clay bust he'd uncovered. "The nose is giving me trouble, and the eyes aren't right. I'll probably have to start over."

He pushed his hood back and crouched to put his face on level with my sculpture. He cocked his head and touched the damp clay. There was a glimmer of light, and the sculpture seemed to writhe and shift under his fingers as he nudged and smoothed the clay along. A pause, and he leaned back, his hand falling away. Now, instead of a half-finished face it was—

"That's me," I blurted out. He nodded, watching me warily as I touched the clay likeness. Here were my almond-shaped eyes, tilted up at the corners and framed by thick lashes my older sisters envied. The soft curves of my full lips and snub nose were captured perfectly, set in a face almost doll-like in its beauty. A beauty that had always outshone the real me, quietly drowning behind a smile.

"Wow," I whispered, leaning closer to trace the arch of a brow, half expecting to see my own warm, brown eyes staring back instead of bare clay. He looked away and down, his shoulders hunched like he expected a blow. "I, um…" I paused, picking what I hoped would be a safe topic. "You never said what you wanted me to call you."

"Adam," he replied, one hand coming up to touch the edge of his hood.

"Adam, then." I stroked the bridge of the nose where a dusting of freckles would've been scattered over pale skin if she were really me. Crumbs of wet clay stuck to my fingers, cool and gritty. "Thank you."

Adam nodded and shifted to hide his hands in his lap. Straightening, I smacked my hands clean on my jeans. He flinched, the sudden movement making his small horns flash and gleam in the lights of my studio as if they were hammered gold. A pointed ear, previously hidden in his wild mane, swiveled toward me.

I jerked back with a squeak. Dark eyes flecked with amber and gold flashed to my face, and his ears flattened among the dark tangles again. "What was…I-I mean, how did you…" I waved toward the clay bust, and his gaze followed the gesture before bouncing back to my face.

"I should go." Adam stood and headed for the window tucked into the wall of my studio space.

"Oh, okay." I trailed after him, watching as he tried the window's latch and slid it open. "Will you come back?"

Adam ran his claws over the windowsill. "I probably shouldn't," he said, his deep voice soft. "It's safer if I don't."

"Safer for who?"

He smiled, an expression filled with such heavy sadness my heart ached. "For both of us."

Then he slipped through the window and was gone.

My breath left me in a shaky rush as my legs gave out, and I slumped to the worn wood floor. If it wasn't for my own face captured in clay staring back at me, I would've chalked the whole night up to being one of my wilder hallucinations.

I hadn't had an episode in weeks, though. The bottle of bitter herbal pills gathered dust with the others, hidden in my kitchen cupboard. In fact, I hadn't taken any pills at all today. Not that there was any choice now. I needed to sleep. Despite my exhaustion, I couldn't stop seeing his face. The teeth, the horns, the tangled fur...his eyes. Dark and deep, and so full of bitter despair.

When I pulled myself together enough to stand, I went straight to my laptop. I hesitated before giving in to the sudden, overwhelming need to *know*. For over an hour, I searched countless websites as I chewed my bottom lip and tried to ignore the queasy feeling in my stomach.

The only references I found mentioning golden horns kept returning to the Greek myths of the Golden Hind or European folklore about the White Beast. Neither of those quite fit, though. According to the articles, golden hinds were always female.

The White Beast was male, but he only appeared as a white animal of some kind. Humans would chase him mindlessly until they died. The Aos Sidhe—powerful, high-caste fae known for their beauty and cruel bargains—sometimes rode him. However, everything I found referred to him as either a huge stag with gold antlers and jewel-like eyes or a wild stallion.

Chris called while I was between articles. I cringed, letting it go to voicemail with a guilty wince. I couldn't talk to him right now. As much as I missed him and wished I could confide in him, Chris didn't know about my hallucinations.

Besides, I had no proof that what I saw was real. Maybe this was all in my head, but how did that explain Adam?

I'd touched him and felt the warmth of his hand. His woodsy scent still clung to me, comforting and frightening.

As I skimmed through a website hosting collections of folklore and faerie tales, I stumbled across something much more likely.

"The Green Man."

I hummed absently, running my thumb along the edge of my dresser. The image of the stone carving in the article was tiny, but I could make out a face with oddly shaped eyes and nose, and a wild beard of leaves framing its eyes and cheeks. Adam wasn't covered in leaves, but something about the image wouldn't leave me alone. After a moment of hesitation, I plugged the new name into my search.

I sifted through pages of links referencing the Green Man, searching for anything to match what I had seen. There wasn't much. The stories circled each other, with an emphasis on the Green Man's attributes being linked to the earth with ties to fertility and charisma. Most repeated the same bits of folklore, while others seemed to be making stuff up as they went. None of them held anything useful.

It was maddening.

I shut my laptop with a firm hand and stalked to my kitchen. I needed to sleep.

Opening the cabinet, I found the pills that would make sure I did. I wavered, staring at the array of orange bottles with their white caps before shaking two out. Adding one of the herbal pills, I filled a glass from the sink and choked them all down.

With a last glance at the clay bust, I went to get ready for bed. Whatever was going on in my head would keep until tomorrow. If I was finally snapping again...well, what was one more night? If this was all real, it would be there in the morning.

Even if Adam wasn't.

***

Morning came, and the clay sculpture was still there. Maybe I hadn't dreamed it up, after all.

Doubt crept in as the days passed. I found myself running my fingers over the unmistakable ridges of claw marks on my window frame. For a week, I played things safe. I stayed away from the bridges when I could and shunned empty streets. The open space of the roof became both a temptation and a curse, and I avoided going up there whenever I could.

If Adam *was* real, I needed to think before I saw him again, but his resemblance to the stone image of the Green Man refused to leave me alone. A creature of folklore and faerie tales, the myth had to come from somewhere.

Everything had a past, a root in reality. Even faerie tales.

Some, though...some really are just stories, I reminded myself firmly when I clocked into work on Friday.

Magic wasn't real. The faeries I remembered playing with, the mermaid who saved me from drowning at the beach, and even the dryads and gnomes who had shown me hidden thickets and ancient orchards on my parents' property were all in my head. Just a lonely kid trying to cope. Dreams and imaginings, and *not* real. Too many shrinks and too many pills had smacked me in the face with the facts over the years. Hoping otherwise was a waste and a trap.

But still... I paused, the dough silky and firm under my hands as I shaped a new loaf. *Is it possible?*

The bustle at the bakery was usually enough to occupy me, but today, Adam dominated my thoughts. I needed to find him. Maybe he could answer some of the questions haunting me. I didn't want to crawl down that dark hole again, but what if he was one of *them*? What if the Good Folk, the faeries in their hills, were real? The very thought made my hands shake, and I pressed them into the floury tabletop until they hurt.

"I'm not crazy," I whispered as the edge bit into my palms. "I'm not."

But half a dozen doctors said otherwise. Maybe I did imagine him.

***

I *was* crazy. The alley stank of fried food going bad and worse. The sour reek of stale beer rose above the other smells from the dumpsters as I approached the spot where I'd seen Adam step out of the shadows. I coughed, gagging while I fought to keep my lunch from making a reappearance.

"Where are you, Adam? How do I find you?" I came to a stop beside a busted bag of trash. An empty beer can bumped against my foot. With a shudder, I kicked it away.

"I can do this." I swallowed back the need to be sick, shoving aside my memories of the last time I'd been here. There had to be some kind of hint as to where he'd gone or how to find him. There had to be.

Laughter echoed around me. I flinched, glancing away from the stretch of broken asphalt under my boots to the safety of the bustling street. "Breathe," I reminded myself as I returned to my search. "Concentrate. If I didn't imagine him, the clues are here somewhere. I need to focus, and—"

Something bounced off my shoulder.

I looked up into a pair of amused dark eyes. "Oh," I squeaked.

Adam freed his claws from the crumbling brickwork and dropped into a shadowy alcove by the cluster of dumpsters. "Hello," he rumbled, wariness shuttering the amusement when I stared at him in silence. The deep hood of his sweatshirt shifted to allow more light as he cocked his head. "Is something wrong?"

"Yes. I-I mean, no. I just wanted to find you and ask if we could talk." He glanced around at the darkened alley, and I blushed. "Not here. Back at my apartment."

His gaze shot to my face, lingering on my reddened cheeks. "Why?"

I stared down at my muddy boots and shrugged helplessly as I scuffed one foot against the broken asphalt. "I don't really know, I guess."

The awkward silence between us stretched, broken by the nearby bar releasing a group of loud, tipsy patrons into the chilly night.

"I just—" I shoved my hands further into my coat pockets, swallowing my nerves as best I could. "Are you one of the Good Folk?" I said in a rush, flinging the words out before I choked on them.

Adam flinched, old brick flaking from his claws on the wall beside him as he turned away.

"Please wait! I'm sorry—"

"Tomorrow night," he whispered as a rowdy group of drunks passed the end of the alley, laughing and trading insults. Adam began to climb. "Leave your window unlocked."

"Tomorrow," I repeated. He glanced at me and nodded, the hint of a smile twitching his lips as he pulled himself over a ledge and disappeared. I huddled into the warmth of my coat with a shiver and headed towards home. I had work to do.

***

There's just no book on how to prepare for something like this.

I peeked over at my studio window for the twelfth time in the last hour. Another peppermint found its way from my pocket, and I crunched the hard candy with nervous energy. All the cleaning was done, and Chris had stopped responding to my texts an hour ago. Each minute ticked by with agonizing slowness, and the thought of standing at my workbench with the window unlocked behind me sparked a sick feeling in my stomach. Any more sweets, and I'd puke, though.

Setting the last few candies from my pocket on the counter, I retreated to the cozy reading nook in my bedroom. My to-be-read shelf was overflowing onto the floor, and I sifted through the haphazard piles as I listened for the scrape of an opening window. The smell of ink and paper soothed the queasiness better than the candies, tempting me to take refuge in the worlds waiting at my fingertips.

I glanced out my bedroom window. It was still fairly light out, thanks to the slow lengthening of daylight hours which heralded every spring. Someone like Adam probably couldn't risk roaming the city until after dark.

Maybe I do have time for a couple chapters. Selecting a new sci-fi novel, I settled into my beanbag chair and let the slow scrape of pages and the weight in my lap ease my nerves.

At first, I ignored the light tapping noise, but when it persisted, I looked up. Adam's glowing eyes peered through my bedroom window. Still half caught up in the story I was reading, I shrieked and fumbled for my bat. He flinched and vanished as my brain caught up with my eyes.

"Wait!" I called out, running to open the window. The latch stuck for a second, and I shoved too hard. "Ow, ow, ow," I chanted when the latch gave way and my hand slipped, gashing open on a hidden bit of metal. "Dammit."

Blood dripped onto the floor. Turning away from the open window, I dug a rag from the full laundry basket by my bed and pressed it to the cut. I should've bought gauze yesterday instead of peppermints. I peered out the window and sank to the floor with a groan.

"I'm such an idiot." I let my head rest against the wall behind me. My hand throbbed, but I couldn't find the energy to do anything about it. I deserved it, anyway.

A low creak pulled my attention back to the window, and my eyes widened. "Oh, um, hello."

A faint smile touched Adam's face, then vanished as he glanced at my hand.

"I, um-it's nothing. I'm not very...it's just a scratch," I finished weakly. I offered him a wan smile and scrambled to my feet. "You're welcome to come in if you want. Someone might see you if you stay out there."

Adam hesitated, still staring at the rag clenched in my hand. He took a deep breath and cocked his head, his hood shifting to allow a little more light. "You're bleeding."

I winced and turned to neaten the stacks of books knocked askew when he startled me. There was another low creak and a scrape of fabric across the old wood of my window frame. A book I'd missed was placed beside me, and I jerked away with a squeak. My shoulder bumped something firm and warm.

"Sorry." Adam's low, rumbling voice behind me was both familiar and frightening. He was so close. His breath warmed the nape of my neck, and I could smell the sharp musk of cedar clinging to him, softened by the cool edge of the spring night. Panic rushed up and choked me. Scooting away, I forced my hands to pick up the book and return it to the correct stack.

Breathe. I reorganized the piles to give myself more time to find my composure. "I-it's okay." I turned and offered him a shaky smile. "I'm sorry. I guess I'm nervous."

My soft admission seemed to strike a chord with him, and some of the tension between us melted away. "Me too," Adam said just as softly and hid his hands in his hooded sweatshirt. I glanced down at his paw-like feet with their calluses and dark, curving claws. Almost human, but different enough to be strange. Just like the rest of him.

"You never answered me, you know," I blurted out when the silence grew unbearably awkward. "Are you one of the Good Folk?"

Adam nodded, his dark eyes glittering from the depths of his hood.

"Oh." I sat hard on the edge of my bed. "Okay." He glanced from me to the window and back, ready to flee. "Am I the only one who's seen you? Are there others?"

Adam looked away again, and the tension returned. He edged over to peer at my collection of succulents beside the window, the low table stained with watermarks and dirt from the clay pots. "No. Yes." He touched the tiny, lone cactus.

"Did you help them too?" I asked, tugging on the end of my low ponytail.

Adam shook his head as he ran his claws over the spines. Green sparks flickered around his fingers.

"Just me?" I whispered, caught by the faint play of light. I almost missed his jerky nod and blurted out my next question before I could stop myself. "Why?"

"Why not?" Adam asked, not looking up.

"Because I'm nobody. Why help me? I mean, I..." I trailed off when he finally glanced at me. The sparks faded as he reached up and pushed back his hood. His gaze dropped to my rag-covered hand, then bounced up to my face, searching for something.

Questions crowded my tongue as I stared at him. I wanted to ask him about my sculpture, about the lights that appeared when he touched my plants. He'd admitted to being one of those beings people once called "the Good Folk". However, the internet and books weren't always right. Maybe it was just another name that didn't mean anything. If I asked about the Green Man, or about magic, I'd probably look stupid. But I couldn't squash the buried hope I carried in my heart. Foolish, damned hope.

I bit my lip, and it was my turn to look away. I twisted the rag around my hand, trying to swallow my questions. The rough cloth dug into the jagged cut, and I dropped it with a sharp gasp. I was bleeding again. I stared at the pooling blood, fighting back tears and choking on the rising swell of panic.

Then Adam's hands were on mine. My heart thudded, and I froze like a startled rabbit, staring as he wrapped the bloodstained rag around my hand with practiced ease. Makeshift bandage secured, he retreated to a more comfortable distance for both of us. My fingers trembled as I touched the unfamiliar knot he'd tied.

"Why me?" I asked again, a familiar frantic edge sharpening my words as Adam folded himself into a seat beside the window. "Those men you stopped...they were searching for something. Is that why they grabbed me? Because of you?"

"You saw me," Adam said after a beat. "You didn't run, even though you were frightened. You spoke to me."

"Oh." It made a horrible kind of sense, and the thought of what could've happened made me nauseous. "You were at the bridge, too. When I fell."

The unspoken question hung in the air between us, waiting. Adam glanced at my hand. "I wanted to make sure you were safe," he whispered, looking away.

I shook my head, at a loss and fumbling for the right words. They never came. At last, Adam sighed and stood. "I...I should go."

I followed him to the window. "Will you come back tomorrow?" I asked in a rush as he gripped the sill.

Adam glanced over his shoulder at me, searching. At last, he nodded.

"Tomorrow, then. I, um..." I wiggled my fingers at him, wincing as the rag bandage flexed against my palm. "Thank you."

Adam smiled and pulled his hood up, hiding his face in shadows again. "You're welcome," he said in a low rumble—and then he was gone.

With shaking hands, I closed the window and latched it. I stood there for a minute with my forehead pressed against the cold glass surrounded by the lingering smell of cedar. Shivering, I double-checked the latch, then headed to the kitchen for a much-needed mug of chamomile tea. Maybe I could avoid pills tonight.

"I did it," I whispered to myself as I found a mug and filled the kettle. A wide grin broke across my face as my accomplishment sank in. It made my cheeks ache, but I couldn't make it leave for once. *He's real*, I marveled as I settled in to wait for the kettle's whistle. I hadn't hallucinated him. Adam wasn't a dream...and he'd be back tomorrow.

Wow.

Chapter Five

The sun took forever to set.

Will he actually come back? I fiddled with the fresh gauze bandage around my hand, then checked the time on my phone, yet again, before picking up my dinner. The grilled cheese sandwich tasted good, but my stomach was a churning mess. I forced down another bite and stared across the roof as I fumbled for my hot chocolate.

"Hello."

I yelped, leaping to my feet and sending my plate flying as I spun around. "Oh, um, hi," I squeaked out as Adam caught the falling plate with its sandwich still intact. He nodded, and the deep hood shifted as he gave my untouched sandwich a curious sniff. "It's grilled cheese, um, with pepper jack cheese. You can try it, if you want." I brushed at the greasy crumbs caught in the thick knit of my sweater.

Adam turned from the plate to me, then looked down at my previously elusive cocoa. "Do you...normally eat up here?" He set the plate beside my mug and pulled himself over the ledge.

"I—no, but sometimes I just need to breathe." The smooth edge of my phone caught the light, and I bent to pick it up. Tapping the screen, I stared at the five missed calls from my parents. My stomach twisted at the reminder of the unpleasant conversation with my mother this morning. With a sigh, I turned to stare at the twinkling city lights.

"You don't like it here."

I flicked a sidelong glance at Adam. "It's...complicated," I said, swallowing the sudden urge to tell him the whole truth.

The city was loud and noisy, and full of the smells of too many people in a small area. There were days I longed for the taste of air not choked with exhaust and city grit. I missed the peace of the country, of being surrounded by the green things and open spaces I'd grown up with. I missed it horribly, but at least in the city my hallucinations were more manageable. Crowded or not, this was where I needed to stay if I wanted to hold on to my sanity. All the pills in the world wouldn't help me if I returned to the woods.

"So." I cleared my throat, fidgeting as I mentally shoved my past back in its box. "Do you want to come in?"

Adam cocked his head. I caught the flash of his eyes within his hood, glowing when they reflected the street lights below. He nodded.

"The window is open. If you give me a minute, I'll meet you inside." Adam turned away, and I watched him drop out of sight before gathering up my dishes and heading for the stairwell.

At my door, I fumbled my key twice in my rush to get inside. My nerves vanished in the wake of my frustration, and I growled. "Come on," I mumbled with a wince, scuffing my knuckles. Finally, the door opened. Inside, I left my dishes in the kitchen and headed straight for the band-aids in my bathroom to cover my new scrapes.

"Are you alright?"

I gasped and spun around. I hadn't even heard him come in. "I, um, yes. It's just a few scrapes."

He lowered his hood, and a faint amusement warmed his dark eyes. "I meant your cut. From yesterday."

"Oh! It's fine, too," I said hastily, smoothing the fresh band-aids over my knuckles. My little bathroom grew more claustrophobic the longer he lingered in the doorway. I shivered and focused on breathing evenly while I tried to ignore that I was trapped. My hands started to shake, and I curled them into fists to hide it, nails biting into my palms.

Adam went still and took a deep breath. Slow and halting, he backed away.

My breath left me in a rush. "Sorry," I whispered as I slipped past him.

"You're scared of me."

"No!" I blurted out, throwing my hands up. I struggled for words to explain before I gave up and slumped onto my couch. "It's not you," I whispered, hiding my face in my hands as old shame made my cheeks burn. The memory of a bruising grip echoed through me. I winced, my stomach clenching.

A low creak made me look up to find Adam watching me. He drew closer. I froze, not daring to move as he crouched an arm's length away. "Then why?"

He sounded so sad and hopeless. It pulled me away from the dark place where my past lurked, and the words I'd needed untangled themselves with a wrench. "I...I don't do good with people I don't know very well, Adam," I whispered after a moment. "I've been hurt in the past by a person I thought I could trust." The panic his closeness inspired soured, and I swallowed hard as my heart spluttered against my ribs. I looked away, fighting to keep my breathing slow and even. "H-he hurt me pretty bad. I—my parents—nobody believed me when I told them what he'd done. For months, they told me it was all in my head. Ever since then, I..."

"Oh," Adam said, his deep voice soft as I trailed off with a shudder. "Is this okay?"

I gave him a wan smile, brittle and trembling. "Yes. Please be patient with me? It's been a long time since I've been able to talk to someone. I don't have many friends."

"Friends..." Adam whispered, tilting his head and making his golden horns flash and gleam against his dark fur. "Are we friends?"

"Do you want to be?" I asked, tucking my feet up on the sagging cushions and hugging my knees.

"I think I would like to try." He stood slowly. "I don't want to scare you, though."

I looked at him. *Really* looked at him. After a minute of scrutiny, he started to fidget, and a shy smile slipped out before I could stop it. Adam stilled, watching as I uncurled and stood. I crossed the meager distance between us and held out my hand. "I'd like to try, too," I said, proud of the even tone I managed, even with my stomach churning from my earlier confession.

Adam hesitated, searching my face for a long moment. I held steady and was rewarded with a sudden, shy smile to match mine as he took my hand. "Okay."

"Okay," I repeated. When he let me go, I remembered my abandoned sandwich. It had cooled, but it was still nice and gooey. I broke it in half to offer part to Adam. He accepted it cautiously, watching me eat before making it vanish in two bites. My offer to make more was turned down with a faint smile and a shake of his head.

"I should go," he said as I added the empty plate to the meager pile in the sink.

"But you just—will you come back soon?" I followed him to the studio window. "Tomorrow?" Adam paused, a question in his eyes. "I have some things I'd like to ask...as a friend."

A smile flashed across his face, a startling slice of white against his dark skin and darker fur. "Tomorrow," he promised, pulling his hood up and slipping out my window.

"See you tomorrow, Adam," I whispered, shutting the window and flipping the latch closed. With a light touch to the cold glass, I headed for the kitchen.

Another sandwich sounded delicious.

***

"What...what are you doing?"

I yelped and spun around, dropping my phone. "Adam! Um, hi..."

Adam slipped through the open window, picking up my phone and returning it before I could shake off my surprise.

"Thank you." My cheeks warmed in embarrassment as I finished the text he'd interrupted and hit send. Adam's curiosity was a tangible thing as he closed the window behind him, and my nerves settled as I tried not to smile. "I was texting Chris. He's going to Cambridge University in England." I laughed, soft and sad. The lonely ache in my chest grew, then faded when I looked up at Adam. "Nothing but the best for Chris. He's really busy, but I thought he might...never mind."

I plopped onto my bed, plugging my phone in to charge. For a beat, I considered the glowing screen before putting it on silent and setting it on my nightstand. Chris wouldn't expect a quick reply this late, anyway.

"He's your..."

"Boyfriend." I drew my legs up and hugged my knees against my chest. "We're trying to make the long-distance thing work, but...it's hard. He's graduating early next year, though."

Adam pushed his hood back and touched one of his golden horns. "You haven't told him about me?"

"No, it's better if I don't. He's kind of the jealous type."

He cocked his head and sank into a cross-legged seat under the window. "He doesn't want you to have friends?"

I shrugged, fiddling with a stray thread on my quilt as I tried to explain. "Mostly he doesn't like it when I talk to other guys, that's all. It's okay. Chris is always worrying about me. Even when we were kids. I used to get picked on a lot, and he would chase the bullies away for me. To be honest, I don't really have friends other than you and Chris." I paused. "Well, and my boss, Sherrie. She's nice to everyone, though."

Adam dropped his gaze to his clawed hands in his lap. "I don't want to cause you trouble for being my friend, Bri."

"It's okay." I gestured to my phone. "When Chris visits, he never stays late anymore—"

"You would lie to him for someone you just met?"

"Yes." I paused, not sure what to do with that guilty revelation. "I guess I would."

"Bri—"

"What about you? What would you do?"

"I don't know." He gestured to his strange features with a shy smile. "It's not easy for me to make friends."

"I guess it would be hard to make friends with folks when you can't let them see the real you."

Adam chuckled and shifted to gaze out my window. "Yes, it is. I have managed it in the past, but it's difficult."

I stared in fascination as faint sparks brightened and faded at his touch while he examined the tiny aloe plant I'd forgotten on the edge of the sill. "If you managed it in the past, why did you let me see you on the roof when I asked? Why take the risk I'd tell people about you?"

"I don't know," he admitted with a wry half-smile as he stroked the spiny leaves. "It's hard to befriend someone based on a lie." Adam glanced over at me, and the wistfulness in his eyes washed over me with a soft sigh. "I guess I was lonely."

A sharp ache shot through me. His gaze returned to my aloe plant, a melancholy mood settling over him with a familiarity I knew far too well. What would it be like to have someone I could trust to be honest with me, always? Had he ever known anyone like that? Maybe, but...maybe not.

"I won't lie if you won't," I offered, shifting on my bed and making the frame squeak.

Adam's dark eyes flicked my way, and a trembling smile tugged my lips. A tension I hadn't noticed until it was gone left his large frame. "I would like that," he said, his voice soft with a timid hope as familiar as his melancholy.

"Are you thirsty?" I asked after a beat, fumbling for something—anything to stifle the awkward urge to hug him. Adam nodded, following as I headed to my tiny kitchen and started pulling tea things out of the cupboards.

Last winter, Sherrie had given her employees a bunch of teas after a nasty cold swept through the bakery. The tins of loose-leaf tea smelled of green things and sunlight. Some held the ghostly sweetness of dried flowers. I couldn't stomach sodas, and most juices were unbearably sweet to me, but I loved tea. Hopefully he did, too.

He lingered at the edge of the linoleum at first, but after several questions about his preferences, Adam came closer to sift through the tea selection. Scent seemed important to him. He sniffed each one and rejected all but two right away. Finally, he slid one tin towards me.

"Mm, peaches are a good choice," I said, savoring the hints of summer fruit, vanilla, and rooibos leaves wafting out of the open container.

"You're ill?"

Confused, I looked up as I added teabags to a pair of mismatched mugs and the kettle began to whistle. The temptation of the open cupboard had drawn Adam closer. One of the hateful orange bottles was dwarfed in his hands.

"It's...it's complicated," I whispered, my happy mood melting away before I could stop it. *No lies.* I sighed and tapped the pills in his hand. "These are to help me sleep." I pointed to the remaining bottles in the cupboard. "Those are supposed to keep me calm or trick my brain into thinking I'm happy. A couple are for headaches." My gaze fell on the largest tucked behind the others, and my explanation stuttered to a halt. "Like I said," I whispered, turning to Adam. "It's complicated."

He frowned, opening the bottle he held as I fell silent. Adam sniffed the pills, then jerked back as if he'd been jabbed with a needle. "These are...this is poison." Eyes wide, he shook his head. "Why—"

"Because sometimes I can't afford to stare at the ceiling every night for weeks on end," I replied, the words bitter and tart as they tripped off my tongue. Taking the bottle from him, I capped it and returned it to the others. "Sometimes, being trapped in nightmares is better than living one. At least the dreams end when I wake up." Closing the cupboard, I offered him a shaky, brittle smile and a steaming mug of tea. "Do you want some honey? I have sugar, too."

For a long minute, Adam stared at me, searching. "Thank you," he said at last, reaching to take the mug.

"It's hot," I warned when he went to taste it. A faint smile quirked his lips, and his tongue darted out to test it before he took a sip.

"Honey is on the left. Sugar is on the counter in the blue bowl," I mumbled, startled by the sudden flash of pink. His tongue looked like a cat's. The shape was broad and almost flat. Another oddity to remind me he wasn't human. "Do you want a spoon?"

Adam paused, the bottle of honey already in his hand. "No, thank you."

Adding honey to my own mug once he was finished, I took a cautious sip. There were thousands of questions I wanted to ask, but the reminder of my own broken past left a bitter taste in my mouth no amount of tea could wash away. What if Adam's was the same?

"Are you..." He looked up as I trailed off. "Are you alone? You said you didn't have any friends, but what about your family?"

Adam flinched and dropped his gaze to the tea in his hands. "They're gone."

"Oh," I said softly, stomach clenching when his melancholy returned. "I'm sorry. I didn't mean to—I'm sorry."

He nodded and looked up. "What about you? Are you alone too?"

"Kind of." I hid behind my mug as I took a sip. "My family and I don't get along," I explained when he only looked puzzled. "It's complicated."

Adam's gaze shot to the closed cupboard, then back to me. I flushed, and he hesitated, glancing around at my sparse furnishings while I fiddled with my spoon. Regular cleaning sprees kept the clutter at bay, and if my belongings were a bit careworn, at least they were mine. Still, even a blind man could tell no one else lived here.

"Humans don't enjoy being alone," he said at last, slow and careful as if feeling his way along.

"Mostly." I took another sip.

"Why aren't you living with your...boyfriend?"

I choked and sputtered, coughing to clear the tea from my lungs. "I-I don't think that would be a good idea," I managed to squeak out at last. "If I did, he would want me to..." I fumbled for words as my face burned. "My parents have strict rules, and there are certain expectations Chris would have if he moved in with me. Even if he did convince them it was okay, I can't be like that. I don't *want* to be. So, I live alone."

Adam seemed to consider my words, and I gulped another mouthful, wincing when I nearly burned my tongue. "What about living with...someone else?"

Sighing, I slipped past him to slump onto one of the barstools. "My parents might be fine with it as long as they approve of the person. Chris would be upset about me living with a stranger, though. Sherrie is my best option if I needed a place to stay, but it would be awkward living with my boss."

He frowned, and I blurted out my next question, eager to move on to something less awkward. "Your horns...are they gold or only gold-colored?"

Adam reached up to touch one, his ears twitching before they went still again. "They're gold." He straightened, a wariness in his dark eyes as sudden tension laced his frame. He looked ready to bolt.

"Oh." My gaze dropped to his clawed hands as he shifted and ran his thumb along the lip of his mug. Several tense minutes stretched between us. "How...how old are you?"

The *thunk* of his mug settling on the bar snapped my attention back to his face. He watched me closely, his expression a blank mask. "You...don't want them."

"Your horns? You mean because they're gold?" I asked, puzzled. He nodded, and I offered him a wan smile. "They're yours, Adam. I know how it feels to have a part of you stolen away. I wouldn't do something so horrible to someone else."

He stared for a moment, then the tension melted away. "Thank you."

I nodded, fiddling with my spoon again.

"I don't know how old I am," he said at last, a wry twist to his lips. "There was a time when I...lost track. For years, I existed only in the moment. I think our ages are close, though."

I hummed and nodded, trying to ignore the uneasy flutter in my stomach as I considered the short gold spikes. "Probably." His expression grew puzzled, and I shrugged, my cheeks warming from more than the tea in my mug. "It's your horns, I guess. They're not very big." Adam reached up to trail a gentle claw tip along one ridge of gold, shooting me an odd look as he let his hand drop back into his lap.

"I'll be turning eighteen in a few months." I waved off Adam's surprise with another sip of tea. "Humans always keep track. Do you have anything you want to, um, ask me? I didn't mean to interrogate you. I just...never mind." I winced, shying away from the question of magic dancing on the tip of my tongue.

It was stupid. Everyone knew magic wasn't real, and yet it was the whole reason I asked him to come back yesterday. The things I'd seen since I was four years old couldn't be explained otherwise—crazy or not. I hadn't dreamed up Adam, after all. Here he was, clearly more than human, and I still couldn't force the words past my lips. But what if I was wrong? What if in asking I ruined everything the way I had in the past? I'd lost friendships to my obsession before.

For a split second, I was back in the woods behind my parent's house with Lila, begging her to believe me. We'd been best friends for years before I breathed a word about magic, about my hallucinations I'd been so certain were real. The tiny gnarled figure hiding in her wild brown hair had grinned at me when she turned to run back to the house. Our friendship had ended in that moment. All because I couldn't keep my mouth shut. Because I couldn't separate fantasy from reality.

The loneliness Adam's presence chased away needled me, and my gut clenched. I couldn't risk it. Not right now. Satisfying my curiosity wasn't worth the chance

I was wrong...not this time. Setting my spoon on the bar, I drank the last of my tea and turned toward Adam, waiting.

He was watching me again. Suddenly I felt exposed, like I was made of glass with every crack and scar visible in horrible, naked clarity. Nudging his empty mug towards me, Adam stepped away, and the exposed feeling faded. He pulled his hood up. "Thank you for the tea. It was good. I should go and let you rest."

"Okay," I said softly, strangely disappointed as I set my mug beside his. I followed him to the studio window and stopped him with a hand on the latch. "Use my bedroom window. It's bigger. I don't mind, honest."

Adam paused, his eyes glittering in the depths of his hood. "I...are you sure?"

I nodded, my smile trembling at the edges as I backed out of his personal space. "Yes, I'm sure."

He followed me to the big window, waiting as I struggled with the stiff latch and pulled it open. Adam eased past me and leaned over the sill. Probably checking for watchers.

"See you soon?"

He chuckled and nodded, reaching up to touch one of the horns hidden under his hood. "Yes...and thank you. It's been a long time since I could trust a human."

"Hey," I said as my smile steadied, "what are friends for? Good night, Adam."

"Goodnight, Bri," he replied and then he slipped out my window and was gone.

I shut the window, catching my aloe plant when it fell and returning it to the little table where it belonged. With a brief touch to its spiny leaves, I knelt to cup my hands over my tiny cactus. I could always ask Adam about magic later. Right now, I wanted to live in this moment.

"Next time," I whispered. "I'll ask next time."

Chapter Six

Spring became summer, and I still couldn't make myself ask Adam about magic. The first few weeks of our friendship were awkward, full of stilted conversation and sudden pauses as we fumbled along. Somehow we managed, and the awkwardness began to fade as our friendship grew. Before long, the sound of Adam's gentle tap on my window became one of the few things that could make me smile after a day of anxiety and pills. Pills I used less and less as the weeks passed. Though, some days were better than others.

***

"Hello."

I looked away from the city lights with a sigh. "Hello, Adam."

"Is...everything okay?" he asked as he found a seat beside me on the ledge edging the rooftop. Not too close, though. He was good about that.

"It was just a long day," I whispered, turning back to stare at the skyline.

"Oh."

I shivered and tugged my sweater closed. Today had been unseasonably chilly and gray for June, the skies dripping rain in a steady trickle until the setting sun burned through the thin clouds. Normally, I would've been in bed ages ago. I was off tomorrow, though, and I was tired of being alone.

Lately, the long days and short nights of summer had kept Adam from visiting more often than not. I hadn't even been sure he was going to come by tonight, but I had hoped he would. With nearly a week having passed since his last visit, I'd missed him.

"How did you know I was awake?"

Adam glanced over at me, his faint and sheepish smile a familiar comfort after such an exhausting day. "I didn't."

"And you came by, anyway?" I wondered aloud, the possibility almost enough to startle me out of my funk. Then my gaze caught on the darkened phone next to me and I faltered. Adam shifted beside me. I looked up with a wan smile. "Sorry, I guess I'm not very good company tonight."

Adam glanced at my phone, then at my hands clutching my navy sweater closed, my knuckles white as the thick knit bit into my fingers. After giving me a long, searching look, he pushed his hood back and waited.

A shuddering sigh ripped loose from the tangle of misery lodged in my chest, and I struggled to swallow back tears. "Chris was supposed to visit this week," I said at last. "He canceled, though. Something must've come up. I-I mean, Chris said he'd be traveling this summer, but when we talked last week, he said he'd been able to free some time after all. He was going to come to New York this weekend. But I guess things just...didn't work out."

"Does that happen a lot?"

"Him being busy?" I mumbled, drawing my legs up to prop my chin on my knees. Adam nodded. "It didn't use to. When we were kids, he was always there. Chris was my first real friend. Someone I thought I could always count on no matter what." I tipped my head back and let my eyes fall closed as I remembered those early days with Chris. "I was seven years old when I met him. He was eleven. It was at a company party for my dad's business, I think. His family had recently moved to the States from England, and he was the only other kid who would talk to me. Chris actually came across the room to give me a rose from one of the tables. Somehow, he charmed my parents into letting us wander around by ourselves."

A soft laugh slipped out as I remembered how the adults loved him. Chris used his advantage ruthlessly. He was the perfect golden prince, and the world was his kingdom.

"I envied him back then. No one ever told him no. He would smile, and the adults would indulge him in anything. After the first day, we were practically inseparable."

I gestured to the city lights around us. "In a way, Chris is the whole reason I'm here. He somehow convinced my parents to let me move out when I turned sixteen. When I came to the city, Chris checked in all the time, making sure I was doing okay. Even after he returned to England to finish his degree, he was always sending me things he thought I needed." I couldn't help but smile at the memories of the extravagant bouquets and small luxuries he insisted on giving me. "That summer, we started dating. It was wonderful, like a dream come true. During his winter break, he asked me to move to England with him, and I just...I couldn't do it. Ever since then, I've hardly seen him."

Adam frowned, and I flushed as I realized how whiny and pathetic I sounded. "But it's okay. It's not as if he abandoned me or anything. He's busy."

Adam cocked his head, his dark eyes flashing in the faint glow of street lights below. "You miss him."

"I think...I mean, what if he never comes back?" I whispered, the hot prickle of tears burning my eyes.

The gentle hand on my shoulder was as welcome as it was surprising. Normally, Adam avoided touching me, but some moments needed more than words. The brief press of his calloused palm steadied me in a way I never expected. Warmth from his skin seeped through my layers to ease the ache in my chest. And just like that, I could breathe again.

"He will come back to you, Bri," Adam assured, his warmth already fading as he pulled away.

"You think so?" I let my legs drop and looked up with a tremulous smile.

Adam nodded, tucking his hands away in his hoodie pocket.

I sighed, drying a few escaping tears on my sleeve as we watched the flash and glitter of the city around us. "I hope you're right."

***

As the days lengthened and the nights became shorter, the number of days between Adam's visits grew until I hardly saw him at all. The lack left me anxious and twitchy. Midsummer was the worst. After a lonely three-week stretch, I started staying up the nights before my days off to hang out with him. We spent most of those late-night hours on the roof. Our conversations wandered aimlessly. We talked about anything and everything into the wee hours of the morning. And while neither of us were anxious to share our pasts, sometimes bits slipped out.

***

"I wish I could see the city the way you do," I said with a wistful sigh, cushioning my head on my hands while the gritty rooftop bit into my shoulders. The lingering heat from the day bled through my old t-shirt, and the warmth was a pleasant counterpoint to the cool night breeze. A soft rustle beside me made me look over to see Adam staring out at the twinkling skyline.

"This way is better," he said, his deep voice soft.

"You don't like it here, either," I whispered, the realization echoing through me.

Adam's gaze met mine, and he looked away.

"Oh." I sat up. "Why do you stay if you don't want to?"

His lips twitched with a faint, wry smile, and he cocked his head, his horns flashing in the light from the street below. "Why do you?"

I flushed. "I–it's better if I'm here. There's something wrong with my head. Do you remember the pills in the cupboard?" He nodded. "I'm sick, Adam. I see...I mean, I..."

For a moment, I was back in my room at my parents' house the day I moved out, staring into knowing eyes that peered at me from the shadows between empty shelves. Icy fingers dug into my chest, and the words died in my throat even as I tried to force them past my lips.

Adam gave me a puzzled look, and his gaze dropped to my hands as an odd spark of recognition flashed across his face. I looked down. My knuckles were white on the hem of my t-shirt, the worn cotton in danger of ripping from my tight grip.

Taking a deep breath, I forced my fingers open and swallowed the confession burning my tongue. I couldn't do it. Not yet. "I-I...well, most of the time, being in the city helps me feel better," I mumbled hastily, offering up the smaller bit of honesty in lieu of the heavier truth sitting like a lump of lead in my stomach. Familiar shame burned my cheeks, and I fixed my attention on the city lights around us with a wince.

"Bri..."

"So, how about you?" I turned to flash him a weak smile. "Why do you stay if you don't like it here?"

Adam sighed and dropped his gaze to his hands resting in his lap. "I don't know. I suppose I stay because I don't have anywhere else to go. Here, at least, I have a friend."

"You don't wonder if there's something better out there?" I asked softly, my nails digging into my palms at the thought of him leaving.

"Sometimes." Adam lifted one hand and watched the play of light on his claws.

"Well, for what it's worth, I'm glad you decided to stay," I said after a few minutes. Adam's hand curled into a fist and dropped back into his lap. He looked over at me. An unspoken question lingered in the quiet between us. Chewing on my bottom lip, I gestured to the glittering sea of lights around us with a shiver. "It's just good to know I'm not as alone in the city as I thought."

Adam's shy smile sparked an answering one from me. "Really?"

"Yes," I said, ignoring the telltale burn in my cheeks at the simple pleasure warming his dark eyes.

"Me, too."

***

We spent the rest of the night talking about sillier things until the gritty rooftop was cold against my jeans, and I couldn't stay awake any longer. Bidding Adam goodnight with a yawn, I headed to bed.

Normally, I would sleep in after one of our late-night talks but not this time. Instead, I was up with the sun, the steady *thunk* and creak of clay hitting my workbench with a musical rhythm.

I had a friend. Sometimes the reality of it snuck up and hit me in unexpected ways. As if I were waiting to wake up and find myself all alone in this city again. But Adam was out there. He wasn't going to leave or disappear either. The thought warmed me. I smiled as I rolled the clay into a ball and set it on my makeshift potter's wheel.

And sometimes friends give each other gifts, I assured myself. Sherrie loved the set of tiny bread plates and dipping bowls I'd made for her. Hopefully, Adam would like his surprise, too.

A bit of jazz music floated through my open window. I hummed along as I dipped my hands in the water bucket by my hip. Giving the battered kick wheel a spin with one foot, I began to shape the clay.

It didn't take long to finish the new mug and make a handle for it. By the end of the day, it was tucked safely out of sight, hidden among other pieces of drying greenware on my studio shelves. It wasn't anything fancy, but it seemed like a good choice.

For days, I fretted over whether I should really give it to him. Finally, I forced myself to add it to the next lot of pieces ready to be glazed and fired. Even once I'd found the perfect glazes for my gift and picked up the finished result at a local kiln a week later, I couldn't help but think maybe the whole idea was a stupid mistake.

***

The worn edge of my workbench dug into my hip as I stared at the new mug I held. I smoothed my thumb over the slick glaze, following the curve of the handle. "I hope he likes it," I mumbled as I wrapped the mug up again and returned it to the box of freshly glazed and fired pieces. Now, I only needed to find the right moment.

Giving the box a shove with my foot, I turned to my workbench. "And this isn't working." I frowned, sinking onto my little stool. The face staring back was half-finished, and I resisted the urge to flatten it into the lump of clay it started as.

Again.

With a low groan, I scrubbed my hands over my face. The little fan by my studio window whirred, and another gust of cool air trickled over me, sending a few stray hairs dancing across my cheeks. I smoothed the wayward strands into my ponytail and sighed.

Chewing on my bottom lip, I glanced at the finished bust watching me from the top shelf, her face serene as mine never was. It had taken me most of the summer and countless questions to find the right combination of glazes to bring her to life, but the results were worth it. Pale skin and warm brown eyes gazed back at me. Colored glazes added the dusting of freckles to the snubbed nose and revealed the full lips were quirked with a hidden smile.

"How did he do it?" I whispered, standing to trace one inky brow and tap her chin. My chin. In a few short strokes, Adam had captured my face that first day as if he'd known me for years, instead of a few scattered moments.

As if by magic.

"No, no, no," I moaned, spinning around and snatching up a damp rag. Attacking the ever-present film of clay dust blanketing my studio corner, I forced down the sudden flush of razor-edged hope. Remembered bits of last week's conversation whispered through my head. I'd come so close that night. I'd almost told Adam everything. But fear had choked me at the last second. Fear and the desperate, greedy desire to keep the one friend I had in this crowded, noisy place.

The frantic swipes of my rag slowed to a stop as I glanced toward my bedroom window. The sunny morning had given way to gray skies on my way home from the potter's studio. I could smell rain every time my fan pulled in another scrap of breeze. A folded towel waited on the edge of my bed for Adam's inevitable tap at my window, ready in case the gathering storm broke before he showed up.

Yes, it was good to have a friend. The questions could wait a little longer.

Humming, I returned to the half-finished bust. Maybe it wasn't hopeless. A faint smile grew as I ran a damp finger along one of the stubby horns, only to falter when a loud knock echoed through my apartment.

The firm, no-nonsense rap was familiar, and I stared at my door for a minute before snatching up a scrap of plastic sheeting. Tossing the old rag into the bucket beside my bin of clay, I covered the half-finished bust I'd been working on and went to open the door.

"Hey, girl," Sherrie caroled as she sailed into my apartment. Tucked under her arm was a sleek white box stamped with her bakery logo. Her keys gave a merry jingle when she set the box on the kitchen bar, and a broad, infectious smile warmed her brown eyes. Brushing a handful of slender black braids over her shoulder, my boss gave the box a perfunctory pat. "I've been experimenting with a few new recipes, and I thought you might enjoy some. How are you, hon?"

"I—uh, good," I said with a nervous smile, accepting her brief hug as I glanced toward my bedroom.

There was a flicker of movement outside my window. I forced myself to turn back to Sherrie before she noticed my wandering attention.

"I'll just—I need to—" I plucked at my apron all smeared with clay and gestured to my bedroom. "I'll be right back," I blurted out and made my escape.

Kicking the door shut behind me, I peeled off the crusty apron and threw it in the hamper. Of all the times for my boss to stop by to check on me, it had to be on a day Adam might show up early. I bit back a groan and went to the open window. The scrape of claws on brick drew my gaze to the side, and my stomach sank.

"Adam, I'm sorry, but you can't be here right now!" I whispered harshly when he glanced over at me. Then we both froze as footsteps and voices echoed up the narrow alley between the buildings. If anyone looked up, they'd see him. Adam was pretty fast when he needed to be, but was he fast enough? Probably not.

"Oh, what's this, girl? Are you working on something new?"

Biting my lip, I backed out of the way and motioned for Adam to be quiet. He glanced toward my bedroom door and nodded, slipping inside seconds before a group of people passed below—loud raucous laughter drifting through my open window. "Don't let her see you, please," I choked out before leaving to see what had caught Sherrie's attention.

She was standing at my workbench with a pile of plastic sheeting tangled around her hands. She held it up with an apologetic grimace and gestured to my stuttering fan. "Sorry, hon. I didn't mean to snoop, but it just kind of blew off, and I couldn't help myself. Did you make this? He's quite striking."

"I—it's not done yet." I glanced at my bedroom before flashing her a trembling smile.

Sherrie chuckled and winked as she handed me the plastic shroud. "Don't look so stricken, now. I can see he still needs some work yet. I expect to see pictures when he's all polished up, you hear?"

"Sure." I assessed the clay portrait of Adam on my workbench, suddenly glad I'd only roughed in the basic planes of his face while I fought with the eyes. Still, it was enough to spark her interest. Sherrie always chatted with her customers about her talented employees. I could only hope she forgot about this before my parents somehow caught wind of it.

I let the plastic sheet fall, kicking it under my workbench to be dealt with later. Sherrie gave my shoulder a gentle squeeze and turned to go as I stared at the clay bust. When her brisk stride faltered, I looked up.

Sherrie had paused beside the kitchen counter. The cupboard above had sagged open at some point. For a moment, she stared at the array of white caps and orange plastic bottles before reaching up and closed the cupboard door with a firm hand.

I winced and resisted the urge to apologize. To make excuses and push her out the door. To hide from the shame of what was wrong with me and avoid the inevitable questions. To start the conversation that would end with me outcast and jobless.

After a beat, Sherrie sighed and flashed me a sadder version of her usual sunny smile, her bright eyes dimmed. "You take care now, you hear? I'll see you on Monday—"

A low creak and a clatter from my bedroom cut her off, and I froze. Sherrie turned toward the sound with a puzzled frown. "What in the world..." she said absently as she strode over to open the door and peered in.

My heart spluttered against my ribs, my nails biting into the sturdy support of the workbench. A flash of eye-glow jerked my attention to the corner between my bed and window, and I almost choked. Adam wasn't watching me, though. His gaze followed Sherrie as she went to the window and checked the latch. I waited for everything to fall apart.

But she only sighed and closed the door behind her as she came to catch me up in a hug and drop a kiss on my temple. With a sunny smile, she pulled her phone from her pocket as it began to ring. "That's the bakery, hon. I expect a full report on those goodies when you come in Monday, you hear? Ciao!"

And then she was answering her phone as she swept out of the door with an absentminded wave and cloud of bakery aroma. With a shuddering sigh, I slumped against my workbench.

"Who was that?"

I jerked upright with a squeak, shooting Adam a wide-eyed look when he appeared a few feet away. He hesitated, and I winced. "Sorry, I...that was my boss, Sherrie. She owns Sweet Haven Bakery, and she's always bringing me food. She says it's because I have a good palate, but I think she just likes to feed people."

Adam nodded, glancing at the cupboard with its array of pill bottles. The door was hanging open again. I flushed and grabbed a screwdriver. When I finished tightening the blasted latch, Adam was crouching in front of my workbench. He touched the clay likeness.

"It's not very good," I said as I joined him. "I know I can't keep it either, but I wanted to try."

Adam nodded, hiding his hands in his hoodie pocket as he stood. It was then he noticed the other face on my shelves. "You finished it?"

I nodded, flashing him a shy smile. "I did."

"Why?"

I fiddled with the hem of my shirt. "I suppose it's because it was a gift from a friend. One I could keep to remind myself I *have* a friend. That I didn't just dream you up because I took the wrong pills."

A slow, sweet smile spilled across Adam's face. He stepped aside, and I covered the unfinished bust of him with the plastic sheeting once again, then moved the whole thing to my shelves. I had a few more weeks before my aunt would stop by for her usual inspection. Maybe I could figure out what I was doing wrong before returning it to my bin of clay.

When I backed away, my foot caught on the box from the potter's studio sitting beside my shelves, and I paused. *Well, now is probably as good a time as any.* I knelt to sort through the collection of freshly finished pieces. Finding what I wanted, I straightened and turned to Adam.

"Here," I mumbled, my cheeks warming as I held it out. "This is for you."

He took the wrapped bundle I thrust at him with a bemused slant to his faint smile, curiosity in his dark eyes as he peeled away the brown butcher paper. "You made this...for me?" he said when the gift was revealed.

Unlike my other mugs, this one was wide and deep, with thick walls and a handle big enough to accommodate his large, paw-like hands. The green and light-brown glazes I'd chosen glimmered with pinpoint flakes of gold.

"Yeah," I said as he turned it over in his hands, staring at the simple gift as if he thought it would vanish. "The studio where I fire my pieces got these new glazes in a couple weeks ago," I explained, watching as the studio lights made the mug shimmer with gold sparks. "They kept reminding me of you, and I thought maybe you'd want to have your own mug to keep here. For when you visit." He was still staring at it, and I bit my lip, fighting the impulse to start apologizing. "Do you like it?" I asked instead.

He nodded. "Thank you," he rumbled, his deep voice soft.

Right on cue, my copper kettle started to warble.

I held out one hand with a grin, giddy with relief. "Ready to try it out? I found some new teas yesterday, and I can smell sweet rolls in the box Sherrie left. I bet she saved me the best ones."

Adam chuckled and nodded. He handed me his new mug, and together we headed into the kitchen to silence the shrieking kettle.

Chapter Seven

The days grew shorter again as summer bled into fall. Chris's travels took him out of the country, and our conversations over texts and phone calls dwindled to the occasional hastily written message. I spent a lot of my free time on the roof or in my studio. His absence was an ache I didn't know how to fill.

With the return of longer nights, Adam's visits became a regular occurrence once again. His presence eased the loneliness Chris left behind. I would hear his gentle tap on the glass a few hours after I got home from work, usually right before bed. Dreary days remained his favorite times to see me, and I found myself looking forward to each one.

More often than not, we ended the night in my bedroom, talking...always talking. Adam's interest in the plants by the window grew as the nights became crisp and chill. I still saw green sparks whenever he touched them, or fiddled with the clay on my workbench, but I couldn't force myself to ask. Every night, I swallowed the questions burning my tongue even as they lodged in my throat. This was too precious.

Nothing could be avoided forever, though. One rain-drenched night, it all came apart.

***

"What are those?" Adam asked, draping his damp towel over the back of my couch.

He'd shown up right as I walked through the door. Dripping from the storm, I'd tossed my purse, stuffed with mail, on the coffee table and rushed to let him in.

After giving him a towel to dry off, I was sorting through the damp bundle for any bills when I saw the familiar address stamped on the tan envelope. My stomach clenched. I pulled the damned thing from the stack, tossing it into the basket with the others waiting for the shredder.

"Bribes. Temptation. Take your pick," I muttered, sorting through the rest and finding only the usual junk.

Adam tilted his head, one brow raised.

"They're from my parents." I dropped the junk mail in the trash. "Chris convinced them to let me move to the city, but I have to give them weekly updates on my job and my expenses until I turn eighteen. I have to prove I can pay my own bills and follow their rules. They send checks every week. If I use the money, even once, I have to come home and see whichever shrink they choose. My aunt is a realtor. She agreed to lease this apartment to me for peanuts after Chris spoke to her. Dad wasn't very happy about that."

"She must really care about you."

I snorted and headed for the kitchen. "Hardly. Dad and Aunt Bridget have been bickering ever since I can remember. She loves my mom, but she's always watching for ways to tweak Dad's pride, and I was a convenient way to make him mad. If he breaks our deal, he'll look foolish. It would be as good as admitting I actually *can* hack it out here on my own. Without their money. Heaven forbid he be wrong."

Adam's brows shot up at my sharp tone. I flushed, jerking open the fridge as he gave the basket of checks a thoughtful look.

For the most part, our pasts were one subject which remained unexplored. Sometimes it created awkward moments, but we managed to find other things to talk about. Just the thought of opening up about my past terrified me. What if it drove him away? I sighed as my anger drained away, leaving me hollow.

"Why?" Adam asked at last as he watched me sort out the ingredients for my dinner.

"Why?" I repeated, setting a pair of cabbages on the counter. Confused, I waved at the basket of checks. "Do you mean why try to bring me back home, or why don't I want to be there?"

"Why don't you want your family, I guess." I hesitated, and a sad smile flickered across Adam's face. "You don't have to tell me if you don't want to, Bri."

I sighed, slumping against the counter. "No, it's okay." I scrubbed my hands over my face, fumbling for the right words and trying to decide how much I should tell him. "I just...I don't belong there, Adam." The gentle admission left a bitter taste in my mouth. "It's hard to explain, but I guess it boils down to them not understanding me at all."

"They don't?" he asked, his deep voice soft.

I straightened and turned back to the cabbages, ripping off the mangled outer leaves with more force than needed. "No, and they don't even want to try, either. They'd rather pack me off to some shrink to 'fix' me, like when I was a kid."

"You were broken?"

I glared over at him but couldn't stop the smile sparked by his mischievous expression. "You're horrible," I muttered, relieved as his odd humor diffused some of the painful tension.

It was only right he should know. After all, I couldn't keep pretending the past had never happened. That it didn't haunt me. Adam deserved to know what he was getting into by being friends with me. I was still broken.

Lightning flashed outside as the storm picked up, the rolling boom of thunder echoing in my ears as fat drops splattered against the glass. A faint creak, and Adam appeared at my shoulder. His sudden closeness startled me, and I dropped my handful of cabbage leaf discards with a squeak. Adam froze, then pulled away, hiding his hands in his hoodie pocket. "Sorry."

"No...no, it's okay," I managed as I pried my heart from my throat. "I'm a little jumpy, I guess."

Adam nodded and tentatively eased closer. When I didn't run away screaming, he grew bolder and asked me to show him how he could help. I explained as I went, chopping and stirring while he peeled onions and garlic from their dry skins.

As the rich smell of cabbage stir-fry filled the kitchen, I waited for Adam to ask about my childhood, but he never did. In the end, I told him anyway. About the loneliness of being far younger than my other siblings. How I'd "imagined" playmates, and the series of shrinks who followed after I told my parents about them. My being banned from the woods...and then being sent to more doctors after I tried to run away the first time.

"They didn't believe you?" Adam asked while I set out some bread I'd gotten from work.

"I was a little kid," I replied tartly, retrieving the butter from the cupboard. "Of course they thought I made it up."

"But...you have the Sight."

I almost dropped the little clay crock. Adam's words echoed through me, the thorny weight of them rooting me in place. The Sight. I swallowed hard, hope and fear a heady muddle in my chest. I was going to be sick. "I-I—what?"

Adam took the butter pot from my nerveless fingers and set it on the bar. "You have the Sight, Bri," he said again, concern softening his deep rumble. "You see the fae and their magic. Some glamourie will be too strong, but you see most of what is hidden. My mother told me about humans like you. It's rare. One of your parents must have passed it on to you. I...Bri?"

I stumbled back, and the edge of the bar banged my ribs. The pain barely registered as I fumbled for one of the barstools with trembling hands, all but falling onto it. "Real?" I whispered, my eyes wide as I searched his gaze for any sign of a cruel trick.

Adam would never do that, I realized as he nodded, worry and bewilderment flickering across his face. No lies, not even to make me feel normal. He was keeping our promise.

I let out a shuddering sigh as I buried my face in my hands. Real, not imagined. I wasn't crazy. I was gifted with an inherited magical Sight. I wasn't crazy, and my parents had probably known it all along. They were *all real*.

"Bri?"

It was too much. I scrambled to my feet and bolted for my bedroom while the world tilted and spun. Collapsing on my bed, I grabbed a pillow and pressed it against my face as I shook and tried to breathe past my whirling thoughts.

It was impossible. It was the only thing possible. Panic was a heartbeat away, but shock held it at bay. Everything I'd ever seen, the creatures of nightmares and dreams, ran through my head in fragments and flashes. All of it was real.

A strangled whimper escaped me. "Breathe," I whispered, tasting salt and copper. "Breathe."

Bit by bit, the maelstrom faded into a familiar numbness. I huddled on my bed while my breathing slowed and steadied. When I finally emerged from my bedroom, Adam was still there. At last, I possessed a name for the little sparks I'd been seeing all along. He had been doing magic. Just like he was right now.

Green lights brightened and faded around Adam's hands as he pressed his palms against the wooden frame of my studio window. I started for the bathroom but stuttered to a halt when leaves and vines made of the same light sprouted from his arms, face, and chest. They sank roots into the wood under his hands, and a faint, earthy sweetness echoed through me.

I shivered, and my eyes drifted closed as the pure peace of an ancient forest wrapped itself around my apartment with a rustling sigh. A low creak jolted through me, and I jumped, eyes wide as I stared up at Adam. He watched me for a long minute and then turned away, pulling his hood up.

"You don't have to go," I whispered when he slid the window open, rain speckling his sweatshirt as he gripped the sill.

Adam's shoulders slumped for a breath, and he kept his gaze on the fat droplets streaking past. "I should."

I crept a few steps closer and stopped to stare at my feet. "It wasn't your fault, Adam. None of it was. Those memories are just...and did my parents know? Did they ever even try to..." I shuddered and looked up. "Please stay. Please."

It seemed like I stood there for an eternity before he slid the window closed again. "Okay," he said at last, lowering his hood.

I heaved a sigh, my numbness fading into an exhausted relief. My world had been turned inside out and upside down in one night, but I didn't have to face it alone. Maybe I could do this. Offering him a small smile, I led the way to the kitchen bar. "Are you hungry?"

"A little," Adam admitted as he trailed after me. "Mostly I hunt. I don't need to eat as often as a human."

"Oh, um…well, stir-fry doesn't have much meat. I hope that's okay." I handed him a plastic fork and grabbed a regular one for myself.

The pan was still hot to my relief, and I filled a plate for each of us as my stomach grumbled with impatience. Adam tested one of my barstools to see if it could handle his weight. At the first ominous creak, he stood again with a sigh, and I bit my lip.

"I'll be right back," I mumbled, setting both plates on the counter and heading for my bedroom.

The roof was our usual place to hang out whenever Adam stayed for a visit. That wasn't an option tonight, thanks to the storm. My tiny couch wasn't much better than the barstools, but the extra beanbag in my reading nook was huge for someone my size. Hopefully it was big enough for him.

I wrestled both beanbags into the living room, my melancholy mood melting away as I struggled with the blasted things. A quick shove to my coffee table, and I had a pretty cozy setup. Well, as long as he didn't mind sitting on the floor in beanbag chairs. Chris would've thrown a fit.

I stilled, my chest tight. I'd hardly talked to Chris outside of text messages in the past month. My eighteenth birthday was in two weeks, and he had promised to come celebrate with me, but it wasn't looking like he'd have time after all. I missed him horribly, but Adam's friendship lessened the ache and made it bearable. With him to lean on, there was a measure of peace while I waited for Chris to return. This was just another moment to survive. It would pass.

My stomach snarled as the smell of food grew stronger, and I looked up with a start at the dull chime of ceramic dishes on wood. Adam set down the last plate and eyed the massive bean-filled cushion with its bright blue cover. Gingerly, he tried it out. The beanbag shifted as he settled and did its best to dump him on the floor. He caught himself and tried again, careful not to puncture it with his claws.

"Sorry, I figured it would be better than sitting on the floor, and, well…never-mind," I muttered under my breath. My cheeks burned while I bit back the rest of the apology and claimed the smaller lavender beanbag for myself, grabbing my fork. I'd just taken a big mouthful when Adam spoke.

"You didn't know?"

I swallowed hastily, coughing when some broth went down the wrong pipe. "Didn't know what?" I choked out, coughing as I reached for my water.

"That you were different," he said, his deep voice soft.

"Did you?" I shot back. My parents had decided I must be sick, then told me as such until they convinced me I was. I was four years old the first time I'd told them about seeing the fae. Did they even try to believe me? Or was it easier for them to get on with their busy lives and continue the lie, instead of considering maybe their own child was telling the truth?

Adam had said my Sight was inherited. Which meant at least one of my parents must've known it wasn't a childish fantasy. That I wasn't sick or crazy. But instead, they stuck to the lie. It had gone on for years, and for what? All those doctors and pills...and the world would never believe I was anything but damaged goods now. Something to be ignored, to be used and tossed aside.

Bitter words crowded my tongue, but Adam's flinch at my harsh tone was enough to wash them away. I shivered, suddenly empty and lost as my anger spluttered and died. Adam wasn't the cause of the mess I'd become, and he didn't deserve to suffer for keeping a promise to a friend, either.

"Adam, I'm sorry. I—"

"No."

Slowly I lowered my fork. Adam turned to gaze out the window as a flash of lightning lit the sky, his plate untouched. "You didn't know?" I whispered, food forgotten. "But how? You're—"

"My mother was half human," he said in a rush, cutting me off. "Most true halfbloods don't have strong magic, and often, they appear human enough. When I was born, I looked human, too, and my mother was able to hide me."

Adam sent me a sidelong glance. "She told me once that glamourie is instinctive for most fae, but it's not always easy. Strong or weak, it's best to change what's already there, rather than to create it from whole cloth."

"How long were you..."

"Normal?" Adam dropped his gaze to his paw-like hands resting in his lap. "I was ten years old when my mother's magic couldn't hide me anymore. We were supposed to go to my father's clan before that happened, but something went wrong. Humans found us."

For a while we sat in silence, each lost in our own broken pasts. Finally, I smiled and reached across the table to touch his arm. "Thank you, Adam."

My smile was shaky and wistful, but it was *real*, and so was his. Slowly, as if to avoid frightening me, Adam took my hand and squeezed gently. "You're welcome."

Chapter Eight

"Why didn't you tell me before? About the magic, I mean."

Adam hesitated and touched the closed flower on my cactus. Faint green light sparked, and the flower bloomed while we watched. "I wasn't sure you would understand or be willing to accept it. You never asked, Bri. I wasn't even sure you could see it until you told me about your past. It was as if you didn't know if you wanted it to be real."

I shivered as he touched a bud on my new miniature rose bush next. It unfurled its petals in a rush of color and turned toward him as if he was the sun. "I...I guess I didn't," I mumbled, remembering the hints and awkward pauses that had once peppered our long conversations.

About two weeks had passed since he told me I possessed the Sight. I half-expected to wake and find I'd dreamed it all up, but this was real.

The bitter herbal pills no longer lurked in my cupboard. Throwing them in the trash had felt liberating, even if it was nerve-wracking to know they were gone. I almost let the others join them, but in the end, I couldn't force myself to do it.

A part of me still longed to be "normal," but this was the truth of who I was. I would be eighteen tomorrow. An adult, for all intents and purposes. I was done with continuing the lie my parents had fed me for years. The fae were real. *Magic* was real. Even if the world insisted otherwise, Adam's friendship proved it to me every day.

I frowned as he coaxed open another rosebud. "How did you know I might have the Sight? You say it's rare."

Adam glanced up, his ears twitching and going still again. He searched my face for a long moment. "You saw me that first night when you spoke to me and then later in the alley," he said at last. "You saw me...and you shouldn't have."

"But you were right *there*," I blurted out, confused.

A faint smile touched his face and vanished, and he turned back to the rose. "Yes, but no one has seen through the magic before."

My gaze went to the hood hanging from Adam's shoulders as he examined the newly opened flowers. "Is that the real reason no one sees your face? Magic?"

Adam nodded, ruffling the tiny rose petals. "It's a glamourie. An illusion. The same way my mother used to hide me, but not as good." He glanced up from the rose trying to twine around his fingers and gave me a wry smile. "Casting glamourie is difficult for me. Darkness at night is easier than most but appearing human is more complicated. I can't manage it for more than a few hours at a time."

"Oh." The half-remembered glimpses of our first meeting flashed past my mind's eye as Adam coaxed the rose to behave, and the sparks of his magic faded. "Could you show me? Please?" He stiffened and turned toward the window, running his claws along the sill. "You don't have to if you don't want to, Adam," I said gently.

He shuddered and drew his hood up, a familiar sweetness heralding the rise of stronger magic than he'd used with my plants. Faint sparks returned to glimmer at the edges of his hood. When Adam turned, I couldn't help my wide-eyed stare.

It was him, but not. This time the lines of his face remained crisp as I took him in. The wild beard was as I remembered it, framing his mouth and jaw in a dark tangle. He looked naked, with pale skin and tousled black hair in place of his usual dusky skin and darker fur. Only his eyes were the same.

"Oh." I drew closer to get a better look. A faint green light rippled over his features, hiding in the shadows and edges unless I focused on it alone. The new face fought for my attention, though if I squinted just right, I could still see the real him. It was somewhat unnerving. The familiar musk of cedar that always clung to him steadied me. He might look like a stranger, but this was still Adam.

Adam's gaze was wary and a little hurt as he watched me approach. After a moment, I frowned. Without considering what I was doing, I reached up and combed my fingers through the thick fur along his jaw, pushing his hood back. His glamourie popped like a soap bubble, and I smiled.

"Much better," I murmured, my hand falling to his shoulder. His eyes went wide, and for a second, I was confused—then realization dawned. "Sorry," I blurted out, snatching my hand away. I'd never really touched him before. His fur looked coarse, but it was silky against my fingers. Was it all so soft?

Adam's ears flicked forward before flattening into his mane as he glanced to the side. "I—it's okay," he rumbled, his deep voice soft. He started to touch his face and then seemed to change his mind, tucking his hands into his hoodie pocket instead.

"Well, I...I better try to get some sleep. I have work in the morning, and Sherrie asked if I could help with the midday rush, too." I tugged the end of my ponytail, twisting the inky strands around my fingers. "You don't mind, do you?"

Adam smiled, a low chuckle slipping out as he pulled his hood up. "Go to sleep, Bri. I'll come back later."

"Thank you, Adam. For everything." I motioned to my own face with a sheepish wince. "I get the feeling you, uh, didn't want to do that. I'm sorry."

"I...I just don't want you to change how you see me. I haven't looked human in a long time," he whispered, his whole body tense as he watched me.

"Adam," I said in a light, chiding tone as I gave him a look of fond exasperation. "Under the illusion you're still you, but...I prefer the truth of who you are. You're incredible. Even if the world can't see it yet."

He was staring at me as if I'd started spouting Greek. A shy smile twitched my lips, and his stunned gaze swept over my face, lingering on my mouth a beat before meeting my eyes. "I...thank you."

"You're welcome," I said firmly. I went to the window and pulled it open, pushing the curtains aside to check for anyone lingering in the alley below.

When I turned around, Adam was still watching me, something unreadable in his dark eyes. Before I could ask him what was wrong, my phone chirped, breaking the moment. With a whispered apology, I brushed past Adam to my dresser and tapped my phone screen to check my messages.

"Oh, it's Chris!" Hastily, I opened the new text. "He's in town. He's...he's taking me to dinner tomorrow night for my birthday." A giddy laugh broke free, and I grinned at Adam. "He says he missed me, and he wanted to surprise me. I guess you were right." I glanced at my phone and back to Adam. "Will I still see you tomorrow? I probably won't be out too late, knowing Chris. You can come by, if you want."

He hesitated, his gaze dropping to my phone. A muddle of emotions flashed across his face, too quick for me to untangle them before they were gone again. Adam met my puzzled look with a faint smile, the gesture oddly wistful as he nodded. "I would like that."

"It's settled then." I hugged my phone to my chest as he swung out of the window. "I'll see you tomorrow."

"Tomorrow," Adam agreed and dropped out of sight. Yawning, I closed the window and locked it.

***

The next day passed in a blur of warm bread and frantic searches for what to wear to dinner. Chris's love of fancy restaurants, especially for special occasions, meant something more formal than my preferred jeans and t-shirt or thick-knit sweater. The longer I sifted through my meager variety of dresses and skirts, the more I wished Adam would come by and soothe my nerves with his deep rumble and gentle presence. At the same time, I prayed he wouldn't. Explaining him to Chris could only end in disaster.

Finally, I settled on a long black skirt slit to the knee on one side and a shimmery red button-up. Simple but elegant. The strappy black heels I chose as a finishing touch were a gift from Chris. Hopefully, I wouldn't embarrass myself trying to walk this time.

I put the heels on and stood with a slight wobble. Careful and slow, I crossed the length of my living room on unsteady feet, trying to readjust to my new footwear. When I passed the window by my studio space, I caught sight of my reflection and flushed. I didn't look like myself at all. The fancy clothes paired with the light makeup hiding my freckles transformed me into a porcelain doll. Even my hair, tamed and pulled into a simple, elegant twist, conspired to make a stranger out of me.

"Maybe I should change."

"You look...different."

I spun around with a squeak, catching myself on the couch when I stumbled on my narrow heels. "Adam?! What are you doing here?"

He leaned against my bedroom door frame, and a faint smile flickered across his face as he took in my appearance. "I wanted to see you before you left," Adam mumbled, distracted by my shoes for a moment before his curious gaze bounced to my face.

I huffed and crossed the living room to glare up at him, my cheeks hot. "For heaven's sake, why?"

Adam cocked his head as he eyed my up-do. Green light sparked when he reached out, and I spotted the rosebud hidden in his palm right as he touched my hair.

I gasped, flinching as my hair suddenly tumbled around my shoulders, several bobby pins falling to the floor with a faint clatter as something twined through it, tugging it away from my face. Trembling, I patted my hair, then brushed past Adam to peer into the mirror over my dresser.

"Oh," I said with a soft sigh, eyes wide as I gaped at my reflection. Instead of being completely restrained in a simple twist, half my hair had been gathered back while the rest was left to hang free. An intricate braided knot, set with tiny red roses surrounding a larger bloom, adorned the back of my head. More tiny flowers studded the swept-up hair at my temples.

Adam chuckled as I twisted this way and that, trying to see everything. "Better?" he asked when I traced a pair of thin braids from my temples to the knot woven with flowers.

"It's beautiful." I turned to beam at him. "How did you..."

"My mother loved wearing flowers in her hair," Adam whispered, his amusement fading into something wistful.

I crossed the room and pressed my hands against his folded arms. "Thank you so much. It's perfect."

Adam hesitated, searching my face for a long moment. "You're welcome," he said at last, his deep voice soft. "Happy Birthday, Bri."

A firm knock echoed through my apartment. My gaze snapped to the delicate gold watch on my wrist. Six o'clock on the nose. It could only be Chris. "I have to go," I whispered as I glanced around the room to make sure I wasn't forgetting anything. "I'll see you when I get back." Adam nodded, and I gave him one last grateful smile before I bolted for the door as Chris knocked again.

Somehow, I reached it without falling victim to my narrow heels. Pausing with one hand on the knob, I took a deep breath to steady my thudding heart and opened the door. "Hello, Chris. I just need to grab my coat, and I'm ready to go."

Chris smiled, frank approval warming his cool blue eyes as his gaze skimmed over my outfit. As usual, even all dolled up, I couldn't help feeling out of place standing next to him. Chris had particular tastes, especially when it came to his appearance, and tonight was no exception. He exuded confidence and expense. His dark gray wool coat showcased his lean frame and broad shoulders. A starched white collar peeked above the neck of his coat, and his black slacks were well-tailored. The crimson scarf he wore could only be silk, with its soft luster, and sleek, glossy dress shoes completed his outfit. Not a hair out of place, he looked like he was about to step out on a catwalk rather than go to a restaurant.

Chris nodded, the light from the hallway making his sandy brown hair gleam. "Go on and grab it then," he said absently as he touched one of the roses in my hair. He glanced around my apartment with a frown. His gaze lingered on my closed bedroom door, and the frown deepened for a moment before melting away. "The car is waiting. I've made reservations for a private table, and we don't want to be late."

I nodded and went to retrieve my coat, snatching up my little black clutch along the way. It barely held my phone, keys, and a tube of lip gloss, but it complimented my outfit and added the kind of touch Chris loved. When I rejoined him by the door, he was eyeing the basket of checks.

"Your parents say hello, by the way," Chris remarked, almost thoughtful. His attention returned to my closed bedroom door.

"Oh."

His gaze snapped to mine, and I forced a smile. With a soft sigh, he pulled me closer, kissing my forehead. The floral musk of his favorite cologne surrounded me, blending with the sweeter scent of Adam's roses in my hair.

Chris smoothed a stray tendril of hair along my cheek and smiled, his warm fingers trailing along my jaw to tip my chin upward. "Happy birthday, Brianna," he murmured, leaning closer. "You look lovely."

Ignoring the uneasy twisting of my stomach, I caught his patently possessive kiss on my lips. "Thank you."

"The flowers are...interesting," he said a minute later while we waited for the elevator doors to open. Chris tugged a bloom free to examine it.

It hurt—as if the flower was rooted in more than my hair. I let him pluck a second one, wincing. "I thought they were a nice touch."

"Hm." He plucked another, his gaze sharpening when he noticed how I flinched. "They're beautiful," he said at last, touching the largest bloom. "Who gave them to you?"

"I—no one," I stammered, Adam's face flashing through my head.

"Really?" Chris's hand dropped away and caught up mine, bringing it to his lips. "Well, I'll have to see if I can match them," he murmured, a curious edge to his usual crooked smile.

Chris kept my hand all the way to the restaurant. Two blocks away, he had our driver make a brief stop at a florist, and I endured him plucking out Adam's flowers to replace them with his own. My scalp still ached by the time we were seated, and only the largest flower remained. Delicate sprays of tiny star-shaped white flowers studded my hair now, and several pale peach blossoms accented the large rose.

"Much better," he murmured, running his hands over my hair and adjusting a bloom here and there. "You are as beautiful as ever, Brianna."

My cheeks warmed at the praise, and I reached for the menu. Chris chuckled and took the elegant stemware at my place setting. He poured it full from a fanciful glass water pitcher beside our table. For a moment, the liquid almost seemed to glow in his hand, but when I paused to look, it was only water.

Chris hummed, considering the filled glass a moment longer. The play of light through the delicate crystal made the water sparkle like fine wine. It was beautiful, and after a second, Chris nodded with an oddly satisfied smile.

"Thank you," I said absently when he returned it to its original place at my elbow. Eyeing the water in my wineglass for another second, I turned my attention to the menu. I skimmed the choices and bit back a wince. Chris loved these kinds of places, but I could barely understand what half the dishes were, and nothing had prices. A sure sign it would be expensive.

"Don't worry, love," he said with a careless wave at the menu as he took his seat. "All their food is wonderful. I've already ordered something for you."

"Oh, okay." I set the menu aside, my stomach a tight knot. It wasn't unusual for him to order for me. He had a knack for knowing what I might like, and his choices were always delicious. In fact, it was a common occurrence when he took me out to dinner. Especially when I couldn't afford the bill. Which begged the question...why did it bother me now?

"So, how have you been?" I blurted out, stifling the need to touch Adam's rose in my hair. "How are things at Cambridge?"

Chris paused and set his menu beside mine with a faint smile. "They're going well, actually. I received several job offers during my travels over the summer, and I've decided to accept one."

"O-oh?" I stammered, caught off guard as I reached for my water. A generous sip had me struggling to remember I was in an upper-class establishment. Spitting the wine I'd mistaken for water back into its glass was simply not done in a place like this. I swallowed and shuddered as it burned down my throat in a sticky, honeyed trail. Was wine supposed to be this sweet?

"Yes," Chris continued, his gaze sharpening when I set my glass aside. "It's not to your liking?"

"I—no, it's fine," I said, flushed from the unfamiliar burn of alcohol in my throat. "I just didn't realize it was...and well, I don't drink. You know that."

"Mm," he hummed noncommittally, sipping from his own glass before nudging mine back to me. "I also remember you mentioning you aren't taking your medications anymore, love. As I see it, the staff here tonight are good friends of mine, so you needn't worry about any trouble there. Why don't you enjoy it while you can? I chose it for you especially, after all." Good manners had my fingers curling around the delicate stem as Chris raised his wineglass in a toast. "To us," he said with a teasing smile.

I blushed and raised my glass, taking a meager sip because he clearly expected it. Whatever was in my glass might look like water, but it was as potent as it was sweet. I resolved to ignore any further nudges to drink. Especially on nerves and an empty stomach. "You mentioned a job offer. Is it in New York?"

"It's in London, actually." Chris took another sip, then frowned when I set my glass aside again. "I'll be moving into a townhouse of my own next month, and..." his smile returned with a smug edge as he leaned closer to caress my cheek, "there's room for two."

I froze, my sluggish brain struggling to catch up. "You mean—"

"Come to England with me, Brianna." It was almost a demand. Part of me wanted to say yes, but I hesitated. The knowledge of my Sight sat like a lead lump in my belly, and I floundered for a beat before I realized it wasn't a question at all. Even if I wanted to leave the home I'd carved out in the city, I couldn't abandon Adam.

Chris was still talking.

"I've already spoken to your parents, and they've given us their blessing. We can apply for your passport tomorrow, now that you're of age. You would have your own room, if you'd prefer. The spare office will make a good studio if you want to continue your hobby, and—"

"I can't," I said softly, cutting him off. My hand went to Adam's rose before I could stop it. "I have a home and a job here. Friends."

"You can get another job, Brianna, and you'd live with me." His blue eyes narrowed and darted from my wineglass to the rose in my hair. He considered my words for a moment, then leaned forward with a faint frown. "What friends?"

"Just...some people I've met around the city."

On the street, in an alley, under a bridge...on a rooftop.

"Is that who gave you the flowers? A friend?"

I hesitated, then nodded. "Yes, they wanted to wish me a good evening."

"A *male* friend, wasn't it?"

I flinched, straightening when Chris sighed and reached for his wine, tilting the glass to watch the liquid sparkle. "A friend, Chris. A good friend."

"So good, you'll abandon a chance for a better life, abandon *me* to live in a shoebox, working a menial job. All to stay with your *friend*."

"I—It's not like that."

"Isn't it?" he asked silkily, setting the glass down with a sharp tap. My stomach clenched at the cold light seeping into his blue eyes as he looked me over. "This was a mistake. I never should've come tonight."

"Chris, I don't—"

He waved off my protest with a sharp-edged smile. "Your parents were right. They told me about your history when we spoke years ago, but I thought... Well, it doesn't matter now, does it?"

I stared. "I—I don't—what did they tell you?"

Chris sighed, concern thick in his voice as our appetizers arrived in a clatter of porcelain plates and quiet murmurs. "Everything, of course. I want to help you, Brianna, but I can't keep waiting for you to realize that."

"Help me? I'm not *sick*, Chris," I choked out in a whisper.

"Yes, you've said as much before." His gaze swept over me. Something sharp and mocking replaced the concern. "I once believed I could help you, but perhaps I was a little too overzealous. You won't even help yourself. Your denial of your illness is as tiring now as it has been in the past. I may have foolishly indulged you then, but I won't get dragged into cleaning up your messes anymore. I'm sorry."

"No, you don't understand. This time is different. I can prove it, Chris. Please, I-I..." I trailed off, suddenly sick to my stomach. I couldn't prove it though, could I? Chris would never believe me without hard evidence, and I couldn't ask Adam to reveal himself to a person who would never see him the way I did. I couldn't sacrifice my friendship—sacrifice Adam—just to disprove the lies my family insisted were truth.

He can never know the truth about Adam...ever, I realized as Chris sipped his wine, one brow raised while he waited for me to continue. I sank back, my shaking hands gripping my seat. "I-I..."

"I thought as much." Chris set his wineglass down and leaned towards me with a pitying smile. "Last chance, Brianna," he said softly, his voice coaxing. "Come with me. Everything will be different in London. We can try again, love. Let me take care of you."

"I can't," I whispered, my voice cracking as I gave him a pleading look, begging him to understand. Chris's expression darkened, and I froze as he stood and walked around our table until he was behind me, his hands gripping my shoulders.

"Are you sure?" he whispered in my ear. I clamped my mouth shut and nodded. Chris's grip tightened painfully for a moment—and he let me go. A sigh of relief was halfway to my lips when a new agony sparked down my neck and along my spine as Adam's rose was torn from my hair.

I swallowed my cry of pain and watched Chris return to his seat. My scalp throbbed in time with my heart.

"Well, then it seems you've left me no choice except goodbye."

Ice slammed through me, and sour heat flooded my mouth. "Goodbye?"

He nodded, watching me in a cold, clinical way I'd seen from too many doctors and therapists who'd only wanted my parents' money. As if I was a bug pinned to a card in its death throes, to be pulled apart and put back together however they pleased.

The ghost of rough hands plucked at me, and I flinched when Chris dropped the handful of crushed petals on the table. A puddle of blood red on the snowy tablecloth.

"I've wasted enough time coddling you, Brianna, and I won't squander any more pandering to your illusions. If you're not even going to try, then neither am I." He sighed and reached for his fork. "Now, eat. We can finish talking about this later."

Later. As if there was more to say. As if my throat wasn't locked too tight to swallow down the sticky-sweet wine at our table, much less any food. My stomach rolled, rebelling at the thought of even trying, and I bit the inside of my cheek as I fought the sudden need to be violently sick. I couldn't stay here another minute.

"Of course," I said faintly, gathering up my purse with a brittle smile. "I just need to use the ladies' room first. I won't be long, I promise."

Chris nodded absently and waved me away, and I fled as quickly as I could without breaking into a run.

Once I left his sight, I bolted. Somehow I managed to convince a waiter to bring me my coat and let me slip out the back door without anyone else the wiser. I had to resort to asking a stranger for directions before I found the right route toward home. I stood out like a sore thumb in my fancy clothes as I stumbled along, but I didn't care. I just wanted to go home.

I walked for what felt like hours before my building finally came into sight. In I went, kicking off my heels the moment I set foot in the lobby and bolting for the stairs. The cold linoleum and metal soothed my aching, bare feet. I was a shaky, shattered mess by the time I reached my door and stumbled into my apartment, tears burning in my eyes.

I sobbed, the numbness from the walk home fading as I tore off my finery and threw it in my closet. Down came my hair, the flowers Chris put in tumbling into the trash as fast as I could pluck them out. Washing off the makeup wasn't enough, and I found myself taking a blistering hot shower as I scrubbed and scrubbed and scrubbed, until I was raw and pink. Clean and dry, I threw on the first decent clothes I touched and headed straight for my workbench.

Restraining my wet hair in a ponytail, I opened the bin underneath and yanked out a fresh ball of clay. Again and again, I slammed it down, throwing all my confusion and pain into wedging the hapless lump. I didn't even pause when the familiar scrape of an opening window sounded from my bedroom.

"Is...everything okay?"

"No," I choked out. Adam sighed, and the worn floorboards creaked as he slipped into my studio space. For a while, he perched in the corner, watching me beat the lump of clay into submission.

"What happened?" he asked when I started to wind down a little, earthen red streaks staining my fingers. "I thought you were happy he'd come back to you."

"He didn't, though," I whispered, letting the clay rest on the table. It was ready for shaping, but I wasn't. "He's...I don't know. He's different. It was like talking to a stranger."

Chris had mocked me, as if I was a child throwing a temper tantrum. As if he had only been indulging me and now it was time I grew up. His casual cruelty had been like sharpened claws digging into my skin, and I couldn't ignore the whisper in the back of my head insisting maybe it wasn't Chris who had become a stranger.

With a shiver, I turned away from my workbench and wrapped my arms around myself, heedless of the clay on my hands. "He...he said he's leaving, and he's not coming back this time. There was a job offer in England, and—" I scrubbed my burning eyes, my voice cracking as I continued. "He says he can't do this anymore. That it was all a mistake. A waste of time."

Gentle hands gripped my arms, and Adam sank into a seat by my workbench, lifting me into his lap as I started sobbing. I pressed my face into the fall of tangled mane spilling over his shoulder and just cried as he told me it would be okay. I wasn't going to be alone always, and hush, hush...don't cry. Please don't...please. His rumbling voice plucked at me, keeping me from retreating into the numb fog seeping through me. It was so tempting, so enticing. To let it wrap around me and push aside the pain. To dream and not feel.

Adam's claws combed my messy ponytail, smoothing it over my shoulders as I huddled closer. My heart ached and bled from the words Chris used to tear it out, mocking its scars. Slow and halting, I told Adam what had happened. The flowers, the romantic birthday dinner at the fancy restaurant, and the betrayal of being told I just wasn't good enough. I was too broken, and Chris was tired of picking up the pieces.

Oh, how it hurt to remember his words backed by the pitying look and his smooth tenor voice. How I wanted to die, to vanish right there in the classy restaurant with its gleaming tableware and snowy tablecloths. It was like the past few months hadn't even happened. All the confidence Adam's friendship had given me, all the stories and moments we'd shared...in one conversation, Chris had broken me as if I were his to throw away. Like I didn't matter and never would.

At last, my tears ran out. Curled up against Adam's warmth, I was falling asleep when he stood. I gasped, started to struggle—then remembered who held me.

"W-what are you doing?" I rasped, my tongue thick and clumsy, and horribly dry.

"You need sleep." He slipped into my bedroom and sat me on the edge of my bed. "Are you thirsty?" I nodded, and Adam brought me a filled glass wet from the dishwasher. He started to hand it to me and paused. His gaze lingered on my splotchy face and shaking hands as I shivered, and he frowned at the glass, concentrating. For a second, the water inside glowed with a soft green light. When it faded, Adam held it out. "Here."

"What did you do to it?" I whispered as I peered into the glass, remembering the fleeting glow I spotted when Chris filled my glass at the restaurant. *Except I probably imagined it. After all, Chris is human, and humans don't have magic*, I reminded myself bitterly. Still, the wine he pressed on me had been so sweet and potent, even though it, too, only looked like water.

"You need to rest," Adam insisted. "It won't affect you like the pills you hate. It's just to help you sleep. Please, drink it."

"Will I dream?"

Adam smiled. "Perhaps."

"Will you stay?" I blurted out when he glanced at the false dawn lightening the sky outside my bedroom window. "Please?"

He hesitated. His gaze dropped to my shaking hands again, and he nodded. Propping himself up in a corner by the window, Adam looked pointedly at the water in my hand. A tiny, trembling smile quirked my lips, and I drank, tasting nothing except water and the faint, sweet tang of his magic as it slid down my throat.

"Thank you, Adam," I mumbled as a different kind of darkness reached for me and I collapsed into my pillows. It was good to know I wasn't alone.

Chapter Nine

I woke to the gentle tick of rain striking my window and the sharp musk of cedar all around me. For a while, I lay there and let it ease the dull pain in my battered heart, still tired despite the deep sleep granted by Adam's gift.

Adam.

My eyes fluttered open, and I turned my head to find he'd moved closer during the night. Now, Adam leaned against my bed, combing the tangles from his mane with his claws. I sucked in a shuddering breath. One ear flicked toward me. He looked up, his hands falling to rest in his lap. "Hello," he said after a moment when I only stared.

"Hi," I rasped, tugging the blankets a little higher. Adam gave me a long, searching look, then returned to his grooming, his silent presence soothing the ache better than words.

"He...he wanted me to go with him," I mumbled into my quilt after a few minutes, half hypnotized as I watched his hands move.

Adam paused and turned, his dark eyes strangely opaque as his hands stilled. "Why didn't you?"

I blinked blearily at Adam and shrugged, rolling over and burrowing into the rumpled bed. "I wanted to stay." *I couldn't leave you behind.* What that meant for our friendship, I had no idea. "When I said I couldn't, he wasn't thrilled about it."

Adam's hand on my shoulder was unexpected enough to startle me but not enough to make me pull away. Something in my chest loosened at the gentle contact, and a few leftover tears leaked out. "It will be okay, Bri."

"But what if it's not?!" I cried out, more tears escaping as I sat up and turned to face him without the blankets hiding me. "I'm not like you. I-I can't—"

"Yes, you can," Adam assured me as I swallowed back another sob. "You won't be alone. I promise."

"Yeah," I whispered past the heavy lump in my throat. I swiped at my wet cheeks and tried to smile. Adam hesitated and ran his thumb along my cheekbone, brushing away the last of my tears. "Can I…" He cocked his head, waiting. I bit my lip and looked away. "Nevermind. I-I should probably get some breakfast."

Adam glanced at the pale gray sky outside my window and smiled. "It may be a little late for breakfast," he said as I unwound my nest of blankets and stumbled over to draw the curtains closed.

I grimaced and nodded, scrubbing at my reddened eyes while I headed for the kitchen. A lone glass sat beside the sink, and I paused, staring at it as the memory of last night flashed through me.

"Bri?"

I gasped and spun around to stare up at Adam with wide eyes, my heart thudding against my ribs.

"Are you okay?"

"You stayed all night," I whispered, fighting for the numb calm of a moment ago.

"You asked me to. Should I go?"

I shook my head violently, curling in on myself as my composure slipped further. "N-no, I don't want t-to be alone."

I gasped as panic rose to choke me. Alone. I *was* alone. What was I thinking, refusing Chris's offer to go with him? I had nothing here to hold me together. No one would care if I disappeared. No one would miss me.

Adam would. I shuddered, the thin whisper of a thought drowning in the morass of panic and guilt and disgust rushing up to wrap me in leaden folds.

"Bri!"

Gentle hands grabbed my arms. Adam's sharp cedar musk cut through the fog, and I found myself held tight while he called my name over and over. "Adam?" I whispered, my voice cracking as something drove back the sick mess trying to pull me under.

"Bri," he replied, his breath warming my icy cheeks as he peered down at me, searching. "Bri, what's wrong?"

And just like that, it was over. I could breathe again. I wasn't alone. Maybe I could do this.

"I—I'm okay," I stammered, staring into his dark eyes. The attack faded with every breath I took. How was he doing this? Because I *was* okay. Careful not to trip over my own feet, I straightened from my huddle on the floor by the sink and stood as Adam let me go. It was gone. The sick swirl of emotion which fueled my attacks took hours to dissipate in the past. But suddenly it was gone as if it had never been.

Adam frowned and leaned closer. "Bri, what..."

I shivered, and a wan smile broke free of my stunned haze. "It's nothing," I whispered. He glanced at the empty glass that had triggered the attack, then back to me. Unspoken questions hung in the air between us, and I gave him a pleading look. I wasn't sure what had happened, and stopped or not, I was still a wrung-out mess. It was almost comforting.

With a low sigh, Adam stepped away to fiddle with the fruit on the bar while I scrounged for something to eat.

He stayed close the rest of the day. Every time the panic tried to return, he was there to chase it away with a touch, a look, or a few words. When he left that night, another bespelled cup of water waited by my bed, and I no longer felt as if I were made of fractured glass.

"Thanks," I whispered, trailing one finger through the condensation beading on the slick surface. The magic inside made my fingertip tingle, and a wobbly smile quirked my lips. I needed rest, but I couldn't bring myself to drink his gift. Instead, I remade my fluffy nest of pillows and blankets and traced lacey shapes in the droplets on the glass. I fell asleep with the tingle of magic nipping my fingers and the faint glow soothing my dry, burning eyes.

Morning came far too early, but I couldn't afford to miss work. I stumbled through my shift, focusing on mixing, kneading, and shaping dough instead of the quivering mess of nerves and emotions I'd become overnight. After I ruined three batches of rolls, Sherrie put me on cleaning duty, and it was a relief. By the time I clocked out for the day, I was too exhausted to think of much besides dinner and bed.

"Ugh," I croaked, hanging up my keys as I let my purse slip from my shoulder. I dropped it on the couch and headed straight for the bathroom. Much to Sherrie's delight, I'd thoroughly scrubbed every nook and cranny in Sweet Haven Bakery as an apology for the bread I'd ruined. Even the storage rooms. My clothes were grungy with crumbs of rancid grease and caked with old flour. I wanted them *off*.

A shower revived me somewhat, and I wrapped myself in the only towel left with a sigh. Living alone meant it didn't matter if my towel was short and threadbare. It was clean and dry, and I had fresh clothes in my bedroom that weren't covered in bakery refuse.

It wasn't until I was crouching by my bed in a clean bra and underwear as I dug through the basket that I realized I should've drawn the curtains first. I shivered, abandoning my search to snatch up my robe. The warm fleece felt good on my chilled skin. I snuggled into the fluffy collar for a minute before I turned toward the window just as there was a light tap on the glass.

I froze, and my head snapped up to see Adam staring back, his eyes wide before he dropped out of sight. I squeaked and fumbled my robe closed, hoping desperately it had hidden enough. I grabbed the first t-shirt and jeans my hands touched and fled to the bathroom, shaking. A few minutes later he tapped on the bathroom door.

"Bri?"

I groaned and huddled into a tighter ball on the damp bath mat.

"I—I'm sorry, Bri," Adam stammered out in a rush. "I didn't...I didn't see anything. Please come out."

My face burned with embarrassment, but I managed to find enough composure to open the door. For a long moment, I just stood there and stared at my bare toes.

"Brianna..."

I flinched and looked up. Adam knelt, concern and a hint of pleading softening his deep rumble. "I'm sorry. I—it really was an accident."

I nodded, a sudden numbness seeping over me. I was at my limit, and the haze settled into my bones like a damp chill. "It's okay." I pushed past him. "Please don't call me that."

"I...it's your name," he said as he followed me to the kitchen.

"Not to you," I whispered, tugging the cabinet open and staring at the pill bottles. "You never call me Brianna. Just Bri."

Adam's footsteps stuttered to a halt. "Oh..."

A humorless smile flickered and faded across my lips, and my focus returned to the orange bottles. I didn't even realize I'd moved until Adam had my wrist and was prying one of the containers from my grip. "Bri, please...don't do this. Let me help. You don't need these anymore."

"I—I don't—I can't..." Hot tears pricked my eyes as my stomach rolled and twisted, a familiar sourness on my tongue. With a keening whine, I jerked my wrist free and lunged toward him, burying my face against his hoodie with a cry. Adam stiffened. Pills clattered to the floor as his arms folded around me. Sobs wracked me, and I let them, pressing my face to the worn fabric of his sweatshirt and breathing in the sharp cedar musk that always clung to him.

Breathe, breathe, breathe, I chanted over and over to myself as the panic attack crested—and broke against Adam's presence. Just like the last one. It was too much, and I shivered as the attack bled away and the world started to fade. "Please...I don't want...to be alone," I whispered. He started to reply, then everything went black.

***

Waking up was more difficult than I remembered it ever being. My eyes burned, and my throat throbbed with a horrible, dry ache. Lingering exhaustion turned my limbs to lead. My head was a pounding mess. I longed to return to the oblivion of sleep, but the ringing chime of my alarm plucked at me. I couldn't find the strength to ignore it.

I tried to swallow and choked, coughing. There was a soft rustle beside me as I was propped up, and a cool glass pressed against my lips. It helped clear my throat, and after a few sips, I opened my crusty eyes to find Adam watching me, concern in his gaze. "Bri..."

"Hi," I croaked, taking the glass from him and giving it a wary glance. It only tasted like plain water, but my tongue was so dry, I wasn't sure if I'd be able to taste his magic right now.

"It's just water," Adam assured me with a slight smile.

"Oh, thank you." I took another sip. He nodded, and I realized he was holding me up, his claws catching on my shirt. I was on my couch. My phone chirped again. "What happened?" I asked with a cough as I sat forward so Adam could have his arm back.

"You fainted," he said, hiding his hands in his hoodie pocket. "I wasn't sure what to do, so I put you here. It's almost dawn. You slept all night."

"You stayed with me."

Adam's shy smile was too brief as he nodded.

"Oh." I glanced around for my phone before spotting it on the coffee table next to me. "Thank you. I should...I should probably get ready for work."

Adam helped me untangle myself from the blankets he'd laid over me last night. I wasn't hungry, but with Adam watching me with such concern in his eyes, I forced myself to gulp down some orange juice and a pair of cream cheese-stuffed croissants I'd made in a fit of boredom last week. They weren't as good as the ones Sherrie sold at her bakery, but at least they were filling.

As I rushed to get ready, Adam lingered on the edges of my routine. His curious glances followed me while I sorted myself out, and when I turned to head out the door, he stopped me.

"Here." Adam pressed a smooth, cloudy white stone into my hand. A silk pouch was next. "Take these. If it gets to be too much, hold the stone and clear your mind if you can. Focus on something that makes you feel safe. Can you do that?" I nodded, and he smiled as he continued. "Keep it in the bag while you're not using it, or the constant magic will make you drunk."

The stone buzzed against my fingers until I slid it into the pouch. "Silk really does insulate magic?" Adam nodded, and I frowned before looking up with wide eyes. "Wait, why are you giving me this?"

He hesitated and glanced towards my studio corner and the window there. For a moment, he was quiet, sudden tension in his big frame. "I need to leave for a few days. I didn't want to go without giving you some kind of help. Something besides your...pills."

I rolled his gift between my palms for a second, then slipped it into my pocket with a nod. "I...okay. Thank you, Adam. Do you know when you'll be back?"

Adam shook his head, and I swallowed back the flicker of fear fluttering through my stomach. "Maybe a few days, or longer."

Questions crowded my tongue. I almost asked them, but the odd wariness in his eyes as we stared at each other stifled the need to know. It was his business, not mine. We were just friends, and he'd already given me so much of himself these past few weeks. I could at least give him this.

"Thank you," I said again, pressing one hand against the hard lump in my pocket with a trembling smile. "I'll...I'll see you soon?" Warmth melted the tense look from Adam's face, and he nodded as he returned my wobbly smile with a wistful one of his own. "Okay." As I yanked the door open, a gentle hand gripped my shoulder.

"I will come back, Bri. I promise."

I laughed, shaky and brittle. "I know, Adam. I'll see you in a few days. Just...just come back safe."

His hand fell away, and the scrape of my bedroom window echoed in my ears as I locked the door behind me.

Please, don't leave me all alone.

Chapter Ten

I spent the rest of the week waiting. The roof, my studio, my bedroom window—they were all so empty now. Without Adam to buffer me, I struggled with one panic attack after another. His gift helped, but I barely used it. I was too worried it would become a crutch, like the pills in my cupboard.

Chris emailed me on the fifth day, claiming my mother asked him to contact me for her. It hurt—seeing him going on as if nothing had happened. He even sent a list of flights to England and advice on what to pack. I closed my laptop without replying.

Extra shifts at work kept me too exhausted to dream at night and ate up the hours in between. Each day was as lonely as the next, but it got a little easier. All told, ten days went by before Adam returned.

I'd taken to eating my dinner on the roof in order to watch for him. It had been a good day. The best one since my disastrous night with Chris. The rooftop still held the sun's heat. Warmth seeped through my jeans while the crisp fall breeze made a mess of my hair. Adam's stone hummed beside me on the roof, glowing faintly as I nibbled on grilled cheese and watched the city lights sparkle.

"Hello."

I choked, scrambling to stand and swallow my buttery mouthful of bread and cheese at the same time. A low chuckle rumbled in my ears as I gulped some tea and looked up into achingly familiar dark eyes.

I stared as I set my mug aside, half expecting him to vanish again. A slow, hesitant smile quirked his lips. Adam tilted his head, and the light from the street below pushed aside the shadows in his hood. He looked...different. Richer, fuller, brighter. Refreshed.

"Adam?" I hesitated for a moment longer before a trembling smile broke across my face. He nodded, his smile widening into a rare grin as I lurched forward to throw my arms around him. Adam hummed and combed his claws through my wind-tangled hair while I buried my face in his worn sweatshirt.

After a minute, I stepped away, letting him go to pick up his gift and press the gleaming stone into his palm. "Thank you for this, but I don't need it anymore. Would you...do you want to come inside?" He nodded, watching as I scooped up my plate and mug and headed for the stairwell. "Race you!"

A low chuckle echoed around me as the door swung shut on my heels, and I laughed. I felt like I had wings on my feet as I all but flew to my apartment and burst through the door. Locking it behind me, I abandoned my dishes on the kitchen bar and bolted for my bedroom, only to find Adam already there. He looked up from his seat beneath my window as I stumbled to a halt, my cactus in his lap.

"No fair," I gasped out past the laughter threatening to bubble forth. I planted my hands on my hips and bit back a giddy smile, a stray giggle slipping free as I tried to glare at him.

Adam grinned up at me and ran his fingers over his spiny captive. "It was your idea," he said with a laugh, and I gave in to the light filling me up, sitting on the edge of my bed as my laughter mingled with his.

When we both quieted, Adam pulled the stone from his hoodie pocket. "Did it help?"

I glanced at the glowing stone. "I didn't really use it, but it did help. I was just—I didn't want to depend on it too much." The pleased look he gave me made me want to hug him again, but I quashed the impulse. "Are you hungry?" I asked instead, bouncing to my feet.

Adam set my cactus among my other plants. He shot his hands a wary glance before curling them into fists and hiding them in his hoodie pocket. "Not...not really, no."

My giddy mood faltered. *Strange.* "I...how about some tea?"

Adam relaxed and nodded. He lowered his hood, and my eyes went wide. His horns had grown. Now they twisted up and back, their ends splitting into three points as they curled over his ears. The jagged edges made him appear wilder, almost feral when paired with his new overabundance of energy. Adam noticed me staring and started to raise his hood.

I caught his wrist. "Wait, it's okay. Please don't hide. They've grown, haven't they?" He nodded, his gaze wary as I let him go and stared at the living metal. "May I...?" I motioned to his gold horns as I trailed off, distracted by how they gleamed against his fur. Adam slowly tilted his head in invitation and became a living statue as he watched me reach out to trace their shape.

"They're *warm*." I inched closer and ran my finger over the longest tip. He flinched, and I squeaked when the point sliced into my finger. "And sharp," I mumbled, sticking the injured digit into my mouth.

Adam rose to his feet and tugged on my wrist until I let him see. "I'm okay," I insisted, wincing when he pressed his thumb to the cut. His touch buzzed and tingled, and when he let me go, the wound was gone. "Oh." I looked up at him, my eyes wide with wonder as a soft smile curled my lips. "Thank you."

His ears twitched and then stilled as his gaze swept my face, catching on my smile before bouncing to my eyes.

"You know, you don't have to do that, either," I blurted out. Adam cocked his head, and I nodded at his deer-like ears. "I noticed sometimes you try to keep them still. You can let them move. I don't mind."

"I...oh," he said, his deep voice soft. I smiled and shrugged, my eyes drawn to his ears as they trembled and flicked to catch a noise I couldn't hear. I started to reach up, and Adam caught my wrist.

"Sorry," I mumbled, my cheeks warming as he let me go. "I-I didn't mean to just...I'm sorry."

Adam nodded and looked away, flattening his ears against his tangled mane as if to hide them. "They're just...sensitive."

"Oh, okay." I gave them a last, wistful look. Adam met my wandering gaze, and I offered a sheepish smile. After a beat, he sighed. The wary tension in his big frame melted away, and I knew I was forgiven. Relieved, I motioned towards the kitchen. "So...tea?"

For hours, we talked, and when it eventually came time for him to go, I found myself swallowing the words asking him to stay. I'd never before realized how lonely my life had become until his friendship filled the empty spaces. Watching Adam slip out my window and into the night was hard, but at least this time I knew I'd see him again soon.

For days, I brimmed with a quiet joy like spring sunlight. I didn't even mind that Adam's visits were shorter than usual. Whatever he'd been gone for left him overflowing with energy, and he couldn't sit still for long. We had two blissful weeks full of silly teasing and quiet conversations over warm bread and tea. I should've known it wasn't going to last.

***

"Food, food, food," I chanted as I tossed my purse on my little couch and made a beeline for the kitchen. A big order had come into the bakery, and I'd skipped lunch in the rush to help Sherrie and the others fill it. I was *starving*.

Halfway through putting together a sandwich, my phone beeped. I paused, setting down my handful of meat and cheese as I peeked at the screen beside my plate. There were several missed calls...and a text from Chris.

"'Stop being childish, Brianna,'" I read aloud, my sandwich forgotten as my stomach churned. "'Your parents are worried about you stopping your medications. Especially your mother. Ignoring the help you need won't change anything. Call your parents. They'll fix it.'"

Fix what? I didn't want to be *fixed*. Another text popped in as I stared, numb. "'You might even lose your job if you insist on neglecting yourself. Perhaps the truth was a bit harsh, but I only wanted to help you, love. I'll be in town next week. Call me when you're ready to be reasonable.'"

No, no, no...

Why would he come back? I was a mistake to him, a failure. He'd tossed me aside and made it plain I was *worthless*. Yet here he was, acting as if everything had been a simple misunderstanding. His words had been so hurtful, but were they really, or was I overreacting? Maybe I should've stayed instead of running like a coward.

"What do I do?" I whimpered. The edge of the countertop bit into my palms, my good mood melting away like the dream it must've been. Clutching my head, I sank to the floor, gasping and rocking as my thoughts scrambled around and around in an endless cycle of self-disgust, confusion, and regret. Suddenly someone was shaking me. A familiar rumbling voice called for me through the churning mess in my head. I cried out as I shied away, and my eyes flew open to find Adam staring back.

"Adam," I choked out and lurched toward him, crawling into his lap without a second thought. "I-I'm sorry," I managed as his body went rigid against mine. "I just...it helps—I mean—"

"Oh," he said, his soft reply bringing my stuttered explanation to a halt. I shuddered and hid my face against his chest as his arms closed around me and pressed us closer. "Is this okay?"

Half sob, half laugh, the strangled sound slipped out as I gave him a sad smile. "Yes, thank you."

Adam nodded, his gaze roaming my face before settling on the wet tracks streaking my cheeks. "You're welcome," he said, and I stared, transfixed, when he leaned across the meager distance.

His breath warmed my cheek as his mouth brushed my skin. Hot and brief, his rough tongue skimmed my jaw, tasting my tears. I shivered, turning toward him when he pulled away—and froze as the tips of his lips touched mine. It was the barest contact, like the gentle brush of butterfly wings. He gasped, caught in the delicate kiss for a second before jerking back and breaking the spell.

"I-I—um—I'm sorry!" My face burned as my mouth tingled, and I resisted the urge to touch my lips.

"I—do you...does this happen a lot?" Adam asked, his ears flattening into his mane as he looked away.

"It depends. Some days are better than others," I admitted, beyond grateful for the change of subject. *Did he—did we just—* I swallowed hard and gestured between us when he glanced down. "I don't know why, but lately, having you here..." I trailed off, and suddenly I had his undivided attention. "Well, when you're here, it's different."

Adam hesitated and cocked his head with a slight frown. "Maybe it's the magic."

"No, it's you...it's always you. I can't explain it, but it's not the magic." I fumbled for the right words, and he waited, dark eyes searching. "I see your magic as green light, but sometimes I can taste it, too. It's sweet and sometimes kind of earthy, but I usually know when it's around. This...is different." I winced and slumped against his chest again, rolling a pinch of loose fabric between my fingers. "Sorry, I know that doesn't sound much better."

"I...it's okay," Adam rumbled, tentatively running his claws through my hair. I shivered and let myself relax as the last traces of my panic attack melted away under his gentle touch. He grew bolder, letting his claws graze my scalp, and my eyes drifted shut.

The first time Adam's nose brushed my temple, I assumed it was an accident. The second time was longer, and I heard him breathe deeply before a great sigh gusted over my shoulder. *Scent is important to him*, I reminded myself, trying to smother the blush threatening to return. I'd been hurt by something he couldn't see and didn't understand. He needed the reassurance his friend was okay as much as I needed him close. Scent spoke truer than words.

"Thank you," I said softly when he nosed my temple again.

Adam paused, and for a brief moment, a low purr vibrated under my cheek. "You're welcome."

Curled up in his arms, I lost track of time, savoring the comfort he offered. My stomach finally growled in protest, and I untangled myself with a wince and a whispered apology.

"Are you hungry?" I asked, giving my abandoned sandwich fixings a queasy look and wrapping them up for later.

"A little." Adam stood and moved out of the way while I flitted about the kitchen.

"Hungry or curious?" I mumbled as I pulled a package of chicken thighs from the fridge and set the oven to preheat.

"Both," he replied with a sheepish smile.

"Fair enough" I handed him a bag of apples with a shy smile in return. "I could use the help."

I explained as I went, showing Adam how to peel and chop the apples as I mixed spices into flour for the chicken. I'd been planning to surprise Chris, but after all that had happened, making it with Adam instead seemed right.

"You know, you never talk about her, but with the kind of person you are...your mother must've been pretty amazing," I said while I dusted each chicken thigh and laid them in the pan.

"She was."

"What did she look like?" I asked as I finished the last piece and went to wash up.

Silence.

"Adam?" I glanced over my shoulder, my hands soapy in the sink. He was just staring at his hands resting on the bar. "Adam—"

"She was beautiful," he whispered. "Not all halfbloods are, but she was." His ears flicked back, and he looked up long enough for me to see the glitter of tears before he turned away.

"Adam," I whispered, shaken. "You don't have to—"

"I want to," Adam said softly, picking up one of the apples waiting to be peeled and cut up. "Someone should remember her besides me."

"Oh...okay." Rinsing, I dried my hands and turned to lean against the sink. For a long time, we simply stood there in my kitchen as he rolled the apple between his palms. Finally, he spoke.

He told me about a proud, beautiful woman with rich brown skin and tiny golden antlers she would hide in her wild curls. Tall, delicate, and fierce, she concealed her deer-like ears and her fae son with glamourie while passing off her brass nails as a fancy polish. When they were taken while traveling to find his father's people, she'd protected him any way she could. In the end, she died ensuring his freedom.

"You said she was a halfblood," I said when he fell silent. "What was her fae half?"

A faint, sad smile flickered across Adam's face, and he reached up to touch one of the golden horns peeking out of his wild mane. "Her mother was a Golden Hind. One of the last on this side of the Hill."

"Oh," I whispered, staring at the gold arching from his brow with new eyes. "They're not horns, are they? They're antlers, because the Hind is a female deer."

Adam nodded, the sad smile returning for a moment before fading away again. "They never would've caught her if not for me. She was very fast."

"It wasn't your fault, Adam. You know that, right? Her dying, I mean."

"I know." Adam set the apple back on the bar, his gaze distant with old memories. His pain tugged at me, and before I could consider what I was doing, I'd crossed the distance between us to draw him into a hug. Adam stiffened and started to pull away.

"It's okay," I whispered. "Friends, remember?" A slow shudder rippled through him, and he folded. I hummed nonsense tunes and held him as he buried his face in my shoulder and tears dampened my shirt. I should've been embarrassed. I should've been fighting down panic with the way Adam clutched me close like he was drowning. I should've, but there was only a deep calm and a need to take away his pain, if only for this moment.

"She must've loved you so much," I whispered, relaxing against him and trusting his grip to keep me from falling. A shaky sigh, and Adam nodded, one of his antlers brushing my cheek. "I never...I-I mean..." I sighed as he straightened, and I let him go.

"Bri?"

"My mother never really made time for me, you know? Even now, all she cares about is how it'll reflect on her if people find out I'm crazy. She never tried to stop any of it. Not even once." I shivered, the tarnished memories breaking the calm I'd found to hold his tears. "It's always been that way, I guess. I was raised by my sisters. My parents were busy all the time, and their public image is everything to them. If it didn't meet their approval, it wasn't allowed. I had a friend, a girl named Lila, but that didn't last long. Nobody wants a crazy five-year-old playing with their kid. Even then, we were expected to act a certain way, so when I started telling people about the faeries in the woods..."

I bit my lip at the dawning realization in his dark eyes. "I just wish things could've been different. The way you talk about your mom...will you tell me more?"

For a long moment, Adam stared at me. At last, he nodded. With a shaky smile, I busied myself with getting the chicken in the oven and prepping the apple crisp. Soon, we were sitting in my room by the window as Adam told me story after story. I closed my eyes and listened, letting his words sink in until he fell silent, out of memories to share.

"Thank you."

My eyes flew open, and I stared at him. "I-I—what? Why are you..."

Adam smiled. "For being a friend and helping me remember."

I nodded, a shy smile curling my lips. "Oh, um, you're welcome. Are you hungry?"

He chuckled and pulled me to my feet as my stomach let out a loud gurgle. "You certainly are," Adam teased as the heavy sadness drifted away to leave him wistful and tired, but happy.

Thankfully his storytelling had contained enough breaks to keep me from burning my dinner, and there was enough to share. I even served some fancy vanilla ice cream—part of an unexpected barter for one of my mugs—to go with the crisp.

The rest of the evening was filled with happier subjects and friendly teasing at Adam's first experience with apple crisp and ice cream. Finally, it was time for him to leave.

"See you tomorrow?" I asked as he opened my bedroom window.

Adam nodded and pulled up his hood. Before I could think too much about it, I hugged him, surrounding myself with the sharpness of cedar. Letting him go again was harder than it should've been, but I managed. Flushed and flustered, I stepped away.

"Tomorrow, then," I mumbled, a strange shyness creeping over me as if I'd been caught with my hand in the cookie jar.

"Tomorrow," Adam promised and leapt into the night.

I shut the window and drifted back to the kitchen to put away my meager leftovers. Halfway through getting ready for bed, I shook off my daze. I was being ridiculous. Adam and I were friends. One evening spent sharing about his mom and an accidental kiss didn't mean anything was changing between us. Not like that, anyway.

The memory of Adam's tears soaking my shirt echoed through me, and I paused as my cheeks warmed. Flustered, I set my hairbrush on my dresser. Sleep. I needed to sleep. Besides, I'd promised to help Sherrie with the lunch rush tomorrow. Whatever was going on in my head would keep until morning. It always did.

Climbing into bed, I rolled over and buried my face in my pillows.

"Friends. We're just friends."

Somehow it didn't sound as convincing as I'd hoped.

Chapter Eleven

"Oh, oh, oh! Somebody's in a good mood."

I jumped and spun around, nearly dumping a cup of flour on the floor. Sherrie flashed me a mischievous grin and tugged the bottom of her hair net over the neat coil of thin braids at her nape.

"Oh, good morning, Sherrie," I managed at last with a sheepish smile. I turned back to the dough I was mixing.

Sherrie grabbed a bowl of risen dough and joined me. "I don't think I've ever seen you smile so much in one morning before, hon." She leaned in close. "Who is he?"

"I, um, don't know what you're talking about," I blurted out, staring at her with wide eyes as heat crept across my cheeks to burn in my ears.

She laughed and winked, her warm brown eyes sparkling as she emptied her bowl on the floury tabletop. "Fine, don't tell me. I know you're not much of a talker. Is he cute?"

"I-I..."

"Whoever he is, he's obviously loads better for you than that trash, Chris."

"Trash?"

Sherrie sighed, a frown wrinkling her dark brows as she kneaded and shaped her dough. "Yeah, hon. Trash. Chris was bad news. You'll be much better without him, trust me. Dumping him was a good move."

"I didn't," I stammered out, my blush draining away as I remembered his hurtful words in the restaurant. "It just wasn't working out, I guess."

Sherrie glanced up, her gaze sharp as she looked me over and pursed her lips. "Let me guess. He said you weren't worth the trouble? A waste of his time?" Speechless, I nodded. "Mm, he seemed the type to try that foolishness with a sweet thing like you. Men who treat a woman that way are always nothing but trouble. Now, I don't stick my nose in other people's business—" I bit back a wince, remembering the opaque look she gave us the first and only time I'd brought Chris to the bakery, "—but trust me, hon. He's not worth listening to, and he's wrong."

A slow grin curled her full lips. "Besides, it seems like your new beau knows how to appreciate a woman." She leaned closer and lowered her voice to a harsh stage whisper. "So...*is* he a cutie or what?"

"I..." My thoughts danced through the past few weeks with Adam, and my blush returned full force.

"Oh, your face! He must be a real looker," she teased as I tried to ignore my flustered nerves and get back to work.

"He's very...striking," I admitted at last, caught in the memory of Adam's gentle smile and the warmth of living metal under my fingers.

"Mm-hm," she hummed as I finished mixing my dough and dumped it onto the floured tabletop. "You got it bad, hon. It's nice to see you happy."

Did I? Was I falling for Adam? But we were just friends...weren't we? Sherrie bustled off to get her loaves in the oven while I kneaded my dough, portioning it into balls and setting it on a shelf to rise. The rest of my double shift passed in a blur. I kept busy, drowning my confusion in my work until the chaos of the lunch rush forced me to set aside my worries and help Sherrie with the customers. At last, three o'clock rolled around, and my long shift was over. Relieved, I cleaned up and said goodbye to Sherrie.

The whole way home, I turned her words over in my head. Could it really be true? As I walked the last block between work and home, my thoughts drifted to yesterday's innocent kiss, and butterflies exploded in my stomach. Maybe Sherrie was right, but more likely it was simple nerves from that kiss. Besides, what Adam and I shared was too precious to risk with something so flighty and fickle as a crush.

My building came into sight, and I quickened my pace. *It'll pass*, I decided, stopping outside my building and digging through my bag for my keys. *It has to.*

"Keys, keys...where are they?" Crouching by the door, I dumped everything into my lap.

No keys.

"Oh no," I moaned. "No, no, no!" I checked pockets and compartments in the worn canvas, but my keys were gone. My hands were shaking by the time I gathered it all up and returned it to my bag.

I kept spares for both, but my new spare building key was in my apartment, and my spare apartment key was stashed on the roof. The roof door was never locked, and the fire escape ladder was always down.

But when I shouldered my purse and circled around to the alley behind my building, I found some industrious soul had drawn the ladder up properly for the first time since I'd moved in.

For a long minute, I stood there and fought to swallow my frustrated tears. Clutching my bag, I mentally went over the route I'd taken to work early this morning. I'd have to retrace my steps and hope my keys showed up. Spinning around, I headed out to the streets once again.

For hours, I searched with no luck. Lunch was a slice of street vendor pizza, and dinner was a cup of ramen at a gas station. Finally, an idea sparked. The sun had finished setting while I'd been paying for my meager dinner. Adam had a knack for finding me, and he had magic. Maybe he could help. There was just one problem.

Where would a forest fae hide in the city?

I turned toward Central Park, and a queasy knot formed in my throat. Gulping down the last of the salty broth, I tossed my foam cup in a nearby trash can. Memories of the one and only time I'd ventured into the park when I first came to the city haunted my nightmares. The fae living in the park had found me as the sun set and chased me. First in one direction, then another. At the time, I thought I'd finally lost it, but now I knew the truth. They were all real.

I forced myself to straighten my shoulders and left the gas station. My nails bit into my palms as I headed for the green shadows and concrete paths I'd once avoided as if my sanity depended on it. Old habits were hard to break, and my heart picked up its pace as I drew nearer. Knowing the fleeting movements among the trees, the half-glimpsed faces, and foreign chatter were real and not hallucinations didn't help, either. In the oldest stories, a lone human was an easy mark—a plaything—for fae creatures, and there was no guarantee Adam would be there.

Not that I have a choice, I reminded myself a little while later when I stood frozen just inside one of the entrances. Eventually, someone would notice me standing around. If I was going to search for Adam, I needed to move.

"Please be here," I whispered. Casting a last desperate glance at the still-bustling street behind me, I picked a random path and followed it.

With every reluctant step, my heart thrummed faster against my ribs like a hummingbird caught in a jar. Deep shadows lingered among the trees, despite the lampposts scattered along the path. More often than not, I was forced to rely on my phone's flashlight. The sounds of the city grew muted the deeper I ventured into the park, and the rustle and sigh of greenery wrapped around me. After a few minutes of encountering nothing worse than a huge moth attracted by the light from my phone, I started to relax. Whatever or whoever had chased me around the park before didn't seem interested in me this time. Best not to keep pushing my luck, though.

"Adam?" I called in a harsh whisper. "Are you here? Can you hear me? I need your help. I—"

A high-pitched, chittering laugh pierced the quiet rustles. The sound sliced through me like nails on a chalkboard. Flinching, I looked about wildly for the source.

"I'm not crazy," I whispered to myself, but the reminder was a cold comfort right now. I might not be crazy, but that meant something really *was* out there.

And it wasn't Adam.

I swallowed a scream when skittering movement jerked my attention to the trees. Two points of sullen glow flickered to life. I froze. Were those...eyes?

The chittering laugh sounded again. This time it was answered by a chorus of faint chirps and whistles. I forced myself to turn around. If I stayed on the path, it would lead me out of the park. The sounds followed me, and I began to walk faster and faster until I was running and out of breath.

Strands of spidery softness brushed my cheek as I ran. I shied away, my stride faltering and my heart in my mouth. Another cobweb hooked into my skin and sent strings of embers down my neck. I whimpered and smacked at the stinging pains, sobbing for breath that burned, each lungful a battle I couldn't win. My tongue started to tingle with numbness, and the trees around me blurred together as I forced myself to keep moving.

There was a low cry from up ahead, and a small body crashed into my legs, knocking me off the asphalt path. I went down hard. One ankle twisted under me, and a harsh burst of pain shot up my leg. Sprawled in the dirt beside the path, I fought the urge to cry and failed, several tears spattering the dirt under my cheek.

"I'm never going to find you, am I?" I rasped, coughing and gasping for breath as my tormentors gathered in the trees above me.

A low warble answered me, followed by a weighty silence filled with the rustle and scrape of several small bodies leaving with a lot of speed and not much care for stealth. I forced myself to my feet, squinting and blinking hard to clear my vision. It didn't do any good. The park around me dimmed into a muddle of blurry smudges and deep shadows. Soon, I wouldn't be able to see anything.

"Dammit," I choked out as more frustrated tears overflowed. I rubbed them out on my shirt. At this rate, I'd never find my way out of the park. And it wasn't as if Adam knew I was here. I would be spending the rest of the night on the street. Blind and alone.

Panic, hot and sour, slammed into me, twisting from my stomach to dig claws into my head. I crumpled—and someone caught me.

I screamed and started to thrash before the familiar cedar musk registered. A tingling warmth bloomed across my face, banishing the spreading numbness in my tongue and bringing a familiar sweetness with it. My vision cleared, and I looked up into dark eyes.

"Adam," I rasped, reaching into his hood to touch his cheek. "You found me."

Adam nodded, his gaze worried. "Is something wrong? Why were you looking for me?"

"I...I-I..." I buried my face against his chest and burst into tears as his presence lifted away the sick feeling in my gut, and my panic attack shattered. After a few minutes, I managed to pull myself together and explain about my lost keys and the fire escape.

"I thought maybe you could help. But I couldn't find you anywhere and then *they* started chasing me and..." I trailed off with a shudder. "Sorry, I didn't mean to fall apart on you. I just—um...it's been a long day."

Adam pulled me into a brief hug as a familiar, eerie warble sounded overhead, followed by a handful of words spoken in a strange language with a high, sharp voice. I flinched, and Adam's arm around my shoulders tightened as he loosed a warning growl. The low rumble, more felt than heard, buzzed against my cheek. The owner of the voice snapped off another string of words, and then we were alone.

"I can probably get you to the roof. Can you find your way out of the park on your own and meet me there?" Adam's deep voice was gentle as he let me go and gave me a searching look. I scrubbed my face dry on my dampened shirt and nodded, offering him a shaky smile and earning a quick grin in return. "Good. Stay on the path, and the sprites will leave you alone this time. When you get home, go to the back alley. I'll be waiting for you."

I nodded, and he led me to a different path. This one, he promised, would bring me out of the park nearer to my apartment than the one I'd been following. With a last assurance I would be okay, he left.

"Okay, let's do this," I whispered, straightening my shoulders and lifting my chin. "Okay." Hitching my bag higher on my shoulder, I headed for home.

Circling my building when I arrived, I ducked into the alley. "Adam?" I whispered, searching the shadows for movement. A chill breeze washed over me, and I shivered, wrinkling my nose at the ripe smell of trash and dead leaves it carried with it.

"Over here." He stepped from behind a dumpster some local kids had managed to tip on its end.

I grinned and ran over, careful not to trip on the black trash bags piled beside it. "So how are we getting to the roof?"

Adam eyed the building and dropped into a crouch. "I'll have to carry you. It'll be easier if you're on my back."

"You want me to ride you?" I squeaked, a faint blush warming my cheeks. "But—"

"It's fine, Bri. I don't mind," he assured me, amusement twitching his lips when he glanced over his shoulder.

"I-I don't—Well, I figured you could drop the fire escape ladder for me or something."

Adam looked up at the rusty stair and winced, shaking his head. "I'm sorry," he said with a sheepish smile. "I don't know how, and there's too much iron. I can't."

"Oh," I said softly, peering up at my usual route. The myth about iron being the bane of the fae wasn't simply a story then. Which explained why Adam had refused a spoon when we first met and continued avoiding silverware whenever he stayed for a meal.

Chewing on my bottom lip, I turned to Adam, giving into defeat as gracefully as I could manage. "Okay." Straightening, I shifted my bag out of the way and slipped my arms around his neck. Some of his mane spilled over my wrist while he adjusted my hold, and I resisted the urge to drag my fingers through it. *His fur is always so soft*, I mused as Adam hitched my legs up around his hips.

"Hang on." He started to climb.

We were nearly halfway there when I realized I could feel him through his hoodie. The ripple and flex of heavily corded muscles pushed against my belly as I clung to his back, between my thighs on his hips. I tried to focus on the ragged sweatshirt he always wore and found myself wondering what Adam looked like under the thick cloth. Did he have fur everywhere, or would there be dark, supple skin, like his face?

The mental image I conjured up flashed through me, sparking a frisson of heat in my belly. My mouth went dry, and Adam's claws slipped. *No, no, no...oh please, no*. I cringed, squirming as he scrambled for a better grip and shot a wide-eyed glance over his shoulder at me.

"I'm okay," I squeaked, hiding my flushed face against the nape of his neck and trying to slow my racing heart.

"Okay," he mumbled, his uncertainty as clear as a shout but not enough to make me look up.

After a beat, Adam continued the climb, and I did my best to pry the images of sleek muscle covered by dark skin and darker fur from my brain. It was hopeless.

The more I tried, the worse it got. By the time we reached the roof, I was in desperate need of a cold shower, and Adam acted as if every gust of wind was a cattle prod.

"Thank you for helping me get home," I blurted out as soon as we were on solid ground and I could let go.

Adam flinched as a playful breeze swirled around us and shot me another odd look. "You're...you're welcome. Are you sure you're okay?"

Are you? I wondered, my blush spreading down my neck and burning in my ears. I could feel the ghost of him pressed against me, and the litany of images and thoughts running through my head grew more and more intimate. "It's nothing, honest. I-I just..."

I just...I think I finally want to be closer to someone...to you, but I never will, I finished silently. I guess I didn't need a cold shower after all. Why would he ever want someone like me? Even after months—years—of striving to pull myself together, I was still broken. Still damaged beyond repair. I had nothing to offer him. Nothing but my heart, and no one wanted a shattered soul. Adam deserved so much more than I could give him.

"Bri?"

I jumped, staring up at him with wide eyes as I suddenly found myself fighting back tears instead of blushes. "I...I have to go," I whispered, my shame and sorrow a choked tangle in my throat.

"Bri, wait!" Adam called after me as I spun away and ran for the stairwell. I shook my head and bolted through the door. I couldn't handle facing him right now. It wasn't until I reached my door and was fumbling for my key that I remembered my spare was stashed on the roof. With Adam.

"No," I whimpered, my pointless search growing more frantic as the sourness of an approaching panic attack twisted my gut.

"Hey, are you apartment 42b?"

Breathe, I told myself as I shoved my turmoil to the back burner as best I could and turned toward the unfamiliar voice. Shaggy blonde hair and sheepish brown eyes marked him as the musician down the hall. He was holding my missing keys.

"Oh," I managed to choke out, "you found my keys. Thank you."

He grinned and tossed them to me, hefting a battered saxophone case. "Nah, it was my girl who found 'em. I guess she saw you leaving and spotted them by your door. Later!"

I forced a brittle smile and a wave as I stuffed the right key in the lock and darted into the safety of my apartment. "Breathe," I whispered. "Just...breathe."

My bag and keys clattered to the floor as I slumped against the door and slid to a seat beside them. "I'm such an idiot," I rasped as the tears finally won out. The sourness in my belly was a leaden lump now, but I wasn't fooled. The lightest nudge would send me crumbling to pieces.

A light tap on my bedroom window drew me out of the haze, and I hesitated. I should apologize, at least. He would worry otherwise. Slow and stiff, I dried my tears as I stood, locking the door. I hung up my things on my way past the kitchen. For once, my stash of pills called to me with a siren's song, promising oblivion for a few precious hours. I stared at the closed cupboard, started to reach—and stepped away as another quiet tap echoed through my apartment. I could always take them later. If I had to.

The window was already open when I walked into the tiny bedroom, but Adam waited outside this time. I didn't invite him in.

"I just wanted to make sure you're alright."

I dropped my gaze to my stockinged toes and nodded. "I'm okay."

He inhaled sharply. "Please don't lie to me, Bri. We promised we wouldn't. Remember?"

"It's complicated," I mumbled, finally relenting and waving him inside.

As Adam slipped through the window, the chaste almost-kiss we'd shared flashed through me again. It made me jittery as it mingled with the knowledge of the panic attack looming over me and my realization on the roof.

I wrung my hands for a moment, then bolted from the bedroom and went to my workbench to pull out a fresh lump of clay. Not even bothering with my apron, I started wedging it against the sturdy wood.

The soft creak of worn floorboards revealed Adam's presence as I did my best to beat out the storm of emotions boiling through me. His proximity was making it difficult, though. I wanted to hide, to yell and scream at him, to cry, to hit him...to ask him to hold me close and kiss me again. A real kiss this time.

Tears were seeping into my mouth, flavored with old clay fragments. My dust mask beckoned, but I ignored it. A headache would be a welcome distraction at this point.

"Bri." I shook my head and threw the clay down again with a satisfying *thunk*. Adam sighed. "I'm sorry."

My hands stuttered to a halt and I turned to stare. "Wh-what?"

"I upset you," he replied with a slight frown at the clay I abused. Adam crept closer and crouched, watching me with dark eyes I could drown in as he touched the tear tracks on my face. "I'm sorry."

He was beautiful.

As if in a dream, I reached out and threaded my fingers through the fur along his cheek. Adam started to smile, then faltered when I leaned closer. "Bri, what—"

I kissed him.

His lips parted under mine with a startled gasp, and his taste flooded my mouth. Earthy, almost like the clay smeared across my hands, but also rich and wild. A sharp tang of sweetness, like the magic he had me drink that one night, and a musky spice. I wasn't the only one trembling when we broke apart.

Holy crow, I can't believe I did that.

I could still taste him on my lips. My warm, tingling lips.

"I—I—" Adam stammered for a second as we stared at each other. I started to lean toward him again—and suddenly I was alone. Only the lingering warmth from his touch testifying he had ever been there.

Chapter Twelve

Almost two weeks passed without a single visit from Adam.

"I'm such an idiot," I whispered, smoothing my thumb over the cheekbone of the new bust I was working on. The bittersweet memory of our kiss still thrummed through me, wonderful and terrifying. Crushes were fickle. What if I had broken things between us on a stupid whim? I missed him horribly, but my window remained stubbornly empty. In the past, even a few days with no visits had felt like an eternity. This was infinitely worse.

Picking up one of my favorite clay shapers, I hesitated and put it back down. Now was as good a time as any to call it a night. Waiting around for someone who wasn't going to show up was pointless.

"Dammit." I leaned against my workbench and swiped at a stray tear. My eyes burned and ached, but crying wouldn't fix what I'd done. Shoving my melancholy aside as best I could, I covered my work with some old plastic sheeting and cleaned up. As I scrubbed the last bits of clay from under my nails, a muffled thump sounded from my bedroom. I froze.

"Adam," I gasped, dropping my nail brush in my scramble to shut the water off. A low creak, and another thud echoed through my apartment. I bolted for my bedroom, my heart in my mouth as I stumbled through the open doorway.

My window hung open. The latch was twisted out of its proper shape, and one glass pane was cracked, but I only had eyes for the dark shape slumped over the sill. "Adam?" I choked out when he didn't move. "Adam!"

Running over, I had barely touched him when he reared up with a snarl. I jumped back, my hands flying up to cover my mouth. His head swung towards me, and his name slipped past my fingers in a harsh whisper. Adam's eyes were blank and unseeing within his hood. Then, a faint frown wrinkled his brow, and he seemed to wake up.

"Bri," he rasped, fumbling for a better grip as he tried to lever himself up. "H-help me." Something dark dripped down the wall as Adam struggled to drag himself over the sill, and my eyes went wide. Blood.

The realization broke my stunned paralysis. Praying I wasn't hurting him further, I grabbed an arm and pulled hard. Adam gasped and finally managed to get the rest of himself through before his strength fled, and he collapsed. There was so much blood. His sweatshirt was soaked with it.

"Where?" I slowed his fall, kicking my colorful rag rug out of danger as he slumped to the floor. Darting over to the window, I slammed it shut and drew the curtains closed. "Adam, where—"

"Stomach and shoulder," Adam choked out as I knelt and fumbled with his hoodie, my hands shaking.

"This needs to come off. I can't see—"

Magic, wild and sweet, slammed into me. I fell backwards, banging my elbow on the windowsill. Adam's head lolled against the floor as his magic spluttered and faded. His eyes fluttered shut, and he went limp.

I needed to stop the bleeding. Maybe even sew him up. My stomach rolled at the thought of pushing a needle through him, but I was already running to raid my apartment for anything I could use. Gathering up my finds, I returned to my bedroom and dumped the armful on my bed. *Needles, thread, clean rags, medical tape, gauze...I can do this.* Half expecting his magic to knock me arse-over-teakettle again, I wrestled Adam's sweatshirt off.

"Um, scissors," I mumbled at the sight of the snug t-shirt he was wearing underneath. There was no way I could get it off him in one piece without his help, and it was ruined anyway. I'd get him a new one later.

The thin fabric parted under my scissors easily. I peeled it away to uncover the source of all the blood and stuttered to a halt.

Short fur gave way to bare skin over his chest and stomach. The smooth expanse was marred by two deep, ragged holes along his belly with a third in his shoulder. A nasty graze curved over his ribs. The blistered scrape wept fluid and smelled of scorched hair, the longer fur around it burned away. The skin surrounding each puncture wound was a torn, reddened mess. It was as if he'd been savaged by his own claws or attacked by a clumsy surgeon. All of them oozed blood in a steady trickle.

"Oh, Adam," I whispered, horrified. "What happened to you?"

The wounds appeared to be at least a few days old, hot to the touch and puffy, already infected. Adam's dark skin was caked with dried crud. Under the fresh blood, it felt brittle and harsh in a way that spoke of a wicked fever.

I ran to the kitchen. A new glazed beauty I'd made for myself was the perfect size. I dumped a double handful of clean rags into the deep bowl and filled it to the brim with the scalding tap water. For hours, I worked feverishly over Adam, rinsing his wounds and cleaning the muck from his skin and matted fur.

Several odd bits of metal popped loose when I flushed a noxious slurry of pus and old blood from each ragged hole. They looked like gunshot wounds, which meant the fragments were...from the spent bullets? I set them aside to figure out later, using tweezers to tease out a few stragglers before I covered each wound with gauze. It took gallons of water to clean him up, and my arms and back were one solid ache before long. When I was done, I could barely lift the bowl as I scrubbed it out and filled it with ice cubes.

"Don't die on me, Adam," I whispered, making crude ice packs with some sandwich baggies. I wrapped them with my last few rags and tucked them around his pulse points. The ugly wounds were hidden under fresh bandages, but the thick gauze pads were already bloodstained. His ragged breathing was painful to hear. I touched his cheek, combing my fingers through the thick fur along his jaw.

Careful not to bump him, I dragged a beanbag over and curled up to wait. Somehow, I fell asleep. I woke up with one hand tangled in Adam's mane. He had shifted toward me during the night. His face pressed into my palm, dry lips scraping my skin. I needed to get him to drink something.

Wiggling my hand free, I stumbled into the kitchen for a mug. After some debate, I grabbed the turkey baster from my drawer instead of a plastic spoon. Adam was shivering in miserable fits and starts when I got back, his fever climbing. I set the water on my dresser and checked the ice packs. With a reckless yank, I pulled the blankets from my bed and piled them on top of him.

I needed a thermometer if I was going to track his fever, but mine had broken weeks ago. The closest ones were at the corner store, but I couldn't leave him right now. I would have to make do.

Through trial and error, I managed to get Adam to drink. I alternated water with broth every few hours as his temperature continued to climb during the night. I ran out of ice, and he started shoving the blankets off. Once, he snapped at me when I tugged them back on, but he didn't wake up.

For three days, I stayed with him. None of my attempts to cool Adam's fever worked. Halfway through the second day, I abandoned the ice packs in favor of trying to sweat the fever out instead.

I guided him to the bathroom during his few lucid moments, then scrambled to change the blankets in the nest I'd made for him before he collapsed again. More of the strange metal fragments appeared each time I checked him, stuck in the mess of pus and blood on the gauze. It was an exhausting blur of bandage changes and exchanging sweat-soaked, bloody blankets for fresh. I called in sick to work, never more thankful for a boss like Sherrie, who accepted my vague explanations without question.

Adam's fever finally broke on the morning of the fourth day.

I left for a short shift at the bakery and prayed he wouldn't relapse. For six hours, I shaped loaves with shaking hands and haunted the grab box for a loaf of rustic artisan bread—Adam's favorite. Luck was with me. One was dropped in just as I was leaving, its bottom scorched. Loot in hand, I raced home.

"Adam?" I called out, stowing my stuff and setting the warm bread on the kitchen counter. "Are you—oh!"

"Hello." He steadied me when I almost tripped and fell. His dark skin still looked faded, but his gaze was clear and alert for the first time in days.

"You—are you going to be...you're bleeding again."

Adam glanced at the bloodstained gauze peeking out of the quilt he'd wrapped around himself. "Oh," he mumbled, letting me tug the blanket down and peel the edge of the bandage aside.

"I need to check this," I said as more blood seeped out onto the gauze. He followed me to the blue beanbag and sat while I retrieved what was left from taking care of him these past few days. At least there was a fresh roll of gauze.

"I-I, um..." Adam cocked his head, and I blushed as I knelt beside him and tugged on the blanket. "This is in the way."

He looked away and slowly let it drop. The old, patchwork quilt pooled in his lap, creating splashes of color against his worn jeans. The faded hues suited him, and somehow the sight brought to mind the night I kissed him. Of the warmth of his cheek on my palm and his taste on my lips.

The heat in my cheeks grew, and I jerked my attention to the pile of first aid supplies in my lap. *This was a lot easier when he was bleeding all over my floor.*

Still, Adam needed me to do this. There was no one else he could ask, and dragging it out would only make it harder. The thought steadied me. I motioned for him to lay back while I sorted out what I would need. A roll of sticky medical tape found its way onto my thumb like an oversized ring, and I fumbled to open the new package of gauze while Adam settled into the beanbag.

I took a deep breath. "Right. Tell me if I hurt you too much, okay?"

Adam nodded, refusing to look at me as I peeled the bandage off his shoulder.

At first, it wasn't too bad. Despite the fresh blood, his shoulder was looking better, and the graze over his ribs was finally starting to heal. Relief hummed through me as I rebandaged them both with fresh gauze.

Tending to the wounds on his stomach was another matter. With each brush of my fingers, Adam flinched like I'd stuck him with a tack. He was still a little hot, but the harsh feeling had gone from his skin, leaving it velvety soft like fine suede or buckskin.

He smelled of musk and cedar as he always did, but underlying that was something earthy and wild, with hints of honey and an exotic spice. The combination made me want to rub my cheek against his skin and breathe him in like a cat with catnip.

A slow shudder rippled through him as I applied the last bit of medical tape over the gauze. I shivered, running my thumb along the edges to make sure it was secure as the velvety warmth of his belly shifted under my fingers. My focus faltered for a second. The sudden urge to taste Adam's skin the same way he'd once tasted my tears arced through me. I froze, snatching my hands away as the calm I'd been clinging to crumbled away and a fresh blush exploded across my face.

"There!" I blurted out and stood in a rush. I needed some air. "I-I'll be back in a minute." I grabbed a laundry basket and fled to the roof before I did something to embarrass us both.

He was *beautiful*. The realization haunted my thoughts every time I looked at him. Even with the doubt from our kiss gnawing on my heart, I ached to touch him.

I slumped against the stairwell door and scrubbed one hand over my burning face. Pulling myself together, I gathered up the laundry I'd hung up to dry before heading to work. The weak October sun warmed the crisp air, soaking into my shoulders as I plucked rags from the makeshift clothesline strung across the roof.

Adam's sweatshirt was ready to come in, too. His scent clung to it even after being washed, and I pressed it to my face with a shudder, breathing him in.

He made it, and he's going to be okay.

Focusing on those two facts, I pushed aside my growing infatuation as best I could and set his hoodie on top of the rag-filled basket. The last thing I wanted to do was drive him away again. The scent embedded in the worn sweatshirt brought back the memory of our brief kiss, his chapped, warm lips, and his startled gasp on my tongue—

I groaned, sinking to the rooftop as memories of caring for a feverish Adam danced through my head. The warm, firm bulge of muscle under my fingers when I changed bloody bandages for fresh. The slick softness of fur and the press of smooth, supple skin on my palms as I coaxed him to his feet. The trusting weight of him as he slumped against me while I helped him to his makeshift bed.

His injuries would need care for a while longer, too. I bit my lip and let my head rest on my knees. Just the thought of touching him again made my heart stutter and my cheeks burn hotter.

"This is normal." I stood and picked up the basket, fumbling with the door. "He almost died, and he's—"

Beautiful. Wild. *Mine.*

"Oh, I'm in so much trouble." I winced, pasting on a polite smile in case I ran into any of the other tenants.

Luck was with me for once. I returned to my apartment to find Adam deeply asleep on the beanbag with my quilt in a colorful puddle at his feet. Setting his sweatshirt next to him, I pulled the blanket up around his shoulders.

I watched him sleep for a few minutes, twisting the hem of my shirt around my fingers as I wrestled with the weight of longing lodged in my chest.

It wasn't just his exotic looks or the sleek muscle shifting under dusky skin and darker fur. Though those certainly didn't hurt. It was as if he was a lodestone, pulling me to him. He was distracting in a way I'd never experienced before. Not even with Chris.

Especially not with Chris.

I fled to my bathroom. A shower was definitely in order. A *cold* shower.

Chapter Thirteen

It took another three days before Adam was healed enough to leave my apartment. A week before he was doing well enough to do away with the constant bandage changes. At first, he wouldn't talk about what happened. Frustrated and almost sick with worry, I finally confronted him with the metal fragments I'd kept from that awful, bloody night.

"These are bullets, aren't they?" I asked softly after another awkward bandage check. The wounds had closed over at last, but the scabs and new skin were fragile. At least we were down to once a night.

Adam paused, his new t-shirt wound around his hands. "Yes," he said, just as soft as he turned away and straightened out the bundle of fabric with a shake.

"What happened to you, Adam? Why did you disappear for so long and come back with bullet holes? Why aren't you healing faster than this?"

He pulled his shirt on with a sigh, covering the fresh bandages. The thin fabric clung to him in interesting ways as he retrieved his hoodie from the couch. I swallowed hard and forced myself to focus on the questions hanging in the air between us. This was important. I couldn't let my new feelings for him distract me. Not right now. "Adam?"

"I went to the mountains." Adam's ears flattened against his mane, his deep voice a quiet rumble, more felt than heard. "Human hunters were in the woods."

"With guns?" Chris hunted, and he always complained about how rifle season wasn't until the end of November. This was October. The only hunters out there should be armed with bows, not guns. "Why would they—"

"They were hunting *me*, Bri."

I gaped at him, eyes wide as a sick feeling pooled in my gut. My thoughts flashed back to the first time he saved me. In the alley. The two men who grabbed me wanted me as some kind of bait, and then Adam had shown up. But...

"Why?"

He looked away, one hand going to his antlers, and my stomach sank. "It...depends. Most want the gold. A few are searching for a beast you humans call—"

"Bigfoot," I said with a groan.

Adam nodded. "Others know what I am. They want to return me to the people who killed my mother...or keep me for themselves."

"How long have you been hunted like this?" I whispered. "Is it even safe for you to be in the city?"

A wry smile twisted his lips, and he slid his hooded sweatshirt over his head, settling it into place with a sigh. "Not really." He paused, his voice heavy with sad resignation when he continued. "It's always been this way for me, Bri. I've been hunted since I escaped five years ago. I haven't been caught yet."

"Why aren't you healing yourself the way you healed my finger?" I asked after digesting the revelation for a long minute. Hunted. Like a beast, and all because he was different. It was horrible.

"The ones who shot me knew what I was and were prepared. They used bullets filled with pieces of iron."

"Bane of the fae," I said softly.

Adam nodded, glancing at the handful of metal fragments. "Arrows are easy to pull out, Bri. Bullets are...harder."

"Oh." Dazed, I looked at the sandwich baggie. How many times had he been shot over the years to learn that? *Too many.*

Strange little disks rested among the jagged chunks. They were dull and rusted...and the perfect size to fill a hollow point. Such small pieces of metal—but enough to kill him if I hadn't been there to go to for help. I'd almost lost him.

The bag slipped from my fingers, and my hands flew to my mouth. A thousand scenarios tumbled through my head. A thousand ways things might've gone differently without my help. Part of me wanted to beg Adam to stay, to never go near the mountains again, but he was wild, not tame. To trap him here would kill him just as surely as those bits of iron.

Besides, it was even more dangerous for him to live with me. Eventually someone would notice—like the men who had tried to use me. He would be right back where he started, or worse.

"Bri?"

My spinning thoughts settled into a numb certainty. I shook my head, my gaze dropping to the bag of metal shards on the floor. Adam couldn't remain in the city if he was ever going to be truly free. He needed to leave. Maybe not today, maybe not next month, or even this year, but soon. I couldn't ask him to stay where he was in danger, not for a simple friendship. Maybe not even for something...more.

The realization left me empty, ready to blow away in the slightest breeze. A husk with a breaking heart. The urge to cry swept over me and set my eyes burning with unshed tears. I looked up at Adam. If I told him how I felt, would it make a difference?

"I'm...it's okay." I straightened and brushed past Adam. For a moment, I wavered before I gave in to the inevitable and headed to the shelves beside my workbench with a wan smile. One way or another, I always came back to the clay.

Adam trailed behind me, watching me touch each of my unfinished pieces before pulling the plastic shroud from the new bust I'd been working on. "Are you sure?"

"No," I whispered as I moved the sculpture to my workbench. Picking up my favorite wooden tool for details, I eyed the clay face. "I will be eventually, though. That's what's important, right?"

He was quiet. I worked with the silence, letting its weight cover me and push down the tangle of emotion lodged in my chest. I desperately wanted to take a chance and tell him what was in my heart. If he left, I didn't want to always wonder what might've been...but what if I was wrong? What if I ruined everything? Could I hope Adam ran from my kiss out of shock rather than revulsion, or was I only seeing what I wanted to? It didn't matter. I had to try.

"I'm sorry I didn't tell you sooner," Adam said at last, his deep, velvety rumble cutting through the constant cycle of fear and longing in my head. "And I'm sorry for leaving."

I nodded and tried to ignore the blush making my cheeks burn as I smoothed the eye I was creating with my thumb and wooden tool. "It's okay," I mumbled, the slight grit of the clay steadying my hands, even if it did nothing to quell the trembling in my voice. "I shouldn't have—I mean, I...dammit!"

I glared at the fresh gash across the clay eye. Adam plucked the worn wood responsible from my fingers and set it aside. The silence stretched for a moment more, waiting. It was now or never.

"I don't want to lose what we have," I finally blurted out. "Our friendship—it's important to me." I looked up and caught a glimpse of his sudden smile, a flash of ivory against his dark skin and darker fur. "But I..." I trailed off as the words stuck in my throat, digging roots into my tongue and tangling themselves into a hopeless knot. Adam waited for me to continue, his brief smile fading while I stood and stared at him, my confession stillborn.

"But?" Adam prompted, a familiar sadness starting to deaden the odd light in his eyes.

"I..." *I dream of you, and I want more...for however long we have left.* I shook my head and dropped my gaze to the clay smeared on my hands.

"Oh," he murmured. My head snapped up as he turned to go.

"Adam, wait!" I choked out.

He paused in my bedroom doorway and sighed. "It's okay, Bri. I understand. I'll go—"

"No!"

Pushing away from the bench, I shot across the distance between us and buried my cold hands in his hooded sweatshirt. The thick material snagged on my clay-smeared skin. I gripped it tight, keeping him here with me.

"Please don't go," I pleaded. "Please don't leave me all alone."

Adam froze. Then his arms were around me, surrounding me with the sharp comfort of cedar and *him*. "Never," he whispered, and I crumpled, my tears breaking free at last.

It was almost midnight before I was able to think about letting go, my tears spent. He had moved us into a sprawled seat under my open bedroom window, the crisp breeze tangling my hair in his fur.

"Better?"

I nodded jerkily and let him shift me in his arms until he could look me in the eye. The silence stretched again, and I realized he was still waiting.

"Please, Bri. What—"

It wasn't graceful or neat. I probably looked like an albino raccoon from all the crying, and I couldn't quite breathe, but it didn't matter. I couldn't lose him like this. I had to try, to take the leap and hope Adam would catch me instead of letting me fall.

Gripping a double handful of worn hoodie, I hauled myself upward to cut him off with a desperate, tearstained kiss. The words I struggled for remained a tangled mess, but I didn't need them anymore. Adam went rigid, his mouth started to pull away—and then he was kissing me back.

Shy and unsure, it was clumsy and over far too quickly. I sighed against his lips, and the strength born of adrenaline melted away. Adam caught me when I swayed, burying his face against my neck.

"Are you sure?" he whispered, his breath warming my collarbone as one of his antlers brushed my cheek.

"No," I whispered back as I burrowed closer, "but I want to try."

***

Eventually Adam left, promising to return in a day or so. He was still a little dazed, and I wasn't much better.

I...I did it. I leaned out my window, wishing I'd been brave enough to ask for a goodbye kiss. The crisp night breeze tangled my hair, tempting me to linger. I didn't have to work in the morning, but exhaustion tugged at me, insistent and demanding. With a yawn, I gave in and closed the window.

I readied for bed in a pleasant fog and slept like the dead. When I finally woke up, I buzzed with fizzy energy. Bemused, I discarded my plans for a lazy day in the studio. Out came dusting rags, broom, and mop. I threw on some of my oldest, comfiest clothes and spent the whole day scrubbing and reorganizing with laughter in my heart.

It had been years since I'd felt this good. I found myself cranking up some catchy music and dancing through my cleaning. By the time evening came around, my apartment was spotless. Dinner simmered on the stove while I conquered the last few dishes I couldn't fit in the dishwasher.

Another favorite song came on, and I hummed the melody, turning up my speaker a notch. Swaying my hips to the beat, I set the last mug upside down on the stove to dry. I sang along as I shimmied and spun—until a low strangled sound brought me screeching to a halt. I whipped around with a squeak, heat flooding my cheeks in a painful rush.

Adam stood rooted at the edge of the linoleum. His dark eyes were wide, his hands clutching the edges of his fallen hood as he took in my ripped-up shorts and faded camisole.

"Hi!" I blurted out, scrambling to adjust my tousled clothing. My skin prickled under his stunned gaze. I tugged at the ratty hem of my shorts, wishing I'd opted for something that left me feeling less exposed. I hadn't expected him until tomorrow, though.

I need a shower. Do I stink? Maybe he won't notice. I pushed my hair out of my face, tucking it back into my sloppy ponytail. My blush crept across my face to warm my ears as I fumbled with my speaker, cutting off the song mid-chorus. The abrupt silence was deafening. Adam just stood and stared.

There was something strange about his eyes...

"I'm going to, um, go change," I mumbled, finally giving into my embarrassment and squeezing past him.

As if we were connected by a thread, his head turned to follow me. Claws brushed my elbow, and I stumbled when his arm snaked around my waist. I froze, my heart thudding against my ribs as a low rumbling growl filled the quiet. Adam's nose skimmed along my neck, and something hot and rough slid over my pulse.

What is he doing?!

I flinched and shied away. He yanked me back. Sharp teeth grazed the curve of my throat as he pinned me against the bar. For a second, reality blurred, and I couldn't remember where I was. Panic slammed through me as my body remembered a different man and how he'd held me down while he violated my trust.

"No!" I screamed, pushing and clawing at my captor until suddenly I was free. My legs gave out as I was let go, and I fell in a clumsy, shaking sprawl. I cried out, cowering and throwing up my hands in defense as I scooted away.

"Bri, I-I..."

I gasped and choked, wrestling with the panic attack and losing, even as I registered it was Adam standing horror-stricken in my kitchen. Not the man who violated me so horribly in the past. It was Adam. I pressed my hands over my mouth to muffle the keening whimper as tears flowed in scalding trails down my face. What...why had he done that? Did I do something wrong? Was it my fault?

"I-I'm sorry! I—" Adam choked, staring at his hands as if they belonged to a stranger. For a moment, we shared a stunned, terrified look before Adam bolted. The sound of him leaving through my bedroom window scraped through me, and I slumped against the cabinets with a sob.

Eventually, the smell of my dinner about to burn roused me from my huddle on the floor. "Breathe," I whispered, my voice a harsh croak. I shuddered and more tears fell as I went through the motions of finishing my meal prep and serving myself.

The food was tasteless and stuck to my tongue like glue, but I forced it down. The amazing mood from earlier was only a dream now, and I went to bed early, all my energy drained away. Somehow it was my fault. Just one day and I'd already ruined it. I was an idiot to think this would work.

For hours, I laid there, staring at the ceiling. When I finally drifted off, nightmares of grasping hands, oppressive weight, and bruising pain followed me. All night, I fought back and failed, waking myself with my own gasping cries and screams. Morning found me huddled on the couch, contemplating whether or not to give in and take some pills to give my body the rest it needed.

Somehow, I made it through that day and the next. Adam didn't come back, and I started to wonder if I should try to find him and apologize. The nightmares returned every night until, almost a week after he'd fled, I woke up with a gasping scream to find myself clutching a familiar cloudy white stone.

I stared at it as the last traces of my dream faded. Shoving my quilt aside, I went to get out of bed and froze. On my nightstand was the silk bag for the stone. Beside it, a glass of water glowed with a faint green light.

"Oh." I set the stone down and ran trembling fingers over the slick glass. It was still wet from the dishwasher.

I was shaking as I snatched up my robe and made my way to the roof. There, perched on the farthest corner, was a familiar figure. "Adam," I whispered, clutching my robe and shivering in the night chill.

He was slumped forward, staring at his clawed hands with enough loathing to turn my stomach. His thoughts were so loud, I was able to walk right up to him before he noticed me. Adam stiffened and peeked over his shoulder, his ears flicking to catch the sounds of my approach. I stuttered to a halt a few feet away.

"Hi," I whispered, standing my ground even as my stomach roiled and twisted, urging me to flee. Adam flinched and looked away, hiding his hands in his hoodie pocket. I hesitated and bit my lip as I inched closer.

"I-I'm so sorry!" I blurted out in a rush.

Adam twisted around to stare with wide eyes at my confession. "I-I—what?"

"I'm sorry!" I sobbed, my tenuous control shattering. I collapsed to the gritty rooftop, scrubbing helplessly at the tears pouring down my cheeks.

A rustle and a soft thud, and I was surrounded by the sharp musk of cedar. Adam started to reach for me, only to stop himself as he stared at his hands in wary disgust.

"It's not your fault, Bri," he choked out as I stared up at him. "I shouldn't have—I didn't mean to—" Adam stopped and shuddered, his hands curling into fists as he turned to go. "I should've known better, but I hoped...I'm sorry," he whispered, and then he was gone.

Not my fault? Of all the things I'd expected him to say, that wasn't even on the list. I sat, stunned as I stared out at the city lights.

"Adam..." I whispered. My tears were spent, but his name on my lips knocked a few stray drops from my wet lashes. Somehow, he didn't blame me for what had happened.

With Chris, it had always been my fault. I was always the one begging forgiveness, but instead, it was *Adam* apologizing to *me*. Why? It was too much for my exhausted brain, and it was cold up there on the roof.

Stumbling, I stood and somehow got myself back to my apartment. As I shucked my robe and crawled into bed, something in my churning gut settled. The memory of Adam afraid to touch me flashed across my mind's eye. I needed to talk to him, but how do you find someone determined to avoid you in a city this big?

I reached out and rubbed my thumb over the stone, its magic buzzing against my fingers. "Please," I whispered as sleep started to pull me under, "don't leave me all alone."

***

Morning came and brought a clearer head with it. I was still an awkward mess, but my focus had shifted. I needed to talk to Adam.

Work passed in a blur of exhaustion. Sherrie pulled me aside at the end of my shift to shove a warm loaf of cinnamon bread wrapped in brown paper into my arms. "You tell that beau of yours he better behave himself, you hear?" she called over her shoulder with a saucy wink as I fumbled for words to thank her. With the warm spice of cinnamon and sugar in my nose, I headed home.

If I was going to find Adam, I needed him to come to me. He'd been on the roof last night. Hopefully, he would be back tonight.

At home, I busied myself with the studio, setting up my little pottery wheel and throwing mugs and a few bowls while I waited for the sun to set. My whole apartment smelled of cinnamon.

When darkness fell, I made a plate of the sweet bread, buttering each thick slice and filling his mug with a fresh brew of the peach tea he'd liked the first time he'd been in my kitchen. It was simple, but hopefully, it would give him the right message.

I miss you.

I left the food by the spot I'd found him last night and went straight back inside. While I fashioned handles for the mugs I'd thrown earlier, I listened. Just as I was about to give up and head to bed, my patience was rewarded.

The slow scrape of the window opening jolted through me, and I dropped the handle I was shaping. "Adam?" I whispered, wiping my hands on a damp rag and running towards my bedroom.

He was waiting for me. The empty plate and mug lay gleaming on my bed as he hovered by the window. "Please don't go," I said in a rush, gripping the door frame with white fingers. "I'm so sorry I—"

"Don't," Adam whispered, touching the edges of his hood. "It wasn't your fault, Bri. It was mine."

"Please stay." I closed the distance between us as my eyes started to burn, and a few stray tears slipped out.

He hesitated a moment before reaching out to brush his thumb along my cheek. Quicker than thought, I grabbed his hand and pressed it flat against my face. Adam's breath caught, and he jerked, but he didn't pull away. Slow and halting, he stepped forward. With a shuddering sigh, I dropped his hand and threw my arms around him, pressing my face to the worn fabric of his hoodie.

I shivered, breathing him in as his arms slowly came to rest around my shoulders. For a long time, I just clung to him. After a while, Adam pulled me down with him into a seat beneath the window.

"You don't hate me."

I shook my head, burrowing closer.

A huge sigh rippled through him, taking his tension with it as he crushed me against his chest. "Thank you. I know I don't—I-I can't—"

"Adam," I croaked, muffled by cloth and muscle. "Please don't. Can't we just put it behind us?"

He went still. "And if I...do it again?"

I pulled away to look him in the eye. "Don't leave if there's a next time. Talk to me. I thought I ruined *everything*." The painful memory dug into me like a festering thorn.

"I...okay." Adam nodded, ducking down to nuzzle my cheek. "Okay."

I shivered and nuzzled back, bumping noses with him. His breath caught, and his gaze flowed over my face as I reached up to trace the line of his cheekbone to his chin and up over his lips. There was something about his eyes...they *glowed*.

Brightening and fading sparks of gold and green light flickered in Adam's eyes when his gaze met mine. A question hung in the air between us, and I rose up on my knees to meet him halfway. His mouth was soft and hesitant, and infinitely gentle. He kissed me like he was afraid I'd shatter and crumble into dust.

"I don't want to scare you again," he murmured against my lips when I tried to press closer.

"Just don't let me forget it's *you*. Last time it was—I remembered *him*, and I-I couldn't..."

Adam's thumb brushed over my lips, and I fell silent as he pushed back his hood. He caught my hand and pressed it to his face, nuzzling my palm. "I can do that," Adam whispered, eyes fluttering shut for a beat. His nostrils flared as he drank in my scent, and he pressed a tender kiss to the inside of my wrist.

I was melting, trembling, *burning* in a way I never had before. I swayed closer as he tilted his head, and my hand slipped from his grip and into his wild mane. My thumb stumbled over the base of one of his antlers. Adam shuddered and caught my wrist, tugging until he could press both my palms against his chest. "D-don't—"

"Oh, sorry," I mumbled with a blush at the glazed look in his eyes. He shivered but didn't object when I stole a kiss, and then another.

I knew I was clumsy and not at all practiced, though Adam didn't seem to mind the way Chris had. Instead, his breath hitched in his throat, and he matched me kiss-for-kiss, even as he was careful to keep a little space between us. Eventually, the slow, hesitant kisses faded away to gentle claws in my hair, and a nose tucked into the crook of my neck.

"I'm glad you came back," I murmured, warm and safe and happy for the first time since he'd stumbled across me dancing in the kitchen.

Adam chuckled and shifted us until he could tuck me against his chest. "Me, too."

"Yeah?" I sighed, humming happily when he resumed running his claws through my hair.

"Yeah."

"Good," I whispered and grinned as his quiet laugh lit up the night.

Chapter Fourteen

"What if I'm too broken?" I asked a few days later. We were up on the roof sitting on the ledge, and it was another perfect, crisp fall night. "What if this is as close as we can get? What then?"

Adam cocked his head. "Close?"

Warmth crept across my face, my stomach fluttering a little when he tucked some of my hair behind my ear. "You know, like if we ever got married." He chuckled, and my blush deepened. "Are you laughing at me?"

Adam shook his head. "No, I just...no one wants to be tied to a beast, Bri."

"You don't think this will last?" I asked, hurt.

He looked away, but I'd already caught sight of the bitter frustration darkening his gaze. "Do you?"

"I want it to," I admitted shyly, leaning around him to watch his face go slack with surprise before he turned to give me a soft look of wonder.

"Really?"

I nodded. "But...I'm damaged goods, Adam. What if I can't be enough? What if I can't—I-I don't—"

Adam smiled and stopped my stammering with his thumb on my lips. "I don't think it would be a good idea. For us to get closer right now, I mean."

"Why?" I asked, my lips tingling from his brief touch.

Adam looked away. His ears twitched back, flattening into his mane. "My magic is earth magic, Bri," he said softly, an awkward tension lacing his big frame as he stared at his hands. "What do you know about the fae humans once called the Green Man?"

"Not much," I admitted. "He has something to do with forests and some of the darker pagan rituals, charisma, and—"

"Fertility magic."

I frowned, then blushed. "Oh...*Oh*, um, so..." I trailed off, and Adam flicked a glance at me before turning away again. "Is that what happened in the kitchen? You can't control it?"

"I've never had to," he whispered, and my own embarrassment faded under an upwelling of sympathy.

"I'm sorry. I didn't realize I was making things difficult for you." I fiddled with the hem of my shirt, remembering his face when he'd found me dancing with more skin on display than he'd ever seen from me before. I glanced down at my loose t-shirt and jeans, and back over at Adam with a sheepish smile. "I guess I should leave a note on my window next time."

Adam huffed a wry laugh, dropping his head into his hands. I scooted closer to lean against his shoulder, and he tensed. "Is this okay?" He shuddered and nodded, but I could feel muscles jumping and twitching under my cheek. I stiffened and peered around his shoulder. "Adam?"

"It's just—it's your scent."

I sniffed my shirt. The breeze had died away, and beneath Adam's cedar musk, I smelled like I always did. It didn't sound as if he was talking about my shampoo, though. "Do I, um, smell good?" I asked in a small voice as I slowly leaned away.

He shuddered again and stood, walking a few paces away. "Yes," he whispered, and the harsh ache in his voice rekindled the fluttering in my stomach.

"Could we cover it up...with your scent? Would that help?" Adam froze and turned slowly, his dark eyes glowing with green and amber lights. I offered him a shy smile as I slid off the ledge and crept up to tug on his hooded sweatshirt. "Let me wear it? Please?"

For a long minute, Adam stared at me. His glowing eyes glittered green and gold. Slow and halting, he reached up and began to tug it off over his head. The t-shirt under it rode up as he maneuvered the hoodie around his antlers. I touched him before I thought about what I was doing.

"Bri," he gasped, freeing himself with a sharp tug and ripping fabric. "Don't—"

Too late.

Skin, hot and supple, pressed against my fingers, and fine, short fur tickled my palm. Then suddenly I was pinned to cold brick, my wrists in an iron grip and a familiar hooded sweatshirt balled up between us. Adam hid his face in my hair, and his harsh breathing warmed my skin.

"Sorry," I whispered as he let me go and thrust the bundle of fabric at me. A low, husky chuckle was my only answer as I pulled the hoodie over my head. I was still trying to locate the sleeve holes when he took my face in his hands and kissed me, slow and sweet.

"Oh..." I gasped against his lips. Adam smiled and kissed me again, careful to maintain the distance between us.

After several more breathless, teasing kisses, he helped me free my arms and roll up the sleeves. I buried my face in the folds of his hooded sweatshirt with a satisfied hum and took a deep breath. "You know," I mumbled as we perched on the roof's edge once more, "you smell really good, too." Adam looked away, and I grinned. "Are you blushing?" He shot me a crooked smile and shook his head. "Yes, you are." Fingering the drawstrings tangled in the heavy fabric, I bit my lip. "I'm sorry. I didn't mean to—"

"It's okay, Bri. Maybe..."

"We should set some ground rules?" I finished breathlessly as the gold and green sparks in his eyes brightened before fading away.

With a faint quirk of his lips, Adam nodded.

"I can't do anything about my scent." I frowned, mulling it over for a moment. "I mean, the hoodie seems to help, but your scent will fade if I keep it. Besides, it's too big for me to wear all the time, and you need it, don't you?" I glanced down at my lap. "I don't want to make things harder for you."

Adam laughed, rich and velvety, and deep. "Your scent will change in a few days, don't worry," he assured me with a fond look while I fought with the sleeves yet again.

"It'll change..." I gaped up at him. "You can smell that?!" I squeaked, my embarrassment rushing back, plus some. Adam flinched, and I buried my face in my hands. "So the first time I kissed you…" I swallowed, sudden panic rising in my throat. "You knew what I—I mean, um—" I whimpered and peeked through my fingers to find him watching me uneasily. "You knew what I wanted to do."

"I-I—no, not at first," Adam said with a wince, tense and ready to bolt. He sighed and turned to stare out at the city lights. "I don't have much past experience to fall back on, Bri. What little I do have was nothing like this."

Adam's ears flicked back, flattening into his mane. His grip on the ledge tightened. He fell silent, and an eerie blankness dropped over his expression. I forgot my own awkward embarrassment in the wake of the humiliation and bewilderment surfacing in his gaze.

He started to speak, and I laid my hand over his, my thumb feathering over his knuckles. "It's okay, Adam. You don't have to explain."

Adam hesitated and gave a jerky nod, the painful tension flowing out of him with a sigh. He let go of the ledge and rested his hands in his lap, staring at his claws. For a long minute, neither of us spoke.

"So…this is all new for you, then." Adam looked up, a kind of hopeful wariness replacing the blank mask he'd hidden behind. I offered up a sheepish smile. "I'm not exactly experienced with any of this either, Adam. My parents were super strict about marriage coming first. Which was probably the only thing we ever agreed on. They didn't even let me talk to boys before I met Chris. It's okay."

Adam nodded, his pinned ears relaxing. When I scooted closer, he let me, leaning into my warmth as his arm curled around my waist. "No one has ever seen me the way you do," he said at last, his voice soft. "At most, I have instinct and a guess."

He shot me a sidelong glance, and my cheeks warmed. "You figured it out after I kissed you, though."

A playful smile cut across his face, flashing sharp teeth. "It was hard not to."

At this rate, I would have a permanent blush tattooed across my cheeks. "So, ground rules, then. I think we can agree most of the time some touching and kissing is okay, but no, um…" I glanced up at Adam, gave his worn jeans a pointed look, and cleared my throat nervously. A low rumble pulled my attention back up to his face, and I swallowed hard. The sparks were back in his eyes.

"Maybe we should talk about this in a few days," I whispered as Adam stared at me with a hunger that had nothing to do with food and everything to do with the way my hip pressed into his thigh.

His heat burned me through the layers of heavy fabric, and I sat transfixed as he swayed closer. Adam didn't kiss me, though. Instead, he dragged his mouth from my jaw to my shoulder in a tingling scrape of lips and teeth and breathed me in.

"Adam..." I shivered, my eyes fluttering shut as he nuzzled my shoulder and began to retrace the path he'd marked, his mouth hot on my skin. "You should. ..probably stop—"

"Or what?" he growled against my neck, sounding as drunk as I felt. I gasped as his nose brushed the shell of my ear. The tickle of his lips along my throat set my nerves singing, and my head fell back as all my muscles went slack. Adam caught me with an approving rumble. Only the gentle prickle of his claws, tangled in the hem of my shirt, kept me from melting into the haze his touch inspired.

"A-Adam?" A huff was my only answer. I blushed as the puff of air slipped past the neck of my t-shirt like a tangible caress. "Adam, we're on my roof. People can see us."

Adam paused. "Keep talking," he rasped, one hand dropped from my waist to grip the ledge as he pressed his face into my shoulder. His ears trembled and flattened themselves into his mane as he visibly tried to pull himself together. The temptation to stroke them nipped at me, and I promptly sat on my hands, my face hot.

"It's a little exposed out here, and my neighbors come out on the roof, too," I said instead. "There's a guy down the hall who brings his wife up a lot. They're newlyweds, and she enjoys stargazing." For almost ten minutes, I babbled about my building, work, my sculptures—anything I could think of to help Adam focus. At last, he let me go, pulling away with a lingering caress along my cheek.

"Thank you," he rumbled, dropping his face into his hands with a sigh.

"Um, you're welcome." I freed my hands from where I'd tucked them under my legs and peeked over at him. "Should I go?"

"Yes—no...stay with me, please. Maybe we should go inside, though."

"Inside? You mean the small space where my scent is everywhere and there are walls and doors to close so people can't see us," I said tartly, trying to ignore the giddy flutter in my belly urging me on. The knowledge that I had the power to take advantage of his instincts buzzed under my skin. It was a heady vintage, but scary, too. We didn't need complications.

Adam flinched and shot me a sheepish look. "When you put it that way…"

"I do," I teased, leaning against his side. "Now behave."

"You first," he growled, and I realized my hand was stroking his thigh.

I snatched it back and stuffed my hands in the vast pocket of his sweatshirt. "Sorry!"

A low chuckle answered me, and Adam covered the lump of my hands with one of his. "It's okay, Bri."

I smiled and snuggled closer. "Good."

***

"Do I still smell…enticing?" I asked a few days later as I stowed my dinner leftovers in the fridge.

Adam glanced over his shoulder and sniffed. He shook his head, a slight wariness in his face. "Good," I said with a shy smile, shoving the sleeves of his hoodie back when they flopped over my wrists again, "because we should really have that talk."

His lips twitched, and he turned away with a nod. "Okay."

I watched Adam fiddle with the scraps of clay on my workbench for a minute, then snuck up behind him. At least I tried. One of his ears flicked towards me, followed by a sidelong glance. "Bri?"

"Just making sure," I teased, slipping my hand under his t-shirt and dragging my fingers through the thick, soft fur along his back.

He jumped and grabbed my wrist. "Bri, please—"

"Sorry!" I said hastily as the familiar sparks glinted in his dark eyes.

Adam sighed and tugged me closer, crouching a bit to put our faces on the same level. "Just because your scent isn't as enticing doesn't mean I'm unaffected by you," he said, his deep voice slow and quiet, despite the fading lights in his eyes.

"Right," I mumbled with a sheepish smile, my face hot.

A faint smile quirked his lips, and I knew I was already forgiven. Adam straightened and pressed a kiss to the knuckles of my captured hand, his claws trailing over my palm as he let me go.

The gentle touch sparked something, sending trails of sensation humming through me like half-heard whispers. I shivered, staring at my freed hand as it hung in the air between us before I forced it down to grip the hem of Adam's hoodie. The worn sweatshirt anchored me, but it wasn't enough to quell the sudden, rising need to get closer to him. A lot closer. It echoed under my skin, insistent and seductive.

Shaking my head a little to clear it, I took a step back and stumbled over a box of mugs. Adam caught my elbow, steadying me before I could fall. The warm pressure of his hand jolted through me, and I jerked away with a gasp, staring up at him.

Adam froze, his gaze dropping to my tightening grip on his hoodie before bouncing up to trace the deepening flush in my cheeks. "Bri?"

"Sorry." I flashed him a trembling smile. "I-I don't know why I did that."

Slowly, he reached for me again. Whisper-soft, his knuckles skimmed along my cheek, and I melted into the gentle caress with a breathy hum. I returned his crooked smile with a shy one of my own as I nuzzled into his palm like an overgrown kitten. Brushing his thumb over the bridge of my nose, he took my face in his hands and gave me a long, searching look.

My skin buzzed and tingled where we touched. I shivered. He was only a breath away, but it wasn't enough. The growing need to be closer to him was getting worse, and my eyes fluttered shut as I tried to push past the hands holding us apart.

"Bri, look at me."

"Hm?" I mumbled as I obeyed, straining against his hold. A faint sweetness teased the edges of my tongue, and I licked my lips, chasing the elusive flavor. I felt drunk, my limbs heavy and my thoughts slow and honeyed under his hands.

His nearness taunted me, and a frustrated whine slipped out before I could stop it.

Adam's eyes went wide, and the sparks returned as his grip tightened, his claws prickling my skin. As if caught in a dream, he started to close the distance between us. Our breath mingled, and his lips feathered over mine in a chaste kiss. The gentle touch arced through me, an earthy sweetness flooding my mouth in a heady rush. I strained closer with a gasp, but Adam pulled away, his movements jerky and stilted as he gently held me back.

He closed his eyes, concentrating. With every passing breath, the overwhelming need to be closer to him faded a little more. Finally, it was gone.

Adam let me go with a sigh and slumped against the wall behind him. I swayed as I came back to myself, the taste of his magic fading away as the world snapped into focus in a dizzy rush. "Oh, I...that was new," I whispered, running trembling hands over my flushed cheeks. "Was your magic doing all that on its own?"

"Not entirely," he admitted, looking away as he slid down the wall to sit on the floor.

I bit my lip, burying my hands in the vast pocket of his hoodie with a wince. "I-I...we *really* should have that talk."

Adam chuckled and glanced up with a sheepish grin. "Yes, we should. Please don't test my control anymore, though. I don't know if I can stop it again."

"The magic or the touching?" I asked, dragging his beanbag over and curling up on the blue cushion before I was tempted to sit in his lap instead.

Adam swallowed hard and closed his eyes with a shudder, his ears flattening into his mane. "Both," he said softly, his voice husky and raw.

"Oh," I whispered, my heart stuttering against my ribs as I stared at him. I sank back into the beanbag, letting it swallow me up while I reached up to tug on the drawstrings at my neck. "Okay, ground rules. Is there anything I should know or at least avoid doing?"

His gaze slid towards me, and I squirmed. "Besides trying to pet you, I mean," I mumbled, pulling the collar of his sweatshirt up to hide my face. Adam made an odd, strangled sound, and I peeked out to find him watching me with a mix of bemusement and chagrin.

"That would be one..." He trailed off, his claws biting into the worn planks of my floor before he hid his hands in his lap.

"And I should probably keep my distance when I'm...enticing." I glanced at the new divots in the faded wood. Adam followed my gaze and flinched, fixing the damage with a brush of his fingers and a flurry of green sparks.

"Probably," he agreed, his deep voice soft as the glow of magic faded.

"Why now, though?" I asked when the awkward silence between us had stretched on too long. "I mean...in the past you touched me, and I touched you, and it was fine. It didn't happen a lot, but when it did, it was never like this. If it wasn't a big deal then, why is it now?"

"I...I don't know," Adam said with a sigh, running his claws through his thick mane. He flicked a glance over me from head to toe, before bouncing back to my face as his hands dropped into his lap. "Maybe because things are different now. The last person to touch me with any kind of real affection was my mother, Bri. I was a little cub then, and she was the only person who didn't think I was a...a monster."

Adam grimaced and dropped his gaze to his hands as they curled into fists. The silence between us stretched, taut with an emotional turmoil I understood all too well. I climbed out of the beanbag and went to kneel in front of Adam.

"Tell me?" My soft whisper seemed to jolt through him, and he stared at me as I pulled his hands into my lap. He dropped his gaze to our joined hands, his dark eyes haunted.

"One other human I've met besides you wasn't afraid of me." His expression went blank, and my stomach clenched. "The people who caught us had a daughter. She was kind to us at first, and I thought she was a friend. Then one day, she brought us drugged food and climbed into my lap."

I stared, horrified by the picture his words painted in my head.

"I stopped her before the drugs became too much. When I pushed her away, I broke her arm. To punish me, she had my mother's antlers cut off." Adam hesitated and shifted to take my hands. He gave me a long, searching look as he continued. "I've never had a true friend who knew and accepted my nature before I met you, Bri. I never expected to find more than friendship, either."

"Oh...so what you're saying is we'll have to make this up as we go," I said, the revelation of his damaged past settling in my heart with a thorny, bittersweet ache.

A slow, sweet smile curled his lips. "I'll try if you will."

"I'd like that," I whispered, and blushed.

Chapter Fifteen

It wasn't that easy, of course. One week passed, then another, and still we fumbled to find the right balance. Every day was an exercise in resisting the temptation to toe the line.

Adam did a better job at it than me, reeling in his magic whenever it broke away from him again and again. It was getting stronger, and there was no one to teach him, but somehow he managed. For the most part.

Watching him struggle was a stark reminder that the distance between us was for the best. Still, I longed for the easy closeness I saw in the couples I passed on the street. The ache it left in my heart pushed me to find little excuses to touch him. To be closer without getting too close.

Some attempts went better than others.

***

"Bri, I don't think—"

I waved the brush at him. "I'll behave if you will," I teased in a singsong voice, only half joking.

Adam eyed the brush, then my playful smile, still wary.

"Please?" I lowered the brush, my confidence melting away. "If it gets to be too much, I'll stop." He hesitated, and a sigh of exasperation slipped out as I glanced at the half-hearted tangles hanging over his shoulder. "It looks like you've been letting birds nest in it."

A muffled snort and a chuckle rewarded my dry observation, and Adam finally gave in. The oversized beanbag cushion shifted as he settled and watched me approach out of the corner of his eye.

"Trust me," I said, gathering his wild mane and started in on the mess.

Adam flinched and twitched his ears out of the way every time I drew near them with the brush. When I made a point of avoiding them and focused on the hidden tangles I was finding with my fingers, he relaxed.

"See?" I teased apart a matted handful. "It's not that bad."

A faint sigh answered me, and a low, growling purr began to rumble through my apartment. My hands faltered for a second, awed delight curling through me. I kept going, humming a silly nonsense tune in time with my brushstrokes. Adam's wild mane smoothed into a waterfall of dark fur, silken and warm. Unable to resist the temptation, I abandoned the brush and savored the flow of it over my fingers.

Behave, I chided myself when I'd indulged long enough. Careful not to pull, I gathered up his mane and tied it back with a scrap of navy and gold ribbon. It probably wouldn't hold for long, but that was okay. Trailing my fingers through the thick ponytail, I resisted the impulse to bury my face against the gleaming fur of his neck and breathe him in.

"Adam, I'm done," I said as I leaned around him. "Told you it would..."

I trailed off as the lack of his rumbling purr finally registered, and I took in the peaceful sight of his sleeping face. "Oh," I whispered, tiptoeing around him to look without craning my neck. One of his ears flicked toward me, but otherwise, he didn't stir as I snuck away to turn off lights and get ready for bed.

Apartment buttoned up for the night, I threw my robe on over my pajamas and crept over to Adam. He had shifted to sprawl on his back, one arm tucked under his head. I watched him for a minute, then crawled onto the beanbag beside him. His sharp cedar musk surrounded me as I sank into the space along his side, my head coming to rest on his shoulder. With a happy sigh, I nuzzled into the curve of his throat, fur tickling my nose. If only I could stay here forever. After a few blissful minutes, I forced myself back to reality and went to leave.

I didn't get far.

As I sat up, Adam sighed and rolled towards me. Without waking at all, he reached out and pulled me down beside him. I froze, my heart thudding against my ribs when he nuzzled my neck.

Warmed by his breath, my skin tingled as his lips brushed over my pulse. The collar of my robe fell open, and he sniffed and nudged his way past the nappy fleece with a sleepy rumble.

"A-Adam?" I whispered, shivering.

His nose pushed the strap of my sleep tank aside and skimmed the line of my shoulder, leaving a trail of goosebumps in its wake. My eyes fluttered closed as his mouth dragged back up along my neck. He reached the corner of my jaw, and his contented sigh curled around the rim of my ear. Heat crept across my face as Adam's arms around me tightened. His claws hooked into my robe, as if he was afraid I'd disappear. At last, he settled.

I...should...wake him up, my hazy brain whispered as I slumped forward, pressing my flushed face to his worn sweatshirt with a sigh.

Even as tired as I was, sleep seemed impossible without pills. Being this close to Adam set my pulse thundering in my ears, my heart trying to leap from my chest every time he shifted beside me. I needed to persuade him to let me go, but all I could think of was how much I wanted to stay there, surrounded by his warmth and the sharp musk of cedar.

Just...a few more minutes, I promised myself—and then his purr started up again, and the world melted away.

***

"Mmm...soft."

Silky and warm, my skin tingled deliciously as something teased me awake. I didn't want to wake up yet, though. A wonderful dream danced on the edge of my sleep-drugged brain, and I batted at it, trying to reel it in.

A low rumble in my ear broke the spell, and the elusive dream slipped away as I was pulled close and wrapped up in sudden, incredible warmth. It banished the morning chill that always invaded my bedroom in colder weather, and I sighed happily. Burrowing into the softness tickling my cheek, I reveled in the rich musk of cedar surrounding me, the heady scent familiar with its hints of honey and clay.

Wait...

I scrubbed the sleep from my eyes with a yawn and blinked blearily at the faded black fabric inches from my nose. *This...is not my bedroom.*

All at once, I was wide awake. I went to roll away, only to have my retreat halted by a warm weight across my legs.

"Oh, you've got to be kidding me," I whispered, stifling a nervous giggle as I registered the prickle of claws along my hip and the scrape of worn denim on one bare foot.

We were still on Adam's beanbag. I was cradled against his chest, his legs tangled with mine.

Doing my best to ignore the scorching blush rising in my cheeks, I tried to wiggle free, provoking a sleepy growl from Adam. His hand slid up to curl around my waist, tangling in my robe as he rolled onto his back, taking me with him. I squeaked, clutching the front of his sweatshirt. A gentle scrape of claws at my waist—and then I was sliding free as the tie on my robe gave way.

I landed on the hardwood floor in a clumsy sprawl. For a minute, I lay there, but the cold floor soon drove me to my feet. Without Adam's heat to hold it at bay, the early morning chill quickly seeped through my thin pajamas. I shivered and tried to rub some warmth into my arms, longing for my robe strewn across his lap.

Adam chose that moment to wake up. With a stretch and a yawn, he sat up and paused. My heart thudded against my ribs, picking up speed while he eyed the pile of nappy fleece in his lap with sleepy befuddlement. I took a halting step back, and the scuff of my bare feet snapped his head up.

"Bri?"

"Good morning," I mumbled, folding my arms over my chest with a wince.

He took in my rumpled pajamas and flushed cheeks, and glanced down at my discarded robe. A dawning realization crept into his dark eyes, banishing the sleepy confusion.

"I...here," he said softly, pointedly not looking my way as he thrust the robe at me.

Glancing down at my thin sleep tank, I snatched the robe out of his hand and crumpled it to my chest. "I, um, thanks." My gut swirled with enough embarrassment to make me nauseous. I stared at my bare toes, wishing my living room floor would open up and swallow me whole.

"What..."

"You fell asleep," I explained, forcing myself to meet his gaze and offering up a shaky smile. "I didn't mean to—" I took a deep breath and blurted out the next bit before I could change my mind. "I didn't mean to stay. When I tried to leave, you grabbed me. I really was going to go to bed and let you sleep, but I couldn't—I just...you wouldn't let me leave," I finished weakly. Adam went still, and I cringed, waiting.

"I...fell asleep," he mumbled, sitting forward and running his fingers through his sleep-mussed mane. One of his claws snagged a hidden tangle, and he winced.

I nodded, freeing one hand from my robe to tug on the end of my bedtime braid. "You were purring," I added in a small voice, barely more than a whisper.

Adam's breath caught. The beanbag chair squeaked as he rose and closed the meager distance between us. He cupped my cheek, and for a long minute, he just stared at me, his thumb brushing along the curve of my bottom lip. The kiss, when it came, was sudden and sweet. A chaste brush of his lips on mine.

I shivered and tilted my chin, deepening the kiss. It wasn't enough. I reached out with my free hand to grip a fistful of worn hoodie, and Adam caught my wrist.

"Don't," he whispered against my lips, freeing himself and weaving his fingers through mine. Dazed, I nodded. He sighed as he pulled me in for another kiss, and another. Each one melted away the awkward tension between us a little more until I couldn't take it any longer.

The robe that had seemed so important a few minutes ago fell to the floor, and I fumbled to pull him closer even as he continued to hold me back. I mewled, wrapping my free hand in his hooded sweatshirt and tugging. Anything to get more of his mouth on my skin. With a last brush of lips, Adam peeled me off and retreated, his breathing as ragged as mine.

"I-I…" I gasped out, realizing what I'd almost done. I stared at him as he watched me with a gnawing hunger making his eyes spark and glow. "I have to go."

I bolted.

"What am I doing?" I moaned in my tiny bathroom, my words a harsh whisper when I caught sight of myself in the mirror, flushed and rumpled.

Starting things you don't have the guts to finish, my inner critic taunted as I got the shower going and laid out my clothes for the day. The faded green henley and pale jeans I'd stuffed in the linen closet last night were a little big, but I didn't care. I wasn't sure I'd make it back in here alone if I faced Adam again so soon.

For the most part, I was shocked by my own boldness. Terrified, even. More so because a growing side of me was screaming to go back. To push him down onto the beanbag and climb into his lap. To pick up where we left off. I could do it easily. The right nudge and his resistance would crumble away.

The memory of him purring me to sleep fluttered free of the roiling mess in my head. My embarrassed fluster faded under a shy blush. "Nobody ever said this would be easy," I reminded myself with a sigh as steam filled the bathroom.

While I showered and brushed my teeth, I found myself wondering if I should apologize. The thought needled me while I dressed in the fading warmth from my shower, resisting the urge to linger in the bathroom. I had to face him sometime. Clutching my towel to my chest, I took a deep breath and forced myself to open the door. When I returned to the living room, Adam was waiting for me.

"I'm sorry—"

His thumb on my lips stopped my apology mid-breath. Slowly, he tugged the damp towel from my hands and wrapped it around my dripping hair. Magic flared around me, and I tasted sweetness on my tongue. When he pulled the towel free, my hair tumbled to my shoulders in a dry, matted tangle. I waited, bewildered as he took my hand and drew me towards the empty beanbag.

"Adam…"

"Please," he whispered, and I caved. The bright blue cushion almost swallowed me when I sat, and my floundering wrung a faint chuckle from Adam. I blushed and sorted myself out, resisting the urge to turn around when he crouched behind me. I was about to give into my curiosity when the familiar scrape of bristles against my scalp pinged through me, and my eyes fluttered shut.

For an hour, he played with my hair. First with the brush, then with his claws. I was half-asleep by the time the gentle tugs and touches eased to a halt.

"I'm sorry."

My eyes flew open as Adam came around to crouch beside me. I grimaced and dropped my gaze to my lap, twisting the hem of my shirt around my fingers. "I should be the one apologizing to you. It was more my fault than yours, you know."

He touched my cheek, and I looked up in time to catch his sudden, wry smile. "I wouldn't say that."

I returned Adam's smile with a rueful glance at the gleaming mane tumbling about his shoulders. "I do. I'm the one who put you in a position where it was a risk. Even after you tried to tell me it wasn't a good idea."

The smile faded. "I let you, though. And I...I don't usually fall asleep so easily," he admitted reluctantly, letting his hand drop.

"Oh," I whispered. "You can't sleep?"

"I don't need to every night." He stood and tugged me free of the floppy cushion, setting me on my feet. "When I do it's...difficult."

"Because you're alone?" I asked, remembering how Adam had pulled me close and refused to let me go, even deeply asleep. He hesitated and nodded. "Sleep here, then," I offered, ignoring the flutter in my stomach at the thought of it.

Adam stiffened and shot me a wide-eyed look. After a beat, what I'd said caught up to me. "Not like that!" I blurted out, my face hot. "I-I mean, I'll stay in my room. I can make a bed for you out here."

Adam relaxed and flashed a sheepish smile. "I'd like that."

"Good." I snagged the brush from the coffee table and motioned for him to follow, my cheeks still a little warm as I headed for the linen closet. "Come on. We can pick out some blankets before I finish getting ready for work."

With a low chuckle, Adam did exactly that.

Chapter Sixteen

"Are you okay?" I asked when Adam picked up my aloe plant for the fifth time and ran his fingers over the spiny leaves.

A jerky nod was my only answer as green sparks flickered around his hands. They started to dim—and then arced, sending rivulets of light crawling up his arms for a breath before going out with a crackle I felt in my chest. Adam flinched, his ears flicking back. He stared at his hands cupping the little clay pot.

The past month had been awkward as winter set in. Adam kept pushing himself harder to find the balance between his magic and his control. Last week, he seemed to have been figuring it out, but something had changed a few days ago. He had started shying away and keeping his distance. At the same time, he couldn't bring himself to stay far from me for long.

Adam's constant battle made him bounce between being his usual tactile self and refusing to even get close to me. After his hasty exit last night, I ended up spending an hour researching fae myths and legends on my laptop before going to bed. This morning's search before I'd left for work at the bakery had unearthed a more mundane possibility that fit with his sudden moodiness.

The answer's been staring me in the face all this time. I glanced up at his antlers. *I hope.*

Running my thumb along the edge of my dresser, I took the plunge. "According to the myths I found, Golden Hinds are always female. How..."

Adam smiled and set my aloe plant down. "My mother was only half, and human blood can have strange effects on fae pairings and children." He touched one of his antlers. "I'm more my father's kind than my mother's. He was a fullblood, a greenman. Whenever I asked her about him, Mother would tell me I resembled him more than her."

I nodded and turned to my laptop. "Yesterday, you said you've been having a hard time getting your magic to settle when you're with me." Silence. I tapped my thumb on my dresser and skimmed the article again, my cheeks warming.

The floor creaked behind me, and Adam's hooded sweatshirt dropped over my head. I stifled a yelp, floundering with the heavy fabric. After a moment, Adam chuckled and helped me sort myself out. Pushing the long sleeves up over my wrists, I pointed at the article I'd found. "Could it be your hind blood reacting to the change in seasons?"

Adam edged closer, breaking the careful distance he'd been maintaining all evening. "I don't know. It's mostly quiet while I'm in the city. Why?"

I bit my lip and tried to ignore his sudden struggle to keep from touching me. "I, um," I stammered as his warm breath fluttered over my pulse and made my skin tingle. It was hard to think with Adam leaning over my shoulder, his fur tickling my neck. Somehow, I gathered my scattered thoughts and forced them past my lips with a tongue gone thick and clumsy.

"I-I know it's winter now and not fall, but it's not unheard of...I mean, I think...I think it's some kind of rut," I blurted out, gasping when he pressed his face against my neck with a soft growl and breathed me in. Something popped and sparked where our skin touched. An earthy sweetness flooded my mouth, dragging a faint moan past my lips. Adam froze, and I squeaked as his warmth vanished, leaving me to scramble to avoid ending up in a pile on the floor. "Adam?"

He stood with his back to me, gripping my windowsill hard enough to bury his claws in the old wood. Muscle rippled beneath Adam's thin t-shirt, standing out in taut ropes along his arms. His ears swiveled towards me. "I should go," he whispered even as he dug his claws in deeper.

"Because you're not sure if you can control it, or because you don't want to scare me?" I shivered, fiddling with the knotted drawstrings at my neck.

Adam shuddered. "Both."

Slow and careful, I shut my laptop and joined him by the window. Adam shied away, shame heavy in his gaze. He stared at me like he expected me to run from him. Twisting the drawstring around my finger, I bit my lip. His nostrils flared as he drank in my scent and turned away with another shudder.

Scent was important to him. Over the past few days, he'd made a point of giving me his hoodie to wear whenever we were together. It settled something in him when I let him surround me with his scent. Maybe I could use that.

"Come here," I said at last, ignoring his flinch when I tugged the hem of his shirt. He hesitated but followed without protest when I snatched my spare pillow from my bed and headed for the living room. With a little persuading, I got Adam to sit in his beanbag chair.

"Here," I mumbled, blushing a bit as I thrust my pillow at him. "I don't have anything with my scent you can wear." I plucked at his hooded sweatshirt hanging off my small frame. "My pillows have been with me all week, though. Maybe it'll help."

Adam took it gingerly and watched me retrieve my hairbrush from the coffee table. "I don't think that will help much, Bri," he admitted shyly, pointing at the brush.

I twirled it in my grip and shrugged. "Let me try?"

"You don't understand, Bri. I-I can't—I mean, I..." Sparks lit his eyes. "I want to touch you," he rasped in a broken, aching whisper. He clutched the pillow, his gaze traveling over my body before settling on my mouth.

I swallowed hard, and Adam turned his face into the pillow while I floundered. Earthy sweetness teased my tongue, the flavors of honey and clay growing stronger. The sudden, overwhelming desire to climb into his lap and drown in him crested over me.

Heat crawled down my neck and burned in my ears as my blush deepened. I took one stumbling step closer before I managed to stop myself. My heart stuttered and leapt, the brush handle biting into my palm as I struggled against the heady draw of Adam's magic.

It lapped at me, rising and falling in wavelets like an incoming tide. His battle for control called to me, but I took a deep breath and pushed away the urge to comfort him. It wouldn't just be a kiss or a touch if I went to him now. It wouldn't stop there. I wasn't ready for that. *We* weren't, and we both knew it.

Breathe, I told myself as I forced my body to circle his hunched form and lift the brush. Focusing on anything but the pulse I could see hammering along his neck, I did my best to soothe Adam's riled instincts without giving in to something more.

Tangles parted beneath the brush, and the heat crawling under my skin gentled. I became caught up in the hypnotic rhythm as I smoothed his ruffled fur. Slowly, his posture eased. His pulse calmed, and the taste of Adam's magic faded into a lingering sweetness as he began to lean into each stroke.

"I'm not getting my pillow back, am I?" I dared to tease when I peeked around his shoulder to find him still nuzzling it. Adam paused and shot me a sidelong glance hazy with sleepy contentment. "I thought so." I resumed my attention to his fur with a soft smile. A rumbling purr started up, only to fade as my touch and scent lulled him to sleep.

Careful not to bump him, I set down the brush. I watched him for a minute and went to retrieve the quilt from my bed. After a bit of fumbling, I draped it over Adam, surrounding him with my scent. One ear twitched, and he sighed, burrowing into the worn, patchwork folds.

"Goodnight," I whispered, then tiptoed off to grab a spare comforter for myself before heading to bed.

***

"Hey, how are you feeling?" I said with a yawn the next morning. Waking up to find Adam sitting under my window was something of a shock. He had my miniature rose in his lap, and green sparks danced around his hands.

"Better, thank you." A faint smile twitched his lips. His gaze skimmed over me before his focus returned to the rose. At some point in the night, he'd reclaimed his hooded sweatshirt from where I'd hung it on my door. My spare pillow was tucked behind his hip, my quilt neatly folded beside him. My laptop was beside him, too. I could only see part of the screen, but it was enough to know Adam had been reading the article I'd tried to show him yesterday.

A sudden blush warmed me as the sight reminded me of his words from last night. Adam's head snapped up, and I winced when the green light of his magic began to flicker and crawl up his arms as his control wavered.

"It's nothing," I mumbled hastily, hiding behind my comforter as he tested the air between us, the sparks fading away. "Is something wrong with my rose?"

Adam hesitated and shook his head. "No, not exactly." He looked down, flicking a glance at his hands before ruffling the tiny blooms the way I would pet a cat. "It's not sick. It's just...it's not happy. Roses hate being trapped in a pot. They need to be free to run wild...to spread roots and grow."

"Oh," I whispered, my embarrassment fading. I sat up, glancing at the rose before meeting his gaze with a sad smile. "Are you talking about the rose, Adam? Or yourself?"

His eyes closed, and he shuddered, clutching the clay pot. "I...I can't stay here, Bri."

"I know," I said softly, looking down at the comforter bunching under my hands. "Ever since you told me about the hunters, I knew you'd have to leave someday. I just hoped we'd have more time."

"You knew?" Adam said, his deep voice soft and confused. I nodded, and my eyes began to burn with unshed tears. "Then...why?"

"Why not?" I whispered with a trembling smile. "I understand it was selfish to tell you how I felt, even though you would have to leave. I just...I couldn't let you go without being sure. I didn't want any more regrets." I sank into my mess of blankets, curling into a ball and rolling over to bury my face in my soft comforter. "I'm glad I did it, but I'll understand if you hate me for it. These past few weeks with you, though...they've been the happiest of my life."

Silence.

Several tears slipped free, and I curled tighter, swallowing the panic threatening to rise. A part of me had known this would happen. Adam would leave because he had to, and I would be all alone. Again.

All of a sudden, gentle claws were tugging the tangles from my hair, combing it aside as Adam peeled the comforter away. "I need to show you something."

"Okay." I rolled over to face him, trembling when he touched the wet trails on my cheek.

"Get dressed and make sure you'll be warm." Adam crouched and tucked his nose against my neck for a second. His warm breath gusted over my skin as he sighed. "Please don't cry, Bri. I could never hate you."

He stood and went to my window, pushing the curtains aside to glance at the gray sky and bruise-colored clouds outside. A big storm had begun to roll in while we talked, blotting out the weak winter sun with the threat of heavy rains. "It'll be dark enough soon but not for long."

"I'll hurry," I promised, scrambling out of bed and snatching up what I needed on my way to the bathroom.

My stomach was queasy with nerves as I dressed and searched for a coat. Adam would worry if I didn't eat, but there wasn't time for breakfast, and the thought of food only made my stomach worse. Just in case, I packed a couple sandwiches and a bottle of water. "Ready," I called out, settling the small backpack and turning to flash Adam a trembling smile.

"Go to the roof," he said, touching the braid I'd used to confine my hair. For a moment, it seemed like he wanted to undo it, but he let his hand drop and pulled up his hood instead. "I'll meet you up there." I nodded and grabbed my keys, locking up with hands that shook. A low growl of thunder muffled Adam's exit behind me.

Once on the roof, I peered up at the looming clouds. "How—" Adam crouched, glancing over his shoulder with a mischievous smile. "Oh," I squeaked, blushing.

"We need to go," he reminded me when I didn't move.

"Right," I said, my voice cracking a bit as my face burned hotter. Wrapping my arms around his neck, I let him rearrange the grip of my hands and knees.

"Hold on." He approached the edge of the roof. I nodded—then buried my face against his shoulder with a muffled shriek when he leapt into thin air.

A low chuckle rumbled beneath me as the world twisted and lurched, and my stomach lodged itself in my throat when we plummeted. Our hard landing jolted through me. My eyes flew open right as Adam swung over the edge of another building, hanging upside down like a bat nearly twenty stories above the street. A whimper slipped out. I scrunched my eyes closed, resolving to keep them shut for the rest of the trip.

Fingers of bitter wind slipped under my hood to lick over my neck. They nipped at my cheeks and freed bits of hair from my braid. I shivered and buried my face against Adam's sweatshirt, letting his sharp cedar scent settle my jumping stomach even as he launched us into space again. He knew what he was doing. I was safe. Adam wouldn't let me fall. Another sudden stop, and the smells of pizza, pastries, and curry teased my nose before being overwhelmed by the sour stink of rotten food. I gagged, and Adam patted my knee before breaking into a slow lope.

We left the dumpster reek behind and traveled for a few minutes before we stopped moving. The musk of damp stone surrounded us along with the bitterness of dead leaves and the lingering, sour-sweet rot of old trash. Adam paused, and I felt him take a few deep breaths. Were we being followed? For a moment, I was back in another alley, and my wrists ached from the harsh bite of a plastic cable tie.

"Breathe," I whispered.

Adam cupped one hand over my cold fingers and gave them a gentle squeeze. I sighed and tried to relax as his low purr rumbled and faded. Even if those men came for me again after all this time, Adam ran them off once before. He wasn't going to abandon me or bring me somewhere dangerous. I took a deep breath of my own and blew it back out, latching onto the promise of safety Adam's presence granted me. My fear mellowed, and I hugged him closer, waiting.

Adam waited another minute before he turned and paced forward again. Something creaked, and we dropped into a place out of the wind, the soft thud of our landing echoing around us. I shivered, huddling into his warmth as he came to a stop, a dank chill seeping through my jeans.

Several minutes passed, and a gentle hand touched my knee, making me jump. Adam hesitated, and I felt him shift to look over his shoulder. "Bri?"

"I'm okay," I said in a rush, opening my eyes and letting go a little too fast. With a squeak, I stumbled and ended up on the ground in a heap.

A quiet series of clicks pulled my attention to Adam. He fiddled with a battered flashlight. "Are you sure?" he asked, pushing back his hood as the feeble glow lit the shadows.

"Yeah." I stood and dusted old leaves and grit from my jeans as I looked around. We were underground. Everything was gray and dingy, paint and decals peeling

from age and neglect. Rows of square pillars squatted at the edge of a familiar set
of rails, their white tiles cracked and yellowed like old teeth.

"Are we in the subway?"

Adam nodded and handed me the flashlight. "It's a part that's been abandoned."

"Oh...what's the flashlight for?"

"Humans don't see well in the dark," he pointed out with a faint smile as he
motioned for me to follow him.

"Of course," I muttered, careful not to shine it in his eyes. We hadn't been
walking long when he pulled me into what appeared to be a shallow alcove. It
turned out to be a short side tunnel leading to a brick wall glittering with faint
green lights. I slowed, squinting, and almost jumped when a battered wooden
door swam into focus as my Sight pierced the glamourie. Adam pushed it open,
and I stuttered to a halt.

"Are you living here?" I squeezed past him, staring.

Brilliant emerald moss covered the stone floor, creating a thick, plush carpet
studded with tiny white flowers. There was a dented card table shoved up to a
broken-down armchair beside the door. A collection of tools and stones were
scattered across the table's surface. A jumbled nest filled one far corner. The
old wooden chest bound with rope beside it was half tucked behind the piled
blankets, its lid propped open. Scattered around the room, glowing clusters of
quartz crystals perched in odd corners. Their soft glow was faint but steady
against moss and weathered concrete.

Here was a glimpse into Adam's life, and I resisted the urge to explore the home
he'd made for himself beneath the city. "Adam?" I said as I turned—and froze as
the flashlight's watery light fell on the far wall.

"It's okay," he said, his deep voice soft as I crept closer. "You can touch them."

"Oh, okay," I whispered, the brittle strength of what must be genuine parch-
ment curled under my fingers. Yellowing scraps and dingy gray clippings from old
newspapers covered the wall. Several shelves edged the wall of pinned articles, the
wooden planks having grown roots to hold themselves in place. Worn, dog-eared
books filled each one. Stacks of loose papers covered the lopsided bench shoved
against the wall beneath them.

I picked up one of the dusty books and set it down, glancing at the articles with a frown. "What's all this? I-I mean, why do you have these? There's so many."

"I've been collecting what I can find about others like me since I could use glamourie. Most of it is a useless mess but not everything." Adam joined me, bumping my shoulder as he stared at the scraps of paper. "I want to go home, Bri. I'm hoping these will help me find the way."

"Home? Weren't you born here, though? How..."

Adam smiled, running his fingers along the edge of one of the faded articles—this one with a blurred picture at the top. "Ever since I was a cub, my mother told me stories about Underhill, the land of faerie. That's where my father's people are, Bri. Fae or not, I don't belong here. Especially when I can't stay glamoured for more than a few hours. Over the past few years, I've found rumors of others living among humans. If I can find them, they may be able to give me answers. Maybe even help me find a way into Underhill."

He caught my hand as I started to reach for a slim book with gilded lettering on its spine. "Bri, you could come with me. I...I would like that. If you would, I mean. I-I—"

You could come with me.

His words echoed through me like the peal of bells. For an endless moment, it was as if someone reached out and wiped away my scars. He needed to leave, but he wanted me to come with him.

I could start over. Here was my chance to leave my family's rules and expectations and my poisonous past behind. A chance to become someone new, but could I really? What would it cost me to leave everything I knew for a place no doubt as strange and as dangerous as the fae themselves? There was always a cost. What if his people wouldn't let me stay? Could I return to the human world? Was the risk worth it? What held me here, anyway?

Adam's words pierced my racing thoughts, leaving a crystalline calm behind. *You could come with me.*

A fresh start. A new chance.

Lightheaded and giddy, I stopped his stammering with a shy smile. "Okay," I whispered thickly, "then I will. Where do we start?"

He stared at me, his dark eyes searching as he reached up to run his thumb along my cheek. After a long, breathless moment, Adam turned back to the wall of pinned articles, his bewildered shock and relief sparking a bittersweet ache in my chest.

"I'm not sure," he admitted at last, a sheepish lilt to his deep voice. He touched one of the stacks of books resting on the shelves rooted to the wall. "The people who imprisoned my mother and I knew we didn't belong in the human world. They probably could send me home, but we can't trust them to do it."

"Because they might try to keep you. A real, live fae at their beck and call," I mumbled, fingering one of the pinned articles. "Is that what they did before? Before you escaped, I mean."

Adam nodded and pulled something off a high shelf. He held it out, and I let him drop it into my hands. It was a collar. Heavy leather and metal with a broken mechanism near the latch. "This is how they controlled me," he rumbled.

"But it's just a collar. You have magic. How was it..."

Adam flexed one hand, and I stifled a squeak when his claws lengthened by several inches. Eyes wide, I watched him fiddle with something inside the jagged metal. Smoke curled up while he worked, smelling of burnt hair and something sharp.

With a final twist, he pushed on something inside the latch, and prongs slid out of the lining with a dull clank. "It's a kind of metal called Cold Iron by the fae. It's poison to...people like me," he explained as he sheathed his claws and showed me his hands. "Really any iron is, but this was forged a particular way. It's more potent."

Indeed, just touching the collar had left raw blisters on his palms. "They really made you wear this?" I whispered, horrified as I turned the cruel device over in my hands.

Adam nodded, and my stomach twisted at the thought of such a thing around his neck. "A beast is meant to be collared and caged. It's what they are. Dangerous and violent, and not human enough to matter."

His words were bitter and tart, the cadence of his soft reply clearly a recitation of something he'd had hammered into him for years. He made as if to continue, but I stopped him with a hand on his arm. "I don't think you're a beast, Adam."

His gaze met mine, and his sad smile told me he still believed he was. "I know."

"If iron is poison to your people, how can you stand living in the city?" I asked, wishing he could see himself the way I did. "Steel and iron are everywhere. You couldn't even touch my fire escape."

Adam plucked the collar from my lax grip and returned it to the shelf. "My human blood helps. It offers me some immunity as long as I don't touch it to my skin. Sometimes I get sick, but my magic is earth and forest magic. Spending a night in Central Park helps. If it gets too bad, I go to the mountains. It's peaceful there. The trees are always happy to see me."

"Oh…" I glanced at the wall with a frown. "You've had these articles for years. Have you ever found anything concrete? Something more than rumors?"

"Not really," he admitted with a faint smile. "Once, before the humans took us, my mother told me about four elemental Gates. Stonehenge was the one she knew best. Mother called it the Gate of Earth. It's where we were going when we were captured. A few of these mention Stonehenge a few times, but I can't reach it on my own. I'm not even sure the Gate still works or how to open it."

"Well," I quipped, dusting my hands off and propping my fists on my hips. "It sounds like a place to start to me."

"But how would we get there?" Adam traced the blisters on his palms before glancing at me with a sigh. "What if I can't open the way once we're there?"

I pursed my lips and eyed the wall of articles, tapping one finger on my chin. "I say we take the chance."

"Bri…"

"It's worth the risk. Your mother was certain enough it would work that she was taking you there herself, even with humans chasing you. I'll do some research online if you want me to, but I think we should try it." My confidence wavered when Adam just stared at me, searching. "Please, Adam. Let me help. I-I don't want to just give up, and…I want to see your home. With you."

He loosed a shuddering sigh and caught my face in his hands, ever gentle as he pressed his forehead to mine. "Me, too."

I beamed up at him, just inches away. "Take me home?" I asked, excitement bubbling up to steal my breath as his gaze warmed and softened.

Adam nodded and led the way.

Chapter Seventeen

The journey home was wilder than the ride to Adam's den, but this time my mind was busy as he raced to beat the worst of the rain. A torrential downpour began as we landed on the roof of my building.

"Meet me inside!" I called over my shoulder as I ran for the stairwell, the driving rain stinging my face. Adam waved and dropped out of sight. Lightning flashed, and thunder followed right on its heels with a deafening rumble. I flinched and ducked inside, my braid dripping down my back.

My first stop once I got to my apartment was the bathroom. I shucked off my shoes and wet socks, and tossed my dripping coat into the tub. I'd take it to the laundry room later. My jeans were a little damp, but I could live with that.

"Tea, tea, tea," I chanted as I hopped first on one foot, then the other, putting on dry socks as I went. A low chuckle followed me, and I turned around with a sheepish smile. "Do you want some?" I asked when Adam joined me in the kitchen.

He cocked his head, his gaze on my wet hair. "Yes, thank you."

I put the kettle on and grabbed my laptop. Setting it up on the bar, I waited impatiently for it to boot up. "Come on." I drummed my fingers on the bar for a minute before heading to the cupboard for mugs and the last of my blackberry tea.

As soon as I sat, I felt the familiar tug of Adam's claws in my hair. Humming, I let him unravel my braid while I opened my browser and brought up travel options. "Hm...we'll need to fly. There are boats, but those would take several days. Of course, to get on a plane to England, you'll need a passport. Or at least something that looks like one. We both will."

The tugs on my hair stopped.

"When people take a picture of you wearing your glamourie, all it shows is the illusion, right?" I asked, scrolling through examples of required documents.

"Yes," Adam said, his deep voice soft. He started playing with my hair again. "Why?"

"This is so illegal, it's not funny," I muttered under my breath as I pulled up pictures of passports. "Getting them the proper way will take up to six weeks. If your magic keeps acting out, we can't afford to wait that long. Besides, you don't exactly have the right paperwork for the application. We'll need to make some or at least have some made. We'll need other papers, too."

"How do we do that?"

I slumped onto the bar, my head coming to rest on my folded arms. "I call in a favor and hope they're feeling generous. I'll need a photo of your human glamourie first, though."

Adam paused, then his touch vanished. The scrape of my bedroom window opening jolted through me, and I sat up, twisting around in my seat. "Wait, where are you going?"

He smiled, but it was stilted and empty. "I know something which might help."

"Okay," I mumbled, and he was gone. Confused, I returned to my laptop and started sifting through ticket prices and flights.

When Adam returned an hour later, I had a simple travel plan sketched out and a pair of cooling mugs resting by my elbow. "So, I was thinking—"

Adam set a small bundle on the bar next to me with a loud clank.

"What's this?"

He just watched me, something unreadable in his dark eyes while he waited for me to give into curiosity. "Open it," he said at last when I didn't move.

It was heavy, shifting with each layer I unwrapped. The last fold fell away, and my eyes went wide with a gasp. "Adam?" I choked out as I gaped at the familiar shapes gleaming on the bar.

"It's okay, Bri." He picked up one of the small golden antlers. The short spike that once peeked out of his wild mane when we first met was now dwarfed in his hand. Adam pressed it into my palm. "I trust you."

The piece of gold was heavy and cold. I touched the pair of nubby button antlers—so much smaller than the other spike resting on the cloth wrapping. I swallowed the sudden lump in my throat as my vision blurred with tears. "These..." I shook my head, trembling. "You shouldn't have to do this, Adam. These are yours—"

"My antlers can be shed and grow back. It's needed, Bri," he whispered, catching my tears and wiping them away with a wistful smile. "Will it help?"

"I—yes, probably, but what if they get greedy and want more than this? I can't hand them over like this, either. Can you...change them?" I asked, staring at the gold in my hand. Adam nodded and cupped his hands around mine. Magic bloomed between us, and when he took his hands away, the gold was a twisted lump. "Wait," I whispered when he went to do the same with the others. "We may not need it."

"Bri," he said, plucking the changed gold from my lax grip and taking my hands in his, "it's okay. It needs to be done." I nodded, watching as Adam reduced the button antlers and the second spike antler to misshapen lumps with a touch and a flicker of green light. "Now what?" he asked as he rewrapped the gold in the dark cloth.

"Now, I see if Lila is willing to hear me out." I slid my laptop closer and brought up my email.

"Who is she?"

I sighed, the old hurt sparking a bittersweet ache in my chest. "Once upon a time, we were best friends. I grew up with her, and we did everything together. Until one day, I told her about my faerie friends in the woods. She told her parents, and they told mine. I think I was maybe five, and she was seven. Our parents weren't happy about it, and for a while, hers made a point of telling people why I wasn't allowed to play with her anymore. She blamed me for the abuse her parents put her through trying to 'cleanse' her of my 'influence.' They didn't want her to be crazy, too."

I glanced over at Adam and shrugged, trying my best to keep the jagged memory from showing in my face. "We kind of made up when I turned twelve. Chris helped me get a chance to talk to her. She was already into some dark things by then, but she admitted it wasn't my fault. Lila said she owed me for the trouble she'd caused both of us."

My fingers flew over my keyboard as I spoke. I reread the brief message asking if she was in town. Our old code for needing to meet. With a nod, I hit send. "Hopefully, she's still as serious about settling old debts as she used to be, because she's our only shot at this. Lila hates owing anyone anything. She knows how to bide her time until people owe *her* favors instead. The last time I ran from my parents, it was a fake ID from her that let me get so far before they found me. I probably would've made it, but she was still living at home then, and her brother ratted me out."

"Then Chris...saved you."

"Yeah," I whispered, swallowing the sick lump from the memories that called to mind. Giving myself a good mental shake, I grabbed my phone. "Picture time," I explained with a wan smile when Adam looked puzzled. He flinched and turned away, pulling his hood up as he followed me to my bedroom. "Can you manage it with the hood down?" I asked, pursing my lips as I peered up at him.

Adam hesitated, then let the hood drop back with a small nod. "I can't keep it up for as long, though," he admitted, following me to stand in front of the window as I drew the curtains shut.

"We'll only need it for a few minutes." I nudged him to the right spot and stood on my bed. The familiar sweetness of his magic bloomed on my tongue. I brought up the camera app on my phone and waited while Adam's features shifted until his human guise gazed back.

I ended up taking several pictures. "Done," I said at last, returning my phone to my pocket before I hopped down. Adam sighed, and his glamourie dissolved in a flurry of green sparks. "This will work, Adam. If Lila comes through for us, I can get us plane tickets for one of the overnight flights out of JFK and—"

"Are you sure?"

I nodded, heading to my laptop to search for possible hotels around Stone-henge. "I can start getting the funds together tomorrow. It'll be a little tight but doable."

"I can—"

"No," I cut in, guessing what he was about to offer. "Tickets won't cost as much as our papers. I can handle it."

"But if you don't have the funds…"

"Actually, we do." Adam looked puzzled until I pointed at the basket of checks with a wry grin. "There should be enough there to get us to England and pay for expenses."

"But what about your parents?"

"They never said I had to come home right away." I turned back to my laptop. "Besides, they'll find it pretty hard to drag me home if I'm in Underhill."

"Bri, you don't need to do that."

"I want to, though." I shut my laptop and scrubbed my hands over my face with a sigh. "You don't know what it's like. To have that basket sitting there, full of poison. I've lived on instant noodles and canned chicken for months at a time because I was too broke to afford both bills and food. I've memorized where all the local food pantries are and exactly what I can get from them and how often. If it wasn't for my aunt letting me live here dirt cheap, I'd be a homeless runaway, because the only way I'm returning to that life is if they come to drag me away themselves." The words were bitter and tart, the caustic flavor burning my tongue.

"Bri…"

"I'll never be free of my past if I stay, Adam. My parents…they'll never let me go," I whispered, staring blankly at the glossy emblem on my laptop as the bitter truth I lived with every day finally broke free.

I curled in on myself, the stool's low backrest digging into my shoulders. "I'm an adult now, according to human laws, but that won't matter to them. They'll eventually find a way to keep me under their thumb if I stay. I just know they will. To my parents, I'll always be defined by what happened to me. By what the doctors did and said. My parents' reputation is everything to them, and they know people. Powerful people who could pull the right strings and convince the world to lock me away.

"I'd never be free again. Just trapped in a gilded cage of lies until my parents figure out how to 'fix' me—if they even bother trying. I've lived that life once before, Adam. I won't go back to it. I can't. Not now, not ever. I *need* to do this. Please."

Adam knelt and cupped my cheek. His thumb brushed over my lips, and I waited with butterflies in my stomach as a faint smile tugged his mouth. "Okay," he rumbled with a last gentle touch, his claw dimpling my bottom lip for a second as he traced its shape.

"Good," I mumbled, catching his wrist as he stood. With a shy smile, I brought his captured hand to my mouth, kissing the fading blisters on his palm.

He froze. I bit my lip with an embarrassed hum and let him go. My cheeks were hot as I jumped off the stool, looking anywhere but him while I went to the basket to sift through the mess of checks. "Even by plane, the trip will be almost nine hours of being trapped in an iron box. Are you up for that?"

Adam chuckled and picked up an orange from the bowl on the bar and rolled it between his palms. "I'll be fine, Bri."

I frowned. "Even maintaining your glamourie the whole time?"

He set the fruit back in the bowl with a wince. "I...don't know."

"Where did you go the first time you gave me the white stone? Was it the mountains?"

He paused and cocked his head. "Yes, why?"

I shrugged. "You were brimming over with this crazy energy when you came back. It was like someone gave you fresh batteries or something." With three checks in hand, I joined him in the kitchen. "Maybe we should go there before we go to England. Give you the best chance possible."

I glanced at his hands resting on the bar and gave him a sheepish smile. "We should probably put you in gloves and shoes for the trip, though. Then the only glamourie you'll have to maintain will be your face."

Adam flinched and turned away.

"What's wrong?" I asked, dropping the checks next to my laptop. I sat and reached out to touch his arm.

Adam shuddered and looked up. "What if my glamourie fails? What if it's not enough? Bri...no one is going to look at me and see anything other than a monster."

"I don't see a monster," I whispered. His gaze softened and warmed as he stepped closer to kiss me with a fierce gentleness that stole my breath.

"I know," Adam murmured against my lips. "Thank you."

"We can do this," I promised him, resisting the impulse to bury my hands in his mane. Adam caged me to the bar with his arms. He pressed his nose into the hollow behind my ear, and I closed my eyes, biting my lip when he nuzzled the curve of my neck.

"Okay," he said at last, pulling away with a last press of his nose to my throat.

"I-I don't suppose you know your shoe size," I said in a breathless voice I hardly recognized as Adam backed away. He chuckled and shook his head, his eyes dark despite the moment we'd shared.

A sense of loss tightened my chest, and I looked away with a wry smile. "You're getting better," I murmured, wrestling with sudden, foolish disappointment.

"Bri?"

"It's nothing. It's stupid."

He waited. With a huff, I relented. "It's good you're figuring out more control over your magic. I just didn't realize how much I would miss them. The sparks in your eyes. It's still new to me, and I like it. Being wanted, I mean."

A gentle grip on my chin tipped my head back, and I offered up a wan smile. "See? It's stupid."

His eyes closed for a moment. When they opened, tiny flecks of light flared and grew as he shifted until he cradled my face in his hands.

"Why?" I whispered, awed tears burning my eyes until the sparks blurred into a muted glow. "Why would someone like you want a nobody like me?"

"Why don't you see the beast everyone else fears when you look at me, Bri?" Adam asked in return, stroking his thumbs along my cheekbones, a wry smile hiding in the corners of his mouth.

"I...I don't know." My words were almost lost in the growling purr buzzing against me. "I guess it all started because you see *me*. No one ever has before."

Adam's eyes widened, and the sparks faltered before brightening as he gathered me close to press a gentle kiss to my trembling mouth. Like butterfly wings, his lips fluttered over my cheeks, my brow, my chin. My eyes closed, and a few tears slipped free as he dusted my face with kisses and nuzzles.

"We're really doing this," I mumbled when he pressed a final kiss between my brows and tucked me against his chest.

He nuzzled the top of my head and sighed. "Yes. Are you sure you want to come with me?"

"Positive."

"Then does it really matter why?"

I smiled and burrowed closer, inhaling his cedar musk with its hints of honey and clay. "No, I guess it doesn't."

Chapter Eighteen

It took a couple days of emailing back and forth before Lila finally agreed to meet me for lunch at a nearby café.

Everything was going well—until I set our plates aside and handed her the makeshift bag of gold. Adam had changed it again at my request. Now, it mimicked bits of scavenged jewelry hammered together, right down to the shapes of broken chains and flattened pendants. Lila's gaze sharpened the moment her hands touched it.

"Where did you get this?" she hissed, giving both lumps a narrow look.

"It's a long story," I said, keeping my voice low. For the thousandth time, I wished Adam could've been here. The little café was almost devoid of people, and the alcove we were in shielded us from the few who were there. It would have been too risky, though. What if his glamourie failed, and she saw the real him?

"Really?" Lila drawled, raising a dark brow at me. She flipped over one chunk of gold before setting it back inside the bag. "You just had this...lying around?"

Shifting my purse in my lap, I held her gaze and gave her a thin-lipped smile. "You could say that."

Lila tsked, her hazel eyes calculating as she held my gaze and tapped the lump she'd been fiddling with. "This is *not* yours, is it? Is it Christopher's?"

"What? No!" I said as she tied the bag shut. "Lila, I promise you none of this is stolen or recycled gifts that'll cause trouble from my family."

"But it's not yours."

I gave her a pleading look. "It's complicated, Lila. Please."

Lila weighed the bag with its burden of gold in one hand and eyed me for a long handful of minutes, each one dropping my stomach a little further. "Are you in trouble?"

"No," I whispered, clutching my empty mug of hot chocolate, "but my friend is. He just wants to go home. I want to help him, but without papers—"

"Okay, I get it," she said in a half-hearted grumble as she cut me off and thrust out her hand. "Give it over."

"Thank you," I said in a rush, lightheaded with relief. I handed over the packet of information she'd asked for in the email.

"Don't thank me, Brianna. After this, you and I are even. We're quits, you got it? No more favors."

"Understood."

Lila flipped the envelope open and checked everything. "You still living in the shoebox?"

I flushed, crossing my arms and swallowing the tart words jumping to my tongue. "Yes."

She smirked and thumbed past my picture to Adam's photo. "An upgrade for you and a full work-up for him. It'll take a while to get everything. I'll drop them at your place when it's done." She held up Adam's picture, and her smirk widened into a crooked grin. "Your boy Christopher must be pissed you're shacking up with a hunk like this." My cheeks heated further, and Lila laughed. "He doesn't know, does he?" she purred, returning the photo to the envelope and tucking it into her purse.

"Chris dumped me. So no, he doesn't," I said with a quiet, defiant look as I leaned back in my seat, the wooden chair biting into my shoulders. Lila nodded, her smug cat-in-the-cream smile adding sour panic to the butterflies in my stomach.

Information was money. Lila and Chris were more acquaintances than friends, but that wouldn't stop her from seeking him out if she wanted to. How much would Chris pay Lila to find out why I refused to go with him to London? What if he tracked down Adam? Time to go.

"I'll be heading out of town in a few weeks to help my friend pack. Can you get them to me by then?"

Lila nodded and waved me away, her dismissal clear. Gathering up my things, I stood and turned to go.

"Brianna?"

I paused and glanced back, my knuckles white where I clutched the strap of my purse.

"Good luck," she said, her expression as somber as I'd ever seen it. "Wherever you're running to, I hope you make it this time."

I nodded and left without another word.

***

I put my two weeks' notice in at Sweet Haven the very next day. Sherrie was a little worried about me quitting so close to the holidays. But she brushed off my stammered apology with a hug and a sad smile, saying she would miss me.

That evening, Adam and I started preparing for the trip to Stonehenge. When I wasn't sorting through what to pack, I finished studio projects and sold off what I could. Bit by bit, I emptied my apartment of the stuff I wouldn't be taking with us.

Adam helped me at first, though the rut made him moody and easily distracted. Sleep eluded him, even with my help, and he became restless whenever we were apart for any length of time. As the days passed, he began to spend more nights in my apartment. Twice, I woke up to find he'd left his usual nest of blankets in the living room to doze propped up beside my bed.

Then came the morning when Adam wasn't there at all. After he'd been gone for almost a week, I fell asleep on his beanbag and woke after midnight to find him curled around me, his face buried against my neck. Deep in an exhausted sleep, he didn't even stir when I wiggled free and fetched my old quilt. I tucked it around him with a yawn and dropped a kiss on his cheek before sneaking off to my own bed. The rut was over. He didn't return to his den again after that night.

My last day at the bakery came and went without fanfare, though Sherrie insisted I take home a box of my favorites. I spent the last week before we planned to leave searching for plane tickets and a good hotel.

Adam took the time to practice maintaining his glamourie and controlling his magic. It had mellowed some since the rut ended, but it was growing stronger and more unpredictable every day.

One snowy night, we went out for a walk to see how long he could maintain the illusion without his hood to help him. We made it all the way to Central Park and even managed a short time among the sleeping trees before it faltered. The mix of effort and restraint left his magic unruly and erratic, and we ended up seeking out a secluded spot to let him cut loose.

We almost found ourselves on the news. The surge of magic caused every ornamental tree in the park to bloom in an instant, covering everything in drifts of white and pink petals. The hasty ride home on Adam's back nearly made me sick. And yet, the queasy stomach was worth seeing the soft look in his eyes as he plucked handfuls of petals from my hair.

One by one, the days passed in a blur of frantic planning, magic, and lazy musings. Before I knew it, it was time to pick up my last check.

***

"Well, I guess this is it," I muttered as I stood waiting outside the office at the rear of the bakery. I could hear Sherrie talking to someone on speakerphone, the low hum of voices barely audible in the noisy bustle of the holiday rush. Taking a deep breath, I went to knock—and a familiar hand caught my wrist and spun me around.

"Brianna, what a surprise."

"Chris," I rasped, my mouth suddenly dry. He lifted my captured hand to his lips and kissed my knuckles. The intimate gesture curdled my stomach. I backed away as he let me go, jerking to a stop when the doorknob bit into my hip. "W-what are you…"

"A little bird told me you would be here today, love," he said, cutting off my question before I could choke out the rest. "I also heard you're leaving the bakery. Did you reconsider my offer?"

"I—no, I didn't," I whispered, wishing I hadn't insisted on coming alone. Adam hadn't been happy about it, but I'd convinced him to stay put. His magic had been unruly all day. The last thing we needed was for him to slip up where he could be caught on camera.

Chris paused, pursing his lips. He looked me over and raised one dark brow. "Are you going home, then? Your parents will be pleased to see you."

I shook my head and gave him a brittle, tight smile. "Sorry, I'm just heading out of town to help a friend for a few weeks. It might take longer, so I thought—"

"Really?" Chris said silkily. "What an interesting coincidence." His gaze held mine as he reached into his coat pocket and pulled out a familiar photograph. My stomach clenched and rolled as he held it up and Adam's human guise stared back. "When my little bird told me you were leaving town with company, I told them they were mistaken. They insisted they'd seen papers you paid some charlatan to forge for you, then they gave me this," he murmured, lowering his voice to a soft whisper as he leaned closer. "Where are you going, Brianna?"

"Why?" I blurted out, glancing at the small picture as he returned it to his pocket. "What do you care where I go? You ended things between us yourself, months ago." I shivered, my nails biting into my palms as I curled them into fists to hide their shaking.

Chris cocked his head, and a brilliant smile lit his face. It made him seem so handsome and charming, even as he looked me over with a low hum. "Everyone makes mistakes, love. I've missed you."

I gaped at him. He reached for me again. His fingers brushed my wrist, snapping me out of my stunned paralysis, and I jerked my hand away. "Don't...I'm sorry, Chris, but I can't..." I shuddered and pulled myself together, forcing a brittle, trembling smile to my lips. "I'm sure you'll find someone in England who suits you better than me, Chris."

Chris frowned and started to speak when the sound of a throat clearing cut through the noise of the bakery. Glancing over my shoulder, relief swamped me at the sight of Sherrie standing in her office doorway behind me. Without sparing me more than a brief glance, she turned her attention to Chris, her dark eyes flinty.

"Charlotte," Chris murmured, straightening with a nod.

"Christopher," she replied, her usually warm voice chilly and biting as she came forward to stand beside me.

"Well, love, it was good to see you," he murmured, giving the lapels of his wool coat a sharp tug and flicking a bit of lint from his jeans. "Perhaps next time, you can introduce me to this important friend of yours."

"I-I don't—"

"Really?" Chris drawled, his gaze sweeping over me again as I paled. "Tell me something, won't you? Who *is* Adam, Brianna?"

"You best be leaving, hon," Sherrie cut in before I could answer, the edge of her polite smile razor sharp. The smudges of flour on her dark skin took on the appearance of warpaint as she squared up with him, radiating a quiet confidence I could only envy. Her shoulder bumped mine as Chris eyed her, his expression cold. For a moment, the tension grew—then Chris turned away.

"Another time, Brianna," he said softly and swept down the corridor toward the bakery shop front. I nodded in a daze, my breath leaving me in a shaky rush as he disappeared around the corner.

Sherrie gave my elbow a gentle squeeze, steadying me. "Thank you," I whispered, hoarse and sick to my stomach as I hid my trembling fists in my coat pockets.

"Anytime, hon. You looked like you needed a rescue." I managed a jerky nod, and Sherrie gave my elbow another squeeze before letting me go. "Adam is your new beau, isn't he? The striking one?"

I blushed, and Sherrie laughed, guiding me into her office with a firm hand on my shoulder. "Oh girl, there's that face again! You tell him the next time he's coming with you, you hear? Heaven only knows when Christopher will pop up next."

She paused, and the humor melted into a quiet, firm look as the door swung shut behind us, muffling the bustle of the bakery. "That boy won't leave you be until someone makes him. Be careful, hon."

"I will," I said, shooting her a grateful smile as I collapsed into the battered loveseat beside her desk.

Getting my check and trying to persuade Sherrie I really didn't need all three boxes of baked goods she pressed on me was a blessed relief after dealing with Chris. With a promise to come by Sweet Haven if I ever needed a job again, I made my escape and headed home.

Two days later, a plain brown envelope showed up in my mail, filled with everything we needed to fool the airlines into letting both of us on a plane.

***

"What now?" Adam asked when I showed him the documents.

"Now, we finish getting ready, and I pay for the tickets. My parents will probably know as soon as I cash their checks. We'll have at least a few days before they'll get suspicious, though. Especially if they're busy. How long do you need in the mountains?"

"Three days." Adam picked up the new passport and traced the tiny photograph of his human guise.

I bit my lip, watching him. Chris had possessed a copy of the same photograph when I ran into him at the bakery. I hadn't told Adam about the encounter then, and it seemed silly to bring it up now. We were leaving soon. Whatever Chris might have planned, it would be too late.

Brushing my worries aside for the moment, I hummed and tapped my chin. "Three days might be hard. We can probably manage at least two, though. Either way, we'll have to leave first thing in the morning if we're going to get back in time for our flight, but...how do we get there?"

Adam chuckled and set the passport on the pile of papers. "I can carry you, Bri. I don't need much, and what I do need is already there."

"Okay, but what about a tent or food?"

He smiled. "Mostly, I hunt, but I have a tent and an old cooler."

"So, food that'll keep and a sleeping bag," I said, picking up a pen and a scrap of paper as I thought aloud.

I went to my cupboards and started sorting through the remaining odds and ends. An old duffel bag served to hold my finds, and I filled it with my choices for our trip. Two cans of peaches and another of baked beans joined some tuna, a tiny salt shaker, and a couple cans of pasta haunting the back corner of my cupboard. I zipped the bag shut, noting down what I could run to the grocery for later tonight. It wasn't much, but Adam assured me it would be enough as he set the bag next to the door.

Sorting through the last of my clothes went even faster. When I set my rolled-up patchwork quilt beside my sleeping bag, I faltered.

This was really happening.

Drifting over to my small studio corner, I stuttered to a halt. Slowly, I ran my hands over the scarred surface of my workbench, one foot tapping the empty space where the bin of clay used to be. The shelves were gone, too. My tools had yet to be disposed of, and I gathered them up. The slim shapes bit into my palms as I wrapped them in a stray grocery bag.

"Keep them," Adam said when I went to set them aside.

I stopped and looked up, the bundle clutched in numb fingers. "They...we don't need them," I whispered as he traced the curve of my cheek.

"You do," he whispered back. With a gentle tug, Adam pulled them from my grip and added them to my other bundles.

"Thank you." I trailed after him to help tuck them into the coil of my rolled-up quilt. "I guess that's everything," I said softly, glancing toward my bedroom.

My books were already gone, and my aunt would probably dispose of the rest of my worn furnishings the minute I was found to be missing. A small stack of letters Adam persuaded me to leave for my family rested on the kitchen bar. My apartment was an empty shell. There was nothing left to keep me here.

A gentle nudge pulled me out of my funk long enough to recognize the brush Adam offered me, and I smiled. "Once more for the road?" I teased, swallowing back my melancholy at the cautious invitation in his dark eyes.

He chuckled and sank into the embrace of his beanbag with a faint smile. "It makes you happy."

A blush warmed my cheeks, and I abandoned the brush to use my hands instead. Adam's low, growling purr buzzed against my skin as I combed through his mane, letting the soft fur slip through my fingers. I bit my lip. "I'm scared."

"I know." His deep voice was riddled with his purr.

"Right." I mumbled, nodding at the reminder of his keen senses. "What if they don't like me, Adam? What if your people won't let me stay with you?" I blurted out, my hands falling away.

Adam's purr faded, and he twisted around to haul me into his lap. I went with a squeak, too surprised to do anything but let him. He tucked me against his chest, and I felt his words as a low rumble. "Then we'll find our own way."

"Okay." I sighed, relaxing in his arms with a faint smile. His nose nuzzled my temple, and his purr started up again. He combed his claws through my hair, freeing it from the messy ponytail I put it in earlier. I melted into his touch and let him push aside my worries for the moment.

Tomorrow would start a new, frightening adventure. No matter what happened over the next few days, I wanted to remember this, always. Adam's heart beating against my cheek, his purr rumbling in my ears, the gentle tug of his claws in my hair. Somehow, without me realizing it, he had become my home.

"Stay with me," I murmured when his hands stilled for a moment, full of hazy contentment and drunk on his soft touches.

Adam's breath caught, and his lips brushed my brow in a kiss that felt like a promise. "Always."

Chapter Nineteen

It took almost an entire day to reach the mountains. We left before dawn, using the darkness and aided by a bit of glamourie to help us go unnoticed in the bustling metropolis of New York City.

I felt like so much baggage huddled on Adam's back. My eyes scrunched closed against the swoops, sudden drops, and short loping runs that were his fastest mode of travel. Several times, we stopped for short breaks to let me eat and move around. He had rigged the duffel bag of food to form a kind of sling to help hold me in place, but I wasn't used to being carried.

By the time dawn lightened the sky, we'd been traveling for several hours. My muscles ached with cramps and shivers. It was a relief when the smells of the city faded, but the freshness of the woods brought a whole new set of worries.

What would I see out here, away from the iron safety I'd clung to for the past two years? My foray into Central Park had been bad enough, and I never saw the sprites themselves. When I was little, it had been different. My innocence had shielded me while it had lasted. Now I knew the truth, but I'd never confronted it. Not really.

Except for Adam, I had yet to face the creatures my Sight showed me and *not* believe I was sick. It was enough to tie my stomach in knots.

"Bri…" Adam reached back to touch the top of my head as he slowed to a halt. "Relax."

"I'm okay," I mumbled into his shoulder, my eyes still closed.

His touch disappeared, and something squeezed my leg. With a strangled yelp, I jerked away and nearly lost my grip as the weight of my backpack overbalanced me. Only the sling he'd made of the duffel bag kept me from taking a tumble.

My eyes flew open, and I looked up to find Adam watching me over his shoulder. He raised a dark brow, his mouth twitching.

"I'm scared," I blurted out, scanning the trees around us. He cocked his head, and I hesitated. "What if I see…"

"Oh." His gaze softened into something that warmed me from the inside out and washed away the bitter edge of panic twisting in my gut. "Bri, they'll stay away unless I go to them. They…don't like me much."

"Why?" I asked, confused and curious in spite of myself. "You're fae, too."

Adam sighed and continued his loping run. "Not entirely." He paused again, his ears flicking to catch the rustles and creaks of the surrounding woods. "Mixed bloods aren't always welcome. Especially when humans are hunting them. It's dangerous for them to be near me, Bri. Fae are usually more cautious than that. They show themselves to you because you hold no threat."

"Do they know I can see them?"

Adam shook his head, sniffing the air before continuing along the narrow game trail we'd been following for the past few hours. "Sighted humans are rare. I wasn't sure you had Sight until you told me about your family."

He ducked a low branch. "Don't tell them if it bothers you to see them. Some fae would show themselves just to upset you if they knew you were bothered by it. A few might even ask you which eye lets you see them so they can blind your Sight. Not all fae think humans are harmless amusements, Bri. You should be careful."

"Fantastic." I hid my face against his shoulder again with a shudder. A light touch to my knee, and Adam broke out into a run. *We must be getting close*, I thought and tightened my grip. My trembling, aching muscles protested bitterly. I bit my lip, swallowing a wince. After another short burst of speed, we stopped.

Adam shifted, and the duffel bag dropped away from where it dug into the backs of my thighs. "Bri, you can let go. We're here."

Here was a secluded clearing bordered by several fallen trees. Beside us, the remains of an old cabin propped itself up against a spreading oak. The neglected building appeared ready to fall apart at the slightest touch, but it didn't budge when Adam shouldered his way past the broken door. He returned with a bundle and a battered cooler.

The bundle proved to be a simple two-person tent. I helped Adam set it up, half expecting to see a fae peeking at me from the trees at any moment. As I gathered my backpack, quilt, and sleeping bag, Adam cleared a nearby patch of ground and knelt. Items in hand, I stopped to watch him.

"Adam, why do you have a tent? It doesn't seem like you need it."

Adam glanced up from the glow of his magic as earth and stone formed a fire pit under his hands. "It's for you," he said, puzzled.

I waved at the drab structure. "I know, but why do *you* have one?"

The confusion cleared from Adam's face, and he chuckled. "When there are humans wandering the forest, I use it to blend in. Even with glamourie, it would be strange for a lone human to be camping without a tent."

"True." I hitched my backpack up higher on my shoulder and unzipped the tent door. The inside looked newer than the outside. A lot drier, too. With a quick check for rocky lumps underfoot, I unrolled my sleeping bag and stowed my backpack out of the way.

With my stuff settled in the tent, I joined Adam by the firepit. He'd found a stout log and sunk it into the ground beside the fire to create a makeshift bench. Grateful we wouldn't have to sit on the cold ground, I sank into the empty space beside Adam with a sigh.

The heat of the crackling flames felt amazing. It had been unseasonably warm over the past few days. The forecast claimed it would last out the week before we saw more cold weather, but the sun had set while we made camp. Nights in the mountains were chilly. Even with a thick sweater and jeans to insulate me, the dropping temperatures nipped at my skin.

I had a coat stashed in the tent with my things, but I was reluctant to leave the bubble of warmth by the fire to get it. After a few minutes of shivers and internal debate, I decided it wasn't worth the effort. Instead, I curled against Adam's side and savored the way his heat bled through the layers between us.

"What do you normally do out here, besides hunt?" I asked as I poked through the pile of unused tinder by my feet. A small pinecone rolled out, sticky with knobs of sap. I tossed it into the fire and grinned when it exploded with a loud pop.

"Whatever I want," Adam rumbled with a faint smile, fiddling with a fraying hole over his knee.

I laughed—then sputtered when he pulled his sweatshirt off and dropped it over my head. "Hey!" I protested, floundering under the abundance of fabric.

Adam chuckled and helped me find the neck and arm holes with a few nudges and tugs. "Better?" he teased, laughter in his eyes.

I fought with my hair for a second, then gave up. "You're horrible," I muttered, biting back a smile as I tucked my cold hands into the warm pocket of his hoodie. A mischievous grin flashed across his face, and my thoughts stuttered to a halt as my cheeks burned. "I-I mean…"

He was different in the woods.

"I'm…going to go to bed," I whispered, then bolted for the tent, a low chuckle following me as I ducked into the sturdy shelter.

I changed in a daze, listening to the quiet rustles of Adam moving around our camp. The sleeping bag wasn't as comfortable as my bed at home, but I was too tired to care by the time I crawled inside and zipped it up. Between Adam's sweatshirt and my old quilt, it was cozy enough. I fell asleep soon after I burrowed into the thin pillow.

***

I woke in the middle of the night to find Adam gone.

Hunting, probably. I yawned and grabbed my bag of toiletries, shuffling to the thicket Adam mentioned on our way here.

The tiny outhouse was in much better condition than the collapsing cabin at our camp, but I didn't linger. On my way back to the tent, I stumbled by the large oak tree. With a whispered curse, I caught myself on rough cloth…with a fraying hole.

"Oh," I croaked.

It was Adam's *clothes*. All of them, except for the hooded sweatshirt I was wearing. I gaped at the draped cloth—then shot across the last bit of open ground, into the tent.

When morning came, I waited until Adam tapped on the door before opening the tent. Muttering a hasty hello, I promised to be right out and ducked back inside, his curious gaze adding to my embarrassed fluster.

Gathering what I needed, I made a quick trip to the outhouse and returned to find a rabbit roasting over the low fire. The rich smell startled a loud rumble from my stomach as I retrieved his sweatshirt. Clutching it against my chest, I joined him on the sunken log by the fire.

"That smells good," I managed, Adam's hoodie a jumbled pile in my lap.

Adam gave me a funny look and turned away with a sheepish twist to his lips. "I...I didn't expect you to wake up last night."

"Oh, I, um...it's okay?" I stared at the sleeves spilling over my knees, my face hot.

A light touch on my cheek made me look up to find Adam watching me, his face a muddle of confusion and concern. "When you said you do anything you want in the mountains, I didn't think you meant running around *naked*!" I blurted out. His eyes went wide, and I dropped my face into my hands with a groan. "Please forget I said that," I mumbled, horrified.

"I-I wasn't naked, Bri."

"I saw your clothes, Adam. I—"

"I know, but I wasn't."

I peeked past my fingers, curious in spite of myself. "So, you were running around the woods in your underwear?"

"I-I—no, not exactly," he muttered, looking away with a wince.

"What—"

"The forest clothes me," he said in a rush.

"It...it does?"

Adam nodded, a soft smile curling his lips. "I can show you—"

"No!" I squeaked, my blush returning with a vengeance at the thought of his clothes flapping in the breeze.

A low chuckle slipped out, and Adam stood. "Not like that, Bri. Watch." He peeled off his shirt and dropped into a crouch, burying his claws in the loam.

Focus, focus, focus, I chanted as I forced my attention from the shift of muscle under silky fur. Faint green sparks danced in the air surrounding Adam, glittering like dust motes in a sunbeam. Tiny green sprouts peppered the ground beneath his fingers, and the air surrounding him rippled as if he were caught in a heat haze. A weighty hush wrapped around us, as if the forest listened to a question my human ears couldn't hear.

A bird called out overhead, and the quiet moment shattered. The rich sweetness of wild honey exploded across my tongue, tempered by the earthy taste of wet clay. With a rustling sigh, vines burst from the ground. They snaked up Adam's arms, burrowing into his fur. When he stood, he really *was* clothed—but in living greenery veined with a faint glow.

"Wow," I said in an awed whisper. Adam watched as I crept up and circled him, staring. Coming back around, I grinned up at him. "This is amazing. Are they magic? Is that why they're glowing?"

I touched the nearest broad leaf. It was like warm silk. I traced the edge, the soft smooth surface slipping under my fingers when I tipped it up to peek at the underside. Intrigued, I stepped closer to get a better look at the glow threading its veins. A loose rock shifted under my foot, and I lurched forward with yelp, catching myself against Adam while he steadied me.

He froze when my hands flattened over his stomach, crumpling the silky-warm leaves. Leaves that were the only thing separating my hands from the short fur and velvety skin beneath them.

I wanted to touch him.

A blistering flush lit my cheeks at the stray thought, and heat crept into my ears. Adam shuddered. When I licked my lips, I almost tasted the magic he kept from me.

"Sorry," I said softly as another slow tremor rippled through his large frame.

"I...it's okay." His hands slid along my arms to cup my elbows as I straightened. I looked up, and my breath caught at the naked *wanting* in his glowing eyes. For a moment, every part of me sang with it.

Adam shuddered again, the sparks brightening even as he pushed me away. It hurt, and I found myself rising up on my toes to close the distance he was putting between us. "Bri, w-we can't—"

"Okay," I whispered, then pressed my face to his neck, breathing him in. He smelled amazing. Cedar and honey, and a wildness that was as intoxicating as the brandy cherries I'd snuck from my mom's cabinet as a kid.

Adam groaned and folded around me as I sighed against his throat. He let go of my arms, burying his hands in my hair. Claws nipped at my scalp as he tipped my head back, and his lips came crashing onto mine. The vines covering Adam vanished in a rush of magic. I gasped, whimpering at the sudden press of bare skin. With a low rumble, he broke free to drag his mouth along my jaw to my ear. He nuzzled my cheek, and the world tilted as he guided me down onto a thick blanket of moss by the fire.

I hardly noticed the change. Adam was letting me *touch* him. The feel of him under my hands while he traced a heated path along my neck fed the fire growing in my blood. His mouth traveled back up to feather over mine in a sweet, teasing kiss ending in an achy, wet slide of lips and teeth.

"Don't stop," I gasped out when he started to pull away. Adam hesitated, and I caught his bottom lip in my teeth, hauling him closer as I smoothed my hands over his belly and swallowed his low moan.

He turned the tables with a sharp nip, and I gasped when he tore his mouth away to bite the crook of my neck with a snarl. I arched against him, crying out as the press of his teeth echoed through me in a heady, sweet ache.

Adam froze and eased back. With a growl of my own, I buried my hands in his mane and halted his retreat with a sharp tug. He shuddered, returning to the tender spot he'd branded on my neck.

"Oh," I whimpered as he switched between lighter nips and rough, teasing bites. I was melting. Each touch *burned,* and it wasn't until my fingers hooked into the waistband of his jeans that we realized just how far our kiss had gone. Ice replaced the fire in my blood, and Adam and I shared a wide-eyed look.

"I-I, um..." Flushed and disheveled, I slowly tugged my fingers from his waistband and pressed them to the thick moss under my hips. "Sorry," I mumbled, all too aware his breathing was as ragged as mine.

"I should...I-I need to..." Adam trailed off, and his hungry gaze dropped to my mouth before finding my neck.

I bit my lip, and one hand crept up to cover the mark I knew must be there. The faint throbbing ache sent sweet shivers down my spine.

"Don't." The boldness of the woods lingered in his dark eyes as they sparked and glowed. "Don't hide it, please."

More heat flooded my cheeks, but I let my hand fall. "Okay," I whispered, drinking in the sight of Adam stripped bare to the waist with sparks glowing in his eyes. The craving to touch him again crested through me, and I trembled at the smoldering look he gave me.

"I need to go," he breathed, a raspy edge to his deep voice. He ran gentle fingers over the tender spot his teeth branded into my skin, and I shivered.

"Don't forget your, um, your clothes," I said, slowly sitting up when he finally pulled away.

With a stiff, jerky nod, Adam pulled his shirt back on and grabbed his hoodie from where I'd left it by the fire. He hesitated, then pulled the rabbit off the flames. "Eat," he said, sheepish.

"Go hunt," I said with a shy smile as my composure returned, "or I won't."

He chuckled and turned away, vanishing into the trees.

"Oh, I'm in trouble." I dug in the cooler for some fruit to go with my roast rabbit breakfast. "So much trouble."

Chapter Twenty

Adam didn't return until nightfall.

For once, I was grateful for the respite. After nearly crossing the line with him, I needed time alone. I needed to think.

We couldn't slip up again. Adam still struggled with control, and I wasn't doing much better. Something had to change. The last thing we needed right now was for me to end up pregnant.

"It's okay, Bri."

I squeaked, tumbling backward off the log. Adam's laugh lit up the woods around us. I flopped back with a stifled groan. Gentle hands pulled me upright, and I reclaimed my seat, my lips twitching at the laughter lingering in his eyes.

"Thanks."

Adam nodded with a soft smile and returned to rummaging through the cooler. He paused, then tossed me an orange.

"I know you keep saying it's okay, but I'm still sorry." I ran my thumb over the orange's bumpy rind. "I...sometimes it's hard for me, too."

Adam plucked the fruit from my hands and cut through the rind with his claws. "We knew it wouldn't be easy, Bri," he pointed out as he handed it back.

I started peeling with a wince. "I know, but...sometimes I just wish I could stop messing up."

"I don't mind your mess-ups," he teased before sobering. "We aren't perfect, but we can make this work. I promise."

"Yeah?" I stuffed an orange section in my mouth and hummed happily when the sunny flavor flooded my tongue.

"Yes." He dropped into a seat on the ground beside my feet with a sigh.

"Good. Um, orange?"

Adam accepted the offered piece of fruit with a slight quirk of his lips and turned toward the fire. The rabbit was long gone, but he'd bagged a small deer while running off our kiss. Somehow he'd rigged three flat stones to create a kind of stove to one side of the flames. Now, strips of meat sizzled and steamed on the hot, smooth surface, cooking in their own fat. It smelled amazing.

"How did you season that, anyway?" I mumbled around my last mouthful of orange. "I smell spices."

"Wild herbs," he said absently, flipping the pieces with his claws and careful flicks of his wrist.

I huffed and threw a piece of rind at him. "I figured that part out myself, smarty pants." I pointed at the thick green paste smeared on the meat. "But we didn't bring anything to make a paste." I paused as Adam began to fidget, and a thought occurred to me. Biting back a smile, I tilted my head. "Adam, did you...did you chew those herbs up to make the paste?"

He flinched, and I snorted out a giggle. "Hush," he growled, shoving me off the sunken log with a sheepish smile, his relief palpable.

Digging through our supplies, I wrapped several sweet potatoes in foil, and Adam buried them in the coals edging our fire. Together we sorted out the odds and ends for our dinner. It was quiet and comfortable, and the awkwardness from earlier finally melted away. Around midnight, I fell asleep by the fire to the sound of Adam's deep voice as he shared a story his mother once told him. I woke the next morning in the tent, tucked into my sleeping bag with Adam's hoodie draped over my shoulders.

"Adam?" I called out, sitting up and pushing the sweatshirt aside. Something fell out of the folds, catching the light. "What in the world?" I picked it up and wiped off the grit.

It was a stone feather carved from labradorite. The beautiful piece rippled through all the shades of green and amber. Brilliant threads of golden brown cut through the subtler colors to make it flash and glow in the sunlight filtering through the tent walls.

"Wow," I whispered, tilting it back and forth to make it shimmer. It was strung on some kind of cord, and I looped it around my neck with a smile.

Bursting out of the tent, I crashed into Adam. He caught me with a smile. "Bri?"

"Sorry!" I blurted out, one hand going to my new necklace.

His gaze followed the movement before bouncing to my face, and his smile softened. "You found it."

"Um, yes I did." I beamed at him. "Thank you. It's beautiful."

For a brief minute, his eyes sparked as he stared at the necklace. "You're welcome." Adam's gaze shifted to the hickey on my neck for a moment before he looked back up. "It suits you."

I blushed. "Thank you. Did you make this?"

Adam nodded and let me go, heading for the oak tree. Reaching into the fork in its trunk, he pulled out a pouch. He hesitated, then crossed the camp and pressed it into my hands.

"I need to hunt," Adam said in a rush as I stared at the leather bag.

"Okay," I whispered as he brushed his thumb over my cheek. He seemed torn, like he was afraid to leave me alone. As if he thought I'd vanish.

"Go hunt," I said after a beat. "We need something for breakfast, at least. I wasn't sure what would keep, so I didn't bring much. We leave tomorrow, okay?" Adam nodded, and I tucked the pouch against my chest with a shy smile. "Well, you better get going. I'll be okay by myself for a bit. I promise."

Slow and halting, he nodded again and turned to go. Twice, he glanced back, and something in my chest coiled a little tighter each time. As soon as he was out of sight, I dove into the tent and tugged the pouch open.

There wasn't much inside. A small golden spike antler, a braided bracelet of ancient, cracking leather...and a carved stone feather strung on a fraying cord. The flowing lines mirrored mine, but it was clear this one had been made by someone else. Its colors were different, too. While mine reminded me of the forests and Adam's eyes, this pendant could've been plucked from a sunny sky. All blues and golds, it was like holding a piece of light in my hand.

Slowly, I set it down. I chose the golden spike antler next, with its strange twisted curves and graceful point. "Ouch," I hissed when I cut my finger on the tip of the slender tine. "Sharp...like Adam's."

These...these had to be his mother's.

"Oh," I gasped, fumbling the antler for a second, my hands shaking. I stared, remembering his stories about her and picturing her as best I could. The antler was a slender, delicate spike, a refined version of Adam's antlers when we first met. A tiny hole was drilled through the base, as if it were meant to be worn by someone. Adam's father, maybe?

I didn't dare risk handling the bracelet more than it took to return it to the pouch. The antler quickly followed, but I stared at the stone feather for a long time before I returned it to the others inside the worn leather bag. Why did Adam's mother have a pendant similar to mine?

The question plagued me for the rest of the day. By the time dusk fell, I'd tried asking Adam several times, but he wouldn't answer. He almost didn't take the pouch back. I insisted though. The contents were far too precious to stay in my keeping.

In an effort to put the mystery from my mind, I pulled out the special treat I'd been saving. "Have you ever tried s'mores?" I asked when Adam met my request for roasting sticks with a puzzled look.

"I...no, I haven't," he said at last while I arranged the chocolate, marshmallows, and graham crackers in easy reach. "What are they?"

"It's a human sweet." I scoured the pile of firewood for decent sticks. "Very messy but good. Help me find some sticks, okay?"

Quickly, I explained the requirements of a good roasting stick, and soon, we found a likely pair. Adam scorched three marshmallows before he got the hang of it. Each sugary torch was extinguished with laughter and the reminder to pay attention to what he was doing. His eventual triumph had me showing him how to layer each piece and bite into his gooey prize without wearing most of it in the process. I wasn't terribly successful.

"Aaugh! I'm melting!" I said with a laugh, catching the oozing chocolate on my tongue. Adam chuckled, watching me with fond amusement while I struggled to contain the mess. "You're no help," I mumbled, swallowing my mouthful of gooey s'more.

A hand caught my wrist. Adam dipped closer and licked away the smear of chocolate and marshmallow, his rough tongue scraping over my palm and along my thumb.

"H-hey, that's mine!" I protested weakly, my cheeks warming. A wolfish grin cut across his face, the laughter in his eyes spurring me into action before I thought better of it.

With a playful growl, I grabbed his hand as he let me go. I licked one chocolate-smeared finger. Then I did the same to his thumb, following a streak of chocolate to his wrist before the implications of what I was doing hit me.

I froze, my face hot as I glanced up, and my breath left me in a rush. Adam stared at me with wide eyes, his mouth slack as sparks lit his gaze. "Oh." A giddy flutter filled my stomach as his shock melted into hunger and set my heart hammering against my ribs. "I'm going to go, um, clean up," I blurted out, scrambling to my feet.

Adam's gaze snapped to my necklace when I stood, my pendant swinging free. I backed away and his attention shifted to the hickey, stark on my pale skin, before meeting my gaze with an impact I felt in my bones. I gasped and bolted for the tent. My fingers barely grasped the edge of the door flap when his arm snaked around my waist. Hot breath bathed my neck, sending goosebumps exploding across my skin as I was pinned to his chest.

Adam's arms tightened. Muscles flexed, and the world blurred for a few breathless moments as he whirled me away from the tent. Rough bark bit into my shoulders when Adam slid to a stop. He pushed me against the broad trunk and kissed me hard, nipping at my bottom lip. His taste filled my mouth, and I whimpered, pressing closer when he jerked the hem of my sweater aside, and his hands slipped beneath my shirt. The scrape of his calloused palms over my skin arced through me. Gentle claws traced the line of my back to leave stinging, *burning* trails of sensation in their wake. I squirmed, arching into him with a soft cry.

I was drowning in him, consuming even as I was consumed by him, and I couldn't remember why this wasn't a good idea.

My arms circled his neck as my knees threatened to buckle, my hands fumbling with his thick mane until I found his antlers. As Adam's mouth broke away to trace the curve of my throat, I ran my fingers along the ridges of living gold until I found the sensitive skin at their base.

A shudder rippled through him at the first touch. I did it again, rough and trembling. His hands dropped to my hips, his claws prickling through my jeans as he yanked me closer and muffled a groan against my neck. I let one hand wander through his mane until I stumbled over his ear pinned flat to the tangled fur. Adam stilled, ragged breathing fluttering over my pulse when my fingers closed over his ear. His grip on my hips tightened, as if he was about to push me away but couldn't quite manage it.

Sensitive, I reminded myself, careful not to squeeze. I rose up on my toes to press a tender kiss to the rim. Short, silky fur tickled my lips as I gave him a gentle nip.

Adam jerked, arching back with a choked cry. He grabbed my wrists, pinning them by my hips. Rough bark scraped up my spine as he lurched forward, and his mouth crashed down on mine, swallowing my startled gasp.

Growling deep in his throat, he kissed me until I melted into him with a sigh. A familiar earthy sweetness flooded my mouth as sharp teeth nipped my bottom lip. The combination dragged a soft mewl out of me, and Adam pressed closer, an approving rumble buzzing against my skin. Another nip, and he broke away to blaze a path along my neck in a tingling scrape of lips and teeth. His rough tongue pressed the hickey at the end of the trail he'd marked. I jerked, whimpering when he nuzzled the tender love bite.

A low, rumbling purr echoed around us, and his mouth clamped down. I felt something start to give way under his teeth—then sudden cold air washed over my burning skin as Adam dropped my wrists and stumbled away.

"I-I..."

"Yeah," I managed in a raw whisper as reality came rushing back with a vengeance. "You should, um, go." Adam hesitated, and a faint moan slipped out. "*Go*," I insisted, clutching the tree behind me.

He went.

Alone, I slumped back with a soft groan. We couldn't stay up here another night. Not together. Not unless we wanted to find ourselves with a lot more complications.

In a daze, I straightened my sweater and tucked my feather pendant beneath the thick, golden knit with trembling fingers. I glanced around and spotted our camp a little ways away. Adam hadn't taken us far, thank goodness. I needed to tend to the fire and clean up the s'mores mess. My hands went to my hair, plucking out bits of bark and a few pine needles as I tried to catch my breath.

A rustling snap jerked my attention to the trees surrounding me while I gathered the mess into a sloppy ponytail. I scanned the woods with a shiver, ready to scold Adam for returning so soon...and choked when a different figure stepped out of the growing gloom.

Chapter Twenty-One

"Chris?" I squeaked, my hands suddenly ice cold. "W-what are you doing here?"

Chris looked me over with a frown, his eyes lingering on my neck. He was dressed for hunting in jeans and worn boots. He wore snug leather gloves, and a carry strap cut across his jacket, the rifle peeking over his shoulder. I stared at the long, slim barrel as I backed away, my nails biting into my palms. How long had he been nearby? Adam would never have left if he'd known Chris was here. Was he alone?

A thousand questions rushed through my head, only to swirl to a halt when a hand caught my wrist, pressing the thick knit of my sweater into my skin. I jerked away, but Chris's rough grip stopped me.

"Are you alone?" Chris asked softly, his fingers digging into my arm as he stared at Adam's love bite. There was something cold and calculating in his eyes when he looked up. In a flash, I was back in the bakery, and he was showing me Adam's picture all over again. I was going to be sick.

"I...no, I'm with a friend," I whispered as panic joined the fear churning my stomach.

"Really? It's dangerous in these woods if you don't know what you're doing." *They shouldn't have left you alone*, his words whispered to me, threat thick and cold beneath his pleasant tone. He paused, then his free hand was at my throat, and Adam's pendant dangled between us. Chris stared at it, his grip on my wrist tightening until I knew I would have bruises.

The rustle of brush heralded the arrival of others, and I froze.

"You were right, boss. We found a tent and an old cabin back that way. It looks like somethin' big been sleeping under the tree. There's a clear trail leadin' this way before it heads up the mountain."

The gray-eyed man from the alley stepped around a stand of evergreens, his partner behind him. Both were dressed for hunting, like Chris, armed with their own rifles. I stared, shaking as the memory of their rough handling arced through me. The dark-eyed man noticed and smirked, his pale fingers tapping the carry strap cutting into his jacket.

Chris nodded, barely sparing them a glance. "Go, then, but not too far. Brianna and I have a great deal to discuss, but I may need your skills. For now, I require...privacy."

The men exchanged a knowing look. The dark-eyed partner leered at me, growling when his partner wacked him in the ribs with a scowl.

"Aye, boss. We'll—"

"Wait. Switch to the impact hollow points with the iron load. If you find anything of note, shoot to kill. No need to take chances, after all." Chris smiled, a wintery light in his blue eyes. "Isn't that right, Brianna? Or is there something you'd like to tell me, hm?" He tugged on my necklace, setting my pendant swaying between us.

Iron, bane of the fae. Why was Chris in the mountains hunting with men who carried iron bullets? The possibilities gnawed at me, and a wave of nausea hit me like a kick in the gut. I prayed it was just a horrible coincidence as I shook my head. Chris's smile flattened, and he made a sharp gesture at the two men. Dismissed, they left hefting their rifles. Rifles loaded with bullets that could kill a fae. Like Adam.

Chris shifted his grip and started walking, dragging me through the trees toward camp as if I weighed nothing. I fought him, yanking and twisting against his grip, but it was no use. He was too strong. Chris stopped beside the old oak tree and jerked me around to face him. The look he gave me was filled with enough venom to make me choke. I shrank away, the fight draining out of me as he forced me closer.

"Where is he?" he asked.

"I-I don't—"

Agony exploded across my face as his fist slammed into me. "Don't lie to me, Brianna."

I struggled to stay on my feet, my head swimming with pain. "I'm not—"

Another punch—this time to my stomach. I choked and coughed, falling to the ground as Chris let me go and started rummaging through our camp. My face was one horrible, throbbing ache. I wheezed for breath and tasted blood. He'd broken my nose.

Chris stepped out of the tent, my phone in one hand. He fiddled with it for a minute, then tossed it aside. Glancing at his own phone, he ducked into the broken-down cabin. I swallowed a sob. My phone...he'd tracked us through my phone. Yet another gift from him, given after I'd left my parents. I never even considered he would use it in such a way. Never imagined he would stoop to that.

He knows, I realized with a sick jolt as Chris came back out and hauled me to my feet. Maybe he didn't know all of it, but he knew enough to bring hired men with iron bullets, and he was searching for *Adam*. Was he the boss the men had mentioned that horrible night in the alley? How far did Chris's lies go?

Adam's last journey to the mountains had ended with him being shot with iron-filled bullets. Was Chris responsible for that, too?

I needed to warn Adam. I couldn't let Chris find him here. For a brief moment, I could taste the sweetness of Adam's magic—then it was gone.

Would he hear me if I screamed? I wondered as Chris assessed me with a flat, dispassionate expression I'd never seen before. His gaze caught on my stone feather again, now splattered with blood from my broken nose. Something flickered in his eyes, and his mouth curled into a thin-lipped snarl before the mask returned.

Would Adam even listen if I told him to run?

It didn't matter, though, I decided as Chris reached for the strap of the hunting rifle slung over his shoulder. I had to try.

"Where—"

My foot lashed out and struck his knee hard. His grip faltered, and I jerked free with strength born of desperation. Chris snatched at me and swore as I bolted for the trees. I gasped and choked while I ran, struggling to breathe with a broken nose and praying the flare of magic wasn't my imagination.

"Adam!" I screamed. A tree root snagged my foot, and I tumbled down a steep embankment and into a shallow creek. Spitting out a mouthful of muddy water and rotten leaves, I crawled out of the icy trickle. "Please be okay," I sobbed, shivering.

I started to stand—and froze as something hard and cold pressed into my ribs.

"Who is Adam, Brianna? Is he the reason you never heeded me the way you were supposed to? Your parents are worried, you know. You should visit them with me next time. Though, perhaps it's best they forget about you completely after this, hm? Your being such a disappointment should make it easy."

The rifle pulled away, and a booted foot rolled me over. I cried out, my heart in my throat as Chris knelt. He grabbed my thigh, his heat burning me through my wet jeans. He dragged me closer and set the rifle aside to touch my broken nose. A slurry of blood and mud clung to his leather gloves, slippery and cool.

"Where are you trying to go?" Chris gave my leg a savage squeeze before retrieving his rifle and flicking the safety off. He raised a brow when I didn't answer and twisted my nose. Something popped out of place, and I screamed, the sudden agony leaving me slumped on the forest floor, sobbing.

"You're in the middle of nowhere, love." A cold smile cut across his face, and Chris let me go as he stood, wiping his bloody hand on his jeans. "No one to hear you except for the beasts and the birds, and the little folk in their hills." He aimed the rifle at my leg. "Who is Adam?"

Magic, rich and sweet, exploded across my tongue as abruptly Adam was *there*. Shoving Chris hard enough to send him flying back up the embankment, he crouched over me and touched the blood on my face.

"Adam," I gasped, clutching his hoodie as Chris stumbled to his feet, watching us with eyes resembling chips of blue ice. "You can't be here! He's hunting you, and they have bullets with iron. You have to go, Adam, please—"

A gentle thumb against my lips stopped my pleading, and right then, I knew he wasn't going to listen to me.

"Who are you?" Adam rumbled, a low snarl weaving through his voice as he turned to Chris. With his clawed hands and feet hidden in the deep loam and his hood up, he almost passed for human.

Almost.

Glowing embers like hot coals flickered, sparking and dying in Adam's eyes as they stared at each other.

"Be careful," I whispered.

Adam gently freed my hands from his sweatshirt and nudged me behind him. He glanced at the rifle Chris held, then back at me. His thumb brushed my nose, and I heaved a sigh of pure relief as the pain stopped cold.

"You must be Adam," Chris remarked absently.

Adam wiped the blood from my mouth and chin with the sleeve of his sweatshirt. Another pulse of magic drove the water from my hair and clothes. At last, Adam turned toward Chris, and I shuddered. Foreign magic, harsh and biting, began to pulse and fade like waves hitting the beach. It seemed to center around Chris, and an answering glimmer sparked between Adam's fingers while he scented the air between them.

"Who are you?" Adam asked again, rising to stand at his full height.

Loathing and a black rage flashed across Chris's face, his lips curling into a sneer before the cold, pleasant mask returned.

"Christopher Thompson," he replied with a shrug, propping his rifle on his shoulder. "I heard Brianna was planning something foolish. I thought I'd come pick up my fiancé before she embarrassed us both." he said with a mocking smile. "Am I too late?"

I choked. "What—"

"Bri is *mine*," Adam cut in, the odd orange lights in his eyes reddening at Chris's false declaration.

"Not anymore," Chris snarled and leveled the rifle at Adam's chest.

The memory of Adam bleeding and feverish on my bedroom floor flashed through me.

"No!" I screamed, scrambling up the steep bank to leap in front of Adam before Chris could put his finger on the trigger. I pressed a hand to Adam's chest and flung the other out toward Chris as if I could stop him by will alone.

Chris paused, his eyes glittering with an edge of madness I never wanted to see again. The dying glow of twilight made their normal deep blue a chilling violet and limned his silvery scar with ruddy light. He was a nightmare come to life, and something in me quailed even as I forced myself to stand my ground.

"Please don't hurt him, Chris," I pleaded, sobbing for breath. "He's—I—"

His gaze shifted from me to the hickey and the blood-stained necklace, then to Adam as the strange presence gathering around us pulsed, bitter and sharp. I risked a glance over my shoulder and swallowed a cry of dismay. Adam's hood had been knocked aside, and not a scrap of glamourie stood between his inhuman features and the icy fury growing in Chris's face.

"Well, I expected better from you, Brianna," Chris drawled in a soft voice that filled me with dread. "Wallowing in filth seemed quite beneath you when we first met. I guess everyone makes mistakes."

The rifle tip had dropped to point at the ground while he spoke but snapped to attention as Adam moved to pull me behind him. For a second, Chris tracked him, then returned to me when I shook Adam off and stumbled further up the muddy bank.

"He isn't a mistake, Chris!" I cried out, finally finding my voice. "Adam is—"

"I can see what he is, Brianna," Chris snapped. "A filthy mongrel creature searching for a woman to rut with and spawn more things like him, twisted and unnatural." His gaze dropped to my pendant, and his grip tightened on his rifle. "Brightfeather scum. Did he say you were special? That he loved you?" Chris sneered, the mask falling away at last to reveal a hatred so deep, there was room for nothing else. "He's a beast. He should be in a cage."

"No! I won't let you take him away!" I screamed, raw and broken as I faced down my most bitter nightmare for Adam's sake.

Chris gave Adam a considering look. "Well now, love," he murmured, his sudden mild tone sending icy fingers licking along my spine, "that changes matters, doesn't it?" Quicker than thought, Chris shifted his aim to Adam and fired twice, but I was already moving.

Time slowed as I stepped between them once more, my arms flung wide. There was a thump against my stomach and chest, followed by a flood of warmth and horrible, tearing pain. Something splattered my cheek, and my knees buckled as the world sped up again.

"Bri!" Adam caught me as I crumpled. His voice was distant already, as if I were underwater. The world faded into darkness like ink spilling over wet paper while I gasped for breath and listened to my heart stutter. I was pressed against something firm and warm, and I was so cold. With a sigh, I slipped into the black—a roar of anguished fury echoing in my ears.

***

I could taste wild honey and clay. The strong flavors lingered, drawing me out of the dark place where I'd been hiding and into the fading twilight. I was laying on a bed of dead leaves and pine needles, and a rock dug into my leg. My eyes were full of grit, and I winced, blinking blearily at the swaying branches overhead. The faint burble of water drew my gaze to the churned-up earth a few feet away, a gnarled tree root jutting out of the mess. Slow and stiff, I sat up—and found a mangled corpse staring back. I gasped, too wrung out to scream as I tried to drag myself away.

"Bri?"

I twisted around and winced when sore muscles screamed in protest across my chest and stomach. Adam knelt beside me, his claws digging furrows in the ground by his knees. Blood soaked his hands, streaking his clothes and fur in thick splatters. I swayed, and he reached for me, only to let his hand fall when he caught sight of his own reddened skin.

"Adam? What happened? Is...is that *Chris*?"

He shuddered and looked away, but not before scarlet sparks flickered in his eyes. I turned back to what was left of the body sprawled on the forest floor and felt my gorge rise. It *was* Chris. His throat was a ragged, red ruin, and his clothes were little more than bloody tatters. Wicked claw marks rent his chest and limbs. Ashen skin and torn flesh gaped wide to expose the white flash of bone and the slick gleam of organs. A few feet away, the two hunters lay together in a bloody, boneless heap.

Blood soaked the surrounding trees and the ground beneath the bodies. The way they'd all been disemboweled and tossed aside like broken dolls spoke of a violence, a black killing rage I'd never seen before. Adam did this?

"I think...I-I think I'm going to be sick," I heard myself say in an eerily calm voice.

"Bri—"

"Stop," I whispered, staring at the blood still seeping into the ground beneath Chris's body. Slow and halting, I stood and edged away until I bumped into a tree. "You...you killed them. All of them."

Adam glared at the corpses, his bloodied hands curling into fists as a low growl rumbled deep in his chest. "Yes."

"Why? I didn't want—I mean, wasn't there another way?" I choked out, caught by those staring, cloudy eyes.

"Like what, Bri? What could we have possibly told any of them that wouldn't have ended with one or both of us in a cage?"

"I-I don't know. Something. They were rotten, horrible people, but they didn't deserve this," I whispered, finally turning to Adam.

He hesitated, confusion stamped plainly on his face. "Those men hurt you, and he was...I thought—"

"You *killed* them, Adam! Chris is *dead*!" I slumped back as the sudden anger drained away, hiding my face in my hands. "What do we do?"

"I don't know," he whispered. For a long moment, we just stood there. The cricket chirrups around us were deafening in the silence.

"Did you love him?" Adam asked, his words a bare whisper.

"What?" I looked up to find him watching me with a shuttered expression.

"He's the one you cried over. The one who hurt you. Did you love him?"

"Why does it matter now, Adam?" I whispered, tears burning my eyes as fear and horror twisted a jagged knife in my gut. "Chris is *dead*, and *you* killed him!"

He jerked, his head snapping back as if I'd slapped him. "He was going to kill you—"

"No, he was going to kill *you*." I straightened in a rush and pointed to the fallen rifle. "If you—"

"You almost died, Bri," Adam snarled, the ember glow sparking in his eyes. "If those bullets had been filled with iron—"

"You didn't even let me finish what I was going to say!" I cried out, frustration and fear boiling over in a morass of out-of-control emotions. "Should I have let him shoot you?!"

"He wouldn't have hit me—"

"You don't know that, Adam!" I screamed, heedless of the tears wetting my cheeks or the possible danger lurking among the trees. "I saw the bullet holes, re-member? You nearly died from iron poisoning from being shot two months ago, and now you're saying he wouldn't have killed you?! Grow up! What happened to no lies, Adam? Tell me, because I just don't get it!"

A snarl ripped through his chest. Adam stepped closer, crowding me back. Before I could stop myself, my hand snapped out and slapped him hard enough to turn his head. Adam stumbled away, his eyes dark once again as he stared at me in shock. "Bri, I—"

"Stop," I choked out, pushing past him on shaky legs to stand over Chris's broken and bloodied body. For a long moment, I stared at his corpse. Finally, I turned to go but paused when the familiar sweetness of Adam's magic touched my tongue. I stared, numb. The earth beneath Chris writhed and glowed...and slowly drew him under the rich loam. Only the rifle remained to show he'd been there at all.

***

At our camp, I threw myself into the tent and started packing. Anything to avoid the world a little longer. No matter how I tried, though, I couldn't banish the thought of what Adam must've looked like tearing into Chris and the others with his claws, his face a twisted snarl. The blood on his hands and clothes painted a stark picture. A map of violence drawn in scarlet.

My stomach clenched and rolled as I remembered how the trees around the mangled corpses had been splattered with thick smears and splashes. I shuddered, and another memory plucked at me while I stuffed an armful of clothes into my backpack, teasing me with muddied flashes. Twin shots, a feral roar...and sticky warmth trickling down my cheek as I struggled to breathe until darkness washed it all away.

Chris shot me.

My hands froze in the act of rolling up my quilt, and one drifted to my sweater. *Twin shots. I stepped in front of Adam, but did Chris miss me, or...*

My fingers skimmed up the thick knit, searching. I found a ragged hole over my ribs, and my breath left me in a rush. Apparently, magic could put my blood back where it belonged but couldn't fix my clothes. I pulled the ruined sweater over my head and shivered when ragged cotton fluttered against my shoulders. Off came the torn t-shirt, and I stared. The back of my shirt was a mess of mangled fabric, and two neat holes marked the front. One was over my belly, the second just to the right of my heart.

"He healed me?" I gasped, shivering in fits and starts. More fragmented memories of falling and horrible pain flashed through me at the sight of my ruined shirt. There wasn't even a single scar.

I let my shirt fall, scrubbing my hands over my face as my world continued to spin merrily on its axis. Who was Adam—I mean, honestly? The gentle, lonely soul who saw me when no one else did, or the violent, savage creature I'd seen evidence of today? Where was the shy, playful person who let me brush his fur and stole kisses...had he ever been real?

Chris had fooled me for years. Was I doing it again? Clinging to a hope and a dream to avoid the reality of who Adam was?

I fingered the ragged holes and threw myself down on my sleeping bag to burrow into the slick fabric with a sob. Chris was dead. The person I thought I knew was a stranger.

Once more, I was alone.

Chapter Twenty-Two

"Why? Why do I keep doing this to myself?" I whispered as I stared at Adam's stone feather.

My tears had run out hours ago, leaving me hollow and drained. I huddled on my sleeping bag and traced the graceful lines of the carved pendant, shivering in the thin t-shirt I'd found to replace my ruined one. It hurt too much to keep Adam's gift around my neck, but I couldn't make myself throw it away. It meant something to him, seeing me wearing it. Despite everything, I still wanted to know why.

My stomach twisted and churned, growling. I needed to eat. Something besides the jerky and trail mix in my backpack. I forced myself to sit up, dragging my backpack closer and digging a navy flannel shirt from my dwindling supply of clean clothes. I pulled it on, not bothering to button it before I tucked the pendant under my pillow and unzipped the tent door. Shivering, I pushed it open and froze when I caught sight of Adam by the fire.

He'd washed the blood from his hands and fur, but his clothes still bore mute testament to what he'd done. His hoodie was balled up in his hands. Adam stared at the bloodstains splattered across the worn fabric, defeat in the slumped lines of his shoulders. His dark eyes didn't waver from their focus, but one ear swiveled towards me when I sucked a sharp breath past my teeth and choked.

A sharp ache shot through me, threatening my numb haze. I snatched my hand back and let the tent snap closed again. Hungry or not, I couldn't face him right now. Stumbling with exhaustion, I collapsed into a huddle on my sleeping bag.

Somehow, I fell asleep. When I woke, it was past midnight, and Adam was gone. On my way back from the outhouse, I realized his clothes were hanging from the oak's branches once more. Except for his hooded sweatshirt. It was a crumpled ball among the gnarled roots, like it had been thrown there.

Staring at the bloodstained bundle, I hunched against the night's chill. A gust of wind rattled the trees and cut through my flannel shirt. I shivered, folding my arms over my stomach, my knuckles white as I clutched the soft, worn fabric.

I was numb. I was hurt. I was mad. Why did Chris have to follow us to the mountains? So much hurt, so much pain...and for what? Because he believed I belonged to him. He'd come to collect me like a stray dog and died for it.

Bri is mine.

A sob choked me, and I crumpled as tears scalded my cheeks. I rocked and cried, everything breaking loose as Adam's words echoed through me. A part of me was giddy with the memory of him saying those words. But it was muffled and distant, drowning under the weight of my confusion. What was I to Adam? What was he to me?

Everything...he's everything, I realized with a moan, burying my face in my hands and slumping until my forehead touched my knees.

My world was shaken, my gravity gone. I was bleeding and floundering in a midnight sea with neither stars nor compass. Lurching to my feet, I turned toward the tent and stumbled to a halt. Adam watched me from the trees, leaves and vines coiling through his fur in wild abandon. He looked so feral, so beautiful...so cold. His gaze held nothing for me as he met my tearful gaze with a stony mask—then vanished.

I stared at the spot he'd been as it started raining, icy drops soaking my shirt. How could I trust him when I couldn't even trust myself? I couldn't.

"I'm sorry," I whispered to the night as I returned to the tent and stripped off my wet clothes. "I don't know what to do."

Rubbing my burning eyes, I put on the purple henley and faded jeans I'd saved for tomorrow and huddled in my sleeping bag. My clothes would be messy and wrinkled from sleeping in them, but I couldn't bring myself to care. More tears leaked out, and I hid my face against my pillow with a choked sob. Sleep. I should try to sleep. With a keening whine, I curled into a ball around my bruised and battered heart and wept until oblivion reached out and dragged me into darkness.

Dawn came, and Adam was nowhere in sight when I stepped out of the tent, packed and ready. His clothes were gone from the oak tree's branches, and the fire pit was filled in with mossy earth. I set my stuff on the sunken log and started breaking down the tent in numb silence.

Did you love him? Adam's words whispered through my head as my hands tugged, folded, and twisted. *I don't know*, I whispered back as I tied the collapsed tent into a tidy bundle.

Could someone like me even trust her heart to recognize real love? Was it supposed to hurt? Was it supposed to settle in your blood, echoing in your pulse and nipping at your bones? Or...was it supposed to be gentler than that?

Had I felt love for Chris? Been in love with him? "I don't know," I choked out, scrubbing fresh tears from my face as I sat back.

Chris had made me feel safe, but so did Adam. However, the safety Chris offered had always come with a price I'd never noticed until today. What was Adam's price? Did he love *me*? Could he? Chris's broken body rose in my mind's eye, his clouded, staring eyes accusing. Could I love Adam after what he'd done? Yesterday morning, I would've said yes without a doubt. Now, every time I thought about it, I only saw Chris's corpse and the foreign red lights in Adam's eyes.

There were stories which spoke of the Green Man being violent and dangerous. Most focused on a kind being benevolent to the humans around them but not all. I'd never seen such darkness in Adam before.

"What do I do?" I whispered, emptying the cooler into the duffel bag and putting it with the tent beside the broken-down cabin.

I can't go back. The realization shook me, but I couldn't deny the truth of it. Even if Sherrie gave me a new job at Sweet Haven and I found another place to live, there would be no sanctuary in the city. By using my parent's money and running, I'd all but locked the cage myself.

Blotting my wet cheeks with my jacket sleeve, I heaved a shuddering sigh and let one hand slip into my pocket to cup my stone feather. Adam may or may not be who I thought he was, but if I wanted freedom from my past, I had to see this through. My only path was forward. *Even if it means I'll always be alone.*

I was almost done packing up camp when Adam dropped into the clearing with a grunt.

"We need to go," he rumbled, not even looking at me. He sorted through our stuff, discarding my sleeping bag along with anything else we could afford to leave behind. Dumping out the duffel bag, he repacked the bag with my quilt and the meager essentials we needed to get on the plane. "Your Chris and his friends weren't here alone. People are searching for them."

"Oh...okay," I mumbled as he handed me my backpack, shivering in spite of my warm jacket.

He's not my *anything*, I wanted to snap, but Adam's distant, closed off expression made the bitter words stick in my throat. Instead, I meekly put on the backpack and clambered onto his back when he crouched. The duffel bag's zipper dug into the backs of my thighs as Adam adjusted the strap, once again turning it into a makeshift sling.

"Close your eyes," he whispered as voices began to filter through the trees.

Wordlessly, I obeyed.

Muscles bunched under me—and then we were *flying*. For a second, I was flung into the moment he caught me when I'd fallen from the bridge. A sob choked me as his hard landing snapped me back to the present, and I pressed my forehead to his shoulder.

While Adam ran, tears trickled from me in a steady stream. One memory after another assaulted me, each opening a fresh wound on my aching heart until I was drowning. Again and again, I tried setting aside what he'd done. To remember *why* I invited him into my life that night on the rooftop...but I could only see the blood.

It was a stark reminder that, despite all the moments and conversations we shared, I'd somehow forgotten reality was nothing like the gentle world of faerie tales found in books.

By the time we reached the city, a numb haze had settled over me with the growing dusk. In the parking garage at the airport, I rearranged the duffel bag, shrinking it down to fit carry-on standards before helping Adam with his shoes and gloves. He was quiet, accepting the socks with an odd expression when I explained what we would be dealing with when we went through security.

It felt like the whole charade was made of rice paper. We joined the crowds and found a free kiosk to print our boarding passes. Adam adjusted his glamourie to hide his bloodstained clothes, but I could still See them.

As would anyone else with the Sight.

Somehow, I managed to hold it together while we endured a pat-down from bored TSA agents. A flash of heady relief broke through when Adam passed through without hesitation.

Adam's glamourie held up under scrutiny, but I could see the constant attention wearing on him. His normal, easy grace was jerky and stilted, and his face settled into an expressionless mask that cracked a little more every time he met my gaze. By the time we boarded our plane and found our seats, the numbness keeping the world at a bearable distance had melted away. I was going to be sick. Adam didn't seem much better. He pulled his hood up, blocking me out and refusing to even look at me at all. It was like traveling with a stranger.

Five hours into trying to sleep through our flight, I couldn't take it anymore and fled to the bathroom. "What a mess," I mumbled, huddling over the tiny sink and trying to swallow back my churning stomach. Panic was a breath away as I fought the need to be sick, my hands shaking as I pressed them into the edges of the metal bowl.

It took me twenty minutes to pull myself together. When I finally exited the bathroom, wrung out and heartsick, I glanced over at our seats. Adam had shifted to a slump against the window, his dark eyes flat and distant when he caught me staring. I flushed and dropped my gaze as a wrinkled hand patted my arm.

"Are you alright, dear?"

I jumped, swallowing a squeak, and turned to find an elderly woman giving me a soft look. "I—yes, I'm fine. It's just been a while since I've been on a plane. Thank you for asking."

"So polite!" she remarked with a chuckle as she fussed with her short, pale curls and picked up her knitting. Pastel green yarn spilled over her lap, clinging to her burgundy cardigan and tan slacks before trailing into the canvas bag at her feet. "Are you traveling alone?"

A faint smile twitched my lips at her gentle prying. "No, I'm...with a friend." My smile faded as I glanced over at Adam, and my stomach clenched.

Her eyes were bright and knowing behind her half-moon glasses as she followed my gaze. Her hands stilled, and she pursed her lips, setting her knitting aside to reach into her bag. "Well, I won't keep you, then. Here, dear. For your friend," she whispered with a sympathetic smile and a nod towards Adam's hunched form. "He doesn't fly well, does he?"

I shook my head, accepting the pre-packaged pills she pressed into my hand. "Thank you."

The woman tutted and waved off my gratitude with another smile. "My late husband never could stand planes. They always made him ill."

With another glance at Adam, I thanked her again and returned to my seat. Adam watched me now, his gaze drifting to the foil packets clutched in my hand as I sat and tried to find a comfortable spot on the stiff cushions. Curiosity washed the dullness from his eyes for a minute, but only a minute. When he glanced up, it was gone. Despite everything tearing me apart, my heart ached at the loss.

"Are you okay?" I whispered, breaking the silence between us for the first time since the plane took off.

Adam flinched and turned toward the window. "No." I winced and dropped my gaze to my lap, fiddling with the pills and pushing them around inside their packaging. Adam sighed. "Everyone keeps staring, and I feel...there's a lot of iron here," he said in a rush, shuddering.

I glanced at his bloodstained jeans before leaning forward to peer past the edge of his hood. A faint green light shimmered over his features and hid in the folds of his clothes. "The glamourie is still working. No one can see you, Adam."

The look he gave me hit like a punch in the gut, full of a heavy sadness. "I know."

My eyes began to burn as tears fought to be free. I fumbled for something, anything to push aside the tangle of emotion lodged in my chest, threatening to strangle my heart with every painful beat. "I..." Hope flickered and died in his eyes, and he turned back to the window. *I see you*, I finished silently, tucking the motion sickness pills into my pocket. *I just...don't know what to do.*

Adam shuddered again, and this time his glamourie flickered as well, tendrils of green light crawling and arcing along the edges of his hood. I stared, my stomach sinking as it rippled, then steadied.

We were still hours away from landing in London. A quick glance up and down the aisle proved only a few passengers were awake. Thankfully, most had their nose buried in either a book or a phone. I looked at Adam. He needed help, but here, there was only me. The painful distance between us yawned wide, and I wavered. Would he even let me try?

Somehow, I plucked up my courage, daring to touch his arm. Adam flinched like I'd burned him and pulled away without even acknowledging me. Ready to duck, I reached up and tugged on his hood instead. He jerked, and his hands flew up to grip the edges as he twisted around to stare at me.

"One shoulder, no waiting," I whispered with a wan smile, pushing my hair away from my neck. He only looked at me. I bit my lip hard enough to taste blood and slipped one hand in my pocket to touch the stone feather hidden there. "I...I do see you, Adam. I'm just...I'm scared," I admitted in a low, harsh whisper as I lost the battle with my tears.

His breath caught at the first one spilling over, and something between us shifted. Slow and halting, Adam touched my cheek as another violent shudder rocked him, and his glamourie fought to hold itself together.

"This doesn't mean we're okay, does it?" he said softly, tracing the silvery trail. I dropped my gaze to my hands fisted in my lap, and he sighed. "I thought so."

Warmth came to rest against the curve of my neck, and a heavy sigh fluttered over my skin. "Thank you," he whispered as he hid his face in my hair and let his glamourie drop.

"You're welcome." I closed my eyes, angling myself until we looked like any other couple asleep on the plane.

I'd missed this so much. I'd never imagined I could be so lonely as I had been today with him beside me and yet completely out of reach. Even tempered by the violence and doubt haunting my thoughts, the press of his cheek on mine soothed the raw places in my heart.

After about an hour, the last of his shudders faded away, and a soft sigh tickled my neck. A few minutes later, the faint taste of his magic bloomed across my tongue once again, a flurry of green sparks marking the rebuilding of his glamourie.

"I'm sorry," I managed when he started pulling away. "I...I need a little time. Can we talk at the hotel? Please?"

Adam nodded and sat back. Giving me a long, searching look, he turned to the window with a sigh.

We were still at least two hours away from arriving in London. Slumping in my seat, I covered my face with my hands and let a few stray tears slip free.

I needed to think.

Chapter Twenty-Three

London in the wintertime was cold, gray, and confusing. Numb with exhaustion and jetlag among strangers in a strange place, I lost myself in the blur of foreign sights and smells.

At seven o'clock in the morning, Gatwick Airport was thick with bustling crowds. Somehow, I managed to get us both through customs and find the right place to hire a car to take us to Amesbury. The expense was higher than I'd expected, but Adam's glamourie was flickering again. A car would be faster than a train or bus.

Our driver was cheerful and friendly, trying his best to draw us into a conversation as he pointed out a few tourist sights on the way. He even mentioned a small general goods store near our hotel. His descriptions were peppered with native words and phrases that were a sharp reminder of how far from home I'd come. In my exhaustion, I struggled to keep up with the flood of information.

At some point during the two-hour drive, the long, sleepless plane ride caught up with me, and I nodded off. When I woke, I was slumped against Adam. His arm circling my shoulders was the only thing keeping me from landing in his lap. I flushed and jerked upright. He let me go, still staring out the window. Our driver didn't notice my lapse, and a few minutes later, he dropped us in front of the hotel with a wave and a grin. Befuddled and groggy, I looked around with wide eyes.

Everywhere were echoes of the familiar, but the differences were just stark enough to make it all the more foreign and confusing. Narrow buildings of brick and stone crowded against each other. Most were built right up to the edge of the sidewalk, while a sparse few possessed tiny yards. A gray tabby cat perched in a nearby window eyed us with a knowing amber gaze.

People passed us in a constant trickle. Several glanced at me and Adam, but most of them ignored us while they went on with their day. A burst of savory smells from the hotel filled the air as a small group of kids left the building beside us in a flurry of chatter. A handful of harried adults followed in their wake. I watched them go. For a minute, the urge to explore pricked at me through my fog as the ebb and flow of Amesbury swirled around us.

First things first, though. We needed food. Preferably something we could take with us through the Gate. Many stories warned about eating faerie food, especially Under-the-Hill, and airplane food didn't satisfy for long. The thought of eating the wrong berries and finding myself transformed into a shrub or rabbit for a year and a day wasn't very appealing. My stomach churned and growled, unhappy with the granola bar and sandwich I'd managed to force down earlier. Adam hadn't eaten at all.

The straps of my backpack bit into my shoulders as we entered our hotel. More savory smells teased my nose and set my stomach rumbling loud enough to make Adam's ears twitch toward me before he flattened them into his mane.

I checked us in and stowed our bags in our room before heading to the front desk. A cheerful, sweet-faced girl there gave me directions to the store our driver had mentioned. Lunch could wait a bit longer. The need to be ready for anything itched at me, and the crowded dining room wasn't an option for Adam, anyway.

Outside once again, I smoothed out the crumpled scrap of paper the girl had written the directions on. Her tidy scrawl wasn't too hard to decipher, thank goodness. After reading it through twice, I started out with Adam following close on my heels.

Our path was simple and straightforward, but I kept having to stop and retrace my steps to the correct road as my attention wandered to the buildings more than the street signs. They were just too short compared to New York, and I found a part of me searching for the skyline I knew in the narrow, grid-like streets. It left me unsettled. All the odd glances Adam was getting weren't helping.

A few of the more curious locals stopped to ask us if we were lost. The most memorable encounter was a young woman with feathery white-blonde hair and pale blue eyes. She spoke in a soft, lilting voice and only looked at Adam, dismissing me with a glance. Something passed between them, and she smiled, tilting her head in a birdlike gesture. In the end, she stepped aside to let us pass, vanishing into the crowd.

It felt like an eternity before I spotted the little shop. When we finally reached it, Adam stopped and caught my wrist.

"We're being followed." He tilted his head toward the street.

I peeked around him and frowned. "I don't see...oh," I whispered as I caught sight of the lanky teenager leaning on a lamppost.

Like the bird woman from earlier, he didn't quite fit in with the people surrounding him. More than anything, he resembled trouble. Dark hair gleamed against pale skin, styled into a careless tumble of short curls that framed sharp, angular features. Slim fingers plucked a lighter from the pocket of his faded jeans. His worn leather jacket had leaves and vines tooled along the sleeves and zipper, a pack of cigarettes peeking out of one pocket. He glanced up and flashed me a crooked smirk as he slipped one between his lips and lit up.

"What should we do?"

"Go inside," Adam said after a moment. Our watcher gave him a jaunty wave and blew smoke rings with lazy confidence. "Wait for me."

I started to protest—then snapped my mouth shut when orange lights flickered in Adam's eyes for a breath. Slowly, I pulled my wrist from his grip and opened the door. "Please, be careful," I whispered, then slipped inside as he strode towards the seeming boy, who flicked sparks and ash onto the sidewalk.

I hurried through the brightly lit aisles, trying to focus while I grabbed foods that would keep and maybe hold up on the trip through the Gate. Dried fruit, beef jerky, bottled waters, and a variety of roasted nuts filled my arms. My trembling hand snatched a few bars of chocolate at the last minute. When I went to pay, I was surprised to find Adam waiting by the counter.

No fresh blood, I realized, checking him over through my lashes. I handed the cashier my choices and swiped my card with a wince. We would run out of funds in a few days if we didn't find a way through the Gate soon, but for now, the machine beeped, and I was given a receipt instead of an apology. When we left the store, the strange boy was nowhere in sight.

Back at our hotel room, I started unloading my bags. Adam closed the door behind us with a firm click, and I looked up at the following *clunk* of the deadbolt sliding home. There was something in his hand.

"Here." Adam tossed me the colorful carton and peeled off his gloves. He dropped them on a small table by the door before pulling a second container from his hoodie pocket. With a glance around the cramped room, he went to the nearest of the four windows while I stood staring blankly at the container. "Put that across the windowsills. Doorways, too."

"Salt?" I pried the top open to peer at the glittering crystals. "Why?"

Adam finished pouring a thin line along the sill and set the carton aside with a grim smile. "Because the woman who stopped us was a fae, same as the boy who was following us. He used some kind of wind magic to get away from me, and he might try to come here next. This will make it harder for them to find us. Salt stops fae magic."

"Won't it stop yours, then?"

Adam pressed his palms to the window frame. Green sparks trickled from his hands and sank into the salted wooden sill of the hotel window. A flash of teeth too sharp to be called a smile cut across his face. "I'm different, Bri."

And then power slammed through me, spiraling from Adam in waves as if he was the eye of a storm only we could feel. I stumbled back, sinking onto the nearest of the two narrow beds in our room in a daze. The whispery rustle of greenery surrounded us, and I gasped, tasting wild honey and clay as his magic sank into my bones to burn in my blood.

I wanted to go to him, wrap my arms around his waist and burrow against his chest. I wanted to touch his face and smooth away the jagged edges of that bitter smile. I wanted to revel in the buzz of his purr against my fingertips and see the weight pulling him down lift away. A weight I had put there with cutting words and an angry slap.

Why, I wondered as vines of light burst from Adam's skin and rooted him to the floor and walls. *How can I still feel this way after what he did to Chris? To those men?*

He had killed in a violent, bloody rage yesterday. He'd gutted Chris and his hired thugs like the deer he'd hunted for our dinner without a hint of remorse.

We'd only spoken a handful of words since...and yet, he felt like home. Even now, he was a lodestone, drawing me to him while I struggled to remain apart. But every step back only made the ache in my heart worse, and I was weary of fighting.

I was still scared, but now I could see what my silence, what my anger and hurt, had done to him. His shuttered gaze. The tense set of his shoulders. The way he half-slumped in defeat even as he poured his magic into protecting us both. Into protecting *me*.

Just like when Chris found us in the mountains, I realized with a start. When Adam had killed to save *me*.

I sucked a breath past my teeth and let it back out in a shuddering sigh as I stood. I was such an idiot. Adam wasn't human, no matter how much he acted like one sometimes. He was fae, raised on the streets and in the mountains, where the rules were harsher and not everything was black and white. I'd tried to fit him into a box I knew, and blinded by the violence of what he'd done, I'd caused him so much pain with my fear of what I hadn't understood. I should've talked to him. I should've trusted him. Instead, I'd lashed out, treating him like the beast he believed himself to be.

Guilt settled like a leaden lump in my stomach as I turned away and started pouring lines of salt across the remaining windows and both doorways. *I have to fix this.*

I finished with the last window, a tiny porthole in the bathroom above the toilet, and returned to the main room. Capping my salt container, I set it on our bags.

Adam didn't move when I edged closer and stood waiting, twisting my fingers together and tugging until the joints ached. I needed to explain, to tell Adam everything and quickly. Before I pushed him too far and lost my chance. Shaking, I brushed the last crumbs of salt from my hands and took the plunge as his power settled around us like a warm velvet cloak.

"I never loved him."

Adam turned away from the window as the vines of light faded. I offered him a wan smile. He watched me, his shuttered expression giving nothing away.

"I mean, maybe a little, when we were kids. Being with Chris made me feel safe and wanted. I was alone for a long time, Adam. Especially after the mess with Lila. Chris stood by me when no one else would."

I dropped my gaze to my fingers clutching the hem of my shirt, and a shaky, bitter laugh slipped out. "He was always well-spoken and confident, and he understood exactly what to do. Even at eleven years old, he knew what he wanted and how to get it. No one ever told him no or how they knew best. He asked, and they just...let him do whatever he wanted. I was desperate, and he was the charming prince from the faerie tales I used to love.

"Then I turned sixteen, and Chris made my dreams come true. He gave me my first taste of freedom, all bought with a fancy dinner, a bottle of wine, and the charm everyone loved. I needed him to stay free, but I didn't love him. I know that now," I whispered, my heart aching more with every word in the face of Adam's cold silence.

"Chris wasn't thrilled when I went off my medications a couple months later. He promised not to tell my parents, though. For a while, everything was perfect and then he asked me to move in with him. I just couldn't do it. I think he was angry when I didn't follow him after he ended things. I didn't need to...because I wasn't alone anymore. I had you."

I looked up and choked back a sob as tears flooded my eyes and made the room blur. Adam closed the yawning distance between us and cupped my face, uselessly trying to stem the flow as they spilled over. "I don't want to lose you, Adam. Not like this," I whispered, my heart in my throat as his thumbs stroked the curve of my cheekbones. I stared into his dark eyes, biting my lip and tasting blood.

"Don't," Adam whispered at last, his stony mask falling away as he touched my mouth and soothed away the small wounds from my teeth. "Chris—those men—that wasn't the first time I've killed humans."

"I-it wasn't?"

Adam shook his head, a rueful twist to his lips. "No, it wasn't. I've...done a lot to survive, to stay free. Most of the time, I was defending myself but not always."

He paused and glanced at his hands where they cradled my face, claws skimming the curve of my cheek. "I was angry for a long time, Bri," he continued in a harsh whisper, his thumb coming to trace the bow of my bottom lip. "Once, I hunted your people as they hunted me, but even then, I was always myself."

His touch faltered, and he looked away with a shudder. "I...I've never lost control like that before. Not since escaping the place where my mother and I were held. The drugs they fed us made it hard to focus. Me more than her after their daughter tried to..."

Another shudder wracked him, and I leaned into his touch, cupping my hands over his as my heart ached in sympathy. Adam met my gaze and nodded wearily, smoothing away the tears I couldn't stop. "They took me from my mother and collared me. After that day, I became the beast they wanted me to be. I lived in the moment, surviving however I could. Somehow, my mother saved me.

"I was barely conscious when it happened. All I remember are flashes. Then I woke up next to my mother's body. I was laying naked in a stream and covered in blood that wasn't mine. It wasn't until later that I learned how much time I'd lost to the madness."

His eyes closed for a minute, his hands dropping away as he left me to stand by the window again. "If...if you would rather stay here—"

"Are you planning to leave me behind?" I rasped, clenching my fists until my knuckles were white as I fought to keep my voice steady, to stay where I was.

"No, I just...I want you to remember you don't have to come if you change your mind," he said, carefully not looking at me.

"Dammit, Adam!" I cried out, suddenly angrier than I'd ever been. "I don't want you to stand there and tell me I have *options*! I don't *want* to leave! I want to *fix* this!" Striding over to him, I gestured to the window as his gaze snapped to mine. "Don't you realize I've had plenty of chances to leave if I'd wanted to? You've been helping me to find strength to be true to myself since you showed up on the roof *months* ago."

I shivered, the fight draining out of me like a popped balloon as I stared at the toes of my muddy shoes. "I'm sorry for blaming you for what happened with Chris. I think...I think I understand now, and I don't want to be that scared little girl anymore. I don't want to give up. I want to make this work...don't you?"

Adam's breath caught, and before I could continue, I found myself being crushed in a hug. "Thank you," he whispered, his breath warming my ear. "I don't know what I would've done if you had decided to...to stay."

"I'm so sorry," I choked out, pressing my face into his sweatshirt and breathing in his familiar musk of cedar. Sheer relief wrenched a watery laugh past the tight knot in my chest. "We made such a mess out of everything. No more crazy secrets for either of us. Deal?"

A low chuckle in my ear was my only warning before he pulled away only to tilt my chin up and capture me with a rough kiss. "Deal," he whispered against my lips and kissed me again.

Gone was the tension and misery that had tainted our whole trip, along with the distance he'd maintained between us since we left the mountains. It was like finding water after days of thirst, sweet and heady. I melted in his arms, my hands buried in his thick mane as I rose on tiptoe to press closer.

With a low rumble, Adam picked me up and pinned me to the wall. I gasped, the unexpected move jolting through me and knocking loose a chunk of common sense as his teeth nipped a trail down my neck.

"Adam," I whispered, my head falling back when he nudged my collar aside to leave another mark with teeth and lips. "We shouldn't...get distracted."

He groaned into my neck and shuddered. "Then you should probably stop," he gasped as I realized I was stroking my thumbs along the edges of his ears.

"This?" I asked with studied innocence. My nails deliberately ruffled the short silky fur before running over the tips and down to the lobe in one lazy caress. Adam growled and caught my wrists, pinned them against the wall.

"W-weren't you just saying we shouldn't get distracted?" he rasped, his deep voice thready and rough. Green and gold sparks brightened his dark eyes as they met mine with enough heat to *burn*.

He looked...

Blushing furiously, I nodded. Adam slumped into me with a sigh. I let my head rest against the wall, caught between being mortified and smug about affecting him so strongly with a simple touch. After a moment, Adam set me on my feet.

"Minx," he muttered with a good-natured growl, checking the salt on the window.

"Tease," I shot back, tossing my rumpled hair over my shoulder with a playful grin. He huffed, and I laughed, delighted and giddy. "So...are we okay, then?" I asked as I sorted the snacks I'd bought earlier, including a large bag of beef jerky, which I tossed to Adam.

He caught it with a smile in his eyes and cocked his head, settling into a tailor's seat against the wall. "Yes?"

I snorted and tore open a bag of pistachios. "You don't sound very sure," I mumbled with a guilty wince, freeing a handful of the salty green nuts from their shells and offering them to Adam.

"I don't want to assume anything." He rolled the nutmeats around in his hand. "*Are* we okay, Bri?"

I smiled and nodded, a light blush warming my cheeks as I sat beside him and gave him another handful of shelled nuts. "Yeah, I think we are."

"Good."

***

"Is that water dripping?" I asked Adam a little while later.

The sound drew me out of the bathroom. I lingered in the doorway, my half-braided hair looped between my fingers as I listened.

Adam looked up from sorting through our bags. His ears swiveled to catch the faint noise before he tugged his hood up. It was getting louder. I joined him as I secured the end of my braid with an elastic. Together we turned towards the door.

The worn wood floor beneath it darkened while we watched, the stain spreading along the thin line of salt there.

"The salt...it's dissolving," I whispered as Adam stepped between me and the door. With a shiver I felt in my bones, Adam's wards collapsed. I flinched and grabbed Adam's arm when he swayed. He shook his head, dazed. "Are you okay? Adam?" He shuddered and straightened, pushing me behind him as the door flew open with a splintering crack.

A gust of wind blasted in, swirling through the room and tearing me away from Adam with gleeful, greedy fingers. He spun and lunged, snagging my sleeve with his claws. I fumbled for his hand. With a shriek of tortured air, a whirlwind formed between us and flung us apart. The rushing winds stole my breath as they sucked me in, spinning me about before they spat me across the room to land in a heap by the door. Gasping and coughing, I tried to stand only to be pinned by a wiry hand on my throat.

"Bri!"

"Well, look at you, lassie," a light mocking voice whispered in my ear. "A little bit like you with a greenman at your beck and call. Must be a woman's touch."

I froze, fighting to breathe past the tight grip. Adam lurched to his feet, and his low growl echoed around us. My captor rocked back, sitting on his heels. I stared. It was him, the boy Adam caught tailing us earlier.

The strange fae smirked, and the chill edge of a knife replaced the hand at my throat. He stood, pulling me to my feet. "I wouldn't fuss too much, laddie. It won't end well for your lover here."

Adam started forward, only to stop when the boy sneered and tightened his grip. The knife dug into my neck.

"So rude, but what can one expect from a mongrel creature? I can smell the human in you. Little more than a beast, you are."

"Leave him alone," I rasped as the barbed insult sparked embers in Adam's eyes.

My captor shifted, glancing from Adam to me. His eyes were an indescribable shade of green, glittering with a sharp-edged mischief as he leaned closer. He smelled of fresh cut hay drying in the sun and withered flowers. "Afraid he'll forget himself?"

"Adam would never hurt me," I whispered, the realization settling in my heart with a soft glow of warmth and certainty.

The mischievous expression grew, and the knife eased off a bit. He grinned at Adam. In a flash, he released my arm to grip my waist and pull me close, the zipper on his leather jacket digging into my hip. Adam snarled, baring his teeth as his gaze shot to the boy's hand when he made as if to slip it under my shirt.

"Having a little trouble with your temper, laddie?" The lanky fae sniggered and pressed the blade harder to my throat. "You shouldn't let your human toy say such things. A person might start thinkin' she means something to you."

Red. Adam's eyes were nothing but a blaze of red and orange light. Beneath his feet, the wooden floor rippled, tiny shoots of green light pushing out to twine around him. I trembled, barely breathing. Every choked pant scraped against the knife.

"Let her go," Adam growled, magic thrumming through his voice with enough power to rattle the walls.

"Easy there, boy. We only wish to talk." With a rustle of his long coat, a tall, dark-haired man sauntered through the open door. He was all lean angles and graceful arrogance, his face set with slanted, amber eyes and high cheekbones. Thin lips twitched upward with a cold smile, and he arched a winged brow at Adam. "Sprig is just a touch...enthusiastic. It's not every day a greenman and his doxie fold wings on our doorstep. Why are you here?"

I gritted my teeth as Adam's answering snarl caused Sprig to tighten his grip. "Adam," I rasped, and he shuddered, the lights in his eyes fading to pinprick embers.

"I'm going home," Adam rumbled after another beat. "If you're only here to talk, let her *go*."

"That'll do, Sprig," the man drawled, the cold smile never leaving his lips. He eyed me with a thoughtful look. Sprig grumbled something sullen and shoved me away, spinning a stone knife around his fingers with a sneer. I coughed and almost stumbled into the new stranger, my lungs aching as I took my first deep breath in far too long. He caught my chin and tilted my head first one way, then the other before caressing my cheek. "She's a pretty thing for a human, after all. No need to bruise the merchandise."

Suddenly Adam was between us, knocking his hand aside. "Bri is *mine*," he snapped.

The man only raised a brow, unperturbed by the violence bubbling under Adam's skin and glowing in his eyes. "You may address me as Kantor. I am the Guardian of the Gate in this land. Why are you here? Your kin have their own ways of slipping Under-the-Hill."

Kantor frowned and snapped his fingers. Adam's hood jerked and fell away, and Kantor smiled. "Ah, Hind blood," he purred, eyeing Adam's golden antlers. "Fascinating."

"Kantor, Guardian of the Gate." Adam's hands curled into fists even as the ember sparks faded from his eyes. "Will you grant us passage Under-the-Hill?"

Kantor straightened his coat with a hum and a sharp-edged smile. "For a price, yes."

"We don't have anything of value," I said softly as I edged closer to grip Adam's back pocket.

"What a pity, child. You are the reason for the toll, after all. He can go when he wishes. Fae bloods have that right. Humans don't." Kantor eyed me, his gaze lingering on my hands and the fresh trail of love bites branded on my pale skin. Reaching past Adam, he flipped my braid away from my neck before either of us could stop him. "Marked after a fashion, but not properly, and neither bound nor claimed. You have no rights among us, mortal girl. Either he pays a price of my choice, or you stay behind. It makes no difference to me."

"That's not—"

"What do you want?" Adam cut in, catching my clenched fist in his hand. Kantor tilted his head and nodded toward the golden antlers nestled in Adam's brow.

"No! Those are his—"

"It's okay, Bri," Adam whispered, squeezing my hand.

Kantor watched our exchange, the cold smile making a reappearance. "Indeed," he murmured, giving the golden branches a hungry look. "When the time comes for you to shed this pair, you will return to the Gate and give them to me in as perfect condition as possible. I don't have a male Hind's antlers in my collection, yet. Those are quite stunted for one your age, but they will have to do, I suppose."

Adam flinched, and I wrapped my free hand around his wrist. "You don't have to do this, Adam. We can find another way—"

"There is no other way, mortal. Every one of the Gates has a Guardian. Each will exact a different price for your passage. Mine is a light one compared to what the others may ask of you. Provided you could find the other Gates, of course." Kantor drew a silver knife from a pocket inside the breast of his coat and turned to Adam. "Well?"

Adam shuddered, a low growl threading his deep voice. "My gold for safe passage through the Gate for Bri and myself."

Kantor nodded. "Yes, I'll even direct the Gate to drop you near your people's territories. Now, have we a bargain?"

Adam glanced at the knife and looked down at me with a nod. "Yes."

Kantor hissed, triumphant, when Adam held out his hand. Kantor's features rippled, and I stared, my mouth falling open when blue-green scales glittered briefly along his cheekbone. Slitted, gold eyes met mine as Kantor caught Adam's wrist and slid the knife across his palm. Licking the blood from the thin blade, Kantor grinned while magic, smelling of rain and tasting of stone and salt, bloomed in the air around us. Adam hissed, and we watched the cut heal with a shimmer, like heat rising from a blacktop in summer. A strange glyph appeared in its stead and glowed for a moment before going dark. "The bargain is struck, greenman. Don't forget."

Adam stared at the mark for a minute and nodded. Looking up at Kantor, he tugged me closer. "When do we leave?"

Kantor tore his gaze from Adam's antlers and glanced at a gold pocket watch he produced out of thin air. "Midnight should do. Come to the standing stones then. Carry this, both of you, and you will not be seen." He tossed something at Adam. "Do *not* be late." Nodding to Sprig, he left.

Sprig flipped his stone knife over his hand and sheathed it in one smooth motion. "See you on the green at midnight, laddie," he said with a wink as he followed Kantor, waving the door closed behind him with a lazy flick of his fingers.

Alone again, I grabbed Adam's marked hand and traced the glyph. "Why?" I whispered. "Why do you keep doing this for me?"

Adam sighed and enfolded me in a hug, nuzzling my temple. "Why not?"

Chapter Twenty-Four

"Are you ready?" Adam asked, emptying the last dustpan of salt into the trash.

"Yes." I checked my things one last time. It had taken some doing, but everything we needed to take with us from the duffel bag was now stuffed into my backpack. All except my quilt, which was strapped to the bottom in lieu of my abandoned sleeping bag. I would carry what we needed, and once we were out of town, Adam would carry me. The delicate, blue-green scale Kantor had given Adam was supposed to hide us somehow, but he hadn't said for how long. Best not to risk it.

"It's strange." I settled the backpack, tugging the straps to make sure they wouldn't dig into my shoulders, and offered him a wan smile. "We came all this way, and we're not even going to see any of it."

Adam paused and cocked his head, his deep hood shifting to show his human guise already in place. "Do you...did you want to?" He retrieved his gloves from the little table by the door, putting them on with some reluctance.

"Yes—no—I don't know, really. Do you think we'll ever come back?" I bit my lip, reaching up to finger the hard lump my stone feather made beneath my shirt. Adam's gaze followed my hand, then bounced to my face, and I flushed. Somehow, returning his gift to its place around my neck had erased the last painful echoes from the wedge Chris's death drove between us. He still wouldn't tell me what it meant, though.

Adam sighed and walked over to cup my face in his hands, his leather gloves smooth and cool on my skin. "Bri, if you want to stay—"

"No." I leaned into his touch, grabbing his wrists before he could pull away. "No, I want to come. I do. I'm just nervous, I guess."

Adam nuzzled my cheek. "Me too," he whispered, his lips brushing against my jaw. His wrists slipped from my grip, and I closed my eyes, letting his closeness settle my nerves as he wrapped himself around me in a hug.

I hummed, pressing my face to his worn hoodie with a sigh. "I love you," I whispered back, my thoughts hazy with the warmth my new certainty of him sent buzzing through me.

Adam stiffened, and I pulled away with a slight frown, confused by his stunned stare. It took a second before realization dawned. I dropped my gaze as a blush blazed across my face.

"I do, you know," I said softly, his continued silence crumbling my confidence. "You're..." I paused and took a deep breath, bracing myself as I flashed him a shy, tremulous smile. "You're everything to me, Adam. I love you, and I want to come with you. I really am sure. I promise."

Adam trembled, his dark eyes wide. His glamourie flickered and crumbled in a flurry of green sparks. He cupped my face in his hands, drawing me in for a soft, sweet kiss. My backpack slid from my shoulders, and I caught the glitter of tears in his eyes before mine fluttered shut.

"You are my heart," he whispered against my lips, his deep voice raw and open.

Now I was crying, too. The salty flavor mingled with his as I wrapped my arms around his neck and kissed him for all I was worth. Pushing Adam's hood back, I tangled my hands in his mane and hummed against his mouth. My heart sang, full of light and overflowing with heady laughter as we kissed in the dying glow of twilight.

"We need to get going," I murmured a little while later, when the honeyed kisses faded into nuzzles and whispered words.

Adam sighed and nodded, pulling his hood up. He stilled, focusing, and his magic rebuilt his glamourie.

Savoring the sweetness lingering on my tongue, I picked up my backpack and put it on as his human guise settled into place. Hopefully, for the last time.

***

Getting out of town was more difficult than I expected.

Human guise or not, Adam garnered a lot of attention once we left the hotel and wandered the darkened town. Just like in New York, the sun going down didn't deter folks from roaming. There were plenty of people to stare and give us curious looks when we passed. Between my constant confusion and Adam's size, we stuck out like sore thumbs.

Again and again, I compared nearby street signs to the pamphlet about Stonehenge I'd gotten at the front desk. The receptionist had scribbled more detailed directions at the bottom. She insisted we wouldn't be able to miss it, but I had my doubts.

"This way." I caught hold of Adam's wrist and tugged him into yet another narrow street. We turned the corner, past a woman with a young boy and their dog. The kid kept sneaking glances at us, his wide-eyed gaze locked on Adam.

Can he see through the glamourie?

A low growl jerked my attention to the dog, also focused solely on Adam. The mutt stepped between us and the boy, and its hackles rose in a thick ridge. Adam tensed beside me.

I shoved the pamphlet into my pocket, grabbing his hand. The woman shot us a curious look, but I just waved and walked faster, Adam right on my heels as we left them behind.

After several random turns onto different streets, we found one void of people. Shivering, I dug my crumpled directions from my pocket and slowed to a stop, flustered. "There has to be a better way to do this," I whispered, eyeing the tiny map.

I glanced around for the signs the receptionist mentioned and pulled my phone from my pocket. Raucous laughter spilled out of a nearby pub as I stared blindly at the darkened screen, trying to think. Suddenly the phone was plucked from my grip.

"Hey!" I squeaked, but my feeble protest went unheeded. Adam tucked my phone into his hoodie pocket and shifted so the night breeze flowed over his face. "Adam?"

"I...I can feel it." Adam flexed his hands in his leather gloves. He started to shift as if to set his feet and stumbled. Glancing at the shoes he wore, Adam grimaced before returning his attention to the playful gust swirling around us. "The Gate. It's faint, but it's this way."

I shivered and huddled into the collar of my coat. The breeze trickled past my scarf to run chill fingers down my neck. "Are you sure?"

Adam hesitated, then nodded, glancing at me with a wry smile. "Cold?"

"Not all of us have our own fur coat," I replied with a huff, shooting him a fond look as I passed. A quiet laugh followed me, and I blushed, muffling my smile against my scarf.

Following Adam's sense of the Gate was slow and maddening. Like a strand of spider silk snapping when tugged too hard, the traces vanished at the slightest distraction. A cat darting across our path. A door slamming shut down the street. The rich smell of roasting meat and potatoes coming from some of the houses.

Our new path took us along empty streets and through cramped alleys. The occasional sign about Stonehenge confirmed we still headed in the right direction, albeit in a roundabout way. We avoided any more curious watchers, but as the minutes crept by, I started to panic. We had over an hour to make it to Stonehenge, but...

"What will Kantor do if we're late?" I hissed when we paused again so Adam could reorient himself.

"I don't know." He turned onto a different street and quickened his stride.

"Fantastic," I muttered, trotting to keep up. "Wait, look over there! Let's go that way." Adam paused and glanced down the long, narrow road I pointed to. A slice of trees and yellowed grasses was visible at the other end. "If we get out of town, we can move faster, right?"

With a nod and a faint smile, he led the way. The open space of the field was such a relief after wandering through the narrow cobblestone streets. I hummed happily, breathing deeply of air thick with the smell of frost and wood-smoke instead of the muddle of scents in town.

"What are you—oh!" I paused, swallowing a laugh at the sight of Adam peeling off the hated gloves with a grimace. The shoes and socks followed. Adam's sigh of relief fogged in the night chill as he stepped onto the matted grasses edging the field.

"Better?" I teased when his human glamourie fell away and he sniffed the air, seeking the call of the Gate once more.

"Yes," Adam replied absently, cocking his head and closing his eyes for a minute. Dropping into a crouch, he buried his claws in the loose soil. There was a ripple in the air, and sparks glittered around his hands and feet. For a brief moment, I Saw the traces of the Gate reaching for him. The faint trail hung in the air and shimmered with countless shades of green and golden brown. Tendrils twined up his arms and caressed his face, sinking into his eyes, nose, and mouth with every breath until he glowed with it. Slowly, he straightened, and the sparks winked out one by one, taking my perception of the Gate's magic with them.

Savoring the faint sweetness of his magic, I edged closer as the last traces of light surrounding him melted away. "Adam?"

He didn't answer, staring off in the direction the glowing trail had gone. Letting my backpack slip from my shoulders, I took his hand, twining my fingers with his. Adam glanced down at me, the distant look in his eyes fading away under a faint smile. He lifted my hand to his lips before letting me go and dropping back into a crouch. I handed him the pack, then clambered onto his back with a relieved sigh of my own.

He stood. "Ready?"

"Ready," I assured him, slipping my hands into the neck of his sweatshirt.

Adam sighed. "Bri..."

"I'm *cold*."

He tugged my hands out with a low chuckle and pressed Kantor's scale to my palm. The scalloped edges bit into my chilled fingers. "Behave. We'll be there soon."

I shivered and huddled closer, burying my face in his silken mane. His warmth and even loping stride lulled me into a half-doze, and I ended up slumped against him. At last, he slowed and jiggled my leg.

"Bri, wake up. We're here."

"Mmph?" I yawned as I slid off, shivering when the night chill replaced his heat.

A chain link fence loomed over us with barbed wire strung along the top. I eyed the strands of razor-sharp metal and huddled against Adam, too sleepy to focus on the problem of the steel fence for longer than a moment. The warmth of his arm around my shoulders fended off the worst of the cold seeping through my jacket. Together, we gazed at the distant shapes of Stonehenge where the Gate must be, waiting.

We hadn't been there long when a familiar, mocking voice cut through the air. The grating tones hit me like a bucket of ice water, banishing my sleepy befuddlement.

"Well now, such sweetness for your mortal toy. I wonder if she's worth a taste. What do you say, lassie? Care to bed a real fae?"

I straightened and spun, swallowing the tart words springing to my tongue. "No," I bit out instead, a polite smile thinning my lips.

"Pity," Sprig muttered, smirking at Adam's warning rumble. Pulling a long-stemmed pipe from inside his coat, he lit the bowl and motioned for us to follow him.

"Where's Kantor?" I whispered, glancing over at the distant, darkened shape of the visitor center as we trailed along the fence line behind Sprig.

"He's here," Adam said, tugging me closer when Sprig motioned for us to stop. The lanky fae gestured, and part of the chain link fence surrounding Stonehenge rippled and melted away. Instead, a pair of slender, twisted trees created a living archway, the heavy wire loops of the fence tangled in their branches. Adam hesitated and touched the nearest gnarled trunk edging the gap. "I can smell his magic, and the Gate...knows him."

Sprig paused, taking a deep draw on his pipe as he eyed Adam. "Not bad, laddie," he drawled, waving us through and reforming the glamourie hiding the gap with a careless gesture. "There may be hope for you yet."

"Don't," Adam murmured when I turned, a sharp reply on my lips. "It's what he wants."

Sprig grinned around the stem of his pipe. Flushed and flustered, I forced myself to follow Adam in silence while Sprig sniggered.

It took longer than I expected to hike across the open field. Sprig led the way, grumbling about mortal weakness between long draws on his pipe. When we reached Stonehenge itself, I stopped beside the last barrier, a low-slung rope strung between slender poles. With a put-upon sigh, Sprig stepped over the little fence and continued on, waving for us to follow.

The stones were huge up close. I stared like the tourist I was, taking it all in as we passed the outer ring. Only Adam's grip on my wrist kept me moving in the right direction. "Wow," I whispered, the awed hush in my voice spurred by the aura of ancient magic growing stronger with each passing minute. It reminded me of a gathering storm or standing on the beach with high tide coming in. Powerful and more than a little frightening.

"Ah, you're here," Kantor murmured, his low voice silky in my ear.

With a squeak, I jerked my attention from the monument around us as Adam let me go. Kantor raised a dark brow at me before eyeing Adam's antlers with a smug, possessive air that twisted in my gut. "You're a bit early, though it's just as well, I suppose." Turning to me, he gestured towards one of the standing stones a few feet away. "A word, mortal?"

"It's okay," Adam assured me when I shot him a queasy look. "He won't harm you, or our bargain will be broken. We—*you*—can trust him for now."

"Indeed," Kantor drawled with a mocking half bow. "Shall we?" I straightened my shoulders and nodded, letting him draw me a few feet away until the upright stone loomed over us. With a twisted gesture and a snap of his fingers, silence draped over us like a heavy blanket. "There are a few things you should consider before you and your lover traverse the Gate."

"I, um...we're not lovers, actually," I stammered out, my face hot as I tried not to think about what I was saying. "Not yet."

"I know," Kantor drawled, pegging my flat stomach with an arch look. "Your belly would already be swollen with his cubs if you were. Such is the result of loving a greenman. However, this may be of some use."

He held out a piece of slate worn flat and smooth with an offset hole. Faint glimmers sparked in the opening, and the whole thing gleamed faintly to my Sight.

"A hagstone," I said in an awed whisper, taking the offered stone. It pulsed when I touched it, and I squeaked, nearly dropping it when a ripple of warmth shot up my arm.

"Good. Magic likes you. That will make the stone's job much easier," he murmured, catching a hold of my wrist. Before I knew what he was doing, he'd pulled out his silver knife and nicked my thumb. I jumped, but his grip was firm and steady as he dipped his finger in my blood and drew a series of glyphs around the opening in the stone. My blood vanished into the worn surface, and Kantor let me go with a satisfied hum.

"Now, tell me, what do you know of these and the magicks they possess?" Kantor cleaned his knife and returned it to his coat.

I stared at the visibly healing cut on my thumb while Kantor produced a silky cord and threaded it through the stone. "They grant true Sight, protection, and healing mostly." I hesitated and glanced up. "Some stories say they're used in love spells."

Kantor snorted. "Mortals are such simpleminded creatures. Yes, when given lover-to-lover, if one possesses a fragment to complete the stone, it will add to your own fertility. I would caution you not to try it. Greenmen are fertile enough among mortal women without help. Perform that bit of foolishness, and you won't birth, you'll *litter*."

"Oh," I whispered, dazed and unsure what to say to that. "Then why are you giving me this?"

He slipped the cord over my head. "Self-interest, of course." He brushed my hands aside and adjusted it until the hagstone rested on my breastbone. "Male hinds, properly known as Golden Harts, are rare, odd creatures—"

"You mean he's not the only one?" I blurted out. Kantor paused and glanced up, one winged brow raised. I winced. "Sorry."

Kantor gave the cord a last tug and straightened, continuing his explanation as if I hadn't spoken. "It is unusual for them to bind themselves to a single mate. A lone female is quite vulnerable, after all. If he feels you are in constant danger, your lover may find himself unable to drop his antlers for some time.

"The hagstone will protect you from most kinds of magic. Now that it has tasted your blood, the stone is attuned to you and will hasten your ability to heal. However, it does have its limits. The stone itself is fragile, and magicks worked on the world around you will still be effective. Do not depend on it overmuch." He paused and pursed his lips. "It will also act as a contraceptive. As long as you wear it against your skin, you will remain barren. This is merely another precaution, of course. I despise waiting."

"We've done fine so far—"

"Have you now?" Kantor said silkily, giving me a measuring look. "Tell me, mortal...have you ever seen him in his element? Among the mountain winds and ancient forests?"

I froze, my blush returning with interest as I thought back on our brief time in the mountains.

"Ah, I see you have an inkling," he purred, smoothing the lapels of his long coat. "Good. When you arrive in Underhill, it will be far worse. Underhill is overflowing with pure magic. It's what the place is made of, after all. It bleeds into the mundane world via what humans call ley lines, giving birth to the weaker magic of the world of Man."

Kantor paused and nodded in Adam's direction. "He has never known such abundance. For a greenman as young as he, it will be...overwhelming. The magic there is not a tame and biddable force. It will test him, seeking an outlet of its own. If his will is not enough to contain it, you may find yourself facing Underhill herself. You need to be ready for whatever such a confrontation will entail."

Kantor's gold eyes caught and held mine. "Understand me well, mortal. Underhill is not fond of your people. It is quite likely she will not take kindly to your presence. Be prepared to do what you must, however unpleasant. I will not be slighted of my prizes due to a mortal's foolish weakness."

A chill skittered along my spine at the threat glittering in his pale eyes. "I thought Underhill was just a place—"

Kantor snorted. "Humans often do. She is our mother-land and the greatest of us. Her presence and will flow through every living thing, on every breath. Do not seek to play her false; your ignorance will not save you should you vex her."

With a thin smile, he gestured to the hagstone. "Now, do *not* remove that until you reach his people and have spoken with the Elders, or my price will be doubled. Understood, mortal?"

I nodded shakily, and he grinned, flashing teeth too sharp and too white to be human, even with his glamourie. "Good. Now, it would be prudent to send you on before the humans discover us here. My magic is needed for opening the Gate, and Sprig will not be able to maintain the keep-away wards for much longer on his own."

Kantor pointed at the hagstone again as I tucked it inside my shirt. "Remember my warning."

"I will." I smoothed my coat down while he dismissed the magic keeping us isolated with a careless snap of his fingers. "Thank—"

"Don't," Adam rumbled in my ear, his hand suddenly over my mouth as he cut off my thanks and muffled my squeak of surprise. "Never thank a fae unless you want them to call it in as a debt owed."

My eyes went wide and shot to Kantor in time to see him curl his lip at Adam. "Spoilsport."

"She is mine to protect," Adam reminded him, tugging me back as Kantor shucked his coat and handed it off to Sprig.

Unbuttoning his cuffs, Kantor rolled his sleeves up with a smirk. "Truth, greenman. See that you do."

Motioning for us to stand at the edge of the inner circle, Kantor stretched out his hands and began a chant in a low voice. The language was like nothing I'd ever heard before, and it was hard to focus on. Almost as if the words themselves were a slippery echo of what he was using to call the magic. They curled through the air like smoke, tearing apart before I could really hear them.

The flow of magic around us pulsed, and a biting wind kicked up. Adam stiffened and shuddered, a low groan wrenched from him as the gathering magic pulsed again. Power thrummed, crackling between the stones before focusing itself on the innermost circle. I shivered, huddling against Adam. My gaze was drawn to Kantor's windblown figure, and I gasped.

I could *See* him.

A crown of graceful ivory horns and glittering blue-green scales rippled in and out of existence as Kantor chanted. His outthrust hands were now tipped with claws and patterned with more scales that shimmered in the glow of his magic. Faint and blurred, a pair of folded leathery wings shadowed his shoulders. A serpentine shape stirred the grass at his feet.

"He's a *dragon*," I whispered, awed.

"Guardians usually are, lassie," Sprig grunted around his pipe. In defiance of the wind swirling about us, the smoke lingered before drifting upwards in lazy loops. The spicy scent from it combined with the rising magic was making me dizzy.

Suddenly, there was a shout and a soundless thunderclap I felt in my chest as the gathered magicks surrounding us surged forward—and the air at the center of the stone circles *ripped*.

"Go!" roared Kantor, his eyes glowing with a light to match the doorway he opened.

We hadn't taken more than a step when someone shouted for us to halt.

"I got'em, laddie. Now git," Sprig hissed and darted past us toward the loud voices.

Adam only hesitated for a moment before scooping me up and bolting for the portal. Brushing past Kantor, we plunged into the light.

Chapter Twenty-Five

It hurt.

Every joint in my body was being pulled apart. Again and again, the magic tried to yank me from Adam's arms. Rivulets of fire snaked along my limbs and pooled in my lungs until I could hardly breathe. I was drowning in magic, dizzy with it as we were tossed like a leaf on the currents of power.

Adam's grip on me tightened, and I buried my face against his hoodie. Each gasping breath burned with magic, and I fought to stay conscious. It went on and on—and then it was a summery midday instead of midnight in the middle of winter as I tumbled onto thick emerald moss and fragrant pine needles.

Without Adam.

"No," I choked out, scrambling to my feet. The overwhelming magic of the portal faded into a background hum. My hands jerked and shook as I dusted bits of greenery from my hair and clothes. I pulled off my jacket to tie it around my waist, scanning the lush forest surrounding me. "Adam?"

A low, strangled groan snapped my head around. Sheer relief made me giddy, and I turned toward the sound, tripping over my backpack. Reaching for it, I paused. Half buried in the moss, the worn bag was covered in green tendrils and slowly sinking out of sight. I stared—then lurched to my feet, grabbing the backpack and yanking it free.

The trees surrounding me were huge and ancient. The mossy ground bordering their gnarled roots gave way to patches of thick undergrowth where the sun broke through the close-knit branches.

I circled one massive trunk, only to find my way barred by a thicket of strange, thorny bushes. I didn't pause, shouldering my backpack and plunging into the jumble of branches. Limbs heavy with berries of blue and violet glass tangled in my clothes. They snatched at my coat as I pushed past, catching in my hair until I was forced to stop and free it from its braid. I fought to get by without harming anything, intent on the rasp of ragged breathing coming from the center of the thicket. Finally, I made it through.

"Adam," I breathed, falling to my knees next to his hunched form. The bushes snapped closed behind me. "Are you—"

"Get away," Adam groaned, pushing me away.

Green light shimmered around him in a rippling haze. His head came up, and I stared, my eyes wide. Adam's mane had grown shaggier and fell to his hips, threaded with vines. Green and gold light filled his eyes from corner to corner, swirling like smoke under glass. With a sharp crack, his antlers began splitting and lengthening even as I watched.

"D-don't touch me," he gasped. Sparks bloomed between his fingers and crawled up his arms in arcing tendrils. "I...it won't stop. I-I can't—"

"No! I'm not leaving you like this, Adam." I inched closer until I could kneel beside him. I reached for him, then jerked my hands back, my nails biting into my palms. "You just have to control it the way you did at my apartment, remember?"

Adam shook his head, his breath coming in ragged pants. He tried shoving me away again, and I caught his wrist for a second before letting it fall. "I'm not going anywhere," I said firmly. "You can do this. Remember the park? Don't let it control you. Don't let it win."

He shuddered, his hands shaking as he yanked his hooded sweatshirt over his head and tossed it aside. His t-shirt followed. With a groan, he buried his claws in the thick moss carpeting the thicket. Earthy sweetness exploded across my tongue, and I scrambled back when vines burst from the ground to flow over him in a rush of light and magic.

They burrowed into Adam's fur and snaked along his legs, rooting themselves in the fabric of his jeans. His claws dug furrows in the mossy ground while he writhed as if trying to escape his own skin. Several vines twined through his antlers. Another wave of magic washed over us, and the pale green tendrils erupted with tiny white flowers.

Adam arched, his head flung back, teeth bared in a silent roar—then the air around us shivered, and he slumped forward like a puppet whose strings had been cut. The sound of his ragged pants filled the thicket. Bit by bit, the changes ground to a halt.

I started to reach for him but hesitated. Was it over? The glow of magic still hung in the air around him. It rippled with a slow, steady pulse. An ancient heartbeat.

Adam's head snapped up. He surged to his feet, turning toward me with a low rumble. His nostrils flared, like a stag scenting a doe, and he stalked forward, the glow in his eyes brightening.

Heavy branches of gold stretched from his temples, creating a crown of graceful points from which flowery vines hung in delicate loops. Thicker vines framed his shoulders and hips, while a riot of slender tendrils wove patterns of pale green through fur and over bare skin.

A flickering light drew my gaze to his brow. A strange, knotted shape formed there, scrawling itself into being until it became a diadem of opalescent light. I stood slowly, fighting the urge to retreat while he circled me.

With Underhill's magic filling him to overflowing, Adam was something else. Something feral and restless.

Dangerous.

Then he shuddered and gasped, stuttering to a halt. "B-bri?"

"I'm okay. Are you..." I started toward him, only to stop and stare. "Adam?"

Something was wrong with his eyes. The last wisps of green and gold faded, eclipsed by a milky glow. A glow that echoed the shifting colors in the crown of light on his brow.

"Bri," Adam rasped, stretching one hand toward me as blood began to ooze from his nose and mouth. "Run."

And he lunged for me with a snarl.

I stumbled back, tripping over my backpack and hitting the ground hard. The clumsy moment saved me. Instead of tearing out my throat, Adam's claws skimmed my cheek as I fell. I cried out, one hand flying up to cover the stinging scratches.

The shallow wounds burned and itched as the hagstone hanging from my neck warmed. I scrambled to my feet, kicking free of the strap looped around my leg. There was a faint clatter, and a hard, thin shape rolled under my heel. Wobbling, I risked a quick glance down while Adam circled me again.

The clay carving tools tucked inside my rolled-up quilt had spilled out. Worn wood and silvery metal gleamed in the dappled sunlight of the thicket.

Wait. Some of those are steel, which is an alloy of iron.

Iron, the bane of the fae.

I dove for them, and Adam pounced. His weight bowled me over, but not before my fingers closed along a metal shaft. I yanked it free as he sent me sprawling, pinning me to the mossy floor of the thicket. The metal carving tool bit into my palm, the promise of it bright in my mind's eye as his hand curled around my neck.

And still, I hesitated.

"Please, Adam," I choked out past his grip on my throat. "I know you don't want to hurt me. Fight it."

Adam chuffed and bared his teeth with a rattling snarl. I had no choice.

"I'm sorry," I whispered.

Gritting my teeth, I brought the carving tool up with every scrap of adrenaline-fueled speed I could muster. Adam roared when the stubby blade pressed against the crown of light on his brow. Iron against magic. The smell of burning flesh and fur made me gag, but for a moment, it was Adam staring down at me—then the crown blazed hotter. A soundless explosion of light rocked the thicket, and I was thrown aside.

I gasped, sucking in air to fill my lungs in ragged pants. Everything hurt as I struggled to my feet. The hagstone's warmth pulsed hotter against my chest, and I cupped one hand over it. Thank goodness it hadn't broken in the struggle. A flicker of movement jerked my attention back to Adam, and I shivered, bracing myself for another attack.

"Your kind are not welcome here."

A chill slid along my spine. It was Adam speaking, but another voice echoed eerily around the familiar rumbling tones.

For a brief moment, I was at Stonehenge, surrounded by the weight of ancient magic rising in a restless tide while Kantor's voice whispered warnings in my ear. Was this...Underhill?

I edged away, then stopped. Somewhere in there was Adam, and I would not abandon him to this...thing. I curled my trembling hands into fists to hide their shaking and straightened, lifting my chin with a defiant glare for the stranger wearing his skin. Whether this was Underhill or not, Adam was mine, and I would fight for him if I had to. Just like he would for me.

"Give him back," I managed past the muddle of fear and anger trying to choke me.

The being reached up to smear the blood oozing from Adam's nose. It considered the crimson stain for a moment before looking me over with a faint frown. "You have no place here in which to make demands, mortal child. Only those who are worthy may ask a boon of me."

"I don't want a boon," I snapped, anger finally overtaking fear. I brandished the carving tool clutched in my hand. "Leave him alone. Let him go!"

A flash of teeth cut across Adam's face—more of a snarl than any smile—and those glowing, milky eyes went to the steel in my hand. "You would fight me for him, then?"

"I will," I affirmed even as the thought of it made my conviction falter. Could I bring myself to fight knowing I'd be hurting Adam, too?

Yes, I realized as the being strode closer. *Adam deserves the chance to choose for himself.*

"You cannot hope to win," it said with Adam's voice, unsheathing his claws with a careless flick of his fingers.

"I don't need to win," I said, searching the white glow for a scrap of green and gold as the truth of my own words dawned on me. "Adam does."

A battle was already being fought, after all. I just need to give him something to tip the balance.

Without looking away, I closed the distance between us and grasped my feather pendant, raising it to my lips. "Come back to me," I whispered to him, the carved stone cool against my mouth.

Adam reached for me, only to falter when his eyes dropped to the necklace. He stared, a frown wrinkling his brow. My heart leapt when, bit by bit, the milky light gave way to threads of green and gold.

"Bri," he rasped, and it was *Adam* who spoke. He trembled with the effort, his muscles twitching as he struggled with the power flooding his body. The blood oozing from his nose and mouth came in a steady trickle now. It dripped from his chin to stain his hands as he reached out to cradle mine. A few stray drops splattered across my necklace.

A flutter of movement drew my attention to the heavy vines framing his shoulders. I stared, horrified. One by one, they were changing, becoming a thorny tangle unlike anything born of his magic before this. The pale green of new growth drained away to a ghostly white, tipped with thorns the color of rust. Droplets of dark blood matted his fur where the wicked points dug into his skin, streaking the pale vines like bloodstained marble.

"Bri, do you trust me?"

"I do." I said softly, forcing myself to meet his gaze. I opened my hand and let the slender length of steel slip from my fingers even as one of the changed vines reached for me.

"I'm sorry," he whispered, shaking as he fought to stay himself while the presence flooding his body continued to wrestle for control.

I cupped his cheek, watching the milky light fill his eyes again. Letting my hand fall, I offered him a trembling smile. "I love you," I replied, as if it was the only thing that mattered.

Maybe in that moment, it was.

Adam shuddered—and then he was all around me, his mouth a sudden, hot shock of sensation at the crook of my neck.

In the mountains, he'd always stopped before he drew blood. This time, his teeth pierced my skin, and something wild and honeyed passed from him to me, sinking into my bones. I gasped, every muscle pulling tight as I arched into him—and the world went white.

***

"Bri, wake up."

The low rumbling in my ear slowly pulled me out of the soothing darkness surrounding me. I sighed, my body buzzing with familiar magic.

Magic.

Adam's magic.

With a gasp, I sat up, my eyes snapping open. "A-Adam?" I cupped my cheek, and my fingers stumbled over smooth, unmarked skin. The stinging scratches were gone. I found the cords around my neck and followed them down to where my carved feather rested beside the hagstone. Safe. Adam moved into my line of sight, and I slumped with giddy relief. "I—Are you..."

"I'm okay," he mumbled, shying away from my outstretched hand.

"Adam—"

"Please, don't," he whispered, flinching when I grabbed his wrist anyway. "I can't...I don't..."

"Adam, it's okay." I lurched to my knees to throw my arms around his neck. "I'm okay. Please don't push me away. Kantor said..." I trailed off with a sigh, snuggling closer as Adam's arms slowly came to rest on my shoulders. "He said it would happen. That the magic here would be different, and you might lose control for a while."

"He...did?"

I nodded, slumping against his chest as my trembling muscles gave out. "What did you do to me, anyway?" I mumbled. Short fur tickled my nose, and I nuzzled the hot skin under my cheek. "I feel all...woozy."

Adam stiffened for a long minute before curling around me with a sigh. His thumb brushed over the tender spot on my neck, and I shivered at the answering pulse of magic. "It's...hard to explain, but this means you are mine to protect. That we're courting." He sounded more than a little sheepish as he pressed his cheek to the top of my head. "I wasn't sure it would work with you being human, but I didn't know what else to do. I'm sorry."

"S'okay," I slurred, humming as I breathed in the cedar musk of his skin. The thorny vines from earlier had vanished, though bits of greenery lingered at his shoulders and hips. Another sigh gusted over me, and he tucked his nose against my neck, his purr rumbling to life.

For nearly an hour, we sat like that while Adam's magic settled under my skin. Once I thought I might be able to walk without falling on my nose, I nudged him. "We need to get moving, or we'll be camping here."

He nodded and stood, setting me on my feet. I swayed, and Adam steadied me before he went to grab his clothes. After discovering he couldn't dismiss the vines clinging to him, Adam gave me the hoodie and tucked his t-shirt in his pocket.

"Will they change back?" I tied the hoodie around my waist, watching him examine the breadth of his larger antlers.

"I...don't know," he mumbled, exploring the new curves and points with careful fingers.

"Kantor is going to be ecstatic," I remarked with a shaky chuckle.

Adam growled and lowered his hands as he shot me a fond look. "You would think of that."

I giggled, still kind of tipsy. "Maybe he'll owe you a favor instead?"

He chuckled and pulled me into his arms to give my ear a playful nip. "Doubtful. Dragons aren't known for being generous."

"Mmm." I ran my hands through the thicker fur along his spine, tracing the vine tendrils I came across.

Carefully, Adam pried me off, catching my wrists with a shiver. "Bri..."

"Sorry," I said with a crooked smile. He let me go and cocked his head. Moving my necklace cords, he tugged my shirt collar down. "What?"

"I..." Adam frowned and traced his bite mark with gentle fingers. Flipping his hand over, he glanced from the glyph on his palm, to my neck.

"Adam, what's wrong?"

"Nothing's wrong. It's...strange."

I blinked and touched my neck. "Strange how?"

"It's glowing."

My eyes went wide, and I stumbled over to where my belongings lay in a small heap along the thorny wall of the thicket. Clay tools were in a jumbled mess on the mossy ground. My jacket was nowhere in sight, but aside from the fresh berry juice stains, my backpack appeared untouched. I dropped to my knees next to the worn bag and wrestled the zipper open to dig out a small mirror.

The spot *was* glowing—but subtly, with an opalescent glimmer.

"Let me see your hand," I whispered, staring at the sight in my mirror. Adam knelt, and I traced Kantor's glyph. It glowed, too, but in shades of blue and sea green instead of the green and gold of Adam's bite. While Kantor's resembled something I might find on ruins of Atlantis, Adam's bite mark mimicked a cascade of leaves, or feathers like my pendant, instead of the teeth marks I'd expected to find.

"That is strange," I mumbled, tapping the glyph on Adam's palm. "What does it mean?"

Adam frowned, closing his hand over my wandering fingers. "I don't—" He straightened, and his head snapped around, his ears swiveling to catch a sound I couldn't hear. "We need to go," he whispered, staring off into the distance, his ears twitching.

Stuffing the mirror back into the backpack along with my clay tools, I undid his hoodie from my waist. With a glance at the surrounding woods, I put it on in place of my missing jacket. Adam stood and reached for me. "Stay close."

I nodded, settling my backpack on my shoulders and latching onto his hand as he led the way out of the thicket. We followed a thin, silvery trail that wound through the massive trees around us. Adam seemed more focused on evading whatever we were running from than speed, but after I tripped on something for the fifth time, he crouched so I could clamber onto his back.

No longer constrained by my human limits, we took to the trees. I clung tight, closing my eyes against the leaps, sudden halts, and heart-stopping drops. Finally, he halted and patted my knee. "Bri, we can camp here."

I opened my eyes to find we were on the ground, a cave opening looming before us. "Is it safe?"

"I'm not sure," Adam admitted as I slid off his back. "The scents are all strange." He tested the air, his nostrils flaring. "Nothing has been here for a few days, but it's possible I could be..."

"Missing something?" I eyed a set of birdlike tracks in the soft dirt by my feet. Adam nodded with a sheepish smile, his gaze drifting to the mark on my neck. "We'll just be careful," I assured him and led the way into what was probably the only shelter for miles.

The cave was dry, if a bit chilly after the sunny warmth of the forest. Drifts of dead leaves and broken branches lay along the walls, but there weren't any signs this place could flood on us. With a little luck, we'd only stay for tonight.

"Is it safe enough to make a fire?" I asked when Adam pointed out a pile of deadfall along the rear wall of our shelter. Adam nodded, and I scrambled to help as he sorted it for the best pieces to get our fire going. Some of it was damp, but we found enough dry logs to start a small blaze.

"Heaven," I moaned, setting down my armful of damp wood near enough to dry in the fire's warmth and taking a seat as close as I dared.

I held my hands out and hummed happily as I watched the flames lick over the glowing pile of wood. The heat felt amazing on my icy hands and cheeks after digging through the back of the cave. I leaned closer, wincing when the hagstone twisted sideways and scraped across my breastbone. With a muttered curse, I pulled the neck of Adam's hoodie down and pushed Kantor's gift aside to check the damage.

"What is that?"

I froze, blinking up at Adam to find his focus on the palm-sized stone. "Kantor gave it to me."

Adam leaned closer for a better look. "A hagstone. This is why Kantor spoke to you?" He traced the opening in the piece of slate with a gentle claw tip.

"He said it was self-interest," I mumbled, resisting the urge to fidget. "He's worried you won't be able to drop your antlers if I'm in danger."

Adam froze for a minute, then straightened. "Oh..." He turned his hand over and touched the glyph. "You said he knew what would happen when we arrived in Underhill."

I nodded, and Adam sighed, shifting his gaze to his clawed fingertips. I scooted forward and caught a hold of his wrists, tugging his hands into my lap. "It's okay, Adam. From what Kantor said, it's normal—"

"Normal? Bri, nothing about what I am is *normal*," Adam cried, clenching his hands into fists and curling his lip in self-disgust. "I *hurt* you, Bri. I almost—"

"But you *didn't*, Adam," I said, soft and insistent. I released his wrists to grab two fistfuls of his mane and forced him to meet my gaze. "You *didn't* kill me. You *won*, Adam. You kept me safe in spite of everything that thing tried to make you do. I trust you with everything precious to me. You and no one else. That thing wasn't you. *You* could *never* hurt me, Adam."

"How can you be so sure?" he asked in a raw, broken whisper. "How can you know I won't lose control, or force you to—"

"Because I *know*, Adam! You have *always* protected me, even when I thought I didn't want you to." I gave his mane a sharp tug, angry tears filling my eyes at the disbelief and despair in his gaze. "You are not a monster, Adam. You never were. Please believe me. Don't let the real monsters who caged you and killed your mom win now that you're finally free! Dammit, Adam! Look where we are!"

I freed one hand and jabbed a pointed finger at the lush forest outside the cave entrance. "We made it to Underhill in spite of everything. Doesn't that count? Shouldn't that mean something?" I shivered and let him go. Swallowing a sob, I offered him a tearful, trembling smile. "And if it doesn't...shouldn't what we have be enough to make the difference? I love you, Adam. *All* of you. I don't care what you are, as long as you're with me. Please, don't give up now. *Please*."

He stared, shuddering as he traced the tear tracks painting my cheeks.

"Please," I whispered.

Slow and halting, Adam nodded. "I'll...I'll try," he whispered back, pulling me into his lap and crushing me close.

"You better," I mumbled into his chest, wiggling closer.

He held me tighter, like I was his only anchor in the storm as he shivered miserably, shaken and lost.

"I love you," I whispered again, just for good measure. Because I could. Because he needed to know he wasn't alone anymore. I'd tell him a thousand—a million times more and beyond if he needed me to. He was everything, and I never wanted him to doubt it again.

Something warm and broken fluttered over my shoulder and then his hands were tilting my face up so he could kiss me. His lips tasted of salt, and as the breeze shifted, I realized my shirt was damp from his tears. Seeking a way to comfort us both, I buried my hands in his mane.

Adam jerked and broke the kiss, his hands chasing mine. "Bri, don't—"

"Trust me?" I asked, giving him a sheepish smile and dragging my fingers through his mane in lieu of the brush buried in our pack.

He shivered, his ears flicking forward before flattening into the abundant fur. Slow and halting, he nodded. Humming, I drew his head down to rest on my shoulder. He sighed, nuzzling my neck before going still as I finger-combed tangles and bits of vegetation from his mane.

"Is this okay?" I asked and promptly swallowed a giggle when his rumbling purr answered me. A faint snort slipped past my guard, and a halfhearted growl interrupted his purr. I grinned at the rebuke, tucking my face against Adam's neck with a sigh. The sharp musk of cedar surrounded me, and I let my eyes drift closed. I was right where I was supposed to be.

Safe.

Chapter Twenty-Six

I was falling asleep when Adam stiffened and looked up. Confused, I blinked at him as he stared out the entrance, and his purr stuttered to a halt.

"What is it?" I whispered, my sleepiness melting away. I scrambled out of his lap and grabbed my backpack.

"I don't..." He cocked his head, ears twitching. "I don't know."

Together, we crept to the cave entrance and peered out. "Do you smell that?" I frowned and inhaled again. A strangely soothing musk teased my nose.

Adam nodded, taking a deep breath as he eyed the forest's edge. It was sweet, but not cloying, and held a strange undertone that made my skin prickle.

"Where is it coming from? It wasn't there earlier...was it?" I stepped past him as I sniffed.

"Bri, wait!"

"It's over here?" I turned toward a tumble of mossy boulders scattered halfway between us and the trees. Slender vines draped over them in webs of pale, silvery green. The smell grew stronger, and when I drifted closer, delicate purple flowers opened along the curling tendrils.

"Oh." I sighed, everything else fading into a distant echo as the flowers swiveled toward me like I was the sun. "They're beautiful," I slurred, reaching to touch them. Before I could, an arm circled my waist, yanking me back.

"Bri, can you hear me? Bri!"

I swayed and looked up with a frown. "Adam?"

His eyes widened as he searched my face, then turned toward the strange plants with a snarl. The flowers hissed, tiny eyes opening in the upper petals. They swayed threateningly, and something sharp glinted at their centers. The musk was overwhelming now. I took a deep breath, and the world around me melted into a dreamy haze as one flower lunged forward and spat a handful of barbs at us.

Adam roared, and a wave of magic hit me broadside. The hagstone around my neck flared to life and pushed back, the colliding forces knocking me to the ground. Several sharp pains pricked my legs as my head cleared in a dizzy rush. I shrank away with a gasp, and more barbs riddled the ground by my feet.

"Adam!"

"Get inside the cave!" he roared, swatting aside the next barrage with another surge of power. "Now!"

"I can't!" I cried, struggling to scoot back, the hagstone hot against my chest. "My legs won't move!"

Adam snatched me up and bolted for the dubious safety of the cave. Held tight in his arms, I screamed as more barbs peppered my useless legs, and another buried itself in his shoulder. Adam stumbled to his knees with a snarl, yanking out the barb with his teeth while he hunched over me.

Something grabbed my calf, and I screamed again when I was yanked from his arms. Adam reached for me, only to be stopped by more of the same vines wound about my leg. They whipped around him, binding his arms while new purple flowers budded and blossomed, unfurling petals to fire their barbs into his neck and shoulders.

"Adam!" I shrieked, struggling to free myself as he swayed and toppled. Our eyes met—and then a strange lassitude crept over me. I fought it hard, gasping Adam's name as his eyes closed, and the vines wrapped his limp form into a green cocoon.

More barbs sank into my legs, and I lost my fight with the darkness flooding my body. As it swept over me, a shadow separated from the blurred shapes surrounding us. It loomed over me, and a clawed hand pushed my hair aside to touch my neck.

"Adam," I whispered.

The world went black.

***

"What is a *human* doing in Underhill? How did she get past the Guardians?"

"That hagstone around her neck reeks of salt and old magicks. It's Kantor's doing, no doubt. Sea dragon mischief. He should never have been allowed guardianship of an Elemental Gate."

"I say we let the boy speak. Even a halfbreed has enough wit to make itself understood."

The voices were loud. The familiar rumbling tones teased me awake, prying me free of the sluggish mess my thoughts had become. I blinked blearily, the shapes of curling leaves and woven vines overhead swimming into focus. Moving was an effort, but I forced myself to sit up, tuning out the bickering voices as I looked around.

I was in a cage made of living plants. Beside me, just out of reach, was Adam, unconscious in a cage of his own.

We were in an antechamber at the far end of an enormous room. Gray, craggy stone walls alternated with whole, living trees, whose roots sank between the smooth, mossy stones making up the floor. Intricate designs covered the walls, some crisp and others worn smooth from countless centuries. Stone, wood—nothing had been spared. Abstract designs framed detailed scenes depicting the greenmen in various moments. Bartering with humans, drinking and dancing, raising children, and even creating these same carvings while life in the enclave swirled past them.

Dazed, I dragged my gaze upward to find the tree branches woven together to create a vaulted ceiling. Several large lights perched on the arching limbs in delicate cages of woven twigs and vines. Unlike the crystals I'd seen in Adam's den under the city, these were polished orbs of perfect, translucent stone. They glowed in their cradles like stars come to earth, brilliant and beautiful.

Swallowing thickly, I turned to Adam's cage while the voices around us grew more agitated. My mouth was dry when I called his name, and I choked, coughing. All conversation ceased, and I shrank back as every eye in the room turned my way.

There were so many—all clearly greenmen with their shaggy fur and vine-covered bodies. They were dressed to varying degrees in breeches, open tunics and vests, and loincloths made of intricately tooled leather and linen. At least one appeared to be clad in nothing but his own fur. Like Adam, none of them wore shoes of any kind.

Scattered among them were those whose forms were leaner and more graceful, their fur shorter and silkier than the wild abundance of the males. They could only be greenwomen, and several of them eyed me with thoughtful consideration. Proud lionesses assessing a house cat.

The large fae sat on tiers forming a semicircle with Adam and I at their center. Each outcropping appeared to be shaped from living stone rather than carved. It was as if they'd grown from the walls, their shapes reminding me of the shelf fungus found on fallen trees. Only a third of the tiers were occupied, but that was more than enough to set my pulse hammering in my throat.

A few of the greenmen shared Adam's dark coloring. Others were black, copper, deep gray, silvery white, and every earthen color in between. A male with brass-colored fur stepped closer. He crouched in front of me with a sharp-edged smile as cold as the icy fear filling my gut.

The greenman cocked his head, looking me over with a smug self-assurance. He flicked a thick braid woven with pale vine tendrils back over his shoulder. A sinuous tattoo of vines and tiny star-shaped flowers framed one of his violet eyes, spilling down his neck in tangled loops before disappearing along his shoulder. He was the only greenman here without even a hint of silver in his fur, and the rich color made for a startling contrast against his tanned skin. He wasn't wearing much, either. Only a pair of dark breeches that clung to him, slashed in several places to allow his fur to show.

"I caught them. I say the mortal is mine by right of that alone," he said in smooth, cultured tones out of place with his feral appearance.

He hummed, giving me another assessing look, his gaze coming to rest on the stone feather dangling below the hagstone around my neck. I shrank away, one trembling hand clutching my pendant. He glanced over at Adam before meeting my eyes with a faint frown. "Still, I wonder...how did a little mortal like you convince the Guardian of the Gate to let you through?"

"I-I—" I stammered, flinching when he leaned closer. He smelled like the flowers in the forest. The sweet musk tempered with the scent of the woods clung to him. It was oddly familiar, but I couldn't place it.

The greenman snorted, curling his lip as he grabbed for my arm. The cage rippled and opened for him, the thick, woody stems bending away as he hauled me out.

"No! Let me go!" I fought, twisting against the stranger's grip and failing to stop him even for a moment.

"Well?" he drawled, prying open my hands to peer at my palms before gripping my jaw and turning my face this way and that. "Dragons are rarely generous, though they are fond of taking you mortal females as lovers. And yet, you have no debt-glyph."

He paused, and something dark flashed across his face. The greenman cupped my chin and forced me to meet his eyes. "Did you bed him in exchange for passage?"

I flushed, anger replacing the fear. His thumb brushed my mouth. Without thinking, I bit him. He snarled, and pain exploded across my face as he backhanded me.

"Hold your temper, boy," another greenman scolded him, his tone sharp. The rest muttered among themselves and stared while I swayed, choking and coughing. A couple of the greenwomen nearest me hissed and snarled at the male who hit me, anger and disgust on their faces.

"Humans are quite frail, and this one is smaller than most," the other greenman continued once his fellow council members quieted. "Her arrival here is a matter for the council to discuss. The lass will answer to the elders of this enclave. Not you." The new speaker was older, dressed in loose breeches and an open tunic. An abundance of silvery hair lightened his copper fur to a pale pink against his dusky skin. He looked me over, searching for something. "Well, lass? What reason have you for coming Under-the-Hill with one of our kin?"

I shuddered and shook my head, stealing a quick glance at Adam's cage. He was waking up at last. His movements were sluggish, and he lifted his head like it was almost too heavy to move.

"Adam," I cried out, renewing my struggles. Blood dripped from my nose and lip to stain my shirt, and Adam's nostrils flared. His head snapped up, the grogginess vanishing when he focused on the greenman with my blood on his knuckles.

"Let. Her. Go," Adam bit out as he stood, growing steadier with every passing moment.

"You have no rights here, yet, halfbreed…and she is not your concern," my captor proclaimed with a sneer. "I captured her, and I say the right is mine. As *she* will be mine. Be silent and know your place, or I will teach it to you."

Red sparks flared in Adam's eyes. My captor hauled me closer with a smirk, and Adam roared, his magic exploding outward in a rush of verdant light.

I was shoved aside as Adam's cage and mine both unraveled with a rustling sigh. Adam lunged forward, and the strange male met him in a crash of tangled limbs just as a firm grip hauled me to my feet.

I struggled against the new greenman, yanking at his hand on my arm. "Leave me alone—"

Suddenly, Adam was *there*.

With a snarl, he slammed into the one holding me, forcing the stranger to let me go. Gathering me in his arms, Adam backed away until he crouched between the remains of the cages.

The greenman he'd blindsided only blinked at us, rubbing a set of shallow claw marks on his arm with a bemused look. The one who had hit me wasn't so blasé. He lunged for us both, and Adam swatted him down with a flare of magic to dwarf all the ones he'd used before. Vines of green light knocked the snarling greenman back several feet, pinning him to the ground in a sprawl while he spat curses and threats.

I huddled beneath Adam as he roared at the stranger. The structure sheltering the whole gathering shook with his fury, the faerie lights dancing in their holders as the branches swayed. Adam crouched lower, almost hiding me from view.

"Are you okay?" Adam growled, glaring at the other male who shook off Adam's magic and struggled to his feet with a snarl.

"Yes," I whispered, burying my face against his neck for a moment and savoring the familiar cedar musk that meant I was safe. For now, anyway.

Adam touched my cheek, and I looked up as a rumble of muttered voices rippled through the gathered greenmen.

"Foolish scut," snapped the copper elder, dropping from his ledge to land between us and the stranger. Curling his lip at him, the elder turned toward us as Adam sat back and settled me in his lap. "It is *not* your choice," he reminded our attacker, his gaze going to my necklace before settling on my neck. "You're blind as well as stupid. Cannae you see she's already marked?"

He brushed my hair from my neck, ignoring my flinch and Adam's warning rumble. His claws skirted the edge of Adam's mark. A mute testimony of our near miss after we found ourselves Under-the-Hill. My cheeks burned as the mark pulsed and hummed under my skin, but I endured the elder's chuckle and gentle prodding.

"What's your name, human?" he asked, an unmistakable slyness dripping from every word.

I hesitated. "What's yours?"

All around us, low chuckles mingled with gasps of outrage and a few snarls. He flashed a roguish grin, showing teeth sharper than Adam's. "You may call me Oldest, lass. Well? What should we call you?"

What, indeed. My birth name would give them power over me if the legends were true. Names were important here.

The cool weight of my necklaces drew my gaze downward, and Chris's voice echoed briefly through my head. Brightfeather scum, he'd said to me. As if it should've meant something. I stared at the carved labradorite feather glowing against the dark purple of my shirt, and a flush of rightness washed over me. I straightened and met Oldest's gaze. One hand went to the stone feather around my neck.

"Bri Brightfeather," I said, my voice soft and firm.

"Impossible!" roared someone in the crowd of Elders. "A human cannot claim a clan name! How dare she—"

"Enough!" Oldest snarled back, and silence reigned for the first time since I woke up. He eyed us both with an odd spark on his gold eyes. "It dinnae harm my clan to name a human, but they are right, lass. You cannae claim it as your own." His bright gaze skimmed over me, lingering on my pale skin and black hair as a mischievous light warmed his gold eyes. "Methinks 'Bri' will do well enough for now, lass."

I nodded, my cheeks warming at his knowing grin.

With an amused huff, Oldest turned to Adam. "Your strength and control are impressive for a halfling, boy. Who taught you the magic of the greenmen?"

"No one," Adam rumbled, his grip on my waist tense.

"Show us your glamourie," demanded a female elder with a magnificent mane that hung past her hips and curled around her shoulders. Silver-streaked black fur gleamed as she leaned forward on her perch to give Adam a measuring look before shooting Oldest an exasperated glare.

Oldest ignored her and circled us, grabbing Adam's wrist to examine Kantor's glyph on his palm. Adam hesitated as Oldest released him and closed his eyes. Green sparks bloomed and faded, and his features shifted. The black-furred elder sat back with a frown. "You appear to have the basic knowledge."

"My mother taught me what she could before she...died." Adam glanced down at me, and I offered him a wan smile. He traced the curve of my cheek, returning my smile though the sad memory dimmed his dark eyes, and continued. "I don't know much, but she gave me what I needed to survive among humans. I can't hold the illusion for longer than a few hours, though."

Yet another of the gathered elders—this one a male with startling white fur and pale skin—leaned forward with a huff as Adam let his glamourie drop. His pale blue eyes were cloudy and unfocused. He was blind.

"I sense a difficulty with your magicks," he drawled in a creaky, dry voice, his nostrils flaring. "They do not heed you as they should. I assume the mortal is the cause of that, yes?"

I flinched and shrank against Adam as I became the subject of sudden scrutiny from several of the predatory fae. It was like being a fat cow in a pack of wolves. I shuddered, and Adam's grip tightened.

"Bri is mine," he warned, tucking me closer. A growl threaded his words and his red-sparked gaze swept the room. To our left, a group of three females all sharing the same ledge grinned at him, returning his warning look with a mischievous invitation that made me flush.

Oldest chuckled. "Peace, boy. We dinnae have interest in taking yon female from you unless you prove unworthy of her. 'Tis a female's right to be wooed by those she chooses, even a mortal such as her."

The elder paused and pushed my hair back, baring Adam's bite mark once again. This time, the whole room took notice. Murmurs and rumbling whispers started up at the sight of the feathery pattern. I tilted my head, resting my forehead on Adam's shoulder as I let them all stare their fill.

A sly grin from Oldest rewarded my patience as hissed arguments and more placid discussions continued. "You have granted her the mark of a female being courted, but she cannae return it, and the bond has yet to be formed. She may choose another, if she wishes," he said at last when talk began to die down. "Females are a tricksy lot, boy. This glyph is incomplete and will remain so until she welcomes you into her bed."

I squeaked and jerked away, my face hot. Oldest chuckled, then addressed the other elders in the council chamber.

"My brothers and sisters, if you do not object, I will bear the burden of our kin and his mortal. Give them over to me, and I will ensure they dinnae cause mischief while their fate is decided. This is not a concern to be weighed by a single council."

The low rumble of voices answering his suggestion almost sounded sulky. I looked away, a flicker of movement drawing my attention to the massive archway at the other end of the room. A mix of younger greenmen and greenwomen lingered there, watching me with more than idle curiosity. My stomach clenched, and I turned back to the gathered elders. Adam spotted the group of young fae, his grip on my waist tightening. The council talked among themselves for another minute, then all seemed to reach an agreement.

"Very well," announced the white-furred fae, resting his blind gaze on Adam and I. "They are yours to mind until the other councils can convene at sunset."

He huffed and turned toward the strange male who remained crouched where he had been pinned earlier by Adam's magic. "You cubs may make yourselves useful," the elder snapped, raising his voice a hair. He beckoned to a pair of younger males among those watching everything from the archway. "Take *that* away before he does something regrettable."

Murmuring and frowning at the pair of us, the other elders left. A young copper female came forward to guide the white one from the hall, and a mismatched pair of males escorted our attacker out. The low growling tones around me blurred together into meaningless noise as I watched him go. Just before he went through the door, he stopped and looked back.

The venom-filled glare he pinned me with settled in my stomach like a leaden lump, and I turned away with a shudder.

Chapter Twenty-Seven

The great hall emptied quickly.

"Walk with me, boy," Oldest murmured once the last of the gawkers left. "Your lady as well. You must have many questions about your father's people."

"I...don't know." Adam stood, pulling me to my feet. "Do you know why it keeps happening?"

"Your magic escaping your control, or the lack of stamina maintaining your glamourie?" Oldest asked, raising a silvery brow. Adam looked away, and his ears flicked back, tension lacing his big frame. Oldest pursed his lips and nodded, his mouth twitching. He led us out through the great archway to a nearby alcove strewn with woven mats and leather cushions around a low wooden table.

Oldest motioned for us to sit as he claimed a massive cushion for himself. "The reason you find glamourie difficult, boy, is because you try too hard to create it." There was a ripple of light, and when it cleared, a wizened old man peered up at us. "Perhaps your mother's human blood limited her magic, but you should suffer no such hardship. Your father's heritage is stronger than you know."

His gaze slid to me, and an amused twinkle sparkled in his eyes as his glamourie dissolved in another flash of light. "As for your struggle with the human, it is simple. You want her. Therefore, your magic will attempt every opportunity to seduce her to you."

Heat slid across my cheeks, and Oldest nodded, a sly smile quirking his lips. "She seems willing enough without such measures. If she were not, you would find it fairly difficult to draw her in without intentionally trying to do so. Magic responds to belief and will, boy, but also hidden desires." Oldest pursed his lips and glanced at me again. "Or perhaps not so hidden."

"So, it's my fault," I said softly, my face hot as I stared at my hands.

A low chuckle pulled my attention back to Oldest. Amusement warmed his golden eyes as he gestured between the two of us. "Peace, lass. The blame dinnae lay with you. Human and Hind blood have always been a potent mix. 'Tis more that he is young and needs time to learn control. Most of our males his age are over a century from winning a mate of their own. Our females are few and demanding." He paused and cocked his head, eyeing me with renewed curiosity. "Humans normally find us frightening, lass."

"He saved me," I said, taking Adam's hand. "He was all alone...and I was, too."

Oldest hummed and nodded toward Adam's antlers. "And the gold?"

I blinked and looked up at Adam with a shy smile. "I didn't want it. I still don't. I only wanted a friend. In the end, he gave me something more precious anyway."

"You love him, yes?"

I straightened and lifted my chin, returning Oldest's amused twinkle with as much calm certainty as I could muster. "Yes," I affirmed, and Adam's purr rumbled and faded.

"Do you know what it means to love a greenman—or any fae?" Oldest asked me before turning to Adam. "And you—do you know what you have chosen in attempting the heart-bond with a human?" Adam fidgeted, and I bit my lip, confused by the undercurrent of his words.

"I see," Oldest murmured. "Human love is nothing like ours, lass. We are fae, and the fae do not change lightly. Not like your people. They resemble butterflies to us. Their lives are short, and they flit from one flower to another, from one love to the next."

He nodded toward Adam. "If you allow yon lad to finish his claim, you will be joined. His life will nurture yours, and your desires will be his. As his heartmate, you will be granted a voice among our people. If you refuse his suit, you cannae dwell with us. You will be cast out to find your own way in the Wilds or returned to your people. Do you understand, lass?"

"I do." I hesitated, and Adam's hand found its way into mine. "What if I accept him, but I can't find a place here?"

Oldest sighed, a sad smile twitching his lips. "I dinnae say there would be no place for you, but you must be certain of your choice. Once you know your heart and choose to sup with us, you cannae go back. Mortals who eat of our table may not leave again. If you try, Underhill will demand payment for the gift you consumed. Such a demand cannae be borne by mortal blood and bone."

"Someone once told me Underhill is alive and thinks." I glanced over at Adam as one hand grasped my pendant. "What if she won't let me stay? When we first arrived, she tried to make Adam kill me," I whispered, my knuckles white around my feather.

Oldest gave me a somber look, and I shivered, suddenly cold at the answer I saw in his gold eyes. "Rage and desire are twins in different dress, lass. Underhill is a fickle creature. Even to those she deems worthy of her favor. More than that, she wishes to protect her children from hunters and fortune-seekers alike. She is not fond of humans, and to raise her hand against you in such a test of will is not unknown to us. The lad did well to mark you as his intended. It may have saved your life."

I bobbed a jerky nod and peeled my fingers open to stare at the shimmering stone carving. Oldest sighed and tapped a gentle claw tip on the pendant. "It dinnae change the truth of choices you will face here. She may yet ask for your blood to feed the Hunt, and many would answer such a call. Tread carefully, lass. Your kind have caused her great pain in the past, and her memory is long."

I nodded and let go of my pendant as my head spun, and a thread of doubt wormed its way in. No matter which way I looked at it, making the wrong choice would hurt more than just me. This was forever with Adam, or the rest of my mortality without him. There would be no second chances.

Oldest huffed, eyeing me. "Good. None of your human caterwauling, lass. Tears weary me, and they cannae change anything. It is the bond you should worry over now. Either accept him fully or don't. While you decide, the council will grant you what safety we can." His sly smile returned, and he stood. "Perhaps a bit of privacy as well, hm?"

***

The set of rooms he brought us to was a far cry from the cave we took shelter in when we arrived in Underhill. It was dry and *warm*, with the sounds of trickling water echoing from the back. Rugged furs and sweet-smelling rushes covered a mossy stone floor much like that in the council chamber. A cozy alcove off to the side cradled a thick cushion heaped with furs and pillows. It resembled a nest some giant bird might leave behind. I resisted the urge to see if the furs were as plush as they looked.

"Rest," Oldest rumbled, a roguish grin cutting across his face. "Your belongings are there." He pointed to a nook beside the door. "If you need anything more, only ask. It will be provided if the council agrees and Underhill wills it so. A private word, boy?"

Adam nodded and glanced at me. I offered him a wan smile. "Go on. If we're really safe here, I'll be okay."

He sighed. "Okay."

I watched them go. As they crossed the threshold, Oldest waved one hand, and a shimmering glow eclipsed the opening.

Alone again.

"Dammit." I retrieved my things, checking to make sure my quilt was still there. It was, but my clay tools were gone, and someone had rifled through our stash of food. The jerky was missing, along with anything sweet, though the bag of trail mix was untouched. I nibbled on handfuls of dried fruit and nuts as I moved everything to the cushion-filled alcove before returning to inspect the magical barrier.

A gentle prod to the shimmer left me with stinging fingers. I was trapped until they came back. Busy hands would help pass the time. Grumbling to push aside the thread of panic nipping at my heart, I started unpacking. If I was stuck here for certain, I might as well make myself at home.

I spent the rest of the time poking through the main chamber's many chests and nooks, and exploring the adjoining rooms. Over the course of an hour, I found a simple bathroom, a small pantry filled with food and hung with extra furs, and a bathing room fed by what smelled like a natural hot spring.

"All this for unwelcome guests?" I trailed my fingers through the small waterfall at the rear of the pool. The water was crystal clear, and I could see straight to the sandy bottom. I itched to jump in and scrub off the past few days of worries and traveling. The memory of being watched in the council hall was enough to quell the impulse, though.

"Bri?"

I gasped and ran back to the main room. "Adam?" He was setting down a bundle of some sort when I reached him. I shivered and hugged him, the velvety skin of his bare chest hot on my cheek. "What took so long?" I asked as I let him go and turned to stare at the shimmering curtain eclipsing the entrance. "Why the barrier? Did he tell you?"

Adam paused, then sank into a tailor's seat on the mossy stone floor. "It's for our protection."

"We're in danger?" I crawled into his lap and burrowed into his warmth.

He sighed. "Not me. Only you." I craned my head back to give him a sharp look. For a minute, Adam just stared at me, one hand smoothing back my hair. "Fae don't have children as easily as humans," he said at last. "There's a chance one of the others would challenge me for you or try to stealing you away with magic."

"Excuse me?" I squeaked, a blush exploding across my face. "They want me for a-a *broodmare*?!"

"You're here and unclaimed," Adam mumbled, staring at the lock of my hair tangled in his claws. "There are old stories of human brides birthing fae children as long as they stay Under-the-Hill. Oldest says it's within their rights to make a bid for your hand."

"Unclaimed," I repeated slowly. "You mean because we haven't..." I trailed off when he glanced up, and his eyes sparked. Adam gave me a sheepish smile and nodded. "Oh, but I'm not—I mean, we're—I'm not for *sale*!"

"It's how they are, Bri. It doesn't mean we have to...I-I mean—"

I stopped him with a look, ignoring my burning cheeks as best I could. Suddenly Oldest's sly smiles and pointed comments about the big nest of furs and pillows made a lot more sense. "Enough, I get it. They're all literal-minded jerks."

Adam's quiet laugh echoed around us, and I offered him a shy smile. He pulled me closer and nuzzled my temple. "So, what do we do?" he whispered as I combed my fingers through the thick fur along his jaw.

"I-I don't suppose they have some kind of marriage ceremony here." A flutter of panic twisted my gut in spite of his nearness.

Adam went rigid, his heart hammering in my ear as we sat there, frozen. "Marriage?" He pulled away to stare at me, eyes wide.

"That's what accepting the bond is, right?" I reached up to touch his mark on my neck. "I don't have magic, and I can't mark you like you did me, but I can do this. Marriage is supposed to be forever, too, isn't it?" I bit my lip. "I don't want to go back, and I don't want to wander Underhill, either. Not without you. If you stay with your people, so do I."

"Bri, I...I marked you because I had no choice. You would've died if I hadn't," Adam admitted, reluctance thick in every word. He brushed his thumb along my cheek. "You don't have to—"

"I know, but you wanted to, didn't you?" I broke in, my heart thrumming against my ribs. I searched Adam's face for any trace of regret. "Well, what if I *want* to be yours and let everyone know you're mine? What if I simply want *you*?" The familiar sparks glinted in his dark eyes, and he looked away as I continued pleading my case, his claws digging into the thick moss covering the floor. "Adam, will you? Human marriages probably don't hold much weight here, but...will you finish the bond? Will you marry me, Adam?"

His breath caught at my words, and his eyes fluttered shut. Twisting around in his lap, I rose to my knees and threw my arms around his neck. Adam's mane was silken against my face, and I pressed my cheek to the abundant fur before pulling back just enough to whisper in one twitching, pointed ear. "I love you. I want to stay with you, here with your people. Please?"

Adam swallowed hard and nodded, his hands trembling as they cradled me. "You're sure?"

"Yes."

His grip tightened, and I gasped as he stood in a rush, carrying me to the tumble of fur and pillows. Setting me down, Adam pressed his forehead to mine with a soft sigh. "Wait for me?"

I nodded, butterflies filling my stomach.

He sat back to gaze at me with glowing eyes. "I'll be back as soon as I've spoken with Oldest, I promise."

"I'll be right here." I glanced at the furs piled around me and paused. "I-I mean—well, maybe not right here, but—"

"Bri..."

I looked up and gasped as his mouth captured mine with a low growl. Sharp teeth nipped my bottom lip as Adam crushed me close, and I melted into his kiss. The furs pressed against my back, and he broke away to hide his face against my neck, his harsh breathing warming my skin.

"I...I should go," he panted, his lips scraping over my stuttering pulse.

"Yeah..." I shivered, nuzzling the edge of his ear before he twitched it out of range with a shudder.

A breathless laugh fluttered along my collarbone, and Adam pulled away to gaze down at me with glowing, hungry eyes. For a long minute, he just stared, taking in the sight of me sprawled among the bedding and furs.

"Wait for me?" he asked again, his deep voice raw and husky.

"Always," I whispered, resisting the urge to pull Adam back down and damn the consequences. Some of it must've shown on my face. A faint smile quirked his lips, and he stood with a reluctant sigh.

"Okay." A last lingering look, and he slipped through the barrier.

Gone. I was alone. Fumbling with one of the plush furs, I pulled it around my shoulders and settled in to wait.

Chapter Twenty-Eight

"A handfasting?" I exchanged a puzzled look with Adam. "Isn't that supposed to be a human ceremony?"

Oldest chuckled. "Aye, lass. Where do you think the humans learned it from?"

We were tucked into the shallow alcove from before, just outside the council chamber. When Adam had returned, Oldest was with him. He'd whisked us away to wait while the council met to discuss our request.

"I—but then what changed?" Oldest raised a silvery brow, and I fought the urge to fidget. "Well, you said the fae don't change, but humans do." He nodded and pursed his lips, waiting. "Which means it must be different here."

"It is, lass," he said with a sly grin. "We dinnae just bind your hands with a pretty ribbon and say pretty words. You will each need to complete a task to prove your mettle...and then seal the bond."

"Oh," I squeaked, stealing a quick glance at Adam to find him watching me with a sheepish expression.

"Bri, we don't have to—"

"No!" I took a deep breath. "No, it's okay," I said, a little calmer this time. "This is how your people do this, right?"

Oldest chuckled. "You have spunk, lass. The last mortal fainted and had to be thrown into the lake." I couldn't help it. I clapped my hands over my mouth at the silly picture his words popped into my head. A muffled snort slipped out instead of the laughter, and Oldest grinned.

"You chose well, boy," he drawled as he settled back and clasped his hands over his belly. "She will fit in well here, in time."

"I hope so," I said with a shy smile. "Do you know what tasks we'll have to do?"

"No." He glanced at Adam. "If you were both fae, you would choose your tasks for one another. As you are not, the council will choose for you. They will not be impossible, and they will benefit your joining, but they will not be of your own choice. As your keeper, I cannae speak in the decision of what they will be."

"Will we be alone?" Adam asked, touching the edge of his hood.

Oldest had helped him banish the persistent vines before taking us to the council hall. His new antlers kept him from raising the hood, and we'd had to cut open the neckline a couple inches to allow for them, but it was reassuring to see him in his worn sweatshirt again. A bit of normalcy amidst the chaos.

"Yes and no." Oldest sighed, eyeing us both. "The council may allow you to ask for help or bring a companion. However, you cannae call upon one another."

"Fantastic," I muttered, leaning into Adam when his arm slipped around my waist.

"It'll be okay, Bri," he said with a faint smile and a gentle caress of his claws along the curve of my cheek. "We can do this."

I straightened, lifting my chin. "Yes, we can," I affirmed, returning his smile with one of my own.

"Forest lords spare me from courting cubs," grumbled Oldest after a second. Flustered, I forgot myself and glared at him. He tipped his head back and laughed, great guffaws as I froze, mortified. "Oh, aye," he wheezed past his laughter. "She'll do, boy. She'll do."

A young greenman with dark gray fur and ebon skin tapped the archway of our alcove. "They're ready to see you and the others." He spoke to Oldest, but his lanky form was tense, and he kept sneaking glances at me and Adam.

Oldest stood and gestured for him to lead the way with a sigh. Without a word, we followed the youngster into the council hall. It was packed. This time, the ledges the elders used were all occupied, and there were cushions scattered along the walls in the adjoining room, filled with watchers.

"We have considered your request," the white-furred elder began as soon as we stopped before the council, "and your right to settle here among us." His blind eyes went to me, and I forced myself to stand tall. He huffed before turning toward Adam. "You, lad, are welcome to take your place in your father's clan. If you wish to bind yourself to the mortal, it will be allowed. Provided you can prove yourself *capable* of keeping her."

The room erupted into noisy discussion. With a huff, the white-furred elder barked for silence. A few greenmen continued muttering among themselves. The black elder stood and glared about the room. Crossing her arms over her chest, she quieted the lingering whispers with a snarl.

"Marriage to a mortal is a serious matter," she snapped, eyeing us with a grumble. "If you are certain it is your desire, then you both will be given tasks and seven days to complete them." She shot Adam a disgruntled look. "Even if you succeed and she accepts your suit, you will still have the challenges to contend with, boy. What say you?"

Adam glanced down at me, and I nodded, my cheeks warming. He smiled before turning to face the council. "What do we need to do?"

The black elder waved to the white ancient, and the venerable greenman settled his blind gaze on us once again. "You, mortal...step forward." I obeyed, my legs somehow steady in spite of my heart trying to leap out of my chest. "Your task will be to seek Underhill's Heart and gain a mark of her favor. You are not limited as to a means or object, but it must be genuine. You may ask for aid from any fae you encounter during your journey once you leave our lands...but you must venture into the Heart itself alone. Do you understand?"

I nodded. "Yes, sir," I managed, my mouth dry as I clenched my hands into fists to hide their shaking. My nails bit into my palms, and I swallowed a wince.

The elder frowned. "Oldest's heartmate will advise you and ensure you're well equipped to accomplish your task. Prove you deserve a place among our people, and you will be welcome as one of us, child. Fail, and you will be dealt with as the council sees fit."

I shivered and raised my chin. "I understand."

After a long pause, he sighed and waved Adam forward while I retreated to stand beside Oldest. "Your task will be different, lad. You come to us not as a cub but as one who wishes to forge a bonding. Yet, you have never faced the trials our young males go through to prove themselves ready for such a thing. Therefore, your task will be twofold. First, you are to find your father's bones, that he may be laid to rest properly among us. Your second task is to seek a gift for your intended as proof of your suitability. What you choose, we leave to you. Do you accept these tasks?"

"I do," Adam rumbled, his hands curling into fists at the mention of his father.

"Good." The elder pointed toward Oldest. "As the head of your father's clan, he will teach you the magic you need for your tasks, but you will go alone. Listen well, for he will only be given a single day to teach you what you must know."

I gasped, my hands flying up to hide my gaping mouth. Oldest chuckled at the stunned look I gave him and nodded. "Aye, lass. 'Tis why the other elders allowed me to become your keeper. Family should mind family, after all."

I nodded, speechless as I searched his face for Adam's likeness and let the rest of the talk swirl past me unheard. "He is my great-great-grandson, lass. You won't find his face in mine," Oldest said gently, his golden eyes softening at my bewilderment. "I imagine he resembles his mother quite well."

"He doesn't really talk about her much, but he told me some stories," I whispered, swallowing back the sad memory. "He said she was beautiful."

"The fae love beautiful things," Oldest said softly, tapping the stone feather around my neck.

I hesitated and touched the feather. "Do you know what this is? Adam won't tell me. His mother had one, too."

Oldest's silvery brows shot up, and a mischievous smile grew. "'Tis a bonding token, lass. One that marks you as a female courted by one of my clan, a Brightfeather. It is usually given after a claiming."

"But we haven't—I mean, he never...do you think he knows?" I asked as I stared down at the beautiful stone pendant.

Oldest chuckled. "Do you?"

I smoothed my thumb over the carving. I'd been wearing the greenman equivalent of an engagement ring all this time. I thought about the first moment Adam saw me wearing it. "Yes," I mumbled, my face hot.

I tucked my pendant back into my shirt as a pale golden female joined us. She examined me with frank interest, plucking at the travel stains on my clothes and eyeing my worn sneakers. Her sea-green eyes warmed with amusement when she caught me staring at the tunic she wore. Stitched to emphasize her lean figure and slashed in several places to allow for her fur to flow freely, it created the illusion she was more naked than clothed. I squirmed at the mere idea of wearing something that bold in public and forced my gaze to her face.

"Hello, child." Her voice was rich and low, not unlike the rumbling tones of the males. "You may call me Treestar."

"I'm Bri." I glanced over at Adam as the elders finished speaking. He looked upset, and I tensed as his gaze met mine. "What did I miss?" I whispered when Oldest joined him. Treestar stopped me from following with a hand on my shoulder.

"Your tasks begin on the morrow at dawn. To be sure you are not tempted to aid one another, you must be separated until your tasks are complete."

"I don't even get to say goodbye?" I choked out, holding Adam's gaze. Oldest leaned close to tell him something.

Treestar sighed. "We can give you a moment, but not alone." Turning to her heartmate as the gathering broke up around us, she raised a pale brow and nodded towards Adam. Oldest eyed me and sighed, waving us over.

I flew into Adam's arms as soon as we drew near enough. He crushed me to him, nuzzling my cheek and whispering encouragement. "We can do this, Bri," he murmured, his lips brushing over my temple.

"I know," I replied with a trembling smile. "I just don't like being apart for so long." I shivered and pulled myself together, drawing him down into a heartfelt kiss. "I love you," I whispered against his lips as Oldest told us our time was up. "I'll come back to you, no matter what. I promise."

"I'll be waiting," Adam rumbled, a teasing smile almost hiding the tense worry in his eyes. With a last caress along my cheek, he let Oldest lead him away.

"Come, child," Treestar murmured, guiding me out of the council hall and past a group of lingering females who chattered at one another and eyed my worn clothes. "We must prepare you for your journey. Dawn will arrive soon enough."

After several twists and turns, we arrived at what I assumed were Treestar's personal chambers. Everything seemed to be chosen to complement her striking coloring. "You can rest here, child," she assured me when I stopped in the doorway, trying not to fidget.

"But aren't these rooms yours? What about my things—"

She cut me off with a low chuckle and knelt by a wooden chest beside the nest of sumptuous, creamy furs. "I no longer have a need for these chambers, child. My love and I keep them for guests or clan members visiting from our sister enclave on the mountain peaks. For now, they are yours. As for your belongings, they will be kept safe. Until your task is complete, you may not use anything but what you are given."

Out of the chest she produced a tunic and long leather vest. Eyeing my worn jeans, she added a pair of heavy breeches to the pile. "These were made for my human guise when I was a cub. They should suit you. You may keep your bonding token, but those unsuitable garments and your hagstone must remain here."

"I guess that means I'll need new shoes, too." I joined her with a sheepish smile and picked up the vest, admiring the vines and star flowers tooled all over the dark leather. Treestar chuckled, and I glanced up in time to catch a pair of matching leather knee boots. I toed off my sneakers and tried one on. The footwear was too big on me, but before I could say anything to Treestar, the leather shifted, and the boot shrank into a perfect fit. I shot Treestar a startled look, and she grinned, nodding. The other boot adjusted itself, too. I slid them off with some reluctance to set them beside the chest, draping the rest of the clothes over the closed lid.

"Now, eat and rest. Dawn is not far off," Treestar said once I finished, gesturing to a table by the door. A tray waited there, filled with roast meat and strange fruits. Tucked beside the meat sat several palm-sized rounds of unleavened bread.

I stared, my empty stomach churning. The trail mix had worn off a while ago, but this wasn't human food. I was playing by fae rules now.

"It's a bit plain," Treestar said with a faint smile, "but that is to be expected." She retrieved the tray and set it by the bed, eyeing the simple meal. "The young ones haven't ventured into the human world yet. Perhaps they fear poisoning you with rich foods?"

A weak laugh bubbled out, and I forced a smile.

Treestar patted my shoulder. "It's time to choose, child. This task will require much of you. You must bear up with nothing less than your whole self. Do you understand?"

I nodded. Treestar pursed her lips and plucked what looked like an apple from the fruit on the tray. If apples were purple and covered in gold bumps. She offered it to me but withdrew when I reached for it. "Once you partake of faerie, you cannot leave again."

"I understand." I swallowed hard and met Treestar's searching gaze with as much determination as I could muster. "I choose this, to stay in Underhill forever. I want Adam and whatever my choice brings us."

Treestar smiled, frank approval in her green eyes. She gave me the fruit and waited. I took a bite.

It was indescribable. A burst of flavor flooded my mouth, the perfect balance of sweet and tart exploding on my tongue. The flesh was seedless but crisp, with enough juice to slake my thirst a million times over. I swallowed hastily and shot Treestar a wide-eyed stare. She chuckled, smug as I devoured the fist-sized fruit.

"Eat. Rest. I will return when it's time."

"You won't...stay with me?" I asked in a small voice, rolling a velvety, black, egg-shaped fruit between my fingers.

She paused and combed her claws through my hair, her nostrils flaring as she took in my scent. Tipping my chin up until I was forced to meet her eyes, she gave me a searching look. "He kept you close, didn't he, child?"

I shrugged, my cheeks warming as Treestar sniffed me again. "Only recently, really...but...I don't want to be alone."

Her sea-colored eyes softened. She nodded and directed me to sit at the edge of the nest before I could explain further.

Setting the tray on a low table next to me, Treestar settled behind me, teasing tangles from my hair while I ate. She started singing when I finished, and I drifted off to gentle tugs on my scalp and her husky voice thrumming in my head. I woke once to find myself curled up in her arms like a baby, her low purr rumbling in my ear. Embarrassment washed over me, but her purr lulled me back to sleep before I could do anything about it.

Dawn found me perched on the edge of the nest of furs, eating a simple breakfast. Treestar insisted on brushing my hair, and now, her low purr rumbled in my ears while she tugged and twisted, braiding it into an ebony crown. When she finished, she helped me dress in the clothes she'd chosen yesterday, all the while keeping up a steady stream of information about what I might encounter and what to avoid during my travels.

Kindle no fires without permission, and pick no fruit, no matter how tempting. Eat only what I brought with me, and follow no lights but my own. The list went on and on. I knew I wouldn't be able to remember half of it. I tried, though.

"What if I fail?" I asked once she finished explaining how to strike a bargain with a fae without leaving myself indebted to them forever. Treestar's hands paused in the act of adjusting the leather vest. I looked up to see her raise one pale brow, and a brief smile twitched her lips.

"There were many elders who hoped to grant you an impossible task. One which would ensure your failure left you at the mercy of the council. However, the real power here belongs to her, child." She tugged the laces until the vest hugged my body. "The council must bow to the will of Underhill when she speaks, and she has made it known to them that she wishes to test you herself. Thus, your task for the elders is a simple thing, rather than an impossible feat." Treestar patted my shoulder, giving it a gentle squeeze. "Many humans have gone before you, seeking Underhill's Heart. You will not fail."

"What do you mean, 'made her will known?'" I asked as she continued to tie and tuck, checking the fit of my new clothes.

Treestar chuckled. "To gain a seat on the councils, you must be an elder with a bonded mate and the strength of will to bear her voice and presence without risking madness. All these make the burden easier, you see. When Oldest brought your request of marriage before the council, Herself spoke not through one elder, but through all of them. They cannot deny her decision."

I gaped at her, my eyes wide as I tried to imagine it. "Oh." At her gesture, I turned slowly and lowered my arms while she stepped back and looked me over. "Is that why some of the elders seemed unhappy?"

"It has been an age since a human dwelled here with us. They forget themselves, and she has reminded them of their place. Tread carefully, child. I will help you as I can, but *you* must complete this task."

"How do I do that?"

She adjusted my necklace until the stone feather hung over my chest, gleaming against the dark leather. "I cannot say, child. Every journey to seek her favor is different." Treestar paused. "Underhill lives, though not in the way you humans see it. She thinks, speaks, and knows...and feels. Finding her Heart will be simple. Follow the path Underhill shows you and do not stray. She wishes to see you, child."

"What if she changes her mind?"

Her thoughtful gaze became mischievous and sly. "You believe I seek to lead you false?"

I winced. "No, I just...I don't know. I don't think she likes me much." I glanced over at my hagstone resting on the folded pile of my human clothes. If only I could bring its protection with me. Treestar's gaze followed mine, and she gave my shoulder a gentle squeeze, calling my attention back to her. The soft look in her eyes teased loose the question at the heart of my unease. "Why would she want to see me, anyway? She tried to kill me."

"And you not only survived her anger but roused her curiosity," Treestar pointed out with a low chuckle. "You are unusual for a human, Bri. Even a Sighted one."

My cheeks burned even as a shy smile broke across my face. Treestar tapped my nose and picked up a belt hung with a weathered leather pouch.

With deft hands, she buckled it over the long vest. "This will help your journey. 'Tis what mortals once called a faerie bag. It has already been filled with food and healing herbs. Only think of what you need, then reach within to retrieve it."

I nodded and traced the curve of carved bone holding it closed. Catching my arm, Treestar held my hand up and slipped a bracelet of jade beads onto my wrist. "The passing of time here can be confusing for mortals. More so for those who travel alone. These will protect you from Underhill's whims, that time may not be stolen from you while you sleep."

I ran my thumb over the string of pale green beads. "What about stolen items?" I asked, remembering my missing jacket and how the forest had tried to take my backpack when we arrived.

Treestar hummed, handing me a long and thin shape bound with silk and leather. "Underhill does not steal from her children. Though these are gifts, anything of ours will not wander away without help. Even so, it would do you well to keep them close. Humans are not the only ones who thieve from their own kind."

I nodded and unwrapped her last gift. It was an old switchblade, worn smooth with age and handling. I pressed the button and stared at the thumb-length blade that popped out of the wood-and-copper handle. The steel probably wasn't as potent as Cold Iron, but it was still deadly to a fae. There was a slim sheath to carry it in, with a pair of straps I could use to fasten the whole thing to my wrist. Setting aside the wrappings, I buckled it on and tugged my sleeve down to hide it.

"All of these gifts have their limits, child. Remember that and use them well," Treestar warned me as I wiggled to settle the new weight of the pouch and knife. "Now, come. It is time."

***

We didn't go to the council chamber like I expected. Instead, Treestar led me through the heart of the greenman enclave to a small gate guarded by several youngsters who stared and whispered at the sight of me. Standing beside the gate itself was the white elder. His copper aide waited a few feet behind him.

"Ah, Treestar. You brought her, then?" he said in his dry, creaky voice, turning his blind gaze toward me.

"I did, Snowfire. She is ready to fulfill her task set by the council. Are you here to see her off?"

He huffed and gestured for his companion to open the gate. "More to assure the others of the council that the lad has not slipped her aid in the night. Foolish scuts, to trust our own kin so little."

"Adam would never do that," I said softly. "Neither would I. We want to do this right, and I won't ruin his chance to finally have a home where he doesn't have to hide."

Snowfire paused. "Is that so, mortal? Very well, then. Bring us proof of your sincerity. Find the Heart, gain your mark of favor, and return to lay it before the council."

I nodded, swallowing my nerves and straightening with a smile that trembled a little less. I could do this.

"Go, child," Treestar murmured when I looked back at her. With a nod to them both, I forced myself to step through the gate.

Chapter Twenty-Nine

I never thought the quiet rustles of the forest could be so unnerving.

The greenmen made their home at the foot of a mountain range thick with trees. Everything was mossy shadows and dappled sunlight scattered with jeweled colors from blossoms and berries. It was easy to get turned around. Paths twisted in on themselves and became dead-ends, and low branches dripped thorny vines that reached for me if I got too close. After nearly stumbling into a swamp of oozy mud, I quickly remembered not to trust the lights.

Especially when they hummed. The will-o'-wisps taunted me while I struggled through the brush, searching for the path Treestar had been sure I'd find. I gave up once evening fell, making camp under a drooping evergreen. Mindful of Treestar's warnings about fires, I ate some dried meat and flatbread from the faerie pouch. More than food hid in the bag's depths. To my relief, I unearthed a blanket just big enough to cover me. Whatever it was made with, the downy stuff was warmer than my old quilt.

I dozed off and on through the night, propped up against the trunk of my shelter. Every little burble and chirp jerked me awake. I only managed a few hours of fitful sleep before the weird song of the will-o'-wisps became too much to ignore.

Pests.

I glared at the bobbing lights. "Go away," I muttered as one drifted closer. It ignored me, circling the tiny lantern I'd found in my pouch.

Despite the will-o'-wisp trickery, I'd made good time. According to Treestar, the pale stone cairns a foot beyond my camp marked the border of greenman territory. The brief rest and bit of food had recharged me, but it was still dark.

The wisp circled the lantern again, chiming. I resisted the impulse to swat it. In spite of using a salve from the pouch, my hand still stung from the last one I'd batted away.

The fuzzy ball of light darted into the crystal globe of the lantern and back out. In again and out again. I glared at it. How was I supposed to light the empty lamp without matches or magic? It didn't have a wick, only a globe that opened when you twisted the top.

The wisp drifted toward the honey-speckled crumbs of my breakfast. I frowned, then gasped as an idea struck me. Swiping a glob of gooey crumbs, I smeared them inside the crystal globe and waited. The wisp drifted back over, and when it went in, I twisted the lantern closed with a grin.

"Caught you," I whispered as it rocketed about. It wasn't much light, but it would be enough until the sun rose higher. Thankfully, the glass also muted the humming just enough to make it bearable.

Picking up the lantern, I packed up my meager camp and set out. By the time the sun was high enough for me to release the wisp, I'd found a small stream to follow but no path.

"Maybe Treestar was wrong?" I wondered aloud as the brush forced me to wade in knee-deep water or lose my only guide in this dense woodland.

A giggle echoed around me. I froze, trying not to flinch when something slithered past my calf for the third time since getting in the water. Palming my switchblade, I scanned the woods surrounding me.

"Hello?" I whispered, shuffling forward again. My heart beat an uneven tattoo in my chest.

Another giggle—this time from downstream.

Mindful of the wisps' earlier trickery, I took my time following the sound. Whenever I paused to feel my way, the unknown creature in the water twined between my ankles. Twice, I had to stop to cut my legs free from bindings that burned when I touched them. Finally, the water level dropped to barely covering my toes, and my unseen watery tormentor left me alone. A rocky ledge loomed along one bank. Seated on its peak was a young girl in a colorful rag dress, who watched me with bright gold eyes.

I gave the fae a wide berth and clambered onto the opposite bank, relieved to finally be out of the water. I turned to peer up at her, my switchblade a reassuring weight in my hand. The fae giggled and cocked her head. Slightly out of focus, a pair of large black fox ears pricked forward, and a plumy tail waved behind her.

Is she a pooka? I wondered as she looked me over with a mischievous smile that rested uneasily with her seeming innocence.

She giggled again. "You're a human."

I nodded, glancing at her ears and tail. "Are you...I mean, you're a pooka, aren't you?"

She blinked and leaned forward with a wide grin showing more sharp teeth than her mouth should hold. My sense of unease grew, running icy fingers down my spine.

"Oooh!" She giggled and clapped. "You're a Sighted human. This will be fun!"

I started to back away when she yipped—and a sharp pinprick of pain lanced through my neck. I gasped, dropping my switchblade and fumbling at the spot as a familiar lassitude began to creep over me. A feathered dart fell from my numb fingers as I crumpled, and the world went black.

***

Everything hurt.

I groaned, blinking blearily at the rough planks inches from my nose. A small window hewn in the wall above me revealed swaying branches framed by a snippet of pale sky.

My hands and feet had been bound, but I could move a little. I tried wiggling and was rewarded with a shooting pain from hips to shoulders that told me I'd been laying like this for a long time. Too long, from the way I ached. Even turning my head sent pain crashing through me as whatever kept me from moving wore off. I managed to roll over and groaned when every muscle seized and spasmed in response.

"Oooh, she's awake, brother!" A pair of bright gold eyes filled my vision, and I jerked away, gasping with pain. The pooka sat back, giggling. "You slept for a long time. It was boring. Now, you'll play with us?"

"I-I...play?" I rasped as another pooka came into my line of sight.

He sniffed me and wrinkled his nose as his sister sat and pulled her tail into her lap. "She smells funny," he mumbled, cocking his head. His fox ears flicked back and forth.

"We were waiting for your lover to come get you, but he didn't show up, and now we're bored. You'll play with us," his sister declared, adjusting a ring of green beads around her tail.

"We're not...lovers..." I trailed off, staring at the bracelet. My bracelet. "H-how many—how long did I sleep?" I gasped out, struggling against the ties on my wrists and ankles.

"It's been three days," grumbled her brother, crossing his arms and leaning against the open doorway.

Piles of random items lay scattered across the small room like it was some kind of magpie's nest. Past the pooka, I could see a low table and a hearth. Another window showed a view of the forest outside. The door beside it was open just enough to reveal a tantalizing glimpse of the river I had been following when they found me.

The pooka followed my gaze. With a scowl, he left the doorway to crouch by my head, cutting off the view to freedom. "This is stupid. Mina said you were Sighted and would be fun."

"You gave her too much night-sap," Mina snapped, her tail bristling around the bracelet.

Three days...I had two days left to find the Heart if I wanted to return by the seventh day. *I don't have time for this*, my mind screamed while the two pooka argued about who's fault my lack of fun was. I twisted and writhed, ignoring the rivulets of pain radiating from my cramping muscles.

"Stop that," they snapped, each grabbing an arm.

I slumped against their hold. "I can't stay," I pleaded, gasping as tears of pain overflowed. "I made a promise. You need to let me go. *Please*."

Silence.

"Will you come back and play with us if we let you go?" chirped Mina, tugging on the arm she held and sending spasms through my shoulder.

"I can try."

She let go of my arm and chirruped something at her brother.

"Not good enough." He untied me, and I managed to sit up. Lingering next to me, he eyed my feather pendant with a sly smile.

I clutched the carved stone, my knuckles going white. "You can't have it," I said, finding my defiance under the aches and pains.

When he pouted, Mina growled and swatted him. "Ren, that's not fun!"

"How about a bargain?" I blurted out before they started bickering again. They froze, then shot me twin mischievous looks, their gold eyes glowing.

"A bargain?" they asked in eerie unison.

"What will you give us for a boon?" Ren asked, eyeing me again.

"Don't you want to know what I need first?" I asked, confused.

Mina grinned. "You seek the Heart."

"H-how did you—" I snapped my mouth shut, flushed and flustered as they broke into twin peals of laughter.

"You just told us," she said between giggles, her gold eyes bright.

Her brother jabbed her and growled. "Mina!"

"What do you want?" I cut in before she could retaliate, wincing as I tried rubbing the aches from my legs. I felt like a wooden puppet, or like the tinman before Dorothy oiled him, stiff and clumsy.

"A game!" Mina chirped. At the same time, Ren said, "A gift," and pointed at my faerie bag.

My hand went to the leather pouch, and I glanced at my bracelet on Mina's tail. "Which one?"

"Both," they said together.

"Okay," I said slowly, thinking hard, "but this has everything I need for my journey. How will I make it to the Heart and back to where I need to be if I give it to you?"

"If Underhill wants you—" Mina chirped.

"—then she will provide for you," her brother finished.

"What do *you* want, mortal?" they asked together.

"A guide to the Heart that can get me there by dawn." I paused and glanced at my bracelet. The switchblade's sheath was missing from its place on my wrist. What else had they taken while I slept? "I want my things returned as well."

Mina pouted, and Ren shook his head. "No." He pointed to my knife dangling by a cord on the wall beside the door. "Iron is not welcome in the Heart."

"And my bracelet?"

He grinned and shrugged. "It's pretty."

Dammit. I growled, fed up with their idea of fun. "I don't have time to play a game right now," I said instead of the tart reply burning my tongue.

"A promise, then," Mina said with a pout. "Promise you will come back and play one of our games with us."

Faerie games didn't seem like something a human would survive. "What kind of game?" I asked warily as I stood with a slight wobble, my aching muscles complaining bitterly.

"A good game for humans. You mortals are too fragile for the best fun," Mina said with a grin.

Ren nodded, his sly smile widening into a grin when I blanched. "Greenmen are jealous spoilsports. Your lover would take our tails and ears if we broke you. Not fun for us and then we wouldn't have a playmate."

"Well, mortal?" Mina said, sidling up to pluck at my faerie bag.

Slow and halting, I removed the belt and held it up. "Fine. My pouch and everything in it with the promise I'll return when I can for the span of one mortal day to play a game with you. A game safe for fragile humans which will not cause me harm in any way. In exchange, you'll provide me a guide to bring me to the Heart before I lose another day. Deal?"

Mina pouted at the limits I set to her promised game, and right then, I knew she'd been hoping to keep me. Like a pet. Not even Adam could've saved me if I'd let her bind me to such a promise. Swallowing back the queasy feeling *that* thought inspired, I waited.

Suddenly wary, they eyed me, exchanging a strange opaque look. "You mustn't take anything from the pouch. We want all of it," they said in eerie unison.

"Agreed, but you have to swear on Underhill herself that you'll do as you promised," I said with a sharp nod, keeping my hope from my face as they eyed me again.

"We have a bargain, mortal," they said at last. "By blood and magic, and Underhill's will, we will guide you to her Heart before another day has passed." With savage grins, they each bit a finger and let the blood fall. Shooting my knife a wistful look, I held out my hand. The pooka twins grabbed my wrist, and I gritted my teeth as they incised a scrawling shape on my palm with sharp claws.

My hand began to burn like I'd dipped it in lye. I choked back a groan, waiting it out as my eyes watered, and my body screamed. Then, like blowing out a candle, the burning stopped, and their glyph faded into a subtle glow of gold and shadows.

"Well?" drawled Ren, a vulpine grin splitting his face as Mina bounced on her toes. I shivered and tossed him the pouch, rubbing my palm. He caught it and lashed it to his waist with a laugh. "Come," he said, grabbing my wrist and hauling me toward the door.

"This way!" Mina added, latching onto my other wrist and joining her brother's efforts.

Together, they hauled me from their den. I caught a glimpse of a small hut set into the side of a hill before they plunged into the woods, setting a pace I could barely keep up with.

Every muscle screamed bitter complaints, but it was run or be dragged. When at last I couldn't take another step, they became a pair of foxes big enough to ride and took turns carrying me. Their pooka magic kept me from falling off, but foxes—no matter how big—were not meant to be ridden. Not by a human. Their prominent spines left bruises, and their silky, wiry fur bit into my hands until they bled. When we finally stopped for good, I collapsed to the ground with a gasp.

"Are you broken?" A cold nose poked my neck, and a long tongue swiped my cheek.

I stumbled to my feet, drying my face on my sleeve and pushing them away. "I hurt too much to be dead," I croaked. Another nudge from a cold nose, and I was snatched up by the back of my vest. I choked, grabbing the collar and struggling to breathe. My captor bounded and leapt—and dropped me.

A muffled shriek burst out of me as I plunged into a reed-rimmed pond. The touch of the cold water was like knives on my aching body, and I gasped, choking on a mouthful of water before floundering to the shallows. I groaned, slumping onto the pebbled shore.

Nimble fingers tugged at my clothes, and I squeaked when my vest was whisked away. "H-hey!" I said, too exhausted and numb to stop them as they divested me of everything except Adam's pendant.

They giggled, using handfuls of bank sand to scrub me with a ferocity that left my skin pink and tender. I wrestled my underwear away from the inquisitive pooka once they finished and put them back on, blushing furiously. My bra was a shredded, muddy mess tangled in the reeds. I shivered and crossed my arms over my chest.

"Hold still!" Mina scolded as they dressed me in something pale and silky.

Delicate, fluttery sleeves brushed my elbows and left my shoulders bare, the hem pooling around my feet. Mina climbed onto Ren's shoulders with a giggle, making me turn and bend my head in order to thread flowers into my crown of braids.

"There," she declared at last. A tiny mirror found its way into my hands. Mina grinned as I stared at her handiwork. The pale purples, blues, and yellows of the tiny blossoms she had used glowed against my black hair, calling answering hues from the silky dress.

"Mortals are always so dirty," said Ren as Mina patted my hair and hopped down. The mirror vanished with a shimmering chime. "This is better."

"Right," I mumbled, my face growing hotter when I glanced down and realized the dress was transparent where it stuck to my wet skin.

Laughter bubbled from the pooka as they spun me around and pointed to a freestanding arch carved with flowers and vines.

"Through there," they said—once more in eerie unison. "She's waiting."

"Tha—okay." I swallowed my thanks before it jumped out. More laughter answered me, and I glanced back to see Mina trying on my clothes while Ren sifted through the pockets. "Fantastic," I mumbled and faced the arch.

A faint glow shimmered within, filling the doorway and growing stronger at my approach. "I can do this," I whispered, cupping my hand over Adam's mark before shifting to cradle my pendant.

Taking a deep breath to steady my pounding heart, I drew myself up and stepped into the light.

Chapter Thirty

Light.

Everything was light, rippling from one color to the next. It was like being inside a diamond. One whose hard-edged brilliance was softened with a pale, dream-like mist. A warm breeze ruffled the stray tendrils at the nape of my neck and flirted with the fluttery sleeves of my dress. Every breath tasted of honey and green things and a heady spice I couldn't name.

Hello, mortal child.

I gasped and spun. The light solidified, and a beautiful grove of lacey trees formed. A pale marble bench whispered into being, and there was a figure sitting on it.

"Hello," I whispered, frozen as I stared helplessly at the woman who could only be Underhill's avatar.

Thick red hair woven with pale, thorny vines fell around her in tangled waves. The wild tresses pooled on the bench before falling to brush her bare feet. Rich and vibrant, her hair glowed with shadows and light of its own as it draped over her body like a wedding veil.

She was clad in a dress so delicate, it was more mist than fabric, revealing more than it covered. It shifted and rustled in a breeze I couldn't feel, the wispy fabric catching on the thorny vines in her hair. The flawless cream of her porcelain skin was offset by a smattering of gold freckles that glittered as if newly minted.

Her eyes were…indescribable. First, they were green, then blue, or were they purple? Every time I thought I knew, the colors changed. Like jewels, they caught the light and returned it, the shifting hues mimicked by the knotted band on her brow. A diadem of opalescent light.

Come, hummed the soundless voice. The woman touched the empty space beside her. *Sit.*

Somehow, I made it to the bench and sank into a seat on the smooth stone. It was warm. Her gaze swept over me, lingering on Adam's mark and the stone feather around my neck. When her brilliant eyes met mine at last, it was like a punch to the gut.

I have been waiting for you, child. It has been centuries since a mortal dared defy my will.

I flushed, swallowing the urge to apologize. Instead, I straightened, matching her look for look. "Adam came here to be free," I said softly, bracing myself for her anger, and yet, hoping I'd chosen the right words. The right mix of bravery and respect. "I had to protect him."

My presence would have caused him no lasting harm. You are brave, though foolish to interfere.

I fell silent, keeping my thoughts behind my teeth while she looked me over again. Angering her was not my goal here. I needed a boon, and she only granted those to whomever she judged worthy. I couldn't afford anything less.

What do you seek in Underhill's Heart?

"A token," I said slowly, a faint prickle creeping across my skin. Her dress rustled around her, and eddies of magic brushed over me. They lapped at my presence with growing strength, leaving me lightheaded and dizzy. "A mark of your favor."

She gave me a long, measuring look, her beautiful face an expressionless mask. *Why? Isn't this one enough?* She tapped Adam's mark, and a prick of pain lanced from my neck to my hips.

I gasped and shook my head. "It's not for me. Not really. I-I mean, his people said I can't marry him without proof of your favor."

Ah...and you would marry a beast?

Anger burned away some of the magic pulling me under, and I straightened with a thin-lipped snarl. "Adam is *not* a beast. He's *mine*."

A laugh like bells and chimes echoed through me, and the woman gripped my chin to turn my face this way and that. Her touch burned worse than the magic surrounding us. I shuddered and fought to breathe under the weight of her regard.

It will not be easy, mortal child, she mused, letting me go and taking my hand. She traced the pooka's glyph, and I bit my lip as a sharp ache crept up my arm. *There are pleasures you cannot imagine...a great many wonders to be found among my children, but there is always a price.*

Her grip tightened, and sudden agony lit me from the inside out like an oil lamp with the wick cranked up. Tears like acid burned trails down my cheeks. Every muscle seized until my body arched, tugging against her grip. I fought for breath as she leaned closer to touch Adam's mark once again.

A deeper pain cut through me, and I screamed as a thin line of warmth spilled down my shoulder. Somehow, I found enough strength to reach up and grab her wrist. "N-no," I choked out. "You can't—"

But I could, mortal child. It is in my power to free him of you, of the pain you will bring him.

"What about what he wants?" I managed to force past my lips, my fingers digging into her wrist. It was like gripping silk over steel. She didn't even seem to notice me trying to stop her, and I gritted my teeth as her fingers dug deeper.

You assume he wants you, kin to one of the creatures who slew his mother? Her hand rose from my neck to touch my face. Bloody fingers scrawled a lacey shape on my brow in idle, looping gestures. *If he asked you to take your leave of him forever, would you accede to his wishes?*

The thought of leaving Adam wrenched at my heart. It hurt worse than the pain she inflicted, and I shivered. "Yes," I whispered, letting my hand drop as she leaned closer.

Why? She trailed a finger through the blood on my neck and touched it to her lips. With a low hum, she licked it clean.

"Because...it would be what he wanted," I said, my voice a broken, aching surrender as my gaze sought hers, pleading. "Adam is everything good in my life. He's everything, but real love doesn't force itself on others. Love must be free to choose, or it isn't really love. If he decided he hated me, I would go. Even if it meant I'd always be alone."

She tilted her head, and her indescribable eyes burned into mine. The pain she pulled from me ceased. I swayed, gasping as the world dimmed for a second. *Can your love weather the centuries by his side?*

"I don't know," I croaked as she let me go to cup my face in hands slick and warm with my blood, "but I want to try."

An aching, breathless moment stretched between us.

It is well, she intoned at last. *Take my blessing and go, but ware, daughter of the Above. Betray him—break his spirit—and I will not be pleased. Though the Wild Hunt slumbers, they will yet answer my call. You may have defied my will, but you would not escape from them, mortal as you are. They hunger for the chase of old, always, and the Hunter is a Power in his own right who knows nothing of human mercy.*

I nodded, and she smiled, leaning forward to press her lips to my brow. It burned like ice and fire. I gasped, fresh tears springing forth. The light around us grew brighter, and the grove began to unravel.

"Wait!" I cried as she faded. "I still need—"

A touch on my hair stilled my tongue, and I winced when the light swelled to an unbearable brightness. I shielded my eyes, but I could see her shadow through my hands. It was as if they'd been turned to glass.

I granted you my blessing. Have you forgotten your words of love so soon? Now go. Mortals may not linger here in my Heart, and your time is spent.

A rush of wind—a moment of weightlessness—and I fell to my knees outside the stone arch.

"Wait—" I spun around, and the words died on my tongue as the shimmering light winked out. I sank back, barely noticing the chill damp seeping through my dress.

I'd failed. I had her blessing to marry Adam but no token to show the council. Just like with my efforts to find the path Treestar insisted would guide me here, I'd fallen short.

"Dammit," I whispered, fighting down tears. A familiar sourness curdled my tongue, and I pushed it aside as I forced myself to my feet. Sitting in the mud and giving into panic and tears wouldn't change anything. I had a promise to keep, which meant going back...if only to say goodbye.

The tears broke through at the thought, and I let them. Mina and her brother were nowhere in sight when I stumbled to the pond to wash the drying smears of blood from my skin. My head pounded, and my body ached as I splashed water over my face and neck. I rubbed at the rusty streaks with a handful of bank sand, my tears a steady trickle.

I scrubbed until my skin was raw. As if the dull pain would wipe away my failure. Adam's mark was a sharper pain whenever my gritty fingers brushed its edges, like a shard of glass digging into my neck. I wanted to touch it, to make sure she really hadn't stolen it from me, but what was the point? I wouldn't be able to keep it, anyway.

Clean and damp, I lurched to my feet and shuffled towards the trees, ever mindful of my bare feet. Something had begun to bubble under my skin while I washed up, and now it nudged me along, tugging me in one particular direction.

A numb haze settled over me, and I gave in to the pull. For hours, I walked. Every time I paused, the tug sharpened as if it was a thread spooling itself up while it dragged me along. I didn't question it, following my uncanny guide first one way and then another. Bit by bit, the steady seep of tears slowed as I struggled through tangled brush and forded streams, until the only evidence I'd been crying lay in the pale salt crusts marking my cheeks.

Each step became a battle. My feet blistered and bled until even mossy ground felt like I trod on broken glass. The razor-blade ache shot up my legs with each step, only dulling slightly when I stopped to tear strips from the hem of my dress and wrap my feet. I ignored my rumbling stomach and growing exhaustion in favor of movement. The sunset burned through the trees around me as day bled into night, and still I walked. *Just one more step*, I told myself again and again as I limped along.

The moon was high above the trees by the time I passed the first pale cairn of stones marking the greenman territory. The memory of my old camp beckoned to me with a promise of fresh water and rest, but I didn't stop. If I did, I'd think about what I was returning to. If I did that, I couldn't be sure I'd be able to continue on.

Dawn found me stumbling through the massive archway of the council hall. Conversations and arguments faded around me, the effect rippling outward from the door as the gathered fae slowly noticed my presence.

Holding my head high, I'd only taken a few wobbly, painful steps toward the waiting elders when the room tilted. I gasped—then the ground rose up to smack my cheek, and the world went black.

***

"Wake up, child. You've slept long enough."

Something cold slid over my eyes and forehead. It eased my burning eyes and pounding head, and I sighed. A low chuckle in my ear and the sudden absence of the soothing coolness prodded me awake at last. I blinked blearily up at a familiar face.

Treestar smiled and tapped my nose. "You need to see the elders and show them your success if you wish it to count. Best not test their generosity further." A sly twinkle lit her green eyes. "It is said another wanderer now stands in the council hall, ready to speak to the elders about a task completed."

"Adam is back?" I rasped, flailing upright and swallowing my barbed confession as her words registered. *They don't know*, I realized, my stomach a queasy knot of nerves. *They can't tell I failed.*

Treestar nodded, giving me a measuring look as she helped me untangle myself and sit up. "Only just. He arrived last night. Oldest tells me he asked after you before he would deign to rest. He should be coming before the council soon. You have been summoned as well. Shall we show them all you yet live?"

I nodded, and Treestar paused, cocking her head and eyeing me with pursed lips. Puzzled, I glanced down. I still wore the silky dress the pooka put me in, though it was clean and mended somehow. The strips of fabric I'd torn from the hem and wrapped around my bloody and blistered feet were gone, along with the pain. Someone had healed my feet while I slept.

I smoothed a few stray hairs from my crown of braids and flushed as I gave my dress a closer look. The thin fabric was no longer transparent from damp skin, but the way it draped wasn't much better. In contrast, my skin was gray with dirt from my journey. Treestar watched me stand and wiggle my toes, amusement warming her green eyes.

"Hm, perhaps a bath first." She guided me into a small chamber off the main room with a firm hand on my shoulder.

Yet again, I was stripped by a fae and scrubbed pink. It was no less embarrassing than the first time. At least, this time, the water was warm, and I didn't have to fight to get my underwear back. Clean and presentable, I found myself waiting in a familiar alcove, trying not to fidget while I waited for the council's summons.

Treestar lounged beside me, watching me closely as I sifted through a bowl of fruit. After a stretch, Oldest joined us. I looked away from the two of them embracing, doing my best to ignore the sharp ache in my heart. I set down the lone peach I'd found and ran my hands over my faerie dress with a sigh. The thin silky fabric clung to me, warmed by my skin. Treestar had insisted I wear it just as I had been when I arrived. I'd never take my bras for granted again.

Finally, I couldn't take it anymore.

"I...I failed, you know," I said, my voice soft. One hand rose to touch Adam's mark and faltered before it could. The murmured conversation behind me died, and I glanced over my shoulder to flash them a wan, trembling smile. "She gave me her blessing, but I was supposed to bring a token of her favor back. What do I do?" Treestar touched my cheek, her green eyes full of understanding I didn't deserve. "They'll never believe I did it, and without the proof—"

"They will, lass. Dinnae fear that," Oldest rumbled. Treestar hummed her agreement, combing my hair with her claws. "She has left her mark on you, and token or nay, they cannae argue with her choice, lass. You are one of us now."

I bit my lip and nodded, fidgeting as their assurance eased some of the queasiness in my stomach. "Why aren't you with Adam? Aren't you—shouldn't you be—"

"He must come before the council alone, lass," Oldest said softly. "'Tis also his wish that I watch over you, to assure your safety."

"Oh," I mumbled, sinking back into the cushions. Treestar left off messing with my hair and squeezed my shoulder. I offered her a wobbly smile and picked up the peach again, forcing myself to take a bite. Maybe there was hope after all. Either way, I couldn't fall apart yet. I had to try.

By the time we were finally summoned, I'd found enough courage to hold myself up when we entered the hall. It was even more crowded than before but quiet, except for the usual low murmur of conversation. As we approached the stone ledges of the council, the crowd parted to reveal a familiar figure already standing before them.

My heart thudded against my ribs as Adam greeted the elders, his rumbling voice loosening something in my chest. The youngster who'd fetched us whispered something to Oldest and scurried away. I barely noticed his odd glance when he flitted past me. Everything in me focused on Adam. A faint itch crept over my skin as I drank in the sight of him. I shivered, rubbing my bare shoulders.

Snowfire stood and nodded to Adam. "Seven days have passed since you were given your task. Your journey in the Above was no simple romp, given what you were charged to do. In spite of the difficulties you encountered there, you have returned to us. Do you also bear that which you were sent to find?"

"I do," Adam replied, his deep voice rough with exhaustion. He removed first one, then a second bundle from where they'd been strapped to his shoulders. Both he laid before the council.

The grumpy black elder leaned forward with a raised brow, the silver streaks peppering her fur gleaming. "What's this? You were only tasked with finding your father's remains. That other is barely fae and is not welcome here."

Adam stiffened, his ears pinning back against his tangled mane. He laid one hand on the smaller of the two bundles. "This is all I could find of my mother's bones. I never knew my father. He died not long after I was born...but my mother loved him." His shoulders slumped, and a faint tremor rippled through him. "I want her to be laid to rest with him. It's my right to ask this," he added when the black elder looked like she would refuse his request.

A slim, golden stranger among the elders stood, cutting off her sister-elder with a sharp gesture. "Peace, Nightwake." She turned to Adam and nodded. "It is your right, cub. I knew your father, and he spoke well of your mother before he died." She paused, her expression growing somber. "Your request is granted...and well done."

Adam bowed his head briefly, tension bleeding away as he straightened and stepped away. Two youngsters came forward and carried the bundles away. As they left, the golden elder beckoned to me while the black elder continued to glower at Adam and mutter.

Straightening, I flinched as the faint itch under my skin became a sharp prickle, nipping the tops of my shoulders and scattering over my nose and cheeks. The worst of it settled on my brow and in Adam's mark on my neck, burning with a painful, searing ache. Tangling my fingers together, I forced myself to ignore it and stepped forward. Adam tensed and glanced my way.

He froze, eyes wide at the sight of me. His gaze swept me from head to toe, snagging on the drape of my dress over my hips and chest before meeting mine. I blushed, a small smile pushing through my nerves as Adam jerked his attention back to the council, but not before I'd caught a glimpse of sparks in his eyes.

"Hello," I said softly when I was close enough.

"Hello," Adam whispered back, his deep voice husky as he shot me a sidelong glance. His mark pulsed, and the spot on my brow answered it with a flood of warmth to wash away the strange prickle biting my skin. I shivered, suddenly feeling as if we were the only two people in the entire hall. I wanted to touch him. To bury my hands in his tangled mane, press my forehead to his, and let his presence wash everything away.

"You were sent to seek Underhill's Heart," the elder said, her lips twitching when we both jumped and turned to face the council with identical guilty expressions. "Did you find what you sought?"

"I did," I replied, my cheeks warming further as ice-blue eyes lingered on my silken dress. I felt naked standing before everyone in something so flimsy, and I forced myself not to fidget as I continued. "My journey brought me to the Heart, and I spoke to Underhill. I gained her blessing, but..." I trailed off and swallowed hard, flicking a quick glance at Adam before dropping my gaze to my toes. "She didn't give me anything to show you as a mark of favor."

"Didn't she now?"

I flinched, and my head shot back up.

Snowfire leaned forward, his blind gaze on me. "How odd that a Sighted human could be so blind." He nodded and waved to Adam. "He sees it, don't you, lad?"

Adam's gaze swept over me again, and he nodded, meeting my bewildered look with a soft smile. "I do," he said in a hushed voice full of warmth and wonder.

My face hot, I shook my head—and a flicker of light caught my eye. Craning my neck around, I glanced at my shoulder and gasped. Gold winked at me. Like the woman Underhill's essence had become to talk to me, the freckles speckling my shoulders glimmered with the pale gold of newly minted coins.

"Oh," I gasped, my hands going to my face to touch the spot where She'd kissed me. A raised shape on my brow met my fingers. I hesitated, then let one hand find Adam's mark. Like my forehead, faint ridges pressed back.

"It's still there," I whispered, tracing the spot over and over. I met Snowfire's clouded eyes with a dazed smile, an upwelling of hope making me weak in the knees. "So, I...did well?"

He nodded and gestured to the gathering filling the council chamber. "You did, little one. Be welcome amongst us as a sister. An honor no mortal has been graced with for quite some time."

Snowfire sat back as the golden elder grinned, her blue eyes sparkling. Nodding to the ancient, she turned to Adam, who had taken a faerie bag from his hoodie pocket. "Well now...I believe you have something for our new sister, hm?"

A whisper of teasing laughter rippled through the gathering around us. Adam reached into the pouch and drew out a bundle that should've been too big to come out of such a small bag, its bulk wrapped in brown paper. He held it out to me, a faint smile warming his dark eyes as he waited. I stepped closer and took the sweet-smelling gift, my eyes burning with unshed tears. Slowly, I ripped off the paper to reveal a familiar box stamped with Sherrie's bakery logo. The rich scents of butter and sugar spiked with cinnamon filled my nose, and I opened the box to discover it was overflowing with all my favorites. Stuffed croissants peeked out from behind a half dozen sweet rolls, and there was even a small loaf of Sherrie's cinnamon bread. Tucked into one corner was a smaller box, its wrapper speckled with crumbs.

With shaking hands, I cradled his gift to my chest and sniffed the smaller package. The sweet musk of peaches, vanilla, and rooibos leaves filled my nose, and I gasped. "How?"

"Sherrie gave me the box," Adam said, his voice soft as he touched the bundle with a shy smile. "She misses you and told me to make sure you're happy."

A watery laugh bubbled out. I closed the box, happy tears spilling over. "She saw you?"

He shook his head. "I wore a glamourie, but...somehow she knew me. She told me where to find the tea, too."

"Do you accept his suit, child?" boomed an elder, his rich brown fur only marked with silver at his jaw and temples.

Speechless, I nodded, and Snowfire stood with a sigh. "Then let those who would challenge his claim come forward."

I shot a startled look at Adam, who nodded with a wry twist to his lips. Oldest appeared and drew me to the side. Two greenmen set to work prying the smooth, mossy stones of the council chamber's floor from their settings to create a circle of bare ground. When they finished, several challengers formed a loose group near Adam. He stripped down to his jeans and handed his discarded clothes to another greenman for safekeeping. Some of the fae left while everything was being made ready, but most found seats and settled in to watch.

Oldest guided me to a spot beside Treestar on a low wooden bench beneath the council ledges. Here, we would have an uninterrupted view of the challenges. The thought made me queasy, but having to wait to find out what had happened would've been so much worse. Smoothing my dress over my knees, I fought the urge to fidget while Oldest eyed the group of challengers.

"Foolish cubs," he rumbled as he seated himself on my other side with an amused huff.

"What do you mean?" I asked, watching the younger males tussle and shout what were probably insults in their tongue.

He gestured to a group of females lounging across the way, talking quietly amongst themselves. "'Tis a display of their prowess and bravery, fighting such a stranger. They hope to impress the ones they plan to court and win their regard."

"And them?" I jerked my chin at the much smaller cluster of older males watching me closely.

Oldest chuckled. "They are the ones fighting to win *you*, lass. To court you without the boy interfering. 'Tis the female's choice in the end, but only those worthy may win the right to woo her."

I flushed. "Why can't I just choose Adam?"

"If he does well enough to please the council, you can," he said, raising a silvery brow as amusement warmed his golden eyes.

"How well does he need to do?" I whispered, glancing over to where Adam spoke with the elders of the three councils.

"Enough to keep you, child," Treestar murmured with a sly smile, tapping my cheek.

Well, that clarifies everything. I swallowed a growl of frustration.

"Have faith...he will do fine," Oldest murmured as Snowfire stood and barked for silence. Adam came forward, and one of the youngsters stepped into the cleared circle to face him.

The challenges had begun.

Chapter Thirty-One

Oldest was right. Out of all the challengers, only the older group gave Adam a serious fight.

The youngsters mostly showed off. All of them were scared of his antlers. Adam used their fear against them, feinting and driving them around the circle until they had enough and called forfeit. He was given a short rest between opponents, but by the time Adam faced the first of the serious challengers, his exhaustion had taken a toll on him. More assured in their skills than the youngsters, they took advantage of it and pushed his limits.

One brazen idiot let his self-confidence get the better of him. As they fought, he boasted about how Adam's antlers would make a fine prize. *Almost as fine a prize as me.* His arrogance was his undoing.

When Adam stumbled after a hefty blow, the greenman made a try for Adam's antlers. They wrestled for a long minute—then Adam wrenched free. The razor tip of one of the gold tines caught his opponent across the neck, and blood sprayed as the wound gaped wide.

The greenman stumbled back—and collapsed, leaving Adam covered in blood as he slumped into a crouch. Three challengers eyed Adam's dripping antlers and left while the remains were taken away.

I shuddered, queasy with nerves, and forced myself to watch as the challenges continued. Adam didn't always win. Most he fought to a standstill. One opponent beat him soundly, only to saunter over to the group of females and offer a token to a slim, raven beauty with flowers in her hair who'd eyed him the whole fight.

When Adam's final challenger stepped forward, I wanted to be sick. It was the greenman who'd yanked me from my cage and tried to claim me.

"Baen," Oldest muttered with a scowl. "He would wait until the last to challenge the boy."

"Is he good?" I whispered as Baen strode into the circle and faced off with Adam.

"He commands the leka vines, lass. 'Tis one of the few magicks allowed within the challenge circle." Oldest growled, eyeing the fae. Baen topped Adam by a head and was correspondingly broader, but he lacked Adam's muscle.

"Wait...are those the vines with the purple flowers? The ones with eyes?" I choked out.

Oldest nodded with a grimace, and Treestar explained. "It takes powerful magic to call and control the leka vines. They are strong and willful. He is not a Master, but he is skilled."

"Can Adam beat him?" I asked as strange magic rose in the challenge circle.

Oldest smirked. "Wait and see, lass."

The power crested, and Baen roared, leka vines erupting from the ground at his feet. With a gesture, he sent them tearing across the challenge circle.

Adam straightened and jumped back, shredding one branch when it twined around his wrist. Twisting to avoid another grasping vine, he looked up in time to spot Baen's attack as the snarling fae followed in the wake of the whipping tendrils.

Again and again, Baen used the leka to snag Adam's arms and legs while they fought, jerking him off balance at every opportunity. Several focused on his face, leaving thin cuts that bled profusely as they bid for a chance to snag his antlers, only to meet Adam's claws instead. Adam moved constantly, one eye always on the vines while he fended off Baen's attacks. It was almost...as if he waited for something.

"He's fast," I mumbled. Adam pivoted around Baen and landed a punch on his ribs, only to be smacked aside by the leka. Baen stumbled and whirled with a snarl.

Oldest grunted, his focus on the fight. "'Tis the Hind blood, lass. He cannae keep it up forever, though."

A leka flower appeared as Adam staggered into the main vine, unfurling its petals to hiss at him. He grunted, and one hand snapped out to rip the flower from the vine. The sentient plant gave an eerie shriek and flung Adam across the circle. He landed in a clumsy sprawl at Baen's feet.

Baen kicked Adam in the ribs with a vicious grin. "Foolish scut." He sneered as Adam rose, blood dripping from between his fingers. "You cannot stop the leka with crude strength."

Vines erupted from the ground by Adam's feet, whipping around him before he could escape. They wove themselves together, creating thick green cables that twined through his antlers with greedy abandon. More living ropes crept up his body and forced him to his knees, yanking his head back.

Adam tried using his claws to cut himself free, but he wasn't fast enough. His arms were pinned, and he jerked with a ragged gasp as his bloody fist was flattened against his thigh. A thick, woody spine jutted out the back of his hand, blood and sap oozing along his fingers to drip down his leg.

"Good lad," Oldest murmured, leaning forward with a sly grin. "Steady now."

A tremor rippled through Adam, and my stomach rolled as I watched the spine sink into his leg to vanish beneath his skin. "What was—"

"'Tis an old trick for those who wish to master the leka for a span and have not the time to take safer paths," Treestar whispered when Oldest cut me off with an abrupt gesture. "The toxins in the spine will grant him control while they linger in his blood. However, they will tax his strength, and he can ill afford that against one such as Baen."

In the challenge circle, Baen grabbed one of Adam's ears and twisted cruelly, smirking at Adam's roar of pain.

Treestar's grip on my shoulder tightened when I jerked forward, my gaze fixed on the fight. "Peace, child. This is the way of it. He risks a great deal for you, to do such a thing in the state he is in," she murmured as Baen let go and backhanded Adam.

Adam's head snapped back, blood dripping from his nose and mouth, painting his chin red. His dark eyes were glassy, and he slumped, coughing.

"Adam!" I gasped, lurching to my feet only to be yanked back down by Treestar.

"He must do this, lass," Oldest hissed. "Have faith in the one you chose."

I fought Treestar's grip, my heart in my throat as Adam gasped for breath and struggled against the tightening vines.

Baen turned to me with a sharp-edged grin, then hit Adam again, his claws raking fresh tracks down Adam's face from brow to chin. Blood splattered the vines, and Adam swayed, his breathing ragged. Baen curled one hand around his throat.

"Adam," I whispered, clutching my pendant. Baen's grip tightened, and Adam jerked in his hold, choking.

Baen bent close to whisper something as he started to etch a bloody mockery of his own tattoo into Adam's face—and thrust him away with a snarl as green light flared, shimmering over Adam's skin. The leka plant shrieked and let him go with an eerie wail, curling away with incredible haste, as if the light burned it.

The carved edges of my feather bit into my palm as Adam fell forward, gasping and choking, to vomit something thick and gray onto the bloody ground. Again and again, he heaved, each spasm bringing up another gush of smoking, putrid mess. He was shaking when he finally rid himself of the last of it and sat back, his movements sluggish. The purple flowers I'd been dreading appeared along the swaying vines, hissing. Adam spat and lurched to his feet.

Blood and sap coated Adam's skin in oozing tracks, and he was limping. The leg poisoned by the spine was swollen, and Adam pressed his palm to the deep puncture now leaking thick, milky fluid.

Baen's gaze snapped to the wound, and comprehension dawned in his violet eyes. Shooting Oldest a look of pure loathing and rage, Baen resumed his attacks with a roar, and Adam was forced to move. The leka waited, swaying and hissing as their master lashed out with claws and magic until Adam had no choice but to close with him or be driven from the circle.

Baen targeted Adam's bad leg at every opportunity. By the time they broke apart again a few moments later, Adam could barely walk.

"Surrender, mongrel," hissed Baen when Adam fell to his knees, panting as blood seeped from half a dozen fresh wounds. "Rescind your claim, and I will let you live. She will be *mine*."

Oldest snorted, and Treestar's hand on my shoulder gave a reassuring squeeze. I leaned into her touch, forcing down the thread of panic Baen's words inspired.

Adam's eyes reddened, and the ground beneath him rippled. With a snarl, he buried his claws in the blood-soaked soil. Magic surged, vines of light bursting from Adam's skin to root themselves in the ground beneath him. Baen lunged forward—and Adam swatted him out of the air with a reckless explosion of power that shredded the flowers swiveling toward him.

The twitching remains of the leka flowers writhed and keened as Adam turned to the battered vines themselves. The red glow in his eyes pulsed brighter, and he growled. The plants squirmed and whipped themselves around their former master while Baen roared and thrashed.

Spitting out a mouthful of blood, Adam lurched to his feet as the leka dragged their new captive closer. He grabbed Baen by his throat and bared his teeth in a reddened snarl, blood seeping from his claws digging into Baen's neck. "Bri is *mine*. If you ever touch her again, I'll kill you."

Baen bared his teeth in return. "This isn't over, yet, halfbreed."

"Forfeit," Adam snapped, tightening his grip as his eyes pulsed brighter. Baen spat, catching Adam across the face.

"You've lost, boy," Oldest called out, standing and crossing his arms over his chest. He raised his voice to be heard by all. "Give your forfeit. Our mortal sister is not yours to court or claim."

"He is right, Baen." Nightwake stood, the black furred elder breaking her sullen silence for the first time since the fight began. "This challenge is ended."

Baen roared—and Adam hit him hard enough to snap his head around. Baen went limp, and Adam let him fall. He swayed, and I ducked out of Treestar's grip, dashing over to throw my arms around Adam as he sank to his knees.

"Adam," I whispered, wiping away the blood and spit smeared across his face with a fold of my skirt.

"Bri," he murmured, nuzzling my cheek with a weary sigh.

"She's yours, lad. If she will still have you," Snowfire declared with a faint smile. Nightwake sat with a snort and an exasperated look for her fellow elder.

"I will," I replied with a grin.

He nodded and motioned for his aide as he turned to go. "Then once you have completed his claim, we will—"

"Wait," Adam rasped. He struggled to his feet and let me steady him when his bad leg refused to hold his weight.

"What now?" snapped Nightwake with a scowl.

"Bri is human," Adam continued, ignoring the jibe. "Some humans have their own customs. If the council allows, I would like to honor the ways of her family and wait until after the handfasting ceremony to seal my claim and forge the bond."

Snowfire paused, barking for silence as the room and elders all started talking at once. "Are you sure you want to risk that, lad? It will leave your intended vulnerable should another challenger come forth."

"Please," I said softly, my cheeks warm. "If it wouldn't be too much to ask, then I'd like to wait, too."

"Very well," Snowfire said after a brief discussion with his fellow council members. "In three days, we will gather in the grove to witness the binding of your lives. You may use the time to rest and recover. Is that all?"

We both nodded, and he turned away with a sigh, allowing the young copper female to guide him from the hall. One by one, the rest trickled out. I buried my face against Adam's chest, heedless of the blood and sap smeared across his skin and matting his fur. Silence fell at last, and someone touched my shoulder.

"Do you have to?" Adam rumbled, his arms around me tightening.

"It's for her protection as much as yours, boy," Oldest replied, his gruff voice gentle.

"I can protect her," Adam insisted. He tried to step away from me and nearly fell when his bad leg buckled. Oldest raised a silvery brow and lashed out as Adam straightened. His fist connected solidly with Adam's jaw, and Oldest caught him as he crumpled.

"Rest, boy," Oldest drawled, throwing Adam's limp form over his shoulder. "And spare me your tongue, lass," he said, giving me a pointed look. I flushed, and he chuckled. "I dinnae have the patience to argue or explain to a lovesick cub. Let Treestar tend you. You need rest of your own."

He waved me away and turned to go. "Three days. It is not long to wait, lass."

Chapter Thirty-Two

"He'll really be okay?" I asked as Treestar led me back to my temporary chambers.

"Aye, our people heal quickly. He just needs rest, child. Oldest would never have succeeded with such a stunt if your love hadn't been exhausted." Pausing at the door to the rooms she'd loaned me, Treestar gave me a fond smile. "He did well, child. You chose wisely. Now, go rest. I will return soon with something to eat. Go."

I nodded and ducked inside, smoothing my hands along my stomach. My dress was already clean of blood and leka sap. "Faerie clothes," I muttered, heading to the bed and plopping into the soft furs with a sigh. "Self-cleaning and self-repairing...and perpetually braless."

Pursing my lips, I got up to rummage through the chest Treestar had taken my questing clothes from. Maybe I could make some kind of breastband.

I found a likely swatch of material and tied it in place, pulling my dress back on with a relieved sigh. As I smoothed the silky material over my hips, I spotted my hagstone necklace in a little cubby above the chest, out of reach.

"There you are," I whispered with a grin. The chest made a perfect stepping stool, and I hopped down with the stone cradled against my stomach, careful not to drop the fragile slate. I settled it around my neck as the sound of footsteps reached me. Startled, I turned and froze.

"Adam?" I whispered as he ducked inside with a glance down the hall. "How did you— You're not supposed to be here."

"I know," he said, drawing closer with a shrug. He paused and glanced at the open doorway, and I blinked when a sparking, rippling barrier sprang up. He turned to me and chuckled. "I wanted to see you. Isn't that okay?"

"I..." I trailed off, squinting. He wasn't limping anymore, and something about the healing wounds on his face and chest didn't seem quite right. There was an elusive shimmer, appearing and vanishing where the glow from the faerie lights touched him. Was it from the barrier? "What about the council?" I asked, sudden unease curling through my gut as he strode toward me.

"What they don't know won't hurt them," he whispered, catching my waist and pulling me in for a rough kiss.

His scent is all wrong, I realized as he bit my bottom lip. He smelled like...flowers.

I jerked away, ducking out of his arms and stumbling back. "Wait, I—"

He grabbed me and threw me onto the bed of furs. I cried out, scooting away from the stranger. Icy fingers wrapped around my heart and squeezed.

"You're not Adam," I croaked past the rising panic, one hand slipping beneath the hagstone to grasp my feather pendant.

The imposter sneered and dropped the illusion. The strange shimmer dissolved, and I stared, unable to look away. Beneath the glamourie hid a face ravaged by magic and violence until it had become almost unrecognizable. Almost—because I did know this face.

"Baen."

With another ripple of magic, his tattoo changed.

No longer was it a graceful, subtly inked sprawl of vines and flowers across his face. Now, a raw tracery was etched into his skin as if he'd been branded. The wound trailed from the cloudy ruin of his left eye and down the side of his neck. There it formed a tangled knot of vines with an open flower in their center, stark against his tawny fur. The familiar shape tugged at me.

"Admiring your handiwork, mortal?" Baen spat, a snarl curling his lip as I stared at his ruined face, frozen. "I should kill you for what your lover did to my popet."

"Popet?" I croaked, horror slowly seeping in as realization dawned on me.

I stared at the blistered and bloodied lines of his tattoo. Without the glamourie adding the leaves and flowers to the twisted shape, every sinuous curl was an eerie echo of the scar Chris always dismissed as an annoying flaw. Baen's scent of musk and flowers filled my nose again, and I swallowed thickly. I was going to be sick. It was impossible. And yet...

"Chris was...w-was—"

"Yes," Baen drawled, leaning closer until he loomed over me. "He was never real." A smirk quirked his lips at my stunned stare, and he chuckled. "Your Chris was a farce, and one I quite enjoyed. Until your mongrel lover destroyed him."

"No," I choked out, my voice little more than a ragged whisper. "I saw the blood. His body—"

"Sidhe magic," he said absently, watching me inch away. "Our distant cousins wield a form of deeper magic your halfbreed would never unravel—callow and untrained halfwit that he is."

With a low growl, Baen grabbed my wrist. His claws dug into my skin until blood ran down my arm, and I was forced to let go of my pendant. Baen yanked the blood-smeared stone feather from my neck along with my hagstone and tossed them aside. The sharp retort of shattering slate accented the clatter of my pendant as he grabbed a handful of my hair, forcing me closer.

"Why?" I gasped. "Why me?"

Baen smiled, cold and cruel. "You are fae-touched, love," he said mockingly, his voice taking on the familiar cadence of Chris's mannerisms for a second. "Centuries ago, one of your ancestors dallied with a fae lover and birthed an abomination. Magic is in your blood, weak though it is."

He let go of my wrist to grasp my chin, his thumb pinching my bottom lip. "Truly, I wasn't sure at first. Many humans ape at having the Sight, but then you drank faerie wine from my popet's hand and still defied me."

With a casual flick, his claw split the skin. Baen grinned at my pained gasp, and I jerked against his hold. "Because of that spark, you will bear me fae children untainted by your human blood as long as you remain in Underhill." He dipped one finger in the beading blood, smearing it over Adam's mark on my neck.

"No," I whispered, hoarse and trembling. I shoved at his chest, the warm tickle of dripping blood itching my arm as I tried to free myself and failed. My mouth ached in tandem with my wrist, sharp and biting. The pain grounded me, and I clung to it like a lifeline even while fear wrapped icy fingers around my throat. "I would never—"

Baen's finger returned to my torn lip, cutting off my words as he pressed until my jaw ached and blood smeared down my chin. "Humans are fickle creatures, so easily turned. Your betrayal will come as no surprise to the council, and Underhill herself will deliver your punishment, even if they absolve you."

Baen's grip on my hair tightened. He ignored my struggles, adding another line over Adam's mark. Leaning closer, his lips brushed my ear, his voice a soft mockery of a lover revealing secrets.

"Do not fear. I will not allow your death. Not yet. While she is vengeful, Underhill will not kill you with my cubs in your belly. She'll only destroy your mind. Without her favor, and marked by betrayal, the old laws will make me your jailor. You will live on, an empty shell that will produce a clan for me. Your lover will be forced to watch it all, and he will be helpless to stop any of it. A fitting punishment for a beast who thought to steal what is mine by right of the hunt. Fight me if you wish. It will do you no good."

A low purr, smug and triumphant, answered the horrified mewl wrenched from me. Baen's weight settled across my legs and pinned me to the furs. A sharp ache shot through my neck as he drew more of his glyph over the gilded, feathery mark Adam had given me. The purr faded, and Baen tipped my chin up, kissing the curve of my throat. "Don't you see, love? You are already mine. You always were. Now, they will all know it."

His words hit me like a bucket of ice water. Fear and anger broke through the numb shell of horror, and I found my voice.

"No!" I twisted against his grip, tears springing to my eyes when his hand in my hair tightened with a cruel wrench. "I love Adam, and I would never want someone like you. I will never be yours!"

Baen hummed, and his free hand on my neck added one last smear of blood to the glyph trying to eat its way into my skin. "Never? We shall see. *Look at me, human.*"

I gagged as Baen's magic crested over me with a harsh, bitter flavor I couldn't—didn't—want to identify. Twisted desire wormed its way under my skin, violating my body and forcing it to betray me. I was going to be sick.

"No!" I screamed, clawing at him even as I burned and ached. He let go of my hair to pin my wrists with a low growl. I yanked against his hold, welcoming the fresh wave of pain from my injured wrist. Anything to drown out the pulse of magic flooding my body. "Let me go!"

"No, I don't think I will." Baen sat back and casually shredded my dress from shoulder to thigh with a harsh drag of claws. He bared my belly, a smug satisfaction in his eyes as he ran a careful claw tip over the skin below my navel in a quick scrawl. A wash of biting tingles flared in the wake of his touch. Languid warmth welled and sank into my hips, wringing a gasp from me.

"And now…" He pinned me beneath him, my struggles smearing blood across the pale furs. "Desire me, human," he hissed in my ear while I gasped for breath. "Your halfblood will never save you again."

He's right, I realized as Baen hooked his claws into the makeshift breastband beneath my ruined dress and began to pull it aside. Adam was badly hurt, and he didn't know where I was. If I waited for rescue, it would come too late. *It's up to me.* Swallowing back the bile, I let my body go pliant.

Baen paused, lowering his head to his glyph on my neck. I whimpered, unable to stop myself from jerking away, but he only laughed. "Good," Baen whispered into my skin. He let go of my breastband to run his claws over my hip. "That's the way, mortal."

Freeing my arms, he sent another pulse of his magic searing through his glyph, wringing a gasp out of me. I forced myself to just take it. Nauseated, I found myself caught between flinching away and leaning into his touch as his magic burrowed deeper and sent heat thudding through me. The pinpoints of gold that had replaced my freckles burned sullenly, like a hot iron pressed to my skin.

Adam, I thought and lunged forward. I sank my teeth into Baen's ear and clamped down until earthy-tasting blood flooded my tongue.

With a roar, Baen reared back, but I held on. Suddenly, I was flying through the air, crashing into the cave wall. I choked and gagged, spitting out my mouthful of flesh as I hunched where I'd fallen. My empty stomach heaved and rolled, and I fought the need to be sick.

"You filthy beast!" he roared, his ear a mangled, bloody mess. His magic darkened the air around him. "How dare you—"

"I am not *yours*," I rasped, stumbling to my feet and wary of bruises. Panic was a breath away, and I fought it down as my stomach roiled. I straightened, wiping his blood from my chin and cradling my injured wrist against my chest.

"Adam is mine, and I am his," I continued, as Baen stalked closer until he loomed over me. "Your magic won't work on me anymore."

He grabbed my arm, and his magic crested over me again with a bitter tartness, searing its way through the glyph he'd scrawled on my skin. It hurt. He wasn't being careful anymore. Not even a mockery of gentleness remained. Only power and pain, and enough magic to make my lungs burn.

I'd endured worse. I wouldn't again, though. Never again.

My eyes slipped closed, and I dove into my memories. I remembered late nights on my rooftop, hesitant kisses, and an underground room full of hope for home. Memories of s'mores and heat, of pain and finding our way back to one another. Adam's love hummed through me, bolstering my strength. I opened my eyes and glared up at Baen with all the defiance I could muster.

"Impossible," Baen hissed. He yanked me closer with a harsh shake. "No mere human—"

"Bri is no mere human," snarled a familiar voice. "She's *mine*."

My heart leapt as a sharp cedar musk reached me, and we both turned to see Adam standing right inside the doorway, Baen's magical barrier a crumple of fading silvery sparks behind him.

Adam limped closer, slow and stiff, his hooded sweatshirt dangling from one hand. Someone had tended to him in the short time we'd been apart. The rips in his blood-stained jeans showed an herb-stuffed bandage around his thigh, and the open wounds were already healing.

His dark eyes skimmed over me as Baen shoved me away, reddening when he came to my savaged wrist and the telling rent in the faerie silk of my dress.

I stumbled, then straightened. Holding my head high, I walked to Adam, shaking and ready to collapse out of sheer relief when I reached him. Adam thrust his hoodie at me, then paused, staring at the bloody scrawl of Baen's glyph on my neck. He met my gaze for a split second before he turned to Baen, his face an expressionless mask.

"How precious," Baen said with a sneer. "The mongrel has come for his pet."

"The council ruled in my favor, and she has made her choice," Adam rumbled, his eyes pulsing brighter. "You have no rights here, Baen. Bri is mine to protect."

"Is she now?" Baen growled. "We shall have to see about that. There aren't any elders to stop me this time, scut. I will have what is mine, even if I have to climb over your corpse to get it!"

Clutching Adam's worn sweatshirt to my chest, I backed away. Baen bared his teeth, and Adam limped forward to meet him. "Be careful," I whispered as they circled.

Baen roared—and Adam blindsided him in a rush of dark fur and glowing red eyes.

Ducking into a shallow nook, I pulled the hooded sweatshirt over my head and watched with a shudder. It was bloody and violent...and *right*. Despite his healing wounds and the exhaustion weighing him down, Adam moved like water around his opponent, like smoke. There and gone, hit and flow away.

Adam soon bled from a dozen fresh cuts, but Baen fared far worse. Enough blood matted his golden fur to transform the vibrant hue into a sickly brown. The vines threading his mane were tattered shreds. With each exchange of blows, Baen's attacks became ever more savage and reckless as he searched for a way to turn the tables on Adam.

"She was mine, and you stole her from me," Baen roared, stumbling when Adam dodged a hit aimed at his ribs. "I will have her back! No mongrel will stop me from claiming my rightful property!"

With a snarl, Adam lashed out and caught Baen across the face with a back-handed blow. Baen reeled, falling to his knees. He struggled to rise, but Adam pinned him to the stone floor. Baen cursed and twisted against his weight as Adam looked up and caught my gaze, a question in his eyes.

I straightened my shoulders and nodded—and it was over. Adam's claws slit Baen's neck from ear to ear, and blood sprayed in a wide arc. With a choked gurgle, Baen collapsed, his throat a ragged, red ruin.

"Adam," I whispered, scrambling over to crouch beside him as he slid off Baen's body and sank to his knees.

His fur was matted with blood, both Baen's and his own. Heedless of the mess and gore, I cupped his cheek as he came back to himself. Like he was waking from a bad dream.

A low, rumbling sigh rushed from him, and Adam pulled me into his arms, careful not to jar my wrist. "Are you—"

"Yes," I whispered, slumping against him. "I'm okay."

Another sigh and Adam folded around me, crushing me close. "Good."

Chapter Thirty-Three

The morning of the ceremony dawned clear and fair.

Treestar woke me and forced me to eat something before she dragged me off to where the other greenwomen waited. I'd spent the last three days learning as much about life in the enclave as they could stuff into me when I wasn't practicing for the handfasting. Experimenting with the pale, translucent clay Treestar found for me had filled my scraps of free time, steadying the worst of my nerves. I missed my pottery wheel and old tools, but Treestar assured me the greenman artisans could help me make new ones if I wished.

Treestar was always nearby now. I was just grateful I was allowed to use the bathroom alone. She hadn't left me once since they pried Adam and me apart again after Baen's attack. On the first night she stayed with me, I apologized. Treestar had only laughed and told me after several centuries of being bonded, her mate could survive a few nights without her.

The council wasn't very happy about how Baen had pulled off such a deception right under their noses. It turned out he'd made an ally among the Aos Sidhe. Striking a bargain with the sly, treacherous fae, he'd exchanged a fae-touched human child for their crafting of Chris—his popet, or faerie doll. Thankfully, the glyph he'd marked me with faded a few hours after he died, because the council was still arguing about whose fault it was. At least no one else would dare make a similar attempt at stealing me away. Not with the council in an uproar and out for blood.

Nightwake joined us as we finished eating lunch. The other greenwomen made room for her, peppering the black-furred elder with questions about the latest news from the council. She scolded them at first but relented after a few minutes of teasing and pouts. Apparently, despite the initial outrage, several elders thought using a doll to safely interact with the world Above was brilliant. She doubted they would get anywhere for a while, though. Only Aos Sidhe could work the magicks needed to create a popet of such quality. Their twisted bargains were best avoided, and the council had forbidden anyone to try until the matter was settled.

Nightwake left soon after that, and the other greenwomen moved on to teasing me about the ceremony to come, and...afterwards. They were relentless, my sudden blushes at the more salacious stories they shared provoking bursts of laughter. It had been a relief when evening finally drew near, and Treestar declared it was time to make me presentable.

"Oldest has been preparing a place for you and your intended to keep as your own, if it pleases you," Treestar told me while I bathed—this time without help. "Your love can show you the way once the ceremony has finished."

Adam had been helping Oldest as part of his lessons. My being attacked in a place of safety had set Adam on edge. It took a great deal of Oldest's time and attention to keep him in check. Hence the new magic lessons.

"I must say, the boy is stronger than we expected." She settled on the ledge bordering the natural hot spring. "Especially for a halfling." Treestar chuckled and nodded when I shot her a startled look, my hair full of soap suds. "Truth, child. It is all Oldest can do to keep apace with him. He learns quickly."

"He's had to," I said softly, dunking my hair to rinse it. "Humans aren't as unobservant as they used to be. Practically everyone can record things on their phones now. Even with glamourie, people notice oddities. From what little he's told me about his life after his mom died, it was learn fast or else."

Treestar nodded and held out a towel. I swam to the edge and climbed out. Amusement warmed her eyes at the way I wrapped it around myself almost before I cleared the water. I blushed and scurried over to the screen she'd set up when I had asked for a private place to change earlier. Between my time with the pooka and these past few days with Treestar, I'd learned the hard way that fae and human ideas of modesty were drastically different.

My requests over the past few days had been considered odd, but at least the greenmen indulged them. Now, I possessed a small chest of human-styled undergarments and clothes. Though some were fae-made, I suspected a department store somewhere was short on quite a bit of inventory. I wouldn't be wearing any of the human-made clothes today, though.

I changed quickly, wrapping a thin robe over simple undergarments of thick, buttery, pixie-woven silk. When I emerged more or less decent, I followed Treestar to take a seat on the edge of the bed.

Treestar had altered the silky faerie dress that now lay draped over the chest of clothes. It still left my shoulders bare, but now the fluttery sleeves brushed the ground when I walked. The dress had an empire waist, too. The bust and bands of my sleeves were adorned with a net of silk knots that somehow reminded me of climbing roses. Delicate stone beadwork only added to the impression. It was beautiful.

"This is really happening," I whispered to myself as Treestar produced several bottles from a smaller chest and sniffed each one before choosing two.

"It is, child. Are you afraid?"

"Not afraid, just...nervous, I guess," I admitted softly, blushing as she peeled off my robe and began rubbing a spicy, musky oil into my skin. Treestar chuckled, pouring a dollop into my hands and pointing to my breasts and belly before starting on my back. My face burned hotter, but I obeyed her silent order as I continued. "There's still so much I don't know. I don't want to disappoint him—"

"Child, he loves you, and he is quite male," she cut in with a tap on my shoulder. "Do what pleases you and he will also be pleased."

"Okay." I swallowed hard and fisted my oily hands in my lap as she circled me and began on my legs. "Do you—I mean, I..."

Treestar paused her ministrations and eyed me with a sly smile. "You will not offend me with your questions, child. Speak freely, hm?"

I gave her a jerky nod, glancing at my feather pendant's graceful shape. "I-I know some of the greenman lore, and I'm human, but I..." I hesitated, watching

Treestar turn my pale skin into something creamy with a porcelain glow. My gold freckles gleamed like precious jewels.

She paused and looked up, wiping the last of the oil off on her own skin as she retrieved the second bottle and sat behind me to untangle my wet hair. "Yes?"

I huffed and shoved my embarrassment aside as best I could. "What do you know about male Hinds?"

Treestar chuckled. "Golden Harts are extremely rare, but they do exist. At one time, they were worshiped by humans as gods. Like many reclusive fae, not much is known about them outside their own people. If you wish to seek answers, you must first find one to ask." She gave a satisfied hum. "Perhaps you will see one soon."

"Do you mean at the ceremony tonight?" I whispered, eyes wide. "Why? How would they even know to come?"

"All fae love gossip, child. It would be more shocking if they hadn't heard about the handfasting in time. They will not be the only fae to join the celebration. The hills are abuzz with excitement. As for the why...your love is their kin. Why not?"

I squirmed, earning a sharp tug and a swat. Dutifully, I straightened and held still as she finished rubbing something into my hair to turn it into a waterfall of warm black silk. "Once, the Harts would bed untouched human maidens to kindle fertility in the lands above. Even now, many of them see your kind as possible allies, despite hunters seeking their gold."

I flinched, and her hands stilled. "Does it matter if I'm not a...maiden?" I whispered, queasy. Silence. I winced and dropped my gaze to my toes, my face hot as shame curled through me.

Treestar smoothed my hair with her claws and came around to grip my chin, forcing me to meet her gaze. "Tell me." Her tone was firm and no nonsense, but her eyes were filled with a gentle sadness that pulled the story from me in halting, stuttered words.

When I finished, she sighed and touched my cheek. "You are strong. Here, we will honor you as you are, as a sister and beloved to one of our kin. Your past will not be known unless you wish it so."

"I'd rather it wasn't," I mumbled. "Adam already knows, and I'd just rather not."

"Then it will not," she assured me, her voice soft.

"Thank you," I whispered as she held out my faerie dress.

"You are one of us now," she said, as if that changed everything. Then again...maybe it did.

***

"There's so many." I stared, my eyes wide as I took it all in.

The grove buzzed with talk and magic. Fae of all sorts mingled with an abundance of greenmen and greenwomen. Several pooka darted through the crowd as they played some kind of game. One of them stopped just short of tripping over a blond boy with pointed ears and tattoos on his arms and shoulders. The boy laughed and shrank in a swirling flash of light, gaining wings and darting into the air.

The pooka yelped and leapt backward, careening off one of its fellows to go crashing into a group of dryads lounging beside three of the strangest oak trees I'd ever seen. And then one of the oak trees stood up and swiped at the giggling pooka. The mischievous fae called out a string of cheerful insults as it scrambled after its fellows. With a low rumble, the oak-man settled beside his brothers among the dryads.

The tree-men with their red-gold eyes were surprising enough, but there were also other, shyer fae who stayed on the fringes of the gathering, sticking to where the surrounding forest offered shade and concealment. Like the scattering of fauns and a solitary pair of brownies with their weathered skin and knowing black eyes.

True to Treestar's prediction earlier, a small group of Hinds lingered by the trees. Their large, dark eyes watching the swirling crowd, their sleek bodies and delicate antlers limned with the fading light. I turned away to see if I could spot Adam in the crush, but Treestar stopped me, pointing.

A larger shape further in the trees stepped forward. I froze as what could only be a Golden Hart stared back at me.

He was all flat, broad features and broad shoulders. His long, tangled mane hung to his hips, his body both sleek and heavy with muscle. Unlike the pale, flirty tunics the females wore, a loincloth of tooled leather and tight-woven linen was his only bit of clothing. His ears flicked forward as he looked me over, and I flushed as green and gold lights brightened his eyes. A faint smile quirked his lips, and he bowed his head for a moment, his great golden antlers flashing in the sun before he melted back into the trees.

I spun to stare up at Treestar, and she nodded, a smug tilt to her lips. "Wow," I whispered, turning back to see if I could glimpse him again.

A brilliant ripple of light and magic pulled my attention to the other end of the cleared space in time to see a massive scaled beast materialize in a rush of saltwater fire. Wings like stained glass crafted with blues and greens stretched overhead, and I gaped at them.

"A dragon?" I squeaked as Treestar followed my gaze.

A low chuckle drew my attention back to her, and she flashed me a vulpine grin. "A friend of yours, I believe. Shall we greet him?"

I spluttered, towed along behind her as she headed for the huge reptile while he furled his wings and settled into a tight coil.

"Kantor?!" I gasped when we halted beside the tumble of blue-green scales. There was a low rumble, and the coils shifted with a slight rasp. A familiar crown of ivory horns appeared. Kantor's massive head dwarfed me. He lowered it, and a gust of breath smelling of salt and wood smoke plastered my dress against my stomach and hips.

"Wow," I whispered while he eyed me with smug amusement in his golden gaze.

"Hello, mortal. I see you no longer wear my gift."

I nodded, my hands flying up to touch my neck. "It served its purpose," I quipped, imitating his haughty tone.

Treestar chuckled, and Kantor sighed as he shifted his bulk, uncoiling a bit to stretch. "Pert child," he drawled. "And what of the bargain? Is your lover taking good care of my prizes?"

A mischievous quirk to my lips kindled suspicion in his gold eyes. I nodded demurely, thinking of the surprise awaiting him. "He is."

Kantor's tail tip flipped back and forth. His head tilted toward me with a considering hum, and my playful confidence faltered. Kantor's eye loomed close, and *something* flickered in its depths. I leaned in, entranced.

"Enough," warned Treestar, breaking the strange haze with her sharp tone. "You are an honored guest, and we acknowledge your right to enter our lands, but do not overset yourself. She is ours now."

He gusted another sigh over me, and I flushed. The lingering magic from a second ago tingled through me, and Adam's mark pulsed in answer. "Yes, I suppose she is. I cannot leave my hoard unguarded for long, but many will want to know of this mortal girl with the brass to kindle a greenman's heart and follow him under-the-hill."

"Hoard?" I croaked, confused and a little dazed by what I'd glimpsed in his eye. It was like a dream, and if I could only remember...

Treestar's sudden grip on my shoulder jolted through me, and the faint memory crumbled to ash. A part of me mourned, while relief swamped me at the same time as she tapped my nose. "Focus, child. Yes, Kantor has a hoard like any other dragon. His is simply more unique than most."

"Indeed," Kantor said with a strange, smug lilt to his voice as he watched us. "The jewel of my collection is of course the Gate, but the lands around it are still precious to me."

"You own the hotel, don't you?" I asked, a faint wry smile on my lips. "That's how you knew Adam and I were there."

"But of course," he said with a sly chuckle. "Your lover's power was a beacon, and my wards rang for days after he entered them." Kantor paused, tilting his head. "The salt was a clever thought but ineffective against one such as myself with an affinity to the great mother sea. However, Sprig was quite vexed to find himself barred from one of my treasures, even so briefly. He despises waiting as much as I do."

"He's...not here?"

Kantor chuckled again. "Do you wish him to be?" I shook my head, my face hot at the thought of dealing with the lewd, aggravating Sprig today of all days.

A shadow eclipsed the westering sun, and we all glanced up to see a slim, opalescent dragon pivot and land down the hill. Kantor rose to his haunches with a rumble, the avarice in his eyes forcing me to bite back a nervous giggle. The new dragon eyed us before settling in for a thorough grooming, the distinctly feminine cast to her graceful head marking her gender as clear as a shout.

"If you please," Kantor murmured, uncoiling with a lazy flex of muscle, "I have other business to attend."

"Of course," Treestar replied tartly, catching my wrist and giving me a gentle tug. "This way, child."

"She's the real reason he came, isn't she?" I whispered with a grin as we left Kantor to his *business*. Treestar just smiled. I laughed, staying close on her heels as we threaded the crowd to reach a series of balanced stones arranged in a loose circle. I glanced around, and my stomach clenched. "Where's Adam?"

Treestar smiled. "He will be here, never fear. Oldest is testing some of what he has been teaching him. Let them have their fun, child."

"So...Adam's going to make an entrance?" I said when she nodded toward Oldest standing with the other elders of the councils. He glanced our way with a sly smile that warmed considerably once he shifted from me to Treestar. "I think he missed you," I squeaked, blushing at all the subtext in the heated look she gave him in return.

"Of course," she said with a teasing smile and a regal tilt of her chin. "Come."

Together, we took a place in the center of the ring of stones and— "Are those mushrooms?" I asked, spotting speckled caps of russet and ocher.

"'Tis a faerie ring, of course," Treestar said with a laugh.

A quick assessment of the clearing revealed we were actually inside several such rings, the last one bordering the entire open space. Faerie rings were said to grow where the faeries held their revels, born from the wild magic stirred when they danced. My lessons over the last few days hadn't mentioned faerie rings, but I already knew many of the human-known myths were true. Silk insulated magic, and iron was the bane of the fae and their gifts. It wasn't difficult to accept faerie rings as real.

I bit my lip and glanced at the corner of the clearing where several large barrels sat. More were added to the spot while I watched. Somehow, I doubted they were filled with spring water.

"Breathe, child. Not a one of us expects you to stay for the dances and drink," Treestar murmured, gripping my shoulders and spinning me around before pointing to the sun beginning to color the sky. "It is time."

I shivered, and she gave my shoulders a gentle squeeze before she stepped away. Adam was nowhere in sight, but as I scanned the crowd, a rush of warmth seared through his mark.

My hand flew up to cover it, and a tug echoed through me. I frowned, turning towards the pull and stuttering to a halt when a faint blur shimmered beside me, just out of reach. The world rippled with light, and Adam appeared with a soft rustle of magic, his glamourie melting away in a flurry of green sparks.

Oh my...

I stared, eyes wide as saucers as I took in this new side of him. He only wore a pair of dark breeches, and a tapestry of whorls and lines in earthy, jewel-like hues had been painted on his skin. The rich colors bled into his fur in places, each glimmering with magic.

Echoing some of the painted lines, green tendrils wove through his mane and circled his upper arms. Thicker vines draped over his shoulders and trailed down his back to frame his hips before twining around his thighs. There the plants stopped, the pale green vivid against the dark cloth of his breeches. The garment replacing his worn jeans was a couple shades darker than his skin and laced along the outside of each leg. From hip to knee, they fit him like a second skin before falling in loose folds over his feet. The outer seam glittered with stone beadwork.

The soft whisper of my name on his lips drew my gaze to his face where pale feathers banded with faint gold streaks trailed from his temples and behind his ears. Some were accented with labradorite, the beautiful stones shimmering with all the shades of earth and sky. When he cocked his head, my stunned gaze snapped to his antlers. The center point of each branch of gold was wrapped with strips of creamy leather from which dangled amber drops. Around his neck, he wore his mother's pendant.

"Hello," I whispered, a flush burning across my cheeks. Adam chuckled and stepped closer.

"It was Oldest's idea," he murmured as my gaze swept over him again, snagging on the streaks of color flowing along his chest and belly before jerking back to his face. "Do you...like it?"

My face burned hotter, and I nodded. A slow, sweet smile quirked his lips, and I smoothed my hands over the silk of my dress. The craving to touch him washed over me. It was stunning to see Adam so much in his element. It brought to mind the last time I'd seen him this free and wild. I licked my lips and tasted the smoky bite of a campfire and the rich sweetness of chocolate and marshmallows.

This is who he really is, I realized as he caught my wrist to press my hand to his face. I watched him take in my scent, and a faint shudder rippled through him. I swayed, another soft touch away from melting into a pile at his feet.

"Easy, now," Oldest warned with a sly wink when he joined Treestar a few feet away. Adam let me go. "Best save such things for later, hm?"

I squeaked, my face on fire. We were attracting sly looks and mutterings from some of the assembled fae. Adam glanced around and stepped away with a low rumble, his ears flicking back. He didn't even try to hide the sparks burning in his dark eyes when he glanced at me. My stomach flip-flopped as my flush grew to make my ears burn along with the rest of me.

Any further embarrassment was forestalled by the arrival of Snowfire. The venerable elder barked for silence and, like always, it was given without delay. I barely noticed when he began to speak, responding to his questions as if in a dream.

Treestar gave me a sharp nudge. I blinked and tore my gaze from Adam's to see her sly smile and raised brow. Straightening, I held out my hand to clasp Adam's. Snowfire huffed, and the ceremony continued as the first cord was tied in place. Red, like the blood I'd given to create it, it was proof of my willingness to give my life for his. My arm ached with a phantom twinge as Treestar secured the knot.

The next cord was a ribbon of pure magic. Adam closed his eyes with a sigh, and I gasped as a cord of green light spun itself into being, tendrils spiraling from Adam's face, chest and arms to weave it. Oldest stepped forward. I stared, my mouth slack as he guided it to twine around our joined hands, his careful gestures nudging it along.

Magic is their lifeblood. I swallowed, blinking back tears as the meaning of this cord, this promise, hit me. Its warmth tingled against my skin like the magic of the cloudy stone he'd given me. Protection. Promise. Life. Adam watched me with a faint smile on his lips, waiting. The smile I gave in return trembled, but the tears falling were happy ones, and I could tell he knew it.

One by one, four elders came forward to add a cord of their own, each marked in some way with their clan symbol. Sunbursts, mountain peaks set with a crescent moon, starflowers, and a snake eating its own tail all marked our joining, until only one cord remained.

A familiar, sweet musk was my only warning before Snowfire touched our clasped hands and leka vines snaked through the wrapped cords. My stomach clenched as writhing tendrils bound us tight until the only way to separate us would be cutting off a limb. Needle points of pain lanced my arm from fingertips to wrist, and I almost bit through my bottom lip when I spotted spiny roots burrowing into my skin.

One of those damned purple flowers budded and blossomed, unfurling delicate petals and opening its eyes with a faint rustle. Rearing up like a cobra, it turned to Adam. The leka vine swayed and hissed as the barbs in its center inched out in an unmistakable threat. Pain tightened Adam's mouth and pinned back his ears, but he held fast, waiting. The flower feinted toward his face, then retreated with a rasp of rough vines.

The queasy chill in my belly grew when the flower swiveled around to hiss at me instead. The roots dug deeper, and I swallowed a cry of pain, tears burning my eyes, but I followed Adam's example and endured. The leka's grip loosened as the pain worsened, and I knew it was testing me. All I had to do to stop the pain was pull away. Instead, I drew myself up and raised my chin. Staring it down, I forced myself to ignore my rolling stomach.

The flower's strange eyes blinked at me once, then closed. With a wriggle and a wrench, the barbed roots pulled free. I shivered, wincing as its grip shifted until it was no tighter or looser than the other cords. The flower lowered with a rustling sigh, draping itself over our clasped hands and stilling with a shudder.

Snowfire's sudden grip on my shoulder sent my heart thudding into my ribs. I remembered myself just in time as he raised our joined hands. "Lives are bound as hands are bound. Two are one," he declared.

The grove erupted into a clamor of roars, hisses, and undulating cries. I flushed, holding my hand up with Adam's and doing my best to ignore the ache of my wounds. Snowfire banished the leka vine and let us go with a nod. Treestar and Oldest came forward to free us. The elders' cords were wound into a bundle and tied with my lifeblood cord, the brilliant red now threaded with gold. Adam's cord had vanished.

Pins and needles radiated up my arm. The buzzing tingle echoed the sharper pains of the thousand tiny cuts from the leka roots as Treestar took the cords away for safekeeping. I hugged my arm to my chest, wincing.

"Here," Adam's voice rumbled in my ear as he took my hand. Warmth sparked between our palms and shot up my arm, healing the little wounds and banishing the ache.

"Thank you," I whispered, shifting in his grip until I could thread my fingers through his. Together, we faced the crowd, holding each other tight as the gathered fae swirled around us and pulled us in.

A rousing tune full of flutes and fiddles started playing, and before I knew it, I was separated from Adam as the dancing began. I kept glimpsing him searching for me while I passed from one partner to another. Laughter and whistles rang in my ears. Once, someone pressed a cup of faerie mead into my hands. Heady and sweet, it was smoother than any human alcohol I'd ever tasted and strong enough to make me dizzy from the first sip. Before I could worry about being rude, or the risk of getting drunk, another fae whisked me back into the dancing crowd. His friend caught my cup, draining it with a grin. Every time I tried slipping away, Adam would vanish, and I would find myself fending off offers of more mead before getting pulled into yet another dance.

At last, a calloused hand gripped my wrist and plucked me from the crowd. My current partner voiced a halfhearted protest, laughing when Adam snarled in response. With a huff, he scooped me up and carried me to the edges of the grove, where Treestar and Oldest waited for us with twin mischievous looks.

"That wasn't funny. You didn't tell me they'd try to keep her," Adam grumbled, setting me on my feet.

Treestar laughed.

Oldest shrugged, patting Adam's shoulder. "Go on, boy. Take your bride and flee before they continue the game. We'll take care of yon crowd until you're out of sight," he said, chuckling.

"A game, huh?" I whispered when Adam took Oldest's words to heart and scooped me up again. "Were they supposed to be trying to get me drunk, too?"

Adam sighed and slowed as we left the noise and crowd behind, the entrance to the enclave coming into sight. "Oldest says it's an old faerie game, keeping the bride dancing all night. A fae would be fine; they don't need sleep like humans do." Pausing, he flashed me a sheepish smile. "He didn't mention anything about the mead, though."

I blushed. He set me down in the large entryway and took my hand, tugging me along. "Here, it's this way."

Chapter Thirty-Four

It was almost too dark for my human eyes as he led me along. Most of the faerie lights in the enclave were dimmed, probably in deference to the fae who planned to overindulge tonight.

Not everyone was out enjoying the revels, though. At one point, we passed the council hall and were treated to the sight of a bunch of greenman cubs sleeping in a pile of cushions under the watchful eye of several older, bonded pairs. A charcoal-gray male sat in a nest of cushions off to the side with several younger cubs cradled in his lap. Nightwake sat beside him, her silver-streaked mane tousled as she dozed with her head on his shoulder. One of the more elderly females beckoned us over so she could whisper something to Adam that made his ears flick back. With a gentle laugh and a wink, she waved us away and returned to her charges.

A few more twists and turns, and we arrived at a familiar set of rooms. Our belongings rested in neat stacks beside the appropriate places, but everything else was just as I remembered from our first stay here. Except for a squat barrel perched on a new ledge by the sleeping alcove.

"What is that?" I asked, peering at the odd addition.

Adam gestured, and a shimmering barrier eclipsed the entrance to our new home, locking out any more sneaky fae and their pranks. He paused, tilting his head as he scented the air. Going to the barrel, Adam pried off the top.

"Oh." Adam chuckled and gave me a sheepish smile. "It's mead."

"They gave us alcohol? Why..." I trailed off, my face hot as the implications caught up with me. "Never mind," I mumbled hastily, darting over to a stray tumble of belongings by the door.

A shiver of magic jerked my attention back to Adam in time to watch the vines he wore vanish in a ripple of light. Reaching up, he started unwinding the leather and amber from his antlers.

"Here," I said softly, going over to him and tapping his arm, "let me help. At least I can see what I'm doing."

Adam chuckled and sank into a crouch, tilting his head to make things easier. "Thank you."

I huffed, undoing first one and then the other. "You could've asked, silly."

He hummed, straightening when I moved on to the feathers in his mane. He caught my wrist. I jumped, looking up with wide eyes. "I didn't want to frighten you."

I flushed and squirmed, tugging my wrist free as I avoided his searching gaze in favor of freeing the feathers from his mane. "I'm not scared, I'm just..." I trailed off. Freeing several of the dangles, I handed them to Adam, careful not to rumple the feathers themselves.

I took a deep breath and forced myself to meet his gaze. "I want to do this right, for you and for myself. You've promised to be mine, and I've promised to be yours. That means no more hiding, Adam. For either of us."

He stared at me for a long moment and nodded. Brightening sparks made his eyes glow while he watched me cross to the feathers awaiting attention. "I...I don't want to scare you, though."

"I'm not scared," I repeated, fumbling with the leather cords securing the last few feathers and tugging them free. "Not of you. You're amazing and beautiful, and everything I never expected I'd ever find. You're everything good in my life, Adam. Please. I don't want you to think you have to play human for me, *ever*."

I pressed the second bundle of feathers and beads into his palm and caught his wrist, running my fingers over his claws. "You're not a monster, Adam." I paused and bit my lip as a deeper blush burned across my face. "You're mine."

Adam's eyes widened, and for a minute, the sparks dimmed before they lit his eyes until all I could see was green and gold. He stood in a rush, the ornaments tumbling to the ground. His hands came up to cradle my face, and he closed the distance between us. I shivered, my eyes fluttering shut when his mouth slanted over mine, and I finally gave in to the craving to touch him.

My fingers skimmed along the streaks of color painting his skin. A growl rumbled against my lips. Adam broke away to nip a trail down my neck as I explored, ruffling fur and scraping my nails over bare skin when I found it. Just as his mouth brushed my shoulder, my wandering hands stumbled over the edge of his breeches, and I hesitated.

Adam shuddered and started to pull away. "Bri..."

"I'm not scared," I insisted as I traced the ridge of beadwork along his hip, my nails catching on one of the invisible stitches in the tightly woven cloth. "I'm...I don't know," I whispered against his neck. "I-I've never done this before. Not like this," I clarified, shying away from the old, bitter memories. That horrible moment of being at a stranger's mercy.

"Me neither," Adam whispered back, shivering when my trembling hands slipped into the heated space between us. His belly pressed into my knuckles, and I found the smooth, flat curve of a buckle where I'd expected leather laces. Again, I hesitated. Adam shifted against me, his lips brushing my temple as I breathed through the nauseating spike of old fear curdling my stomach. "Bri, do you trust me?"

"Yes," I breathed, my eyes fluttering closed. Adam lowered his head to nuzzle my neck. He sighed—and I gasped at the heady flush of magic buzzing over my skin, fizzing and sweet and earthy. It was *Adam*.

I arched into him with a cry as he bit down on his mark. My head fell back, and Adam dragged his teeth along my pulse, his tongue soothing each stinging nip. I melted against him, a low growling purr buzzing beneath my fingers. Fingers that were suddenly nimble and steady as they latched onto the bronze buckle.

Mine, my thoughts sang, and I popped it loose. With a tug and a twist, I pulled the bit of metal free to toss it aside. The soft thud and ringing chime as it hit the stone floor echoed through me.

Adam growled. Then he was picking me up, cold stone biting into my shoulders as he pinned me to a nearby wall. His hands tangled in the hem of my dress, rucking it up around my hips. He paused, and my nerves resurfaced as the heady buzz of his magic faltered. I shoved them aside. Instead, I focused on his touch, squirming when his claws nipped my skin through the faerie silk.

"Adam?"

"I-I'm not sure if I can...Tell me if I frighten you, Bri. Promise me you will," Adam rasped, his deep voice a raw, aching whisper. He shuddered, his hands dropping away to dig his claws in the stone behind me. Adam kept me there with the press of his hips as his eyes pulsed brighter.

"I promise," I whispered, my hands tracing the whorls and streaks painted over his cheeks and brow before giving in to temptation and burying themselves in his mane.

I stumbled across the bases of his antlers and scraped my nails over the sensitive skin. He groaned, folding around me as I let my fingers wander until I found one of his ears and pressed closer to run my lips along the edge.

Stone flaked away from his claws, and a growl thrummed against me. Adam lurched closer as if he were trying to climb inside my skin. Drunk on the power rising from him in thick, honeyed waves, I gripped Adam's mane and tugged his head back to capture his mouth in a teasing, aching kiss.

"Mine," I gasped when he broke away to nip a trail down my neck.

"Always," Adam growled—and sank his teeth into his mark, loosing his magic with a snarl.

Mine.

***

I woke surrounded by languid warmth. The soft furs were a scattered tumble around my shins, but the heat pressed against me from shoulder to thigh warded off any chill. Adam was *warm*.

Biting back a shy smile, I rolled over and opened my eyes to the sight of him deeply asleep, a hint of a smile hiding in the curve of his lips. His magic fizzed under my skin, making me feel a little tipsy. I could still taste the faerie mead we'd shared earlier on my tongue. The rich sweetness recalled memories of what followed, and I flushed, curling up to Adam's warmth and letting my head rest on his shoulder. In spite of the past few hours, the craving to touch him continued to burn in my blood, and I let my hands wander, marveling that he was *mine*.

A low, rumbling sigh gusted over me as I traced the line of his hip, fur tickling my palm. "Mmm...Bri?" I hummed, absently tracing the faded scars marring his belly. "What are you doing?" Adam rumbled under my ear.

I blushed, ruffling the short, fine fur that followed the contours of his stomach before giving way to smooth, supple skin. "I'm just...happy," I whispered, propping my chin on my free hand so I could see his face.

Adam watched me with a sleepy smile, a blissful contentment simmering in his dark eyes. My blushes deepened as my wandering hand found the scar over his ribs, and Adam's purr rumbled to life. He shifted to grip my waist and pulled me up until I was sprawled on top of him. "Good," he sighed, eyes drifting closed.

I relaxed against him with an embarrassed hum. There was an undeniable rightness to this easy affection. And yet, being able to touch him whenever I wanted and soak in the feeling of him snug beside me without worry...it would take some getting used to. I shifted, letting my head come to rest on his chest as his purr slowly faded. With his heartbeat thrumming in my ear, I slipped back into dreams.

***

The next time I woke, Adam was watching me.

"Hello," I mumbled, resisting the urge to hide behind the pale, spotted fur I'd tugged up over my chest.

Adam chuckled and touched my cheek as I blushed, trailing his claws over the reddened skin. The paint had vanished from his body on its own at some point in the night, but I could tell he had bathed while I slept. His fur was damp, and the mineral scent of the hot spring clung to him.

"How long have you been watching me sleep?"

Adam tilted his head and sat back, his gaze sweeping over me. A faint smile quirked his lips. "Not long." He brushed his thumb over the trail of hickeys running from my ear to disappear beneath the fur. "Are you..."

"I'm okay," I assured him, trying not to squirm as his gentle touch triggered a cascade of recent memories.

What an understatement. I felt amazing, but at the same time, I didn't feel much different. I didn't feel the heady connection to him Treestar said I would once the bond was complete. Maybe I had done something wrong, somehow.

The thought of asking was too embarrassing just yet, though, and I slipped away to the bathroom with a muttered excuse and another blush. The clear waters of the hot spring winked at me on my way back, and I paused. Glancing towards the main room where Adam waited, I let the fur drop and plunged in with a happy sigh. The welcome heat soothed aches I hadn't known were there until they were melting away. It was heavenly.

I didn't linger for too long, though. Clean and wrapped in a silken robe, I returned to find someone had left us food. Adam was waiting for me, a small mug in one hand.

"I need to ask you something." I paused, eyeing the tray, and my stomach gurgled loud enough to make one of Adam's ears twitch forward. "Last night was amazing, and you were..." Adam cocked his head, and I fiddled with ties of my robe as I joined him in the pile furs with a wince.

"Did I do something wrong?" I blurted out, my face hot as I realized he was still naked under the furs scattered across his lap. I forced my gaze to his face in time to catch his surprise and watched understanding warm his dark eyes. "I-I just...Treestar told me about how being heart-bonded felt. I just—I don't—"

Adam chuckled and set his mug on the tray with the food. I picked up one of the rounds of bread and took a bite as I lost my nerve. It was filled with a sweet, spicy meat, and I devoured it in three bites, suddenly starving. Adam handed me another, a grin flashing across his face when I made that one disappear, too, and licked my fingers clean.

"It's okay, Bri," Adam assured me, his gaze dropping to my robe and sparking. He paused, and I glanced down as he dragged his gaze back up with a low rumble.

In my rush to get back, I'd forgotten to dry off, and the silky material of my robe clung to my wet skin.

"It takes more than one night to settle the bond once it's accepted," Adam said, his deep voice husky as his gaze wandered once more.

I flushed, resisting the urge to hide. Instead, I smoothed the damp silk over my lap. "Oh?"

Adam nodded. Combing my hair away from my face with his claws, he rose to close the meager distance between us.

"So, we, um...should try again?" I said, running my hands along his neck and over his chest. His heat seared my fingertips as I traced the paths once marked by paint and magic.

A low, rumbling purr buzzed beneath my hands, and I caught his shy smile on my lips. "I will if you will," Adam murmured, brushing his mouth back and forth against mine in teasing touches.

"I'd like that," I whispered and laughed when he tumbled me into the tangled furs with a playful growl.

His kisses tasted of happiness and mead, rich and sweet. If this was a hint of what our future held for us, I never wanted it to end.

It would never be easy, and I knew there were days ahead where I would wonder if we were better off apart, but I didn't care. We would get through them, as we had with every other challenge that tried to come between us. This was worth the fight. At long last, I was home.

"I love you."

Thank you for reading Brightfeather!

I hope you enjoyed reading Bri and Adam's story as much as I enjoyed writing it. Brightfeather is a standalone novel, but it shares a world with many other stories waiting too unfold.

To stay up-to-date with new releases, come hang out with me on Instagram at @h.hounshell.author, join my reader's group on Facebook, Chosen by Underhill, or check out my website HannahHounshellAuthor.com

As an indie author, every review makes a difference and helps readers find this book. Please consider leaving an honest review on Goodreads, Amazon, or whatever platform you use.

Thanks again!

***

The way to Underhill will return with Book One of the Spriten Chronicles

~Coming soon~

Acknowledgements

No book is brought to life without the hands of others helping to lift it up. The first person I want to thank is my dad, without whom this journey would've been much harder, and taken years longer. Thank you, Dad.

Many thanks to my critique partners and alpha readers. Monica, who threatened me several times when I ran out of new chapters and left her dangling from yet another mini-cliffhanger. Daphne and Lexis, who bounced ideas or talked me off ledges, no matter how chaotic their lives were. Alissa, for calling me out on the massive plot holes I tried to ignore and giving me the idea for the unexpected plot twist that solved half of them. And for my editor, Addison of Avocado Tree Press, who took on a "kissing book" without turning a hair and lent me his critical eye to really make this story shine. You guys are the unsung heroes of the writing in Brightfeather, who gave me the tools I needed to make it something worth reading. Thank you.

And I'll never forget my awesome beta readers. Kaylin, Lyndsey, Emily, Suzy, Christine, and so many more...I want to express my gratitude for your comments and enthusiasm for my debut. Whenever I doubt myself, I look back on the words you left for me, and I know I can do this after all. You're amazing.

Last, but certainly not least, a huge heartfelt thank you to my Father in Heaven, who shoved me out of my funk and into my notebook one night in the middle of doing dishes. Without you, Lord, I wouldn't be here. While I will forever be running behind on chores, there are no regrets. Thank you.

About the Author

Hannah Hounshell is an artist-turned-author living with her husband in the wilds of rural Ohio, where coyotes sing and the odd faerie ring of mushrooms may appear in your yard overnight. She spends her days chasing after her two gremlins, shooing the cats out of the clean laundry, and crafting new stories in between cups of tea and sketchbook meanderings. You can find her hanging out on Instagram as @h.hounshell.author. *Brightfeather* is her debut novel.